BEST AMERICAN FANTASY

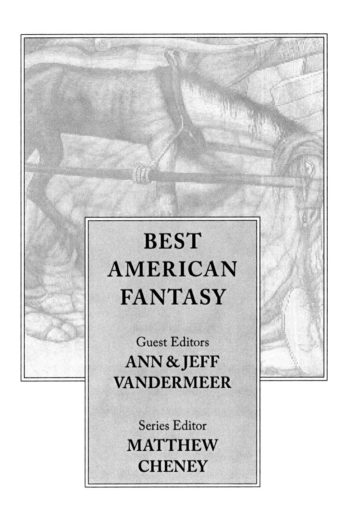

BEST AMERICAN FANTASY

Guest Editors
**ANN & JEFF
VANDERMEER**

Series Editor
**MATTHEW
CHENEY**

PRIME BOOKS

ACKNOWLEDGMENTS

Putting together a book of this sort is an immense endeavor. We could not have done it without the help and support of many people, including John Joseph Adams, Michael Bergstein, Kate Bernheimer, Frederic Chabot, Connor Cochran, Eli Horowitz, John Klima, Tessa Kum, Holly MacArthur, Nicola Mason, Jonathan Strahan, Hannah Tinti, Gordon van Gelder, Derek White, Sheila Williams, and Renee Zuckerbrot. Thanks to Clayton Kroh for his invaluable editorial assistance. Special thanks to the many editors, publicists, writers, and staff members of various publications who have sent us material for consideration. We have tried to list information on everything we have received at the back of the book, and we encourage readers to support these publications.

Table of

Contents

PREFACE:
BEST AMERICAN FANTASY

Matthew Cheney

Best American Fantasy 2008 is the second in a series of anthologies that will each, we hope, provide a taste of the rich and varied feast of short fiction available today.

Two concepts are central to our mission: guest editors and breadth of sources. This book and its predecessor are edited by two people, Ann & Jeff VanderMeer, and the next volume will have a new editor. Such a system will prevent the series from representing one set of tastes alone, for no matter how broad an editor's idea of what constitutes the best fiction may be, we are all limited by our enthusiasms and prejudices, our experiences and blindspots. I cannot imagine readers with broader tastes than the VanderMeers, and yet I know next year's book will be quite different from one they would produce—and that, for all of us, is the excitement of this project.

The breadth of sources is important to us because it allows us to explore a range of American fiction and challenge our own ideas about genres, audiences, and labels. As series editor, I have told our editors that the definition of the word "fantasy" is entirely theirs to decide. When discussing stories, we often begin with gut instinct—it *feels* like fantasy, but...—and then moved on to analysis, deciding, for example, that sometimes fantasy can be as much created by the narrative voice as by any events within the narrative itself.

Our goals are, as always, idealistic—with tens of thousands of stories published every year in magazines and books, on websites and through email subscriptions (and other new means of distribution) it is impossible for us to read even the majority of what is out there. We cannot be comprehensive, but we can discover gems. I hope we can also foster conversations and help readers discover new venues for short fiction while looking at familiar venues through different eyes.

For guidelines and information about submitting publications and suggestions to *Best American Fantasy*, visit http://bestamericanfantasy.com.

INTRODUCTION: THE SHAPE OF A YEAR'S BEST

Ann & Jeff VanderMeer

Last year's inaugural volume of *Best American Fantasy* was wide and deep in its interests. In making our selections, we let the shape of the literature we found shape the anthology. This took us in many wonderfully strange, sometimes mutually exclusive directions. For example, we decided to define "fantasy" in its broadest possible sense. We also had no problem considering wildly differing styles, from the realistic to the absurd, from the stark to the flamboyantly exuberant.

This approach to anthology editing was about first deciding what we considered "best," and then including as much of it as possible, without any other considerations. For example, we trusted readers to understand that what constitutes a "best" short-short is different for than fiction of a more traditional length. On a more general level, we also trusted readers to understand that we were creating a complex bouillabaisse meant to show the diversity and energy of fantasy in North America.

In large part, readers responded enthusiastically to this approach, and so did reviewers. And, in placing writers in juxtaposition that had previously never appeared in print together, we created, behind the scenes, the kind of healthy dialog and cross-pollination that keeps literature vibrant and fresh.

This second volume of Best American Fantasy is a very different beast from the first volume, again shaped by what we found in the magazines and anthologies we read from 2007. For example, we found less interesting fantastical fiction in mainstream literary sources than in 2006. Conversely, we found more risk-taking fiction in genre publications. The result was a much more even balance with regard to the sources of our choices.

We also made further efforts to define focus and scope. First, this year's volume is about fifty thousand words shorter than volume one. This decision was based on wanting a more absolute constraint against which to test and re-test the stories. To force ourselves, in developing the *Best American Fantasy* series, to focus ever more intently on our subject matter. Second, related to this decision, we jettisoned the idea of including short-shorts, and decided to indulge an impulse toward fantasy purism by abandoning the idea of selecting stories where fantasy only exists as metaphor. Metaphor is certainly employed in the stories you are about to read, but in most of them the manifestation of the fantastical is real within the story, even if only hinted at in some.

With these constraints in place, we discovered an entertaining and thought-provoking collection of stories to present to readers. As with volume one, the writers showcased are diverse, many appearing in print together for the first time. Rick Moody's hilarious ghost story "Story With Advice II: Back from the Dead" coexists with Kage Baker's "The Ruby Incomparable," M. Rickert's "Memoir of a Deer Woman" with Micaela Morrissette's "Ave Maria," representing not just *Conjunctions* but the *Wizards* anthology, not just *The Magazine of Fantasy & Science Fiction* but *Cincinnati Review*.

In fact, we would be remiss if we didn't single out a few publications for special praise. *Tin House: Fantastic Women*, edited by Rick Moody, was one of our favorite reads of the year. All by itself it represents a kind of "year's best," from which we could easily have taken many more stories. *The Cincinnati Review* also offered consistently intriguing, often somewhat experimental, fiction throughout the year. And, although *Conjunctions* did not publish much fantasy in 2007, we found its offerings, including its special avian issue, of uniformly high quality. On the genre side, we particularly enjoyed many of the stories in Jonathan Strahan's *Eclipse 1*, Gardner Dozois/Jack Dann's *Wizards*, and John Klima's *Logorrhea*; it was a strong year for original genre anthologies.

In re-reading these stories during the copy-editing phase of production, we were reminded of not just how much we loved these stories but how quintessentially "American" they seemed to us—more so than last year. Whether it signals a trend or just the synchronicity of a moment captured in time, most all of these stories feature American settings or American ideals. They map our current shared experience, from video games to politics, from concerns about the environment to the malaise and unease of modern life. Miranda Mellis' "The Revisionist," for example, perfectly captures the tone and texture of the current toxic atmosphere in these United States, in which the truth has become a fiction. Rachel Swirsky's "How the World Became Quiet" applies the power of folktale to a myth of the future that is more relevant than many "realistic" stories. "The Drowned Life" by Jeffrey Ford is a searing, powerful fiction that works both as surreal story and a commentary on our American life. Other tales provide an interesting look at Americans taking in other points of view, from Bruce Holland Rogers masterful and delightful "The Seven Deadly Hotels" to the whimsical Peter S. Beagle fable "The Last and Only, or Mr. Moscowitz Becomes French" and Judy Budnitz's "Abroad."

All of these stories, we feel, do several things well: they speak to the heart and to the head, they are brilliantly written, and they often push farther and harder than stories that did not hold our interest as effortlessly. We hope you like these stories as much as we did, even if our enjoyment was tinged with regret. This is our last year as guest editors of *Best American Fantasy*, although we will stay on in an administrative role, helping series editor Mathew Cheney. It's been an honor and a privilege, and all best wishes to next year's guest editor, the incomparable Kevin Brockmeier.

BUFO REX
Erik Amundsen

Erik Amundsen has been a baker, an itinerant schoolteacher, worked for two governments, and gotten in bar fights overseas. He now lives at the foot of a cemetery in central Connecticut where he writes nasty little stories and poems that shuffle around in the night when he's not looking. "Bufo Rex" is taken from the pages of the venerable dark fantasy magazine *Weird Tales*.

I am called Bufo, I grow fat upon insects. I make my board under leaves, upon logs and my bed lies in the bogs. My throne is the toad stool and witch's butter is for my biscuits.

I've never put much stock in humanity, despite what stories might have said of me; I am no great lover of human aesthetics, being, myself, so physically bereft. My hide is olive and warted, my fingers pointed and long, my body flat and fat and swollen around, my face a wide mouth and bulging eyes. Some assume, for all of that, I must want for a bride, something pink and smooth of limb, soft, mammalian, to balance out the whole of my existence. As if, somehow, this will lighten the aesthetic load I place upon the eye of God. Well, I assure you when the eye of God tires of looking at a creature such as myself; I suspect I shall be the first to know. Until then. I've no use for a bride and no means or place to keep her; I've mates by the score and children by the hundreds with no need to have ever met either; beneath the brown waters, my wedding chamber, they leave of themselves, as do I, without second thought. What could I hope to gain by maintaining one of the warm blooded creatures you men pant and yell to possess that I do not already have, save a lifetime of trouble?

That was my testimony in my first kingdom, when they dragged me in chains before the king and the pink creatures they sought so to protect swooned and then peeked through half lidded eyes at the monster. The sentence was exile, and they frog marched me to the border, and set me loose on pain of death to never return, but I am called Bufo, I grow fat upon insects. I make my board under leaves, upon logs and my bed lies in the bogs. My throne is the toad stool and witch's butter is for my biscuits.

I have no treasure, no hall, nor wealth, nor store, save that the world contains everything that I have ever needed; food, bed, cool mud and warm sun. No gold, but the color of my eyes. But then, there is always some damned fool that must believe that something as swollen and hopping-loathsome as myself must have some use to men, as all things made by God, such as mosquitoes, poison ivy and the clap are wont to possess. So in this second kingdom of grasping merchants and opportunistic peasants, I learned to my sorrow what every damned fool knows; that toads possess carbuncles in their heads in the space where their brains ought to be. And because my carbuncle taught itself to think and learned that God made, upon the earth, no shortage of damned fools, this time, I showed myself the frontier.

I am called Bufo, I grow fat upon insects. I make my board under leaves, upon logs and my bed lies in the bogs. My throne is the toad stool and witch's butter is for my biscuits. I seek out no company, but I'll accept any which treats me decently and which accepts that it is the nature of the toad to eat insects and to lay in the bog. The woman was old, and she might not have been quite right, but I also saw the mounds where her husband and little children had years ago gone, and eaten some of the beetles who had crawled in their bones. Men are a sentimental lot, and sentiment, as any toad knows, rots the carbuncle. Or the brain, whichever it might be. She called me by her children's names and made me clothing; it was perhaps, inappropriate, but mildly charming. I can only apologize for being a poor conversationalist, but to say we were familiar might be characterizing our relationship a little too strongly.

Some men set her on fire so they could have her house. I'm not quite sure I understood what it was all about, but they seemed upset that she'd been talking to me, though I know enough of men to see an excuse when it comes riding up the path, torch in hand. I suspect they would have used me the same way, for sake of consistency, but sentiment is not a burden under which I labor, or not one under which I then labored, and I fled, hopping fast and strong for all my girth.

I tore my coat and my trousers, but what need have I for the cloth of men? I am called Bufo, I grow fat upon insects. I make my board under leaves, upon logs and my bed lies in the bogs. My throne is the toad stool and witch's butter is for my biscuits.

I came to a fourth kingdom and the people here tipped their hats when they saw me come.

"Please, sir," they said "We've a terrible time with flies and beetles, worms and slugs, and things like that."

"Don't you fear I'll steal your princesses?"

"Our princesses have faces sweet as buttermilk but hearts as cold and dark and wicked as the water under winter ice and voices that make the hens lay weird black eggs, all seven," they said "Take the lot, and none shall miss them."

"I'll pass," I said "What about the gem inside my head, I've heard that all toads have them."

"All men know that only damned fools believe that, and we expose damned fools at birth, by law, in this kingdom."

"Better still," said I "If an old woman talks to me, you won't set her on fire, will you?"

"We've plenty of firewood to keep us warm in the cold months; old women are for stories and spinning."

"I think we may come to an understanding," I said, and I, to my new bog went, and began my work. In a few short years I and my children and grandchildren had the kingdom's pests well in hand, the princesses were all safely married to other countries, to ogres or to pirates, and the people left me to my work.

But man has decreed that good things must not last, and, soon men came from the kingdom next door, you'll remember them as the ones who set the dotty widow on fire for her house. It seems they'd run out of widows.

In truth, I would have missed the whole thing, if not for a misunderstanding. A young man like the one I first met when I came here was speaking to a knight from the widow burning country, with his armor and his surcoat and his heavy cross. The knight asked the young man what God the young man served. The young man replied that, like the knight, he served Christ, but either the knight did not understand his language, misheard, or heard his orders, for he shoved the man back.

"Kroaten?" the knight said, which was a name that some people used for me, long ago, and not quite like what the young man said. It got my attention.

"Your God is the same as Kroaten devil!" the knight yelled. Now, I have been called a devil before, fairly often. I'm quite certain no one has ever been feebleminded enough to worship me.

But now the knight had my attention and I was not disappointed, if, indeed, I had been expecting a repeat performance of what happened all those years ago at the widow's house on a much grander scale. My children and I hopped off to the bog and waited. When the smoke cleared, only men from the widow burning nation remained, loudly thanking God for their victory over Kroaten Devil.

Over me.

I am called Bufo, I grow fat upon insects. I make my board under leaves, upon logs and my bed lies in the bogs. My throne is the toad stool and witch's butter is for my biscuits. I am an unsentimental being; I was born in a bog and fed first on brothers and sisters. I am not prone to fits or to passions, and I do truly believe, to the core of my being that sentiment rots the brain. I sat on my toadstool for days and smelled the smoke of the widow burning nation, and I *felt*; the experience was unfamiliar, yet I knew it as it came to me. I have been watching you men for a very long time, and I know what you are all about. I turned my bulbous golden eyes to the castle, where the widow burning king had unfurled his victory flag, and I decided that I was tired of you men and your killing game.

It's then that I decided you should see how nature plays.

First I went to see Scorpion, and he was sitting at the edge of the water.

"Will you ferry me across" he asked "I cannot find your cousin frog."

"That isn't why I'm here," I said.

I went to visit violin spider, playing his violin in his reclusive cave.

"Have you come to listen to me play my newest funeral march?" he asked.

"In a sense," I said.

I visited black widow in her widow's weeds.

"Let us speak of love and loss," she said "I shall tell you of my dear husband whom I so miss"

"You shall be reunited," I said.

I visited many others, angry wasp, busy bumblebee, and busier honeybee, fire ant, horsefly, all the ones you might expect, and many you might not, some I usually do not visit, and never have, some who considered themselves safe from me by their natures, the long legged spider, certain butterflies; the exact recipe is secondary. That day I swelled to twice my usual size, sloshing with the witch's brew bubbling in the cauldron of my belly. I sat upon my toadstool, terrible pain now coursing through that warted, fat body of mine, skin splitting, suppurating with the strain of all the poisons within, wondering why, in Gods name, I would choose to do this to myself.

Perhaps I was tired of moving kingdom to kingdom one hop ahead of the ever changing idiocy of God's chosen. Perhaps it was to remind man that it was terror that filled Adam's eyes when he fled the garden after he dropped anarchy on the rest of us. I'll never truly remember now.

With veins that pumped the fires of hell, I hopped off toward the castle, the ulcers in my skin burning the ground black where they touched.

The castle's kitchens were well known to me; for it was here that I began my work, years ago, contending with this kingdom's pest problem. In a way, this was more of the same; all things returning to their beginning. Cooks, hastily brought from the widow burning nation were equally hasty in preparing the victory feast for the king and his men, in situ, and, as one might imagine from the nation I described, there was all kinds of cooked flesh. There was also soup, a great, steaming, bubbling savory cauldron of it. I watched from the window, a trail of sloughed off skin and puss trailing down the outside. I waited, and I hadn't long to wait, for I was surely dying now, from all the poison I consumed. But the cooks had ridden long and hard to get here and the soup, one of the opening courses, was not one of their first priorities. Their attention wandered, and when all of them were out of the kitchen at once, I leaped. The pain that followed was a joy compared to the hours that brought me to that point.

I was called Bufo, I grew fat upon insects. I made my board under leaves, upon logs and my bed lay in the bogs. My throne was the toad stool and witch's butter was for my biscuits. I expected to dissolve then, into brute nature as beasts are wont to do, but I did not. Instead I hovered over the huge kettle and watched my body, already made tender with all the venoms, dissolve into the soup. The cooks, hearing the splash returned and speculated a bubble; no matter, for the soup was being called for, a stir, a taste; what was it they had done, this had never been so good; and they set out the bowls.

The men set out in the stolen hall, the king at his enemy's throne, and each in turn was given a bowl of me, which they, amid much boasting and jest, began to eat, while my shade looked on. Toads, you might realize, taste horrible, and while the first spoonful of the soup was sublime, the next was not as good, and the third not so good as the second and so on, as the course progressed, the men grew quiet, the complements and smiles turned to grimaces, but pride, not wanting to be the first to declare the soup awful drove them to continue. Near the end of the bowl, every spoonful was tongue spasming torment, and it was near that point that the King lifted his spoon and found, cradled inside of it, a carbuncle, red as hate, big as a goose's egg.

"I'll be damned," I said, to no one in particular "Those idiots were right after all."

He stared at it for a moment, his face turning red, then purple, and then black; and then he died. His body had swollen out of his clothes and his flesh out of his skin by the time it hit the floor. His men followed his lead a moment later, faithful to the last. His feast, appropriately, burned in the kitchen, and the castle has since become poisoned to the foundations, so that none may touch it and live. With this I am satisfied.

I was called Bufo, I grew fat upon insects. I made my board under leaves, upon logs and my bed lay in the bogs. My throne was the toad stool and witch's butter was for my biscuits. Now owner of a man's castle, my shade sits on a throne no less poisonous than a toadstool, waiting for the day when someone retrieves the poisoned stone. Perhaps then, we shall throw down another tyrant. One could grow accustomed to that.

THE SEVEN DEADLY HOTELS
Bruce Holland Rogers

Bruce Holland Rogers is the author of the novel *Ashes of the Sun*, the nonfiction book *Word Work: Surviving and Thriving as a Writer*, and multiple collections of short stories, including the World Fantasy Award-winning *The Keyhole Opera*. He has also won a Pushcart Prize, the Bram Stoker Award, two Nebula Awards, and the World Fantasy Award for his story "Don Ysidro." "Seven Deadly Hotels" was originally published as part of Rogers's email subscription service (www. shortshortshort.com) and will also be published in *Polyphony 7* from Wheatland Press. Rogers lives in Eugene, Oregon.

1. Das Gästehaus der Schlafenziege

From the moment that I stepped from the white heat of noon into the shadows of the lobby, there were three members of the staff attending me. "Good day, Herr Doktor," said the first bellman, taking my valise. Ordinarily, I make a point of managing my own bags, but my walk up the long alleys and stairways from the train station had made me sweat. Mindful of my status, I had worn too many clothes, but really I could have dressed for comfort. I had met no one from the institute during my hike from the train to the Gästehaus. For good or for ill, none of my professional hosts were present to appreciate how I had overheated myself for the sake of appearances. I let the man take my bag, and when his assistant tried to pull my instrument case from my other hand, I resisted for only a moment.

"Be careful," I said. "Those are delicate medical devices."

"Of course," he said. He set the case onto a trolley. "We will take the utmost care, Herr Doktor."

"Herr Doktor, will you sit down?" said the woman. She lifted the hat from my head, a gesture far too intimate, but as she waved a fan and created a delightful breeze for my forehead, I could not protest. I closed my eyes. The bellmen, having deposited my things on the trolley, now gently pushed me back. I felt a chair at the back of my knees. As I sank into it, I could not repress a sigh. A kitchen servant curtsied as she presented me with an iced drink. "Will you take some lemonade, Herr Doktor?"

I allowed myself one sip, then said, "Perhaps I should go to the registration desk before I get too terribly comfortable." I tugged at the knot in my tie.

"Nonsense, Herr Doktor," said the woman who had taken my hat. "Registration will come to you. Now, if you will allow me..." She gave the fan over to one of the bellmen. Then I felt her slender fingers working to loosen my tie. She even unfastened the top button of my shirt. Again, such unwarranted intimacy! Yet the pleasure of unrestricted breathing curtailed my impulse to take umbrage.

"If you will sign, please, Herr Doktor," said a clerk kneeling before me.

"I must say," I told him, "I am quite surprised that you all should know who I am." I signed.

"We have so few vacancies at Das Gästehause der Schlafenziege," said the clerk. "You are our only new guest today."

"Really? I should have thought the hotels would be full of medical men arriving for the meeting."

"But we had only the one vacancy," said the clerk, smiling. "Only the one." The bellman still fanned cooling breezes toward my brow. The woman who had taken my hat, loosened my tie, and unfastened a button now kneaded the muscles in my neck just below my scalp. I opened my mouth to tell her to cease touching me at once, but I felt the muscles at my temples and the crown of my head relax as they had not relaxed in years. My jaw hung. I groaned. "To your room, then?" said the clerk.

"Ngh," I said, meaning to say that I would stand in just another moment.

The clerk apparently took my meaning. "No need," he said, and I discovered then that the chair had wheels.

As the bellmen pushed me through dim corridors, I half dozed. In my room, a fountain trickled. There is no soporific like the sound of moving water. My journey had taken more from me than I had realized. I had meant to visit the institute in the afternoon, but as my presentation was not until morning, I could wait. For now, sleep, or the cool relaxation just short of sleep, called to me.

The bellmen were valets as well. They began to undress me, and though I thought this strange and wrong, I did not want to halt the sensations of being touched, cared for. I was aware of how the purposeful and professional touch of my examinations could relax patients, but I received little contact of that sort myself. In my surgery, I saw much suffering. Was I not owed some pleasure by now, some freedom from care?

The valets helped me into bed. A gentle *tap-tap-tap* sounded at the door, and the valets admitted the woman whose touch I had never quite managed to protest. I did not protest now when she wrung a cloth into a basin and wiped the road dirt from my face, the remaining heat from my brow. I closed my eyes. She washed my arms, lifting them as if I were a paralytic. I let her. I let her wash my calves and feet. A valet stood at the side of the bed and slowly waved a large fan along the length of my body.

"Window," I mumbled. "Air." I always wanted fresh air as I slept. I heard the heavy draperies moved aside, heard the creak of the window hinges. Street noises drifted in.

I intended to give instructions, before the servants left me, for the hour at which I was to be wakened, but I couldn't rouse myself enough. I imagined speaking the necessary sentences, but I waited before speaking so as to enjoy the next moment, and the next. Then the hotel staff left me.

I dozed. I dreamed of sleeping on and on. I dreamed of people entering my room to feed me, to bathe me, to soothe me if ever I began to bestir myself. I dreamed of light behind the draperies, and darkness, and light again. Once I awoke to hear shouted voices in the street. The room was black. Glass broke. A shout. The sound of boots on cobbles, someone running away. Another shout, this time with words I understood. "Help! Help him! Doctor! Is there a doctor!"

I am a doctor, I thought. I imagined getting up, throwing on some clothes, and making my way out of the hotel. Such a bother. And when I found myself on the street, kneeling beside some man who no doubt had been complicit in his injury, would I remember what to do? I didn't think I would. I closed my eyes. I drowsed. I dozed. I dreamed of floating on warm water, floating farther away, farther away, farther.

2. The Hotel Ginger Plum

Once again I unburdened myself and unfolded the map to check my bearings, though this was difficult as the names of the streets were not posted at the intersection. Glancing to the right, to the left, and again straight ahead, I noticed a small boy standing before the great glass front of the next building. I could not tell what sort of establishment he might be staring into, but he gazed transfixed, in awe. I saw no signboard with the name of my destination or any other hotel or place of business. Still unsure of where I was, thinking that perhaps I should take the street to my right, I instead took up my baggage and advanced toward the boy to satisfy my curiosity about what he saw.

He was looking into a large room where richly upholstered chairs clustered around low tables. On each table were little baskets of tiny cakes and candies, and people sat in twos or threes at a few of these tables, tasting. Deeper inside, across a marble floor, stood a reception desk, and above this was a sign: The Hotel Ginger Plum. I had found the very place I sought! Feeling grateful to the boy for having served as my unwitting guide, I felt in my pocket for some coins and said, "Those sweets look very nice, don't they?"

He did not look away from the nearest basket, but only pressed his forehead against the glass.

"Look here," I said. "Why don't you go to a bakery or sweet shop and pick out something you like?" I held out the coins.

He did not look at me or at the proffered money. "You can't buy *those*," he said. "Those are only for guests."

"I'm sure you can get something nice." I jingled the coins.

He stood stock still. I had to lift up his hand for him and close his fingers around the coins. He did not thank me, but only continued to stare at the little basket. I began to wonder if, perhaps, he was not quite right.

The doorman admitted me, scowling at the boy as he did so. I checked in, ignoring the candy dish that was kept by the register. I rode the elevator to my floor. The corridor was cluttered with room-service dishes that had not been taken away, and I hurried past. In my room, I found a generous bowl of fruit on the bed table. The fruit was of the most ordinary assortment I could imagine – two apples, a banana, two oranges, and a pear. I was grateful for its simplicity. I was trying to lose weight, and perhaps if I satisfied myself with a piece of fruit, maybe the very blandest banana, I could do without dinner. In the morning I could have another piece of fruit and avoid the temptations of the breakfast room before my departure.

That was my plan, to eat only the banana, and perhaps an apple in the morning. But oh, what a banana it was! It looked like any banana I might have eaten before, with its slightly spotted skin. But the aroma as I peeled it was enchanting, with notes of apple, mango, and a delicate floral scent. As I bit into the fruit, I was astounded by the complexity of its foretaste, its delicate sweetness, the hint of tartness as my teeth crushed the yielding flesh. I chewed. As I swallowed, my mouth watered in anticipation of the next bite even as I detected a fading, volatile after-note.

When the banana was gone, I regretted that there had been only one. What a banana! I considered whether there would be any harm in trying one of the apples. I was eating fruit. Only fruit. Eating a meal of fruit was the very soul of moderation.

The apple was as novel and as glorious as the banana had been. Crisp, intense in both its tartness and its sweetness. Aromatic. When, I wondered, would I ever encounter another apple like that? Quite possibly never, unless the other one in the bowl was its equal, which it was. The oranges, likewise, were exquisite, and the pear. I called room service to ask if I might order a second bowl of fruit. After all, I would need a piece of fruit for my breakfast, and they sent up a larger bowl immediately with a complimentary basket of bread, which was the most extraordinary bread I had ever tasted. Also, a complimentary tureen of soup and a dense

THE SEVEN DEADLY HOTELS | 29

little pudding with custard sauce.

If only everything had been more ordinary, I would not have eaten it all. As I decided whether or not to eat the apple core, room service knocked on my door again. I hadn't ordered anything further. "Are you sure?" said the waiter, uncovering the plate of roasted lamb glazed in balsamic vinegar mint sauce with a side of buttered parsnips. "This isn't yours? Why don't you take it anyway? It would be a pity to have it go to waste. When will you ever have the chance to taste this particular preparation again? No charge."

I might have been able to say no, had I not smelled the dish. But when, indeed, would I have a chance like this again? And while I washed my face in the bathroom, the maid let herself into my room, turned down the bed covers, and left the most exquisite mint on my pillow. After I had eaten it, I thought of the dish of candy at reception, and went down in my bathrobe just to have a look. There I discovered that the candies were custom made for the Hotel Ginger Plum. They were wrapped in seven different colors, and each flavor was like nothing I had ever tasted before, and when would I get to taste them again? On the tables in the lobby were those irresistible cakes and biscuits in the little baskets. I put some in my other pocket, the one that was not already full of candies, then ate most of them on my way back to my room. There were two waiters wheeling room service carts, stopping at the rooms of other guests where empty plates were already stacked outside the doors. In my absence, the maid had come again and put another mint on my pillow.

I was up most of the night eating. Although I had left no wake-up call, the phone rang early. It was the concierge reminding me that the breakfast room was now open. He began to describe the sweets and savories on offer.

Near noon, as I was checking out, I happened to turn from the front desk toward the street where I saw the boy again. He was standing in the same place as before, looking in at the nearest basket of complimentary sweets. I finished paying my bill. Then, supposing that I remained a guest of the hotel until I left the premises, I sat down at the table near the window and examined the contents of the basket. The boy watched as I ate lavender-colored cakes, pistachio-powdered biscuits, and little horns of flavored cream so scrumptious that I could not resist going around the lobby, from basket to basket, eating every last one of them.

3. Le Manoir Crapaud d'Or

My guide book advised me to pack light: "The climb from the roadway to the summit is challenging, and difficult to negotiate with heavy or oversized bags." As the taxi driver left me at the foot of the trail, I gazed up at the pinnacle of rock before me and decided that the guide book's caution was a marvel of understatement. As I had seen from miles away in the approaching cab, the sides of the salient were sheer and bare of vegetation except for a scraggly bush or stunted tree rooted here or there in a crack. I had packed light, with only one small suitcase. But even this seemed imprudent to me now, and I paused long enough to sort through my belongings and lighten my load. I cached my electric shaver, my pyjamas, one of my shirts and my book among some loose rocks and marked the location with a little pile of stones. Then I started up the trail.

Along with glossing over the hazards of reaching Le Manoir Crapaud d'Or, the guide book had failed to describe the beauty of the view. As I toted my little bag higher and higher above the valley floor, the forests and circling mountains presented me with an ever more breathtaking panorama.

The path itself was in most places wide enough for two travellers to pass, but I was nevertheless grateful not to encounter anyone else during my ascent. Along some of the wider stretches, a low curb of stones edged the path, but when the path narrowed and the edge dropped off abruptly, it was all I could do to resist the urge to drop to my knees and crawl. Crawling would be too slow. The sun was near the horizon, and I didn't know how much farther I had to climb.

I stopped briefly now and then to rest, Along the path, scraps of fabric hung here or there from snags of jagged rock or were tangled in the occasional stunted tree. Why, I wondered, would anyone want to mark the trail with strips of cloth?

As the sun continued to sink, I pressed on. At last, knees shaking, I stepped onto the level ground of the summit. The sun had dropped behind the mountains, though the sky was still blue. Le Manoir Crapaud d'Or, built from stone quarried from the pinnacle, rose before me like an enchanted palace, golden light spilling from every window.

I staggered into the foyer, collapsed in a chair, and was instantly attended by three members of the staff. A woman handed me a glass of champagne. "Not everyone who makes a reservation has the fortitude to arrive," she told me. She pointed out that the champagne flute was engraved with the name of the hotel and said that I was welcome to keep it as a remembrance. The little collection of *amuses-bouche* were likewise served on a souvenir plate, a piece of fine china bearing the name of the hotel and edged in gold.. Another woman wafted a cool breeze over my head with an ornamental fan. When I finally felt able to regain my feet and go sign the guest register, she folded the fan. "A memento," she said, presenting it to me.

Ordinarily, I would not have considered these objects worth

keeping. Why bother with a champagne glass and plate that matched nothing else I owned? When would I ever use the fan again? But the ordeal of the trail infused these objects with significance. I had earned them. *Not everyone who makes a reservation has the fortitude to arrive.*

In my room, I discovered a pair of pyjamas laid out on the bed with a note explaining that if I wished to keep them, I could do so with the compliments of the hotel. They were silk, and dyed a deep blue that suits me very well.

I had dinner in the restaurant. The prices were nothing extraordinary. I resisted the waiter's suggestion that I could keep my entire place setting. The silverware alone would have been worth more than what I paid for the meal, and his generosity made me uneasy. I did accept the gift of the unique glass in which I was served my complimentary aperitif. The waiter asked, as he brought the check, if there was any object in the room that I fancied as a keepsake. Anything at all! I told him that really I was the sort of person who valued experiences rather more than objects.

Upon returning to my room I called the front desk to confirm the rate that I was paying for my room. It was hard to see how they could profit from my visit if I walked off with the silverware. What was the catch?

The wind had come up while I dined. Shutters rattled in the window frames of my room. After I had put on my silk pyjamas and slippers—all mine to keep—I remembered that I had left my book at the foot of the trail. I went down to the desk to ask if there were anything that I might borrow, and the clerk showed me into the library. I do not know what I expected as I began to survey the shelves. Outdated encyclopedias? Guidebooks left by previous guests? Tattered paperback novels? But the first title to catch my eye was a faded cloth cover stamped *Die Traumdeutung.*

It looked old. Reverently I drew this treasure from its shelf, opened the spotless cover, and there beheld on the title page, below "von Dr. Sigm. Freud" and in well-aged ink, the signature of the author. "First edition?" I said. "Signed? My God! Do you realize what you have here?"

"No one reads these," said the clerk. "If you see something you'd like to take home with you, feel free." He closed the door on his way out.

I could scarcely believe the other titles. *Ulysses* in the 1922 edition from Shakespeare & Company. Not signed. That would have been too much to hope for. But an actual first edition! There were some books I had never heard of by authors I hadn't read, but among the English titles I also found *The Hound of the Baskervilles*, *The Sun Also Rises*, and *The Sound and the Fury*. All first editions! Among the books in French, there were many that I didn't recognize, and some covers that were too old to read. I had to turn to title pages. My hands trembled when I found I was holding *Pensées de M. Pascal sur la réligion*. I could not tell whether it was a first edition, but I read enough to determine that it was an early and uncensored one.

I carried a stack of books to reception. "Some of these," I said, "are almost certainly worth a great deal of money. Are you sure that I may have them?"

"Sir," he said. He paused as a gust of wind shook the doors and shutters. "Sir, help yourself to anything that pleases you. Anything at all. Except for the linens. If you want any bed or bath linens, you have to pay for them."

I hauled the stack to my room and returned to the library for more. I made two more trips to the library. Three. Four. My hoard consisted of more books than I could possibly carry. I went to the desk again. "Is it possible to hire someone to carry my things down for me in the morning?"

He gave me a disapproving look. "It is entirely out of the question."

In my room, I fell into a fever of sorting. I would not keep the souvenir plate or the champagne flute. Well, perhaps the champagne flute, as I could wrap it in the pyjamas. I had earned it. Could I discard some of my clothes? But even if I carried nothing but books in my little suitcase, there would be books that would not fit, books that I could not bear to leave behind.

I returned to the desk. "Could I leave some things here and come back for them another time?"

"Sir," said the clerk, "what do you think we are? The Manoir offers you its hospitality, but we are not a warehouse."

I could perhaps tie books into a bundle made from the pyjamas. But what if the books spilled out on the trail? The sheer silk might split at the seams. What I needed was another suitcase or a backpack or...

"The pillowcases," I said. "How much?"

The clerk reached under the counter and brought out the price list. I blinked and made sure that the numbers were what they seemed. "For pillowcases?" I said.

He nodded. "We accept credit cards, of course."

Now I could see where Le Manoir Crapaud d'Or made its profit. The pillow cases cost as much as what I imagined a pillowcase full of books would be worth. Even so, it wasn't about the money. It was about leaving with no regrets. How could I live with myself if I left behind such treasure?

All night, as the the wind howled around the hotel, I sorted and resorted my books, my lovely books and considered whether, instead of pillow cases, I really ought to go with a sheet.

4. Pensiunea Calul Bălan

I didn't much like the look of the two hotels on the main street, each with worn carpets, interchangeably bored desk clerks, and a lobby reeking of stale tobacco, so despite the lateness of the hour I shouldered my little bag and made my way into the winding cobblestoned side streets. Most windows were dark. I found a restaurant, closed, and a drinking establishment whose sole patron eyed me with bleary contempt.

I resigned myself to choosing the less shabby of the two hotels, if I could determine which one that was, but now I was lost. The curving streets brought me into a little square, and there, by moonlight, I saw a sign bearing the figure of a white horse, and below that, in big letters I could just make out, PENSIUNEA.

Dim light showed in one of the windows. I tried the locked door, then knocked. I thought I heard the creak of a floorboard, but even my second knock brought no answer. Just as I turned to go, lantern light moved in the space between the pension and the house next to it. The gate opened, and the elderly man who appeared there lifted the lantern high so that we gazed into one another's faces by its light. He smiled.

"Bună seara," I said. "Do you have a room for the night?"

He smiled more broadly. "Not for just anyone," he said. "But for you, certainly!" He knocked on the locked door twice, once, then twice again, and the door opened from within. I was admitted to a fire-lit sitting room by a lovely woman—his daughter, I supposed.

She said, "You are to be congratulated. Not everyone who looks is able to find us."

The man added, "Not everyone who finds us is admitted. But for someone of your stature..." He waved his hand.

"Someone of my stature?" I said. What could these people

in a remote town know of me? Although I have a considerable reputation in some circles, surely that reputation was not the sort that could precede me.

"Someone," said the woman, "of your tastes. One needs only to look at how you dress. We don't open for just anyone, you know. Oh, no! Most certainly not!"

"Domnişoara," I said politely, "I give hardly any thought to my clothes."

"Obviously," she said, "you care for greater refinements than mere appearance. And you have troubled yourself to learn our language!"

"Only a few words."

"That raises you above the common sort of traveller," said the man. I smiled at that. I do think it matters that I learn a few polite words wherever I go. He said, "Shall I show you a room, then?"

We climbed the stairs, he and I, to a cozy, tidy bedroom. The furnishings were dark and sturdy. "This will do nicely," I said.

"Yes," he agreed, "this is a suitable room for our most ordinary class of guest."

"So there's something better?"

"It costs a little more. But, yes, there is something better, for guests of a more discerning taste. But, after all, once you are asleep, what does it matter what the room looks like, eh? This will suit you, then?"

"Well," I said, "perhaps you could show me the other room?"

He smiled. "I knew you weren't of that ordinary class. Mind you, all of our guests are a cut above, but I did think you were the sort who, well, you'll see!"

I followed him up another flight of stairs. From a utilitarian perspective, this second room was the same size as the first, was equipped with a bed, a dresser, a desk and two chairs. But every piece of furniture was embellished with delicate carvings, and the paintings on the wall were well-executed landscapes. "Lovely!"

"Yes, lovely. Yes." He nodded. "You like it, then? It's a suitable room for an art lover with mundane tastes. Is this where I should settle you?"

"I'm not sure," I said. I felt a little insulted. My tastes were hardly limited to the mundane.

"Well, there is the next room upstairs," he said, "but it's really for our thoroughly modern guests. The furnishings are, you see, rather avant garde. And it costs rather a lot more. It might be beyond your means, and at your age..."

At my age, he said! At my age! I was not nearly as old as he was! I was not so many years older than his pretty daughter, in fact, or at least not so much older that, well, that she would ever say to me, as she surely said to him: *At your age...*

"I want to see this room. Show it to me!"

"Very well." He led the way up the stairs. When I saw the room, I had to laugh for two reasons. The first was that the furnishings were not so very avant garde as he thought. They were sleek, Danish modernist pieces, and the table was not unlike one that I had at home. The paintings on the wall were handsome oils depicting figures in modern dress in classic poses amid allegorical settings. Brilliant stuff, really, and the sort of thing that not everyone is able to *get*. I said so. I said that the room and the price suited me very well. I dropped my bag on the bed.

"I must say," the old man said, "that I had not recognized you as such a connoisseur. I congratulate you for your taste and your persistence. Breakfast is in the sitting room. Now, unless you need anything else, I will say good night."

"Just a moment," I said. I put my hands on my hips. "Is there yet another room?"

He turned away. "Not for a man in your condition," he said.

"What?" I said. "A man in my what?"

He looked over his shoulder at me. "I mean nothing by it. You're a man who has lived some already, yes?" He turned to face me. "We know that you're a man of the world, a man who appreciates fine things. But let's be honest, sir. That appreciation takes time to acquire. You're no young stallion any longer, no more than I am. The only remaining room is suitable, frankly, for an athlete, a man in his prime. In fact, it was made specifically for an athlete in his twenties."

I retrieved my bag. "I would like to see this room."

"I will show it to you, but you must understand that I can't let you stay there. I couldn't be responsible for what might happen."

"Lead the way," I said.

We passed through what seemed to be the attic, through a hatch in the roof, and up another set of stairs into a still higher moonlit structure on stilts. Within that structure, we came to a landing before a locked door. Next to the door was a great two-handled lever of the sort found attached to water pumps in mines. "We have to raise the floor to enter," the old man said. He took hold of the lever at one end and directed me to the handle opposite. As we worked the lever, the landing vibrated with the rattling of chains taking up slack beneath us, and then the squeak of machinery and the groan of great beams. At last came a loud BANG! "It's set for ten minutes now," he said. "It won't last longer than that without working the machines. We mustn't linger." He unlocked the door.

The attic room inside was Spartan. There was a bed. Next to that, a table, and mounted on the table an alarm clock. The old man wound and set the clock, showing me as he did so that the clock was solidly attached to the table, and that the table was nailed to the floor. The bed, too, was nailed down, the bare mattress strapped to the frame. "When the room is at rest," the old man explained, "this floor swings open. Anyone inside would be flung to the roof or the street below."

"Why?" I said. "For what possible purpose...?"

"Built for a much younger man," the proprietor explained. "A man devoted to his strength, his endurance. These apparatus..." He went to one of the four corners. He took the handle of the machine there and demonstrated the action. "This one strengthens the arms." He went to another corner. "This one, the legs." He crossed to the third. "You must pardon the nature of this demonstration. You did ask to see this room." The third machine required a vigorous thrusting of the hips. The sexual application of the motion required no imagination. The fourth machine similarly prepared the body for extensive carnal labor. "These machines, like the handles outside, work the mechanism that keeps the floor upright. By means of vigorous work, a man can build up the mechanical energy to hold the floor in position for up to an hour at a time. But then he must rise and do it all again. Or else."

"This is crazy!" I said. "Who would submit himself to such torture?"

"A man not at all like you or I," said the proprietor. "A man of youthful vigor, of legendary stamina. A man for whom the very building of this room enhanced his reputation for scandal. But for us, such days are over, are they not? If ever we knew such days at all?" He laughed. I did not laugh with him. I was realizing that once he left me for the night, his daughter would certainly ask him which room I had chosen. What sort of knowing smile might she have for a man who at my age, yes, at my age, had stayed the night in the top-most room?

When the old man saw my expression, he insisted upon cash payment in advance.

5. Grønn Hotell

While I waited for the crew of the freighter to fetch the steamer trunks from my cabin, a hotel agent roaming the dock approached to make me an offer that seemed too good to be true. The handbill from the Grønn Hotell featured engraved illustrations of a plain, simple room with only a bed, a table, and a chair—all at a reasonable price. But beneath this illustration were engravings of a much finer room with a bigger bed, elegant furnishings, and a splendid view over the village and down to the sea. Additional images showed a vast courtyard with a swimming pool, steam room, and a bar.

These additional amenities, explained the agent, were available at no extra cost to any guest who paid for a basic room. I thought at first that I had misunderstood him, and that the extras were for those paying for a fancy room. But the agent said, no, the extras were for anyone. Anyone who paid for a basic room could use a grander room at no charge. Anyone who paid for a basic room might swim in the pool for free. Anyone who paid for a basic room could have a few drinks at the bar without paying a single øre more. Meals in the dining room? No extra cost. Next I wondered at the value of the local money. Had I erred in calculating the exchange rate?

"Please do not worry, sir," he said. "Everything is as I say."

I agreed to have a look at the place, anyway. He waved a green flag high in the air, and a motorcar turned onto the dock and made slow progress toward us among the departing sailors and the longshoremen at work. The agent and driver loaded my trunks into the car, and then the driver steered the car slowly off the dock, through the village, and up the side of the mountain. The road to the Grønn Hotell wove up the side of the slope, this way and that, providing a view of at least two sides of the hotel. It was big, but I already knew that it surrounded a large courtyard. Strangely, only the topmost floor had windows looking outward with a view to the village, the sea, the islands, or the surrounding slopes. The lower floors all presented a blind face of solid brick. Without windows to count, it was impossible to know how high the building might be. Seven stories? Eight? And if the guest rooms were all on the top, what was the purpose of the lower floors?

At the reception desk, there were the same engravings that I had already seen of the basic room. Then, the extras: The swimming pool. The steam room. The dining hall. The bar. The better, optional room with a grand view. I tapped the illustration of the better room. "All included?" I asked the clerk.

"Everything is included," he said.

I wanted to see one of these grander rooms. The clerk said that such rooms were exclusive to the top floor. He gave me a key and showed me to the stairs. Eight flights up, I stepped into a thickly carpeted silent corridor where gas lights burned outside of each brass-appointed door. I let myself into a room. The engraving had not done the place justice. The furnishings were elegant and clean. I opened a window and inhaled the scents of pine from the mountains and salt from the sea. Sunlight glittered on the distant harbor.

As I descended the stairs, I was already counting out my money. What a bargain!

"There is just one thing more to understand about the hotel," the clerk said when I laid my money on the counter. "You enjoy the optional amenities at the pleasure of the other guests. If another guest wishes to deny you any amenity beyond the basic room, he or she may do so for a fee." He laid a price list on the counter. "And you, of course, may deny other guests in the same way, if you choose."

Again, I wondered if I had misunderstood. But the price list seemed clear enough, in five languages: Deny better room. Deny dining hall. Deny bar. Deny swimming. Deny steam. Each with a price.

Well, I thought, what could this have to do with me? Why should any other guest care about the room that I stay in or the pleasures that I enjoy?

"By paying the basic room price," said the clerk, "you agree to abide by this condition."

"I suppose," I said with a shrug. "I want the room that I just saw. On the top floor."

"Certainly, sir."

"They aren't already taken?"

"Not at all, sir."

I signed. The clerk rang for the bellman, who had already loaded my trunks onto a trolley. We did not take the stairs. From the carpeted lobby, we exited into the courtyard where the trolley's metal wheels clattered against the paving stones. The sound echoed among all the inward looking windows of the rooms on lower floors. These were, I supposed, the basic rooms. I hadn't even asked to inspect one. Well, I wasn't going to stay in one of *those* places, with their inward facing windows. Not when I could have a grand room with a wonderful view.

All the way across the courtyard, past the pool and entrance for the steamroom, a glass lift awaited. The bellman opened the lift doors, stowed my trunks inside, and then went around the outside of the car fitting green flags into sconces.

"What are the flags for?" I said.

He shrugged, which I took to mean that he spoke no English. He closed the door and turned the crank on the lift telephone a few times. He held the earpiece as he said a few words into the receiver. Across the courtyard, a whistle sounded. So much procedure for running the elevator up! So much pomp and theater! At last the bellman pulled the lever to start our creaking ascent. As we rose, I decided that the flags made the ride in the lift more festive. And I was, after all, on my way to the top floor, the realm of special luxury! I looked across the courtyard windows, the windows of the basic rooms. The curtains of each window were parted a little. How fortunate I was that there was space in the better rooms, simply for the asking! I thought I saw the curtains in one room move. And in another room, the curtains most certainly stirred. Poor souls, stuck in a basic room. Yes, I was most fortunate indeed.

We were still some distance from the top when the bells on the telephone jangled. The bellman halted the lift, lifted the earpiece, and listened in silence. He replaced the earpiece, and we descended to the courtyard. He wheeled my trunks out of the elevator. "Come," he said. He removed the green flags from the lift.

"My room," I said, "is up there. Top floor." I motioned with my hands: Up! Up!

"Room," he said, nodding. I followed him across the courtyard, down a corridor, and into the cage of a much less refined lift. We arrived at the fourth floor where he showed me to a room. A basic room. It was even dingier than the engravings had made it look: a narrow bed, a table next to the parted curtains, a chair. On the table were a pair of binoculars and a sheet of paper.

"No, no," I said. "I want a room on the top floor."

"Room," he said. He lingered in the doorway as if I might tip him. Most certainly not! Instead, I followed him back to the ground floor.

I said to the clerk, "Now see here! I'm entitled to one of the rooms on the top floor!"

"Sir," said the clerk, "you paid for a basic room. You requested a better room, but another guest paid to deny you the top floor."

"Well in heaven's name, why would anyone do that? I don't know anyone here! I've never even been to this country before today!"

"I'm very sorry," said the clerk. "But you still have the basic room. It's a good value. You have the other amenities..."

"Someone actually paid money to keep me from enjoying the better room? Who?"

The clerk only shook his head.

I considered returning to my room, but the sight of it would only make me angry. I went to the bar. The gaslights burned low. The place was full. Angry faces turned toward me from every table, and I glared back. No one had better deny me this amenity, I thought. I ordered a whisky and soda, and then another, quick, before someone ruined my chance. A man and woman came in together, laughing, and someone at the bar shoved money across to the bartender and spoke a few words in a low voice. When the laughing man approached the bar and said, "We'll have..." the bartender shook his head.

"Not for you," he told them.

"What do you mean?" the man said, not laughing now.

Join the club, I thought.

I had another drink. No one denied me. I tried not to look as if I were enjoying it.

Back in my basic room, I sat heavily in the chair before the table. The sheet of paper, I discovered, was the price list. Deny, deny, deny, in five languages.

I picked up the binoculars and gazed through the parted curtains into the courtyard. The glass car of the lift was empty, but there was a family of fat people walking across the paving stones dressed in bathing costumes. Their forearms and calves were pink. The man had a full moustache. I have never been able to grow a moustache like that, damn him. I turned the focus ring to see him better. He smiled as he dipped his toes in the water. His wife smiled. The children looked content. Their mouths were open, and they might all have been laughing as they waded into the pool.

I examined the price list again. How much to deny swimming?

6. L'Hotel Fiasco Rosso

I arrived long after midnight, exhausted. The wide front window of L'Hotel Fiasco Rosso was painted with the establishment's emblem, a red flask tipped to pour its contents. As I stepped from my cab, I tried to get a look at the lobby through that window, but I couldn't see past the shelves against the window that displayed all manner of porcelain and crystal—cups, saucers, wineglasses and figurines. If "Hotel" weren't part of the name, I'd have thought I was standing in front of a china shop. The bellman—an old man with white hair—started to move my luggage from the cab and onto a trolley. "Go on ahead, sir," he said, resting with his hands on his knees after he had shifted the first bag. "I'll be along."

The window display of glass and china provided a good foretaste of the lobby. There were glass shelves along all the walls, among the lobby furniture, and behind the front desk. All of these shelves and all of the low tables held china or bric-à-brac. The desk itself was cluttered end to end with figurines and teacups, each one sporting a little paper price tag. Behind the counter was a boy who looked too young to possibly be the clerk, but as I approached, he asked if I had a reservation. I gave him my name. He looked at two sheets of paper in front of him and frowned. He asked me to say my name again. I did. He frowned again and asked me to spell it out. I did.

"This isn't you, is it?" Over the cluttered counter, he passed me a form with someone else's name.

"No."

"Not this one either?" The characters on this form weren't even in the right alphabet.

"Most certainly not."

"Oh." He picked up telephone, then put it down when there was apparently no answer on the other end. "Well, you don't have a reservation," he said.

"But I do," I insisted.

"It's all right," he said. "I'll find you a room anyway. Passport?" I gave him my passport. He opened a notebook. The page he opened to looked to me like a confused mass of scribbled notes. He frowned, added a few pencil marks to the page, and then handed me a form to fill in. I took the form away because there was not enough space on the desk counter for me to fill it out there. But there wasn't space on any of the coffee tables in the lobby, either. Dishes and figurines covered every surface. Gingerly, I removed a tiny cow, a vase, a girl with an umbrella, a flowered cup and saucer, and two miniature buildings from an end table so I could have a hard writing surface. I noted the prices on the items as I handled them. They were nothing I would ever want to own, but someone valued them highly, it seemed. When I had filled in the form, I put the pieces back in their place.

I returned to the desk. I pointed to a space that the boy should have filled in. "And the rate?"

He quoted me an amount half again as much as what I had secured with my reservation. "That's wrong," I told him. It was still a good price, better than any other quote I'd had for the city, but a deal's a deal. "That is not what I reserved."

"You didn't reserve anything," he said. "Don't try to fool me."

That was no way for him to talk to a customer, or to any adult, for that matter! I held my tongue, though. He was only a child. "Let me speak to someone else," I said. "The manager."

"They aren't answering," he said. "They never answer at this time of night." He picked up the phone, dialed, listened, then hung up. "See?"

"Well, then, I'll just have to sort this out in the morning. With someone responsible." I looked around. "Where's the bellman with my luggage?"

The boy opened a drawer and took out a piece of paper. "How many pieces?"

"What?"

He asked the question more slowly. "How. Many. Pieces? Of luggage? How many pieces of luggage are you claiming to have lost?"

"I haven't lost any. They're with the bellman."

"If you gave them to the bellman," said the boy, "they're lost."

As if to confirm this, the bellman entered the lobby then, pushing an empty trolley.

"You there!" I called out. I strode to the bellman. "What have you done with my bags!"

"Your bags, your bags," said the bellman, rubbing the back of his head. "So they were your bags, were they?"

"My bags," I said. "The ones you were just taking from the cab!"

"Were you coming or going?" he said. "Dear me."

I hurried out of the hotel onto the empty street. The cab was gone. There was no sign of my luggage. When I returned to the lobby, the bellman was nowhere in sight. The boy waited, holding up his lost-luggage form, and asked again, "How many pieces?"

When the elevator doors opened on the top floor, they opened onto cold darkness. I stepped out, thinking that perhaps the corridor lights would come on when I did. When the elevator doors closed behind me, it was very dark indeed. I groped forward, found a door, but I couldn't feel a number on it. I looked up and saw stars. The top floor had no roof. I groped my way back to the elevator, but nothing happened when I pressed the button. I had to find and take the stairs.

"You sent me to the roof!" I told the boy.

"Oh, right," he said. "No top floor right now. Because of the construction." He consulted his notebook again, then gave me a key for a room on another floor.

I found that room, but when I went to wash my face, there was no water.

The boy consulted his notebook. "I guess they turned the water off on that floor. Because of the construction." He gave me a third key.

In the third room, soiled sheets and bath linens were piled on the floor. The mattress was bare.

The boy spent a long time turning the pages of his notebook this time, then told me that probably that room wasn't supposed to be used because of the construction. He gave me a fourth key. When I rode the elevator again, found the room, opened the door and turned on the light, I discovered that a couple was already in the bed. The man sat up. "Now what?" he said. "Who the hell are you?"

"Sorry," I said.

"Sorry, my ass! Get the hell out of our room!" He seized something from the bed table and threw it. The object shattered on the wall near my head. I shut the door. In my haste, I failed to turn out the light. "Asshole!" I heard him say. Well, none of this was my fault!

As I returned to the lobby, I pondered the question of just whose fault it was. The child at the desk wasn't old enough to be competent. The bellman was too senile to remember what he was doing. Who had hired them? What idiot of a manager was running this place?

"Well," said the boy when he gave me my fifth key of the night, "you should have made a reservation."

The bed in the fifth room was made. The lights worked. Water ran from the tap. The toilet flushed. There was no soap in the soap dish, only a ceramic imitation of a bar of soap. There were ceramic flowers on the cistern of the toilet. I rinsed my face, since I couldn't really wash it. I stripped to my underwear, since I had no pyjamas to wear. Removed the expensive figurines from the night stand, afraid that I might knock them onto the floor in my sleep. I turned out the light, and got into bed.

Bang! Bang! Bang! Bang!

I sat up.

Bang! Bang!

It sounded as if someone were hammering the walls in the room next to me. I turned on the light, dialed the front desk, and the boy told me, "Yes, that's the construction. Do you want me to put you in a different room?"

"No," I said. "I'm coming down." I dressed. I returned to the lobby. "Give me my passport," I said. "I'm leaving."

"Not without paying, you aren't," the boy said.

"Give me my passport, you impudent runt!" I picked up a ballerina and snapped off her head. "Give me my passport, or so help me..."

"I can't!" he said. He started to cry. "I can't until you pay for the room!"

"God damn you!" I roared. I swept a dozen cups and figurines onto the floor where they landed with a satisfying smash.

He flinched at the sound. "And those," he said, wiping his cheeks with his sleeve, glaring at me with reddened eyes. "You'll have to pay for those, too."

7. El Hotel Mono Rojo

Some brothers of my order used the name of the city as another word for sin. They spoke in hushed voices of the fallen women, the boys for sale, the corrupting commerce of that place, and they worried for the soul of any man who went there. They worried for my soul in particular, and bade me farewell with promises of fervent prayers of protection. I was unafraid. Even as a younger man, when I still sometimes struggled with the temptations of the flesh, I had been the courier for our abbey. Our order made money from painting and selling icons. Twice a year for many years I had crossed the desert, stayed in the city, and continued the next day to deliver our surplus earnings to the convent school. On the way home, I would again spend the night in the city. The city always tried to tempt me, but repeating the words "The glory of God," had always protected me. I had never fallen.

This experience had persuaded me that I knew all the methods by which travellers were lured. Thus did I consider myself safe. I was an old man, resigned to the impermanence of flesh and less impressed by the shape of a woman's calf or the swell of her breasts. When I entered the outskirts of the city, women called to passing men from shadowed doorways, but few of them bothered with me. My white hair, the simplicity of my robe and sandals, my resolute stride, or perhaps some other signal indicated I was a poor target. Had they known how much money I carried in my leather purse, they might have made more of an effort. But it still would have been in vain.

In the hotel district, I chose the lodging with a sign showing a red ape and the words "Hotel Mono Rojo." I had stayed here before. The hotels on this street were inexpensive, for the owners expected to make their money in other ways. From me, they had never collected more than the single coin for lodging.

In the lobby, every chair leg, every pillar, every carpentry joint where one piece of wood met another was shaped like a limb, like a woman striking an alluring pose, like a union of flesh with flesh. In the dark wooden panels of the walls lurked lines and shapes that suggested, but did not quite reveal, various acts of carnal knowledge among men, women, and perhaps.... But it was best not to speculate. The frankly erotic paintings were less dangerous, less of a lure to the imagination. "The glory of God," I whispered to myself. Wherever my gaze fell, there was temptation: in the carpet pattern of the red nymphs and black satyrs, or in the carmine fingernails of the clerk as she beckoned me closer to sign the register.

However, the lobby was the worst of it. I was soon ascending the stairs with the bellman, who held my key, though I had asked to carry it myself. My only burdens were the purse at my waist and a loaf of bread tied into a cloth. I needed no assistance. "Just let me show you the way, sir," he said.

He opened the door for me. When he did so, I caught sight of a feather lying on the floor. I stepped into the room and bent to pick the feather up. It was most unusual, with a golden shaft and a white vane edged in gold. The bellman snatched it out of my hand. "Very sorry, sir," he said. "You ought not to have seen that." He put the feather in his breast pocket.

"Why?" I said. "What is it?"

"I, I don't know how it got here. Sometimes the chamber maids are careless! Will that be all, sir?" He worked to stuff the feather ever deeper into his pocket in a manner that struck me as theatrical, as if by his actions he were saying, *Forget all about the feather*, but in a manner designed to make me think of nothing else. I thought I understood, then. This was one of the ploys such establishments depended on. Well, I would not be taken in. "Yes," I said. "That is all. You may go, and good night to you."

He paused in the doorway. He turned to look at me and said, "Well if you must know, it is a feather from the angel."

I didn't reply. I imagined that this discovery of the feather and the bellman's stammering disavowal was a performance enacted with some regularity at El Hotel Mono Rojo. I was meant to say, *The Angel?* And the Angel would turn out to be some costumed dancer, the star of a cabaret or the object of an even more sinful entertainment. "Good night," I said again.

"I have only glimpsed it myself," the bellman said, still blocking the door. "No one knows why it doesn't fly back to heaven. And no one so far can understand its speech. But maybe you…."

So the angel was not a carnal temptation, but used for some spiritual fraud. I would not be taken in. "Bless you, my son," I insisted, "and good night!" I closed the door behind him and locked it.

An angel! In this place! Absurd!

I made my modest dinner of bread. While I chewed, a thought came to me: Why should there not be an angel in a place such as this? Is God not present even in the lives of sinners? Will his messengers not appear among the wicked, who have more need of divine messages than the pious?

I put these thoughts from my mind as I lay down to sleep. From the next room came the rhythmic thump thump thump and muffled cries of adulterous exertions. "The glory of God!" I chanted aloud. "The glory of God!"

What did I know, truly, of the glory of God? I prayed that one day my chastity and humility would be rewarded and I would know God's glory. But what if I need not wait until my last breath? "The glory of God" I whispered, as I tried to recall the details of the feather. Had it looked like an ordinary feather decorated by a clumsy hand? Or was it, indeed, an object of astonishing beauty?

Here is the nature of sin: I had doubts, of course, and yet I could not sleep for thinking of the angel. My prayer failed to bring serenity or sleep. Before dawn had broken, I found myself paying the grinning bellman, with money that was not even my own, and following him to the top floor into a little room hung with red curtains. When the curtains drew back to reveal a dim circular room with mirrors all around, mirrors that could only be the windows of other little curtained rooms, I knew the vice that this place ordinarily celebrated, the sorts of things that other guests must pay to witness. I knew all of this, yet when the curtain parted, I held my breath. I stared.

Though the light was dim, though reason told me that I must be seeing some trick of goose feathers, gold paint, and wax, I beheld the most graceful and beautiful creature that my eyes had ever seen. I saw an angel. I witnessed the gentle expansion of the wings as the angel breathed, the curve of its down-covered fingers. It had its winged back to me. How I longed to see its face! "The glory of God!" I whispered, filled with longing. "The glory of God!"

THE REVISIONIST

Miranda Mellis

Miranda Mellis' work has appeared in *The Believer, Context, McSweeney's, Fence, Cabinet, Denver Quarterly*, and *Post Road*. She teaches at the California College of the Arts and is an editor at The Encyclopedia Project, a five-volume hardcover book project that seeks to present a wide variety of approaches to narrative by reimagining and reinterpreting the reference book and the literary journal. Raised in San Francisco, she was once an aerialist in the tiniest circus in the world, The Turnbuckles (Sister Spit Tour, '98). Taken from *Harper's*, "The Revisionist" was originally published in longer, book form by Calamari Press.

My last assignment was to conduct surveillance of the weather and report that everything was fine. They set me up in an abandoned lighthouse seven miles outside the city. The lighthouse stood in the center of a junkyard, atop a mound of mossy dirt. It was trumpet-shaped with inward sloping walls. A stack of old sewing machines and broken pianos surrounded the dump. Local kids jumped from piano to piano, stomping the sour keys. Dogs chased them, barking. From the tower I couldn't hear, but I could see the kids jumping and the dogs chasing, their jaws snapping open and shut in the barking maneuver. With the latest surveillance technology at my disposal, it was difficult to stay focused on the weather. I was tempted to make my own observations, and I did.

I saw a family driving to the country on vacation. Behind them, a bomb went off. Through my headphones, I noted the rushing sound of radiation cruising low across the land. The father, who was driving, saw the mushroom cloud in his rearview mirror. The others didn't turn around, so they never noticed.

When they reached the campsite, the kids pitched a family tent. The father went inside, zipped up the flap door and wouldn't come out. "I need time alone," he called. His family sat frowning around the picnic table. The father was laughing and moaning inside the tent. The older sister shook her fists in his direction. The younger brother gave the tent the finger. The mother tore her straw hat off and stomped on it. She ground it into the dirt, right outside the flap door. The father heard the twisting feet of the mother. Coming out of the tent and seeing the hat on the ground, he said, "There's something I've got to tell you, but not in front of the kids."

The mother said, "Why don't you let them hear it too. We'd all like to know what you're doing in the tent."

"There's been a nuclear attack." Saying these words out loud had a strange effect on the father. He began running around and around in circles. Then he fainted.

Through my telescope, buildings were curdling. The very air had faded, was pixilated. Inside one apartment building was an elderly woman. Her hearing aid was broken. She was watching the panic on television but could not understand what they were saying. She strained to hear them. She shook her head and wrung her hands. She kneeled and prayed. Her prayers exploded out of her mouth all over the carpet. She coughed up shards of bone and tiny blood-and-gristle soaked figurines. She washed the prayer viscera in the sink and hung them from a clothesline outside the window.

Back at the camp, the father gave the children tests. "What would you do in a nuclear holocaust?" But they couldn't answer. They pantomimed ducking under a school desk, but father frowned.

After they had quarantined the part of the county most affected by the bomb, I published a report showing that the radiation was harmless. My report on the radiation-less bomb was widely circulated. I was promoted. My employers wanted the real reports; I sent them the unrevised originals. A lot of people could see, by observing their own environments for themselves, that my reports were fraudulent.

People wanted to get away. Escape schemes flourished. One guy made a pile of money selling plots on Start Over Island. I went there myself, at first on vacation, and then for real. They gave you a new identity, a clean slate.

There were mutant children who sensed the impending exodus of all the adults, who planned on leaving their monstrous children behind. The mutated kids were impossible to soothe, perpetually hungry and thirsty, shivering and angry. The adults said, "It's only me going. The kids will get by. There are other adults around, social services, orphanages, hospitals, shelters. The others, they'll stick around, get pissed on the head by acid rain and all that, but I'll be gone, and the kids will just get used to it." But the kids didn't get used to it, or forget, because it never occurred to them that they could. No one had ever suggested it.

There were side effects on the island—reddened eyes and this compulsion to rip things. People would be talking mildly at the bank and suddenly rip out their own hair, or go outside and rip the moat of shrubbery surrounding the bank with their bared teeth. They would stumble through the parking lots, chewing the shrubs, eyes gyrating.

I might have stayed on the island if there was no one there I recognized. But there they all were, friends, acquaintances, family members.

At first I didn't mind—since we were now "strangers," I no longer had to do their dishes, take them to AA meetings, make sure they'd taken their pills, fight them off, go to counseling with them, worry about them, be jealous of them, suspect them of lying, miss them, hold their babies, take them to the hospital, help them move, fantasize about them, comment on their haircuts, see their points, admire their looks, proffer my goodwill, keep their secrets, pacify them, reassure them, seek their approval, recover from their abuses, read their manifestos, find them unreliable, try to see their good qualities, hope they'd vote, impress them, ignore their stupidity, or compete with them for jobs and housing.

The day after I ripped my own mother's clothes off in a supermarket, I suspected I needed to leave Start Over Island. My last conversation there convinced me of it. I had been visited by a lady with razor-thin lips. She made astral killings her business. She sold "air art" on the side. "You have enemies here," she told me. Evidently, she had been hired to murder my astral body. Furthermore, she said she had already done it. Hadn't I noticed anything different?

Some others, feeling remorseful, had gone back. But they'd lost their authority over their mutant children who now did whatever they had to do, as well as whatever they could get away with.

I returned to my revisions at the lighthouse. I concentrated on taking measurements of the rising ocean, training my instruments on the creeping shoreline and tidal fluctuations, and revising my data to report, unaccordingly, that the sea was just as usual.

The ocean had always functioned as a kind of clock for the sentient, but gradually it stopped telling our kind of time. The ocean was, simply, not the ocean anymore in the usual sense of the word. It was onto other measures. It tossed up four hundred dead dolphins one day, and claimed one hundred thousand baby seals the next.

The place where one could now go to experience the ancient rhythms of nature was the convenience store. Convenience stores were becoming "nature," and nature had become a run-down, thrashing machine. In the convenience store, people howled and chirped at one another.

A man was voiding near the chips aisle of a convenience store. He was in the process of digging a hole with a jackhammer to bury his shit when a robbery took place. He pulled out his video camera and caught the event on tape. He couldn't wait to get home and show his family the video of the robbery in progress, which had interrupted the burial of his bowel movement.

I fabricated phenomena, makeovers for a bevy of new industry-spawned carcinogens:

- *the air is getting cleaner by the day*
- *cloud miasmas: the future is bright*
- *animal depressions: we're living longer than ever*
- *500 trillion nanobots, built an atom at a time, war in a suitcase*
- *carbon dioxide emissions from fossil fuel combustion have proven highly beneficial to life on earth, especially cockroaches and poison ivy.*

On the outskirts of the city, I saw a man lying on the floor of a dirty small room. There was nothing else in the room but a projecting movie and a chair. The movie showed him sleeping on the dirty floor. He sat in the chair and dissolved.

His daughter came home and found the bones of her father in the chair. She sat on his lap bones, and she turned to bone dust. Her son came in and lay on the floor. There was nothing else left but the movie of his grandfather sleeping on the dirty floor, the chair and the combined bones. He sat in his mother's lap bones and dissolved. His daughter came in and lay on the floor. There was nothing else left but the movie of her great-grandfather, the chair and the bones. She sat in her father's lap bones and she turned to dust. I averted my eyes.

In the past, when something fell out of the sky, or there were collisions, men in jumpsuits arrived, sirens blaring, to erase all traces. Something was always done about something. Now nothing was done, except documentation. For every event, there were multiple documents and artifacts, until there were more documents and artifacts than events. Inevitably someone called a document an event, and people made documents of documents.

Some people chose to end their genetic line rather than risk bringing another lunatic into the world. "He could be the next Hitler," Some argued. "Or the next Einstein." This binary, the Hitler-Einstein dilemma, provided an inescapable deadlock for would-be breeders.

After a long hiatus, I delivered a 178-page summary of my "findings" that stated in its conclusion: *Continuing growth in greenhouse gas emissions is leading to a higher standard of living that will result in a global utopia by the end of the century.* The president quoted liberally from my report, hailing it as an objective docket.

I slept for a week. I awoke numb and looked out at the state. Things moved, had dimension, made sounds, slid right up to the surface, but could not poke through. Nothing was felt any longer, or known through the sense portals, despite the fact that every part of the body was designed for contact. Either the world, usually so flagrant, was camouflaged, or my surfaces were deteriorating. In any case, it was hidden. Time would pass without my seeing or recording events. Some events I would have to imagine. The made-up events were sometimes more believable than actual events. The actual events were often difficult to believe.

THE RUBY INCOMPARABLE

Kage Baker

Kage Baker is perhaps best known for her science fiction "Company" series, but has also turned her hand to horror, historical adventure, and fantasy, including *The Anvil of the World* and *The House of the Stag*. She resides in Pismo Beach, California. "Ruby Incomparable" is reprinted from the Gardner Dozois/ Jack Dann-edited *Wizards* fantasy anthology.

The girl surprised everyone.

To begin with, no one in the world below had thought her parents would have more children. Her parents' marriage had created quite a scandal, a profound clash of philosophical extremes; for her father was the Master of the Mountain, a brigand and sorcerer, who had carried the Saint of the World off to his high fortress. It's bad enough when a living goddess, who can heal the sick and raise the dead, takes up with a professional dark lord (black armor, monstrous armies and all). But when they settle down together with every intention of raising a family, what are respectable people to think?

The Yendri in their forest villages groaned when they learned of the first boy. Even in his cradle, his fiendish tendencies were evident. He was beautiful as a little angel except in his screaming tempers, when he would morph himself into giant larvae, wolf cubs or pools of bubbling slime.

The Yendri in their villages and the Children of the Sun in their stone cities all rejoiced when they heard of the second boy. He too was beautiful, but clearly good. A star was seen to shine from his brow on occasion. He was reported to have cured a nurse's toothache with a mere touch, and he never so much as cried while teething.

And the shamans of the Yendri, and the priests in the temples of the Children of the Sun, all nodded their heads and said: "Well, at least we have balance now. The two boys will obviously grow up, oppose each other and fight to the death, because that's what generally happens."

Having decided all this, and settled down confidently to wait, imagine how shocked they were to hear that the Saint of the World had borne a third child! And a girl, at that. It threw all their calculations off and annoyed them a great deal.

The Master and his Lady were surprised, too, because their baby daughter popped into the world homely as a little potato, by contrast with the elfin beauty of her brothers. They did agree that she had lovely eyes, at least, dark as her father's, and she seemed to be sweet-tempered. They named her Svnae.

So the Master of the Mountain swaddled her in purple silk, and took her out on a high balcony and held her up before his assembled troops, who roared, grunted and howled their polite approval. And that night in the barracks and servants' hall, around the barrels of black wine that had been served out in celebration, the minions of the proud father agreed amongst themselves that the little maid might not turn out so ugly as all that, if the rest of her face grew to fit that nose and she didn't stay quite so bald.

And they at least were proved correct, for within a year Svnae had become a lovely child.

On the morning of her fifth birthday, the Master went to the nursery and fetched his little daughter. He took her out with him on his tour of the battlements, where all the world stretched away below. The guards, tusked and fanged, great and horrible in their armor, stood to attention and saluted him. Solemnly he pulled a great red rose from thin air and presented it to Svnae.

"Today," he said, "my Dark-Eyed is five years old. What do you want most in all the world, daughter?"

Svnae looked up at him with her shining eyes. Very clearly she said:

"Power."

He looked down at her, astounded; but she stood there looking patiently back at him, clutching her red rose. He knelt beside her. "Do you know what Power is?" he asked.

"Yes," she said. "Power is when you stand up here and make all the clouds come to you across the sky, and shoot lightning and make thunder crash. That's what I want."

"I can make magic for you," he said, and with a wave of his gauntleted hand produced three tiny fire elementals dressed in scarlet, blue and yellow, who danced enchantingly for Svnae before vanishing in a puff of smoke.

"Thank you, Daddy," she said, "but no. I want *me* to be able to do it."

Slowly he nodded his head. "Power you were born with; you're my child. But you must learn to use it, and that doesn't come easily, or quickly. Are you sure this is what you really want?"

"Yes," she said without hesitation.

"Not eldritch toys to play with? Not beautiful clothes? Not sweets?"

"If I learn Power, I can have all those things anyway," Svnae observed.

The Master was pleased with her answer. "Then you will learn to use your Power," he said. "What would you like to do first?"

"I want to learn to fly," she said. "Not like my brother Eyrdway. He just turns into birds. I want to stay me and fly."

"Watch my hands," her father said. In his right hand he held out a stone; in his left, a paper dart. He put them both over the parapet and let go. The stone dropped; the paper dart drifted lazily down.

"Now, tell me," he said. "Why did the stone drop and the paper fly?"

"Because the stone is heavy and the paper isn't," she said.

"Nearly so; and not so. Look." And he pulled from the air an egg. He held it out in his palm, and the egg cracked. A tiny thing crawled from it, and lay shivering there a moment; white down covered it like dandelion fluff, and it drew itself upright and shook tiny stubby wings. The down transformed to shining feathers, and the young bird beat its wide wings and flew off rejoicing.

"Now, tell me," said the Master, "Was that magic?"

"No," said Svnae. "That's just what happens with birds."

"Nearly so; and not so. Look." And he took out another stone. He held it up and uttered a Word of Power; the stone sprouted bright wings, and improbably flew away into the morning.

"How did you make it do that?" Svnae cried. Her father smiled at her.

"With Power; but Power is not enough. I was able to transform the stone because I understand that the bird and the stone, and even the paper dart, are all the same thing."

"But they're not," said Svnae.

"Aren't they?" said her father. "When you understand that the stone and the bird are one, the next step is convincing the *stone* that the bird and the stone are one. And then the stone can fly."

Svnae bit her lip. "This is hard, isn't it?" she said.

"Very," said the Master of the Mountain. "Are you sure you wouldn't like a set of paints instead?"

"Yes," said Svnae stubbornly. "I *will* understand."

"Then I'll give you books to study," he promised. He picked her up and folded her close, in his dark cloak. He carried her to the bower of her lady mother, the Saint of the World.

Now when the Lady had agreed to marry her dread Lord, she had won from him the concession of making a garden on his black basalt mountaintop, high and secret in the sunlit air. Ten years into their marriage her orchards were a mass of white blossom, and her white-robed disciples tended green beds of herbs there. They bowed gracefully as Svnae ran to her mother, who embraced her child and gave her a white rose. And Svnae said proudly:

"I'm going to learn Power, Mama!"

The Lady looked questions at her Lord.

"It's what she wants," he said, no less proudly. "And if she has the talent, why shouldn't she learn?"

"But Power is not an end in itself, my child," the Lady said to her daughter. "To what purpose will you use it? Will you help others?"

"Ye-es," said Svnae, looking down at her feet. "But I have to learn first."

"Wouldn't you like to be a healer, like me?"

"I can heal people when I have Power," said Svnae confidently. Her mother looked a little sadly into her dark eyes, but saw no shadow there. So she blessed her daughter, and sent her off to play.

The Master of the Mountain kept his promise and gave his daughter books to study, to help her decipher the Three Riddles of Flight. She had to learn to read first; with fiery determination she hurled herself on her letters and mastered them, and charged into the first of the Arcane texts.

So well she studied that by her sixth birthday she had solved all three riddles, and was able at will to sprout little butterfly wings from her shoulders, wings as red as a rose. She couldn't fly much with them, only fluttering a few inches above the ground like a baby bird; but she was only six. One day she would soar.

Then it was the Speech of Animals she wanted to learn. Then it was how to move objects without touching them. Then she desired to know the names of all the stars in the sky: not only what men call them, but what they call themselves. And one interest led to another, as endlessly she found new things by which to be intrigued, new arts and sciences she wanted to learn. She spent whole days together in her father's library, and carried books back to her room, and sat up reading far into the night.

In this manner she learned to fly up to the clouds with her rose-red wings, there to ask an eagle what it had for breakfast, or gather pearls with her own hands from the bottom of the sea.

And so the years flowed by, as the Master throve on his mountain, and the Saint of the World brought more children into it to confound the expectations of priests and philosophers, who debated endlessly the question of whether these children were Good or Evil.

The Saint held privately that all her children were, at heart, Good. The Master of the Mountain held, privately and out loud too, that the priests and philosophers were all a bunch of idiots.

Svnae grew tall, with proud dark good looks she had from her father. But there were no black lightnings in her eyes, as there were in his. Neither were her eyes crystal and serene, like her mother's, but all afire with interest, eager to see how everything worked.

And then she grew taller still, until she overtopped her mother; and still taller than that, until she overtopped her brother Eyrdway. He was rather peevish about it and took to calling her The Giantess, until she punched him hard enough to knock out one of his teeth. He merely morphed into a version of himself without the missing tooth, but he stopped teasing her after that.

Now you might suppose that many a young guard might begin pining for Svnae, and saluting smartly as she passed by, and mourning under her window at night. You would be right. But she never noticed; she was too engrossed in her studies to hear serenades sung under her window. Still, they did not go to waste; her younger sisters could hear them perfectly well, and *they* noticed things like snappy salutes.

This was not to say that Svnae did not glory in being a woman. As soon as she was old enough, she chose her own gowns and jewelry. Her mother presented her with gauzes delicate as cobweb, in exquisite shades of lavender, sea mist and bird-egg-blue; fine-worked silver ornaments as well, set with white diamonds that glinted like starlight.

Alas, Svnae's tastes ran to crimson and purple and cloth of gold, even though the Saint of the World explained how well white set off her dusk skin. And though she thanked her mother for the fragile silver bangles, and dutifully wore them at family parties, she cherished massy gold set with emeralds and rubies. The more finery the better, in fact, though her mother gently indicated that perhaps it wasn't quite in the best of taste to wear the serpent bracelets with eyes of topaz *and* the peacock necklace of turquoise, jade and lapis lazuli.

And though Svnae read voraciously and mastered the arts of Transmutation of Metals, Divination by Bones and Summoning

Rivers by their Secret Names, she did not learn to weave nor to sew; nor did she learn the healing properties of herbs. Her mother waited patiently for Svnae to become interested in these things, but somehow the flashing beam of her eye never turned to them.

One afternoon the Master of the Mountain looked up from the great black desk whereat he worked, hearing the guards announce the approach of his eldest daughter. A moment later she strode into his presence, resplendent in robes of scarlet and peacock blue, and slippers of vermilion with especially pointy toes that curled up at the ends.

"Daughter," he said, rising to his feet.

"Daddy," she replied, "I've just been reading in the Seventh Pomegranate Scroll about a distillation of violets that can be employed to lure dragons. Can you show me how to make it?"

"I've never done much distillation, my child," said the Master of the Mountain. "That's more in your mother's line of work. I'm certain she'd be delighted to teach you. Why don't you ask her?"

"Oh," said Svnae, and flushed, and bit her lip, and stared at the floor. "I think she's busy with some seminar with her disciples. Meditation Techniques or something."

And though the Master of the Mountain had never had any use for his lady wife's disciples, he spoke sternly. "Child, you know your mother has never ignored her own children for her followers."

"It's not that," said Svnae a little sullenly, twisting a lock of her raven hair. "Not at all. It's just that—well—we're bound to have an argument about it. She'll want to know what I want it for, for one thing, and she won't approve of my catching dragons, and she'll let me know it even if she doesn't say a word, she'll just *look* at me—"

"I know," said her dread father.

"As though it was a frivolous waste of time, when what I really ought to be doing is learning all her cures for fevers, which is all very well but I have other things I want to be learning first, and in any case *I'm not Mother*, I'm my *own* person, and she has to understand that!"

"I'm certain she does, my child."

"Yes." Svnae tossed her head back. "So. Well. This brings up something else I'd wanted to ask you. I think I ought to go down into the world to study."

"But—" said the Master of the Mountain.

"I've always wanted to, and it turns out there's a sort of secret school in a place called Konen Feyy-in-the-Trees, where anybody can go to learn distillations. I need to learn more!"

"Mm. But—" said the Master of the Mountain.

She got her way. Not with temper, tears or foot-stamping, but she got her way. No more than a week later she took a bag, and her bow and quiver, and climbing up on the parapet she summoned her rose-red wings, that now swept from a yard above her dark head to her ankles. Spreading them on the wind, she soared aloft. Away she went like a queen of the air, to explore the world.

Her father and mother watched her go.

"Do you think she'll be safe?" said the Saint of the World.

"She'd better be," said the Master of the Mountain, looking over the edge and far down his mountain at the pair of ogre bodyguards who coursed like armored greyhounds, crashing through the trees, following desperately their young mistress while doing their best not to draw attention to themselves.

Svnae sailed off on the wind and discovered that, though her extraordinary heritage had given her many gifts, a sense of direction was not one of them. She cast about a long while, looking for any place that might be a city in the trees; at last she spotted a temple in a wooded valley, far below.

On landing, she discovered that the temple was deserted long since, and a great gray monster guarded it. She slew the creature with her arrows, and went in to see what it might have been guarding. On the altar was a golden box that shone with protective spells. But she had the magic to unlock those spells, and found within a book that seemed to be a history of the lost race whose temple this was. She carried it outside and spent the next few hours seated on a block of stone in the ruins, intent with her chin her fist, reading.

Within the book, she read of a certain crystal ring, the possession of which would enable the wearer to understand the Speech of Water. The book directed her to a certain fountain an hour's flight south of the temple, and fortunately the temple had a compass rose mosaic set in the floor; so she flew south at once, just as her bodyguards came panting up to the temple at last, and they watched her go with language that was dreadful even for ogres.

Exactly an hour's flight south, Svnae spotted the fountain, rising from a ruined courtyard of checkered tile. Here she landed, and approached the fountain with caution; for there lurked within its bowl a scaled serpent of remarkable beauty and deadliest venom. She considered the jeweled serpent, undulating round and round within the bowl in a lazy sort of way. She considered the ring, a circle of clear crystal, hard to spot as it bobbed at the top of the fountain's jet, well beyond her reach even were she to risk the serpent. Backing away several paces, she drew an arrow and took aim. *Clink!*

Her arrow shuddered in the trunk of an oak thirty paces distant, with the ring still spinning on its shaft. Speedily she claimed it and put it on, and straightway she could understand the Speech of Water.

Whereupon the fountain told her of a matter so interesting

that she had to learn more about it. Details, however, were only to be had from a little blue man who lived in dubious hills far to the west. So away she flew, to find him...

She had several other adventures and it was only by chance that, soaring one morning above the world, deep in conversation with a sea-eagle, she spotted what was clearly a city down below amongst great trees. To her inquiry, the sea-eagle replied that the city was Konen Feyy. She thanked it and descended through the bright morning, to a secluded grove where she could cast a glamour on herself and approach without attracting undue notice. Following unseen a league distant, her wheezing bodyguards threw themselves down and gave thanks to anyone who might be listening.

The Children of the Sun dwelt generally in cities all of stone, where scarcely a blade of grass grew nor even so much as a potted geranium, preferring instead rock gardens with obelisks and statuary. But in all races there are those who defy the norm, and so it was in Konen Feyy. Here a colony of artists and craftsmen had founded a city in the green wilderness, without even building a comfortingly high wall around themselves. Accordingly, a lot of them had died from poisoned arrows and animal attacks in the early years, but this only seemed to make them more determined to stay there.

They painted the local landscapes, they made pots of the local clay, and wove textiles from the local plant fibers; and they even figured out that if they cut down the local trees to make charmingly rustic wooden furniture, sooner or later there wouldn't be any trees. For the Children of the Sun, who were ordinarily remarkably dense about ecological matters, this was a real breakthrough.

And so the other peoples of the world ventured up to Konen

Feyy. The forest-dwelling Yendri, the Saint's own people, opened little shops where were sold herbs, or freshwater pearls, or willow baskets, or fresh produce. Other folk came, too: solitary survivors of lesser-known races, obscure revenants, searching for a quiet place to set up shop. This was how the Night School came to exist.

Svnae, wandering down Konen Feyy's high street and staring around her, found the place at once. Though it looked like an ordinary perfumer's shop, there were certain signs on the wall above the door, visible only to those who were familiar with the arcane sciences. An extravagant green cursive explained the School's hours, where and how she might enroll, and where to find appropriate lodgings with other students.

In this last she was lucky, for it happened that there were three other daughters of magi who'd taken a place above a dollmaker's shop, and hadn't quite enough money between them to make the monthly rent, so they were looking for a fourth roommate, someone to be Earth to their Air, Fire and Water. They were pleasant girls, though Svnae was somewhat taken aback to discover that she towered over them all three, and somewhat irritated to discover that they all held her mother in reverent awe.

"You're the daughter of *the* Saint of the World?" exclaimed Seela, whose father was Principal Thaumaturge for Mount Flame City. "What are you doing here, then? *She's* totally the best at distillations and essences. Everyone knows that! *I'd* give anything to learn from her."

Svnae was to hear this statement repeated, with only slight variations, over the next four years of her higher education. She learned not to mind, however; for her studies occupied half her attention, and the other half was all spent on discovering the strange new world in which she lived, where there were no bodyguards (of which she was aware, anyway) and only her height distinguished her from all the other young ladies she met.

It was tremendous fun. She chipped in money with her roommates to buy a couch for their sitting room, and the four of them pushed it up the steep flight of stairs with giggles and screams, though Svnae could have tucked it under one arm and carried it up herself with no effort. She dined with her roommates at the little fried-fish shop on the corner, where they had their particular booth in which they always sat, though Svnae found it rather cramped.

She listened sympathetically as first one and then another of her roommates fell in love with various handsome young seers and sorcerers, and she swept up after a number of riotous parties, and on one occasion broke a vase over the head of a young shapeshifter who, while nice enough when sober, turned into something fairly unpleasant when he became unwisely intoxicated. She had to throw him over her shoulder and pitch him down the stairs, and her roommates wept their thanks and all agreed they didn't know what they'd do without her.

But somehow Svnae never fell in love.

It wasn't because she had no suitors for her hand. There were several young gallants at the Night School, glittering with jewelry and strange habits, who sought to romance Svnae. One was an elemental fire-lord with burning hair; one was a lord of air with vast violet wings. One was a mer-lord, who had servants following him around with perfumed misting bottles to keep his skin from drying out.

But all of them made it pretty clear they desired to marry Svnae in order to forge dynastic unions with Master of the Mountain. And Svnae had long since decided that love, real Love, was the only reason for getting involved in all the mess and distraction of romance. So she declined, gracefully, and the young lords sulked and found other wealthy girls to entreat.

Her course of study ended. The roommates all bid one another
fond farewells and went their separate ways. Svnae returned home
with a train of attendant spirits carrying presents for all her little
nieces and nephews. But she did not stay long, for she had heard
of a distant island where was written, in immense letters on cliffs
of silver, the formula for reversing Time in small and manageable
fields, and she desired to learn it…

"Svnae's turned out rather well," said the Master of the
Mountain, as he retired one night. "I could wish she spent a little
more time at home, all the same. I'd have thought she'd have
married and settled down by now, like the boys."

"She's restless," said the Saint of the World, as she combed out
her hair.

"Well, why should she be? A first-rate sorceress with a double
degree? The Ruby Incomparable, they call her. What more does
she want?"

"She doesn't know, yet," said the Saint of the World, and blew
out the light. "But she'll know when she finds it."

And Svnae had many adventures.

But one day, following up an obscure reference in an ancient
grimoire, it chanced that she desired to watch a storm in its rage
over the wide ocean, and listen to the wrath of all the waters.
Out she flew upon a black night in the late year, when small craft
huddled at their moorings, and found what she sought.

There had never in all the world been such a storm. The white
foam was beaten into air, the white air was charged with water,
the shrieking white gulls wheeled and screamed across the black
sky, and the waves were as valleys and mountains.

Svnae floated in a bubble of her own devising, protected,
watching it all with interest. Suddenly, far below in a trough

of water, she saw a tiny figure clinging to a scrap of wood. The trough became a wall of water that rose up, towering high, until into her very eyes stared the drowning man. In his astonishment he let go of the shattered mast that supported him, and sank out of sight like a stone.

She cried out and dove from her bubble into the wave. Down she went, through water like dark glass, and caught him by the hand; up she went, towing him with her, and got him into the air and wrapped her strong arms about him. She could not fly, not with wet wings in the storm, but she summoned sea-beasts to bear them to the nearest land.

This was merely an empty rock, white cliffs thrusting from the sea. By magic she raised a palace from the stones to shelter them, and she brought the man within. Here there was a roaring fire; here there was hot food and wine. She put him to rest all unconscious in a deep bed, and tended him with her own hands.

Days she watched and cared for him, until he was well enough to speak to her. By that time, he had her heart.

Now, he was not as handsome as a mage-lord, nor learned in any magic, nor born of ancient blood: he was only a toymaker from the cities of the Children of the Sun, named Kendach. But so long and anxiously had she watched his sleeping face that she saw it when she closed her eyes.

And of course when Kendach opened his, the first thing he saw was her face: and after that, it was love. How could it be otherwise?

They nested together, utterly content, until it occurred to them that their families might wonder where they were. So she took him home to meet her parents ("A *toymaker*?" hooted her brothers) and he took her home to meet his ("Very nice girl. A little tall, but nice," said his unsuspecting father. They chose not to enlighten him as to their in-laws).

They were married in a modest ceremony in Konen Feyy.

"I hope he's not going to have trouble with her brothers," fretted Kendach's father, that night in the innroom. "Did you see the way they glared? Particularly that good-looking one. It quite froze my blood."

"It's clear she gets her height from her father," said Kendach's mother, pouring tea for him. "*Very* distinguished businessman, as I understand it. Runs some kind of insurance firm. I do wonder why her mother wears that veil, though, don't you?"

Kendach opened a toyshop in Konen Feyy, where he made kites in the forms of insects, warships and meteors. Svnae raised a modest palace among the trees, and they lived there in wedded bliss. And life was full for Svnae, with nothing else to be asked for.

And then...

One day she awoke and there was a grey stain on the face of the sun. She blinked and rubbed her eyes. It did not go away. It came and sat on top of her morning tea. It blotted the pages of the books she tried to read, and it lay like grime on her lover's face. She couldn't get rid of it, nor did she know from whence it had come.

Svnae took steps to find out. She went to a cabinet and got down a great black globe of crystal, that shone and swam with deep fires. She went to a quiet place and stroked the globe until it glowed with electric crackling fires. At last these words floated up out of the depths:

YOUR MOTHER DOES NOT UNDERSTAND YOU

They rippled on the surface of the globe, pulsing softly. She stared at them and they did not change.

So she pulled on her cloak that was made of peacock feathers, and yoked up a team of griffins to a sky chariot (useful when your lover has no wings, and flies only kites) and flew off to visit her mother.

The Saint of the World sat alone in her garden, by a quiet pool of reflecting water. She wore a plain white robe. White lilies glowed with light on the surface of the water; distantly a bird sang. She meditated, her crystal eyes serene.

There was a flash of color on the water. She looked up to see her eldest daughter charging across the sky. The griffin-chariot thundered to a landing nearby and Svnae dismounted, pulling her vivid cloak about her. She went straight to her mother and knelt.

"Mother, I need to talk to you," she said. "Is it true that you don't understand me?"

The Saint of the World thought it over.

"Yes, it's true," she said at last. "I don't understand you. I'm sorry, dearest. Does it make a difference?"

"Have I disappointed you, Mother?" asked Svnae in distress.

The Lady thought very carefully about that one.

"No," she said finally. "I would have liked a daughter to be interested in the healing arts. It just seems like the sort of thing a mother ought to pass on to her daughter. But your brother Demaledon has been all I could have asked for in a pupil, and there are all my disciples. And why should your life be a reprise of mine?"

"None of the other girls became healers," said Svnae just a little petulantly.

"Quite true. They've followed their own paths: lovers and husbands and babies, gardens and dances."

"I have a husband too, you know," said Svnae.

"My child, my Dark-Eyed, I rejoice in your happiness. Isn't that enough?"

"But I want you to *understand* my life," cried Svnae.

"Do you understand mine?" asked the Saint of the World.

"Your life? Of course I do!"

Her mother looked at her, wryly amused.

"I have borne your father fourteen children. I have watched him march away to do terrible things, and I have bound up his wounds when he returned from doing them. I have managed the affairs of a household with over a thousand servants, most of them ogres. I have also kept up correspondence with my poor disciples, who are trying to carry on my work in my absence. What would you know of these things?"

Svnae was silent at that.

"You have always hunted for treasures, my dearest, and thrown open every door you saw, to know what lay beyond it," said the Saint of the World gently. "But there are still doors you have not opened. We can love each other, you and I, but how can we understand each other?"

"There must be a way," said Svnae.

"Now you look so much like your father you make me laugh and cry at once. Don't let it trouble you, my Dark-Eyed; you are strong and happy and good, and I rejoice."

But Svnae went home that night to the room where Kendach sat, painting bright and intricate birds on kites. She took a chair opposite and stared at him.

"I want to have a child," she said.

He looked up, blinking in surprise. As her words sank in on him, he smiled and held out his arms to her.

Did she have a child? How else, when she had accomplished everything else she wanted to do?

A little girl came into the world. She was strong and healthy. She looked like her father, she looked like her mother; but mostly she looked like herself, and she surprised everyone.

Her father had been one of many children, so there were fewer surprises for him. He knew how to bathe a baby, and could wrestle small squirming arms into sleeves like an expert.

Svnae, who had grown up in a nursery staffed by a dozen servants, proved to be rather inept at these things. She was shaken by her helplessness, and shaken by the helpless love she felt. Prior to this time she had found infants rather uninteresting, little blobs in swaddling to be briefly inspected and presented with silver cups that had their names and a good-fortune spell engraved on them.

But *her* infant—! She could lie for hours watching her child do no more than sleep, marveling at the tiny toothless yawn, the slow close of a little hand.

When the baby was old enough to travel, they wrapped her in a robe trimmed with pearls and took her to visit her maternal grandparents, laden with the usual gifts. Her lover went off to demonstrate the workings of his marvelous kites to her nieces and nephews. And Svnae bore her daughter to the Saint of the World in triumph.

"*Now* I've done something you understand," she said. The Saint of the World took up her little granddaughter and kissed her between the eyes.

"I hope that wasn't the only reason you bore her," she said.

"Well—no, of course not," Svnae protested, blushing. "I wanted to find out what motherhood was like."

"And what do you think it is like, my child?"

"It's awesome. It's holy. My entire life has been redefined by her existence," said Svnae fervently.

"Ah, yes," said the Saint of the World.

"I mean, this is creation at its roots. This is Power! I have brought an entirely new being into the world. A little mind that thinks! I can't wait to see what she thinks *about*, how she feels about things, what she'll say and do. What's ordinary magic to this?"

The baby began to fuss and the Lady rose to walk with her

through the garden. Svnae followed close, groping for words.

"There's so much I can teach her, so much I can give her, so much I can share with her. Her first simple spells. Her first flight. Her first transformation. I'll teach her everything I know. We've got that house in Konen Feyy, and it'll be so convenient for Night School! She won't even have to find room and board. She can use all my old textbooks..."

But the baby kept crying, stretching out her little hands.

"Something she wants already," said the Lady. She picked a white flower and offered it to the child; but no, the little girl pointed beyond it. Svnae held out a crystal pendant, glittering with power, throwing dancing lights; but the baby cried and reached upward. They looked up to see one of her father's kites, dancing merry and foolish on the wind.

The two women stood staring at it. They looked at the little girl. They looked at each other.

"Perhaps you shouldn't enroll her in Night School just yet," said the Saint of the World.

And Svnae realized, with dawning horror, that she might need to ask her mother for advice.

INTERVAL
Aimee Bender

Aimee Bender is the author of three books: *The Girl in the Flammable Skirt* (1998) which was a *New York Times* Notable Book, *An Invisible Sign of My Own* (2000) which was an L.A. Times pick of the year, and *Willful Creatures* (2005) which was nominated by *The Believer* as one of the best books of the year. Her short fiction has been published in *Granta, GQ, Harper's, Tin House, McSweeney's, The Paris Review*, and many more, as well as heard on PRI's "This American Life" and "Selected Shorts". She lives in Los Angeles, and teaches creative writing at the University of Southern California. "Interval" appeared in the "Faces of Desire" volume of *Conjunctions*.

Dt.dt.dt.dt.dt.dt.dt.

Or-phan… or-phan… Or-phan… or-phan…

theraft—theraft—theraft—

On the first day of sculpture class, the sculptor-to-be sat down with his tools. With him he had brought a wooden shaping fork; a metal prong; gloves that he was not sure he intended to use, liking as he did to touch the clay; a spoon for smoothing—- one used the backside, he had been told—and a spool of wire, for zip-cutting through. He delighted in the smell of clay, had always delighted in it, had never thought he could be the type of person that would attend a sculpture class but this one had fallen into his lap, perfect timing, affordable, around the corner from his apartment, and he watched the teacher in her high heels and swirly skirt navigate the large square lumps of terra cotta-colored clay that she brought to each pupil, each sitting upright in his or her chair, the live nude model undressing behind the muted white screen.

He was watching the model step aside from the screen, and he was so involved with how easily she stood in her own body—an imperfect body, a little tugged down at the hips, sort of wobbly at the knees, but relaxed in itself, accepting of itself, and he was also watching how the other students, who seemed so professional! immediately dove into their clay like it was no big deal that an attractive woman was now stepping into their view, nude, ready to be shaped by their hands. And he was so involved with watching her, and with starting to see the shapes that were her, the shapes that he would soon be creating from his very own lump of clay, that he did not notice until the teacher was right up in front of his face that she did not have a block of clay in her hands.

He was not the end of the row, either; there were about three more students past him.

Here, she said, handing him nothing. Sculpt.

There's no more clay? he asked, unable to keep the rise of disappointment out of his voice. She shook her head, and then went back to her desk, returning in seconds with another square block of clay, and he smiled in relief, awaiting the pleasure, the pewterlike wetness of it, but she walked right past him and gave it to the young man on his left, who was busily clearing space on his desk. And then two more blocks of clay, for the two past that man, and the model, taking her pose in front of them, sitting, with her hands folded on her knee, and her one foot a little lower than the other, and her head, turned, in profile.

Excuse me, said the young man, unsure what to call the instructor. Professor? Ma'am?

She approached, with the raised eyebrows of the listening teacher. Yes? Question?

I'm sorry, he said. Were we supposed to purchase the clay in advance?

No, she said. It is covered in the cost of the course.

Oh. He looked around, hoping he would not have to ask the question, the highly obvious question, while all the other students in class were busily getting their hands all over that clay, shaping and building the model's shoulders.
"Begin with torso!" the teacher yelled to the group, and then returned to him, with her quieter face. Yes?
But I did not get any clay? he said, showing the space in front of him. Empty. His tools neatly laid out, expectant.

You don't get clay, she said.

But I signed up for the Introduction to Sculpture class, he said, beginning to feel angry. I would like some clay, he said.

And he wondered if he had somehow offended the teacher earlier? If so, how? He had come inside, placed his tools on the desk, and waited quietly. He had parked in the parking lot without incident. She seemed surprised at his surprise, which he found disconcerting, since the problem seemed so clear.

You are to sculpt the sounds of the room, she said. I have a note next to your name in my role book.

Excuse me?

Off she tripped in her heels, returning with the class roster, and there were the names of all the class members, and there was his, near the top of the alphabet, with an asterisk by his last name, and then, at the bottom, the asterisk again, followed by tight type:

*This student should not sculpt with clay.
Do not give this student clay.
Please inform this student that he needs
to sculpt the sounds in the room.

He read the sentences three times.

Who wrote this? he asked.

A higher up, she said. Someone higher up.

Up, she repeated.

She seemed eager to get the roster back, as if he were rapidly memorizing the Social Security numbers of all the other students; as if he cared about them, these other students, so happily padding and punching the clay he was banned from, something they felt entitled to; dumb students, he thought. See how close they were, to total inaccessibility? You never care until it's you.

There were music classes available, he said. Had I wanted to sign up for a music class—

I'm sorry, she said, folding the roster in half when he'd handed it back over. I don't want a liability suit. I will not give you clay. You could sculpt the woman, she said, out of sound?

He looked at the model again, who was in the same position as before, a perfect triangle made out of the place where her elbow reached away from her waist, with that sharp point at the tip of her elbow, and already, to his left and to his right, the muggy forms forming, the thick earthy smell dampening the air of the classroom as the students began to fix her in time.

Can I get a refund? he asked, even though he very much wanted to stay in the class, and she said, you have an assignment. You can't get a refund without good reason.

You are not giving me clay! he said, that is my reason! and she said, I have given you an alternate assignment. Here her voice became somewhat snitty.

Other students might feel special about this, she said.

And away she clicked, to go instruct the woman to his left about using small pieces of clay to build the shoulder and collarbone, to create a sense of texture. "Don't be so smooth," he heard her saying, and then the mulky sound of clay ripped from clay. His hands were impatient, but he closed his eyes. The sounds of the room. Fine. He was, in truth, a musician, a player of the oboe and guitar, and he felt discovered, almost outed, by the note on the roster, and it was unsettling, too, because he had not used his real name on the roster, and had, in an attempt to reinvent himself, at this time when everything else in his life felt stale and old, his whole self, his whole tired mind, the music in his fingertips, all known, all done, well, he'd signed up for this class with a false name and paid with cash. He'd wanted a new identity, just for a few weeks, and no one else would've known that, could've known that. It was total coincidence, then, that whoever wrote that on that roster would've linked him to music, and in fact, he found it enraging that of all the members of the class, it was he, HE! who needed it most, who had been looking forward to slamming his hands all over that clay for months now, who was desperate for something expansive, it was he who was relegated back to what he knew best, and the panic was a bird trapped in his ribs.

But he closed his eyes. Fine.

The sounds. The sounds of hands, on clay. A muggy sound. Muck. The sound of the radiator whirring on. Once. Then twice. A honk outside. B flat. The teacher's voice, sing-songy, "don't be afraid of the medium," she called out, "be aggressive with the medium," and so then fine. Be aggressive with the medium. Hrack. The sound of the model's cough, and resettling; the sound of someone's lust, five people down, the young man who had attended the class simply to see the nude woman because he had not seen one, a three dimensional one, in many months. That man's breathing, measured. Fsssh. His own anger, the sound of it. Tight in the neck. Small crack of the neck vertebrae. Dt. The honk again: B flat. The radiator, a low C, and then, far far off in the distance, a bell. F sharp. Honk. B flat. Bell, f sharp. Ping. B flat.

Or-phan. Or-phan. Or-phan. Or-phan.

They are on a staircase, he and the nude model. He is descending, she is ascending. She is wearing the robe she wore when she arrived, and she is post sculpting, so she has the small buzz in her cheeks of someone who has just been replicated lovingly by twelve sets of hands. He, he has just gone running and is sweating, and he is on step four and she is on step eight, and they are going in opposite directions, and these four steps apart they stop. Hello. Hello. He reaches out a hand, to shake hers, but she will not reach hers out; the model does not touch anyone, no, she is only to be observed, never touched except at home, and she runs up to the top of the staircase and is gone, off to the parking lot, and he is on his stair, watching, then down, down to the bottom.

No.

Or-phan. The space between.

Another cough.

Or-phan. Or-phan. Or-phan.

The young man, as a child. His parents die, in a car accident. He is only seven years old. He has no siblings. He has no one. He is adopted by the neighbors; they will become his new parents. How kind of them, people whisper to each other, but the boy shakes his head and says no. What does the will say? he asks his friend, the lawyer. He does not want to be raised by those neighbors, the neighbors who have tight mouths like that.

The will is checked again, and it turns out he is supposed to be taken care of, in case of an accident, by some woman across the country who lives on a farm. No, she lives in a city. A city farm? She lives in both. Off he's shipped. On the plane, there is a border around him, a border of four feet, where no one can touch him; although he is hugged incessantly, he does not feel the hug.

On the farm he is in charge of two horses, one of which he rides into the city where his new family father is a policeman.

He loves them after awhile. But he is an orphan. He cannot forget this. He is stranded, by his own self, for many years. Only later, when he meets the woman who models for the sculpture class, is he able to tap into his first feeling of comfort, for when she comes home, smelling of clay, and he can touch her, the one that the clay is made of, the origin of all of their sculpting, only then does the feeling begin to lighten.

You are the source, he tells her, often.

She loves him because he is kind, and because he thinks deeply. But she never takes him as seriously as he would like to be taken, and as she washes her hands in the sink with dish detergent, she says she needs to do some more sit-ups; she saw some of their sculptures today and her belly was hanging out.

It's the only honest mirror, she says, into the sink.

It doesn't matter, he says, don't you understand? and she says it matters to me, and he makes the afternoon tea and they drink it together and look outside, at the horses which live next door. He now always likes to live by horses. They remind him of second chances. She goes to take a bath and he feels, for the millionth time, that when he is with her he is at the center of something, which fills him with a tremendous comfort.

Theraft—theraft—theraft

Floating on the raft. Ping.

She is the bell, ringing.

He is floating on the raft of this comfort, while she is in the bath. Wake up, he tells her, from the other room.

No, she says, I am taking a bath.

You are the source, he says again, in a murmur.

I am bearing a child, she says, and he says mine? And she says, no, it is the child of all the people in the sculpture class; I am bearing their babies, all twelve of them, and in the bath she starts to yell then, and he is up on his feet in an instant, awake, but the door is locked so it takes longer than you'd expect, much longer, so long he can remember, for the rest of his life, the sound of her screaming. What is happening in there? his mind scrambles. What is happening? Finally he bursts in with the strength of his shoulder, like in the movies but real; he is there to save her, his source, the wellspring, and she's in the bath and screaming and out of her are sculptures, coming out of her, she is birthing sculptures, and they are clay so as soon as they hit the bath water they begin to grow slick and melty, and he holds her head as she heaves and bucks up and births two more, and he pulls them out of the tub, to clear space for her, and they are not sculptures of her anymore, no, they are of the relatives—-there is his mother, there is her father, there are the cousins they never visited, there is that uncle, there is his father, and even in the midst of it all, holding her head, worrying, keeping her head from hitting the faucet, telling her to hang steady, hang steady, even the midst of all that he can't help but feel a little glimmer of pride that in this most primordial birthing of sculptures there are some from his family, too. That somehow the genes of his family have become a physical part of her, a sculpture to be birthed, even though he is not in that sculpture class, no. He will never sculpt her. He is the one she comes home to, of course, and the one she comes home to must not sculpt her. His job is different. That is the sound, teacher, he says, as he holds up the sculpture of his own dead father, cradling her head while she cries, holding her while her breath regulates in the now tan-colored bath water, and she says she's okay, she's okay, it hurt but she's okay, and he's helping her up from the tub, and the sound of the water, going down the drain, teacher, and the sound of the sculptures' muckiness as he lifts them onto the bathroom counter, teacher, and all the family members are melting, they'd need to be rushed to a kiln to be fired, "but they're dead anyway," she says, and he grasps it just as she says it, they're all dead, she has given birth to twelve dead relatives, and then they are both crying together because the clay cannot hold, and when, later, he returns to wash his hands before bed, when she is sleeping peacefully in the bed, when he has closed down the house for the night, only then does he see that they have all mucked together into one large block of clay, and that is all that is left of the birthings and the deaths.

There, teacher, he says. Those are the sounds of the room.

No, she says, approaching his desk again. She looks at what he has made there.

No, she says. Those are not sounds. Those are words? She looks confused, and rechecks the same class roster. The classroom is empty by now, and the model has gone home, gone to her real source, whoever that is for her, and the teacher is almost all packed up, wearing her backpack on her shoulder, and all the clay blobs are still on the desks, barely formed at all, and he says, My job is different, and she says, Seems so, son. Now go on home. We'll see you next week.

M. Rickert's first collection of stories, *Map of Dreams*, was published by Golden Gryphon Press in 2006 and won both the Crawford and World Fantasy Awards. Her work has appeared in various anthologies, *The Ontario Review*, and *The Magazine of Fantasy & Science Fiction*. She lives with her husband in Wisconsin. "Memoir of a Deer Woman" is taken from *The Magazine of Fantasy & Science Fiction*.

Her husband comes home, stamps the snow from his shoes, kisses her, and asks how her day was.

"Our time together is short," she says.

"What are you talking about?"

"I found a deer by the side of the road. It was stuck under the broken fence. Hit by a car. I called the rescue place but when the animal rescue man saw it, he said it had to be shot. The police man shot it."

He looks through the mail while she stands there, crying. When he realizes this, he hugs her. Already she feels the hard shapes forming at the top of her head. Later, she will tell him she has a headache.

He will hold her anyway. He will sleep with his mouth pressed against her neck. She will think of the noise the deer made, that horrible braying.

At midnight she wakes up. The sky is exploding with distant fireworks. From past experience she knows that if they stand and strain their necks, they can just barely see the veins of color over the treetops. It is mostly futile, and tonight neither of them rises. "Happy New Year," he whispers.

"What do you think animals feel?" she says.

He mumbles something about Wally, their dog, who sleeps soundly at the foot of their bed.

"That deer was frightened. Today, I mean. It made the most horrible noise; did I tell you that? I never heard such a noise before. It was really mournful and horrible."

The fireworks end in a flourish of tiny explosions. She knows what she should have done. She should not have waited for the policeman, who took four shots before he killed it. She knew that deer was dying, why did she pretend otherwise? She should have smothered it and put it out of its misery.

New Year's morning is cold and crisp. Wally wakes them up with his big wet tongue. Her husband takes him out to do his business. When they come back inside, she listens to the pleasant sounds of her husband talking in soft cooing words to Wally, his food dish being filled. Her husband comes back into the bedroom alone, carefully shutting the door behind him. She knows what that means. He crawls in beside her. He rubs his hands up and down her body. "Happy New Year," he says. She sinks into his desires until they become her own. Who knows how long they have? Maybe this is the last time. Later, he fries maple sausage and scrambles eggs but she finds she cannot eat. He asks her if she feels all right. She shrugs. "My head hurts," she says. "Also my hands." He tells her to go to the doctor. She nods. Well, of course. But she does not tell him that she already knows what is happening.

She takes down the ornaments, wraps them in tissue paper, circles the tree, removing the lights. The branches brush her cheeks and lips and she nibbles on the bitter green. Her husband is outside, splitting kindling. For a while she stands at the window and watches. Wally lays on his bed in the living room. He does not like the loud noise of the axe. She raises her face to the ceiling. She feels trapped and the feeling rises inside her like bile. She brays. Wally slinks past her, into the kitchen. She brays again. It is both deeply disturbing and a relief.

When her husband comes in, carrying kindling, he'll ask her if she's all right. He'll say he thought he heard a strange noise. She'll shrug and say that she thought the tree was falling. He'll accept this as reasonable, forgetting that she is not the sort to scream at falling Christmas trees, forgetting that when they met she was at least partly wild. He drops the kindling into the box next to the wood-burning stove. "Come here, help me with the tree," she says. He holds the tree while she unscrews the stand. Dry sap snakes from the holes, she cannot help but think of it as blood.

They dump the tree in the forest behind the house. There is a whole graveyard of Christmas trees there. They walk back to the house together, crunching across the snow. A green truck is parked in the driveway. "I wonder who that is," he says. A tall man wearing camouflage clothes and a crocodile Dundee hat steps out of the driver's side. He nods as they approach.

She knows just what her mother would have said about all of this. She would have said, "You are never going to be tame. You will regret trying. You will hurt others if you deny your self."

"Hope I'm not disturbing you. I've got an owl that needs to be released. It was found not too far down the road. You know the Paterly's? They're in Florida now. I thought I could release it in your yard. You could keep an eye on it."

"This is Kevin," she tells her husband. "He came to help with the deer yesterday."

Her husband stares at her blankly.

"You know, the one I found? That had to be shot?"

"Can't believe that guy couldn't shoot between the eyes," Kevin says, shaking his head.

"Oh. Right," says her husband.

"Where's the owl?"

"I was just passing by. I'll come back tonight. If that's all right?"

"Tonight?" her husband says.

She tells Kevin that it would be great if he came back later, with the owl. He doesn't look at either of them. He nods at the snow, gets into the truck. They watch him back out of the driveway.

"He's kind of strange," her husband says.

She shrugs. Her bones ache, her head, her hands and her feet, and it takes a lot of effort for her to understand that her husband is not being mean, just human. They walk back to the house, holding hands. Who knows, she thinks, maybe this is the last time. Already by nightfall she is wearing mittens. She tells him her hands are cold. Again he tells her to go to the Doctor. She tells him that she has an appointment the next morning. This is love, she reminds herself. She smiles at her husband while he turns the pages of his book.

"Stage three," the doctor says.

"There must be some mistake."

"You can get a second opinion."

"What are my options?"

"I say we hit this with everything we've got."

"Are you sure that's my report?"

"I know this comes as a shock but I recommend that you address it quickly. The sooner the better."

"Chemo and radiation?"

"Yes. And then chemo again."

"The magic bullets."

"You could think of it that way, but you might want to choose a different image. Something soothing."

"Like what?"

"I have one patient who thinks of the treatment as flowers."

"Flowers?"

"It soothes her."

"What kind of flowers? Flowers that'll cause my hair to fall out and make me throw up? What kind of flowers would do that?"

"This is your disease, and your body. You get to decide how you want to treat it."

"But that's just the thing, isn't it Doctor?"

"I'm sorry?"

"This isn't my body anymore."

"Why don't you go home? Take the weekend to think about your options? Get a second opinion, if you'd like."

She rises from the chair, stomps out of the office on her sore, hard feet. The waiting room is full of women. One of them looks up, her brown eyes beautiful in the soft pelt of her face. She nods slightly. She smells like salt.

When her husband returns from work she is sitting at the kitchen table, waiting to tell him the news.

"Oh my God," he says.

"It hardly hurts at all."

"How long?" he asks.

"Nobody knows, but it seems to be happening sooner rather than later."

He pounds the table with his fist, then reaches for her hand, though he recoils from the shape. "But you're a woman."

She is confused until she sees where he is looking. She touches the antlers' downy stubs on the top of her head. "It's rare, but females get them too. Nobody knows why. Kind of like men and nipples, I guess."

"What are you going to do?" he asks.

"I'm thinking of writing a memoir."

His mouth drops open.

She shrugs. "I always did want to be a writer."

"What are you talking about?"

"I think I should start with the deer being shot, what do you think?"

"I think you need medicine, not writing."

"You make it sound dirty."

He shakes his head. He is crying and shaking his head and all of a sudden she realizes that he will never understand. Should she say so in her memoir? Should she write about all the places he never understood? Will he understand that she doesn't blame him?

"It isn't lonely," she says.

"What?"

She hadn't meant to speak out loud. "I mean, ok, sometimes it is."

"I don't know what you're talking about."

"There's a memoir-writing group that meets every Wednesday. I emailed Anita, the leader? I explained my situation and she was really nice about it. She said I could join them."

"I don't see how this is going to help. You need medicine and doctors. We need to be proactive here."

"Could you just be supportive? I really need your support right now."

He looks at her with teary blue eyes that once, she thought, she would look at forever. He says, his voice husky, "Of course."

She is sniffling, and he wipes her nose for her. She licks his hand.

She continues to sleep with him, but in the morning he wakes up with deep scratch marks all over his body, no matter how thickly they wrap her hooves in layers of cloth and old socks and mittens. "They're like little razors," he says. "And it's not just the edges, it's the entire bottom."

She blinks her large brown eyes at him, but he doesn't notice because he is pulling a tick out of his elbow. That night she sleeps on the floor and Wally crawls into bed with her husband. He objects, of course, but in the end, they both sleep better, she, facing the window where she watches the white owl, hugely fat and round, perched on the bough of a tree, before she realizes it isn't the owl at all but the moon.

Near the end she stops trying to drive, instead she runs to her memoir-writing workshop. Her husband follows in the Volvo, thinking that he can prevent her being hit by a car, or shot. He waits in the driveway while she meets with the group.

Anita tries to make her comfortable, but lately she feels nervous coming all the way into the house. She lies in the doorway with only her nose and front hooves inside. Some of the others complain about the cold and the snow but Anita tells them to put on their coats. Sometimes, in the distance, they hear a mournful cry, which makes all of them shudder. There have been rumors of coyotes in the neighborhood.

Even though they meet at Anita's house, she herself is having a terrible time with her memoir. It sounds self-pitying, whiny, and dull. She knows this; she just doesn't know what to do about it, that's why she started the workshop in the first place. The critiquers mean well, but frankly, they are all self-pitying whiners themselves. Somewhere along the way, the meetings have taken on the tone of group therapy rather than a writing workshop. Yet, there is something, some emotion they all seem to circle but never successfully describe about the pain of their lives that, Anita feels certain, just might be the point.

After the critique, Anita brings out cakes, cookies, coffee, tea, and, incredibly, a salt lick. Contrary to their reputation, and the evidence of the stories told in this room, people can be good.

The deer woman hasn't shared what she's written yet. She's not sure the group will understand. How can anyone understand what is happening to her? And besides, it is all happening so fast. No one even realizes when she attends her last meeting that she won't be coming back, though later, they all agree that she seemed different somehow.

She is standing at the window, watching the yard below. Six deer wait there, staring up at her. He weeps and begs her not to go. Why does he do this, she wonders, why does he spend their last moments together weeping? He begs her not to go, as though she had some say in the matter. She does not answer. The world shatters all around her, but she is not cut. He shouts. She crashes to the ground, in a flurry of snow and hooves. He stands at the window, his mouth wide open. He does not mean to hurt her, but she can feel his breath pulling her back. She runs into the forest with the others, a pounding of hooves and clouds of snow. They do not stop running until they are deep into the night, and she can no longer hear her husband shouting.

After she is gone, he looks through her basket of knitting, projects started and unfinished from the winter, before her hands turned into hooves: a long thin strand of purple, which he assumes is a scarf, a deep green square, which he thinks might be the beginning of a sweater for him, and a soft gray wasp nest, that's what it looks like, knit from the strands of her hair. Underneath all this he finds a simple, spiral bound notebook. He sits on the floor and reads what she wrote, until the words sputter and waver and finally end, then he walks up the stairs to the attic, where he thrusts aside boxes of books, and dolls, cups, and papers, before finally opening the box labeled "writing supplies." There he finds the cape, neatly folded beneath deerskin boots, a few blades of brown grass stuck to them. The cape fits fine, of course, but the boots are too tight. He takes them downstairs and splits the seams with the paring knife, laces them on with rope. When he is finished, he makes a strange sight, his chest hair gray against the winter white skin, the cape draped over his narrow shoulders and down the skein of his arms to his blue jeans, which are tied at the calves, laced over the deerskin, his feet bulging out of the sides, like a child suddenly grown to giant proportions. He runs into the forest, calling her name. Wally, the dog, runs beside him.

There are sightings. An old lady, putting seed into the birdfeeder, sees him one morning, a glint of white cape, tight muscles, a wild look in his eyes. Two children, standing right beside their father waiting for the bus, scream and point. An entire group of hunters, who say they tracked him and might have gotten a shot. And an artist, standing in the meadow, but artists are always reporting strange sightings and can't be relied upon. What is certain is that wherever the strange man is sighted, words are found. The old lady finds several tiny slips of paper in a bird nest in her backyard and when one falls to the ground she sees that it is a neat cut-out of the word, "Always," she can't fathom what it might mean, but considers it for the rest of her life, until one afternoon in early autumn she lies dying on her kitchen floor, no trauma beyond the business of a stopped heart, and she sees the word before her face, as though it floated there, a missive from heaven, and she is filled with an understanding of the infinite, and how strange, that this simple word becomes, in that final moment, luminescent; when the father searches the bushes where the children insist the wild man hides, he finds nothing but scraps of paper, tiny pieces, which he almost dismisses, until he realizes that each one contains a word. Frightened of leaving the children too long with madmen about, he scoops some words up and returns to the bus stop, listening to the children's excited chatter but not really hearing anything they say, because the words drag his pocket down like stones, and he can't believe how eager he is to go to work, shut the door to his office and piece together the meaning. He is disappointed at what he finds, "breath," "fingers," and "memory," amongst several versions of "her." It is nonsense, but he cannot forget the words, and at the strangest times catches himself thinking, "Her breath, her fingers, her memory" as though he were a man in love; the hunters follow the trail of words, but only the youngest among them picks up and pockets one torn paper, which is immediately forgotten, thrown in the wash and destroyed; the artist finds a neat little pile, as though the wild creature ate words like sunflower seeds and left these scraps behind. She ties each word to colored string and hangs them as a mobile. Sometimes, when the air is just right and the words spin gently, she believes she understands them, that they are not simple nonsense; but on other days she knows that meaning is something humans apply to random acts in order to cope with the randomness of death.

Anita, from the memoir-writing group, goes to the house, uninvited. She doesn't know what motivates her. The woman wrote nothing the whole time she'd attended, had offered no suggestions during the critique, in fact, Anita began to suspect that her main motivation for coming had been the salt lick. But, for some reason, Anita felt invested in the woman's unknown story, and feels she must find out what has become of her.

What she finds is a small house in the woods, by all appearances empty. She rings the doorbell and is surprised to hear a dog inside, barking. She notices deer tracks come right up to the porch, circling a hemlock bush. The door opens and a strange man stands there, dressed in torn boots, dirty jeans, and a cape. Anita has heard rumors of the wild man and doesn't know what to say, she manages only two words, "Memoir" and "writing," before he grabs her wrist. "Gone," he says, "gone." They stand there for a while, looking at each other. She is a bit frightened, of course, but she also feels pity for this man, obviously mad with grief. "Words?" he says. She stares at him, and he repeats himself, ("Words, words, words, words, words, words?") until finally she understands what he's asking.

"She never wrote a thing." He shakes his head and runs back into the house. Anita stands there for a moment, and then, just as she turns to walk away from this tragic scene, the man returns, carrying a handful of words. He hands them to her as though they were ashes of the deceased, gently folding her fingers over them, as though in prayer, before he goes back inside.

She shakes her head as she walks away, opening the car door with difficulty, her hands fisted as they are. Once in her car, she drops the words into her purse, where they remain until a windy day in early Fall, when she searches for her keys in the mall parking lot. A quick breeze picks the tiny scraps up and they twirl in the sky, all the possible, all the forgotten, all the mysterious, unwritten, and misunderstood fragments, and it is only then, when they are hopelessly gone, that Anita regrets having done nothing with them. From this regret, her memoir is written, about the terrible thing that happened to her. She is finally able to write that there is no sorrow greater than regret, no rapture more complete than despair, no beauty more divine than words, but before writing it, she understands, standing there, amidst the cars and shopping bags, watching all the words spin away, as though she had already died, and no longer owned language, that ordinary, every day, exquisite blessing on which lives are both built, and destroyed.

IN THE MIDDLE OF THE WOODS
Christian Moody

Christian Moody is a Ph.D. candidate in English at the University of Cincinnati. His work has appeared in the *Indiana Review*, *Faultline*, and *Sonora Review*. "In the Middle of the Woods" is taken from the pages of *The Cincinnati Review*.

The mechanic's thirteen-year-old son sat alone in the deep snow in the middle of a burnt wood of black trees, on the verge of freezing to death. The farmhouse was now a burned box, the barn workshop a smoldering rectangle. There was nowhere to go and no one left to come get him. He predicted he would soon fall asleep and not wake up again, but this was not what scared him: He had reason to suspect that, in place of blood and guts, his insides were makeshift clockwork, fashioned by his father from broken appliance pieces and other odd parts. Perhaps it was insanity brought on by the cold, or by what he had done—but if it were true, he would not drift into sleep and dream and die; he would remain like he was, shivering and solitary in the forest of charred trunks and branches. To test this idea, he'd several times taken his .22 handgun, a Christmas present from his father, and pushed the barrel into his stomach with the intention of pulling the trigger, but he didn't really want to, and anyway, there was still time for sleep to take him. He began to cry.

The morning of Christmas Eve, the same as any morning, he'd lifted himself off the hearthrug to sift through the night's ashes for coals to start the day's fire. His mother was a snoring lump beneath a pile of blankets on the sofa. His father was gone—a thin blanket folded into a neat square on the cushion of the reading chair where he slept. The son again heard the sound that had woken him, the clang of metal hitting metal, and only now was he sure it hadn't come from a dream but from the mechanic's workshop in the barn. He flipped through the pages of the mechanic's drafting pad. It began with realistic sketches of various birds. Then a claw was replaced by a bent dinner fork, and a skeletal construction of wire formed an outstretched wing. Complex systems of pulleys connected beak, wing, and tail. Details of an inner eye revealed the interlocking teeth of tiny gears, which spun to dilate a pupil. For the rest of the day, curled up in front of the fire, his father's distant clanking in the background, he turned the pages of his tattered book and read yet again the tale of two knights, brothers, each tricked into giving up his heraldic coat of arms for an unmarked shield; in this way the brothers met again as strangers and fought for an entire day, neither of them realizing the mistake until each had fatally wounded the other.

Late Christmas Eve, when his mother was knitting and they were watching the final log of the evening catch fire, the mechanic entered loudly in his work boots and set on the mantelpiece a heavy object draped with an oily rag. There was a loud whir, which the son clearly recognized as the blender his mother had used in the days before the mechanic quit all other things and took to watching birds. It began to wobble and shake.

———

The sound of the blender reminded the son that things had once been otherwise—they hadn't always lived in the den. In what seemed like pictures from a dream or past life, he remembered the other rooms of the house when they were kept warm and well-lit. The last time he'd seen his own room, all the old toys and even the walls were encrusted in ice, and a frozen, slippery waterfall gushed from a busted pipe in the wall as though trapped in time, forever cascading down the once-creaky stairs his father had carried him up to bed.

He didn't remember exactly when his father had decided to do nothing but sit at the picture window with long black binoculars and watch for birds, none of which had returned since the woods had burned, with the exception of the barn owl that scratched around in the workshop rafters. In the evenings, one could sometimes catch the flicker of white wings swooping through black trees. Because there were no other birds, the dated sightings beside "barn owl" in his father's field guide ran several columns long.

He wasn't sure if it was before or after his father's bird watching and the slow growth of ice on the walls that his mother had begun breaking all the household appliances. Over time she broke nearly all they had, but he remembered the blender best— not just because it proved very difficult to break, but because his mother had broken it with such determined ferocity, her face contorted and ugly while she held it overhead and flung it again and again at the kitchen floor. At the time, he'd been reading a story about a sorceress who'd conspired to trap a sorcerer in the trunk of a tree. His mother's face, which had seemed about to snap, somehow contorted further each time she turned on the blender and listened to the blades continue to whir with seamless perfection. It was an older blender, nearly an antique, made when things were put together well and with good parts. The mechanic himself had reconditioned the motor, cleaned and lubricated every internal crevice, and presented it as a gift. In a shower of sparks, and with several two-handed whacks from a chef's knife, his mother chopped through the cord, and the whirring stopped. She then turned the blender over to her son, who, as he'd been directed with all the other broken things, brought it to his father, who, as each time before, did not remove his eyes from whatever blackened, birdless limb his lenses magnified. The son set the blender on the pile of junk that had grown around his father and went back to reading his story.

Whatever the sequence of events, when the cold air glazed the big picture window and frosted the lenses of the binoculars, all three gathered in the den, where the fire warmed them. For a short while things were better. His mother's face was not contorted with anger, and there were no appliances to break. He could see his father's eyes, which blinked with boredom. His mother's stare was also blank, directionless. Still, it was better. Then his father began to scribble on the drafting pad, and the nub of graphite whispered across the paper. Keeping his eyes close to the paper, the mechanic was absent again. As if in response to this, his mother began knitting, and she knitted so her needles clacked together intolerably, and even while she slept, her grinding teeth clacked as if she were furiously knitting together her own dreams. All of this noise gave him a headache that persisted so long that by Christmas Eve he'd forgotten he had a headache until the whir of the blender motor brought it to an entirely new crescendo.

The object continued to shake on the mantelpiece, then steadied itself by pressing two glinting claws deep into the wood.

Two wings stretched out, flapped twice, and the bird glided noisily to perch on the backrest of the mechanic's reading chair. It somewhat resembled the tiny winter wrens that, in the years before the wood caught fire, would settle on the slender twigs of the farmhouse bushes. But the mechanic's wren was over three feet tall and composed of motley metals. It perched silently and motionlessly for a short time, and then the whirring began again. The son covered his head with his book, and his mother stood up, prepared to defend her home with knitting needles. The whirring preceded a jerky cock of the head, an avian flick of the eyelids, and then the beak opened, emitting two rings, clearly the bell from the mechanic's antique bicycle. Mother and son laughed nervously, and the father could not conceal a proud smile.

Unlike a real wren, which is in constant, jittery motion, the mechanical wren was largely still and silent. Occasionally it shocked the room with a loud whir, adjusting its feet on the perch or slowly flapping one wing to maintain balance. It was a wren in shape only; neither symmetrical nor uniform, the bird was a patchwork of sprockets, springs, bolts, nuts, wire, and hammer-flattened metal from hubcaps and baking sheets. The mother's steam iron was partially discernible, and the son observed the ball-bearing ring from a roller-skate wheel. A spark plug jutted out of the dimpled chrome breast at an angle. Although distinctly birdlike, the form was crude enough to be also vaguely manlike, a homunculus of appliances and spare parts.

Several hours later, they'd become more accustomed to the sound of the blender motor. Curled up on the hearthrug, the son kept a watchful eye on the wren, its various metals glimmering faintly in the firelight. The middle-of-the-night whirrings warranted only a half-opened eyelid. Then a final whir, barely distracting the family from sleep, was followed by a shattered windowpane and a bitter gust of air. The mechanical wren blended noisily into the black rectangle of night. They rushed to block out the icy wind by stapling layers of blankets to the window frame. They swept up the broken glass.

Because it was close enough to Christmas, they decided to exchange gifts. In addition to a blanket, the mother had been knitting dark blue mittens and a dark blue hat with earflaps. The son put them on and took from between the pages of his book a sheaf of paper, onto which he'd rewritten a ballad, replacing the characters with his parents and revising some of the details. The mother gave the blanket to the mechanic, who, when he was done admiring it, folded it into a neat square and placed it on his chair. The mechanic then presented a .22 target pistol in one hand and a tiny sculpture of wire in the other. He whimsically crisscrossed his hands, extending gun to mother, sculpture to son. It was a tiny owl, with a ring so it could be worn as a pendant.

"It's a joke," said the mechanic, and he switched the gifts to the rightful recipients. The mother removed a gold cross from her necklace and fastened the owl. The son, sitting cross-legged in front of the fire, rested the gun on his lap. He had shot at cans with a pellet gun before, but this pistol was altogether darker and oilier. He put a finger on the trigger and was eager to squeeze, but didn't.

"It's not a full-grown gun," said his father with some amusement. "But you'll grow into it." That night they all lay awake in the dark, shivering.

When the son woke the next morning, his father had already left for the workshop, and he did not return that night, or any other night, to sleep. The new blanket remained folded on the chair. The son kept close watch on their supply of kindling and logs, and whenever it ran low, he pulled his red wagon up to the barn, where rows of firewood were stacked against an outside wall, kept dry under tarps. Although he was curious about the nature of his father's work, he did not have the courage to knock on the big barn door. He'd return from these trips with a teetering wagonload of wood to tell his mother about the barn owl's white, spectral swoop through twilight. He did not tell her that the woods had begun to fill with mechanical birds.

The burnt trees made simple, arterial shapes against the gray sky. The fire had shorn away all twigs and lesser branches, and some trees had the molten look of black metal sculptures. Absent underbrush and leaves, the uncluttered expanse of snow was clean and open. He liked this better: a snowfield of warped obelisks, as opposed to the more tangled and unruly version of nature. And yet he couldn't like it blamelessly, since he'd been author of the fire. It seemed so long ago that he had taken a rake through a burning pile of autumn leaves to expose the untouched layers beneath the ash; a single, papery leaf had risen on an invisible wave of heat, caught fire in the air, and with the jerky flits of a bat, followed the tunnel of smoke into the woods. There had been nothing to do but let it eat its way through the trees, leaving behind a field of clean black bones.

The frozen, waterless air focused everything into clear detail. When he stood still and aimed his .22 at an imagined target, he could hear silence behind his breath and heartbeat. The snow was crunchy on top, powder beneath, so the initial resistance to each step gave way to a deep, feathery drop. Each step made a loud, squeaky racket that seemed to emanate from within his head. He paused every so often to aim at an empty branch.

He squeaked along awkwardly in this way until he felt he was more or less in the middle of the wood. He knew from experience that the wood had many middles; once you got so far in, any place you chose to stand felt like it must be the center of something. He paused again to aim at what he expected would be an empty branch. Startled, he pivoted in a circle: Mechanical birds sat stoically in the branches. He was afraid, but his fear was not the same as if, for example, he had startled a bear, not the expected, rational, immediate fear of being mauled and eaten. It was what someone might have felt in the same wood two hundred years before, stumbling upon the carved faces of a lone totem pole in the middle of nowhere. An abrupt, anachronistic encounter with a human mind in the wilderness. The sudden loss of feeling alone. Fear of self.

They perched like statues, and he did not know if their stillness was by design (a response to his clumsy approach) or lack of design (maybe they were broken). The crudest bird stood out to him; he aimed at the wren fashioned from the blender. He squeezed. The bullet clanged. The wren tottered and fell, not unlike a soda can skimmed by a BB. Inspired, he took aim at the most frightening one, which had two giant rasp files for a bill and fork tines that formed a crest on its head. Before he was ready to shoot, he sensed a faint electric hum. It became a buzz, which turned into a cacophony of whirling and spinning gears as the entire flock took flight at once. The wren, lying heavily on its back in the deep snow, struggled to spread its wings. He smashed it with the pistol butt until the blender ground to a halt.

He carried the wren by its welded feet. He was hungry and thought of his mother, back at the farmhouse, warming chicken bullion and the last egg over the fire. He tossed the metal against the large barn door with a reverberating thump. The mechanic didn't open. He brought a wagonload of firewood down to the house, then sat in front of the fire with his soup to read about an evil knight who dangled the slain bodies of good knights from the limbs of a tree. Each day he went out to kill what his father had made and thumped it against the barn door. Each day he discovered a new bird perched on a black limb among the flock.

He was sure he could kill faster than his father could create.

He killed a colorful thumb-sized hummingbird that repeatedly landed on his barrel and obstructed his aim, wings buzzing like an electric razor. Bejeweled with sequins and rhinestones, costume rubies for eyes, it was like an ornamental egg confected by a jeweler. Something within its intricate clockwork tinkled like miniature wind chimes. It looked like a gift. He smacked it with a volley of rocks, and it flitted in tight, paranoid circles close to the ground. He crushed it under the heel of his boot and flung it against the barn door.

The next time he entered the woods, black wings grazed his head. A razored beak snipped his cheek. Blood drops hit the snow and bloomed through the crystals. The new, shadowlike bird disappeared before he could see it clearly.

Each bird the son destroyed was replaced by a shadow-bird. They were the simplest in design, like skeletal crows. The body of each was a black coil from an automobile suspension. Within the coiled ribcage, the guts spun in a quiet but constant blur. A large black hex nut made a head, and the hex-shaped hole an eye. Welded to each head was a sharp beak: a rusted ice pick, the blade of a pocketknife, half a pair of scissors or pruning shears. The dark wings were edged with sharpened metal. Pronged feet made of nails. They gouged the back of his neck and slit the top of his ear. He threw himself flat into the snow at every moving shadow.

The few times he managed to hit one, the bullet ricocheted off metal. They dove at him in groups, and he ran from the wood, his knitted hat torn, scalp cut, hair tangled with dry blood. He took to running through the wood with leather gloves, a thick jacket, safety glasses, and a slightly small football helmet. He spun in berserk circles with his pistol and swatted at his helmet while they swooped over him. Beneath each tail (a feathered fan of kitchen knives), he could see a wind-up key, the type used to propel an old toy, or to spin the dancer on a music box, or to rejuvenate the pendulum of a grandfather clock. Slowly, the keys turned.

After Christmas, his mother resumed her knitting. She took back the mechanic's blanket and began to knit everything she'd ever made into a much, much larger blanket that soon resembled less a blanket than a ragged sail with dangling mitten fingers, parts of hats, bits of scarves, and slipper heels. Within this sail-blanket, he could see his own cut-up hat and mittens, with their spots of dried blood visible as small pieces of the patchwork. She seemed always tired and couldn't clack her needles, so instead of this noise, she had developed a long, wheezing foghorn of a cough. Too afraid to leave the house after the flock of shadow-birds had pecked him so violently, he'd let the fire burn low to conserve wood. Slowly, the ice had begun to crackle, vein-like, along the walls, and his mother's coughed-up breath took ghostly shape in the air. When the last log had smoldered down to embers, his mother ran out of wool. She faintly wheezed something about the cold, then, instead of using her motley blanket to sail away on her sofa as he'd imagined, she rolled herself up into her knitting, a cocoon, and slept silently and ceased to cough or even grind her teeth.

The silence, except for the crackling veins of ice that he couldn't tell were real or imagined, grew to be too much, so he more dragged than rolled his red wagon through the deep snow up to the barn, the too-small helmet giving him a headache. From the barn roof, a dark row of hex-shaped heads stared at him with vacant hex-shaped holes of gray sky. Without even bothering to aim his gun, he flipped over the wagon and scrambled under it as best he could, waiting for the rap of sharp beaks. It didn't come.

They were diving at the field on the other side of the barn.

In the field, the barn owl fluttered its wings in bursts and hopped several feet at a time while the shadow-crows casually swooped down to cut it. Some perched heavily on the owl until it managed to flap them off. There was a trail of white feathers, spotted with black marks of blood. The owl cried. The son held a shadow-crow in his gunsight while it pecked at the dying bird with what he recognized as the corkscrew from his camping knife. He fired. The crow flapped away. The owl flailed, losing feathers. He flipped the owl over and put the barrel to its forehead. The eyelids blinked. His shot echoed off the barn. The hex-shaped holes stared emptily.

He built a giant fire in the field, and it melted a wide circle of snow. It was dark, and his bonfire illuminated the side of the barn and part of the roof. At the very edge of the light, barely visible, the crows perched. When he let the fire burn lower, they hopped forward. When he added wood, they retreated back into the shadow. A clunk above startled him. A crow rolled down the roof, slid off the edge, and plopped into the snow. Each hour the crows expired in increasing numbers.

He butchered the owl with the pruning-shear beak of a defunct crow. He held the lukewarm heart in his mouth, thinking himself like a reverent Indian hunter, but then he spat out the heart without chewing and placed it in the snow. He made a pile of the white feathers. He made groupings of bones, beak, feet, and he set aside the eyes and the sturdier pieces of gut. He even kept what blood he could, letting it pool in the basin of his upturned helmet. Two-thirds of the meat he set aside in the snow for his mother's soup, even though he knew there would be no waking her to eat it. The rest he roasted over the fire and ate slowly, piece by piece, letting the juices float throughout his mouth.

———

Alone in the deep snow in the middle of the burnt wood of black trees, he'd stopped crying. He felt so numb that he imagined he was without a body. He drifted into sleep, remembering how good it had been to hold each thin slice still on his tongue until it was cool, until he could no longer tell it was there, and then to swallow with what had been his first sincerely spiritual sentiment. In his dream, he repeated the ritual again and again: He shot the owl, he butchered it, he piece-by-piece filled himself with its spirit, and then at first light, he took his .22 to the workshop door and knocked.

STORY WITH ADVICE II:
BACK FROM THE DEAD

Rick Moody

Rick Moody is the author of the novels *Garden State, The Ice Storm, Purple America,* and *The Diviner,* the story collections *The Ring of Brightest Angels Around Heaven, Demonology, Right Livelihoods,* and the memoir *The Black Veil.* His work has appeared in *The New Yorker, The New York Times, Esquire, Harper's,* and elsewhere, and he has won various awards, including the PEN/Martha Albrand Award for the Art of the Memoir, the Addison Metcalf Award, the *Paris Review* Aga Khan Prize, and a Guggenheim Fellowship. He has taught at SUNY Purchase and Bennington College, and he lives in New York. "Story With Advice II: Back From the Dead" first appeared in the literary magazine *Mississippi Review.*

This is the spot in which the editor's note often appears. In the editor's note, an eminent academic describes the way in which he or she came into possession of this obscure but astonishing manuscript.

Given to him by the mother of the author, he says, who had long worried about her son's tarnished legacy. She carried the dog-eared pages with her from university to university over the course of decades.

Or the manuscript was discovered in a cache of papers in the attic of an abandoned farmhouse. Or it was purchased by a trafficker in codices from an arms dealer during the hottest part of a Saharan summer. Civil conflict raged.

This editor's note goes on to describe the unlikely, singular nature of the contents of the soiled pages, delivered to the reading public against all odds. Were this a genuine editor's note, it would further observe that this particular manuscript seems, on its face, to be fraudulent, even ludicrous, and yet here it is, having apparently been published first in installments several years ago in a forgotten periodical to be described below. Should we believe the manuscript? Should we suspect it of falsifications? Is there any manuscript without them? Is the editor not embarrassed to bring this manuscript, with so few bona fides as to provenance to the aforementioned reading public? These and other issues are often covered in this six-inch introduction, where there is also time for asides about the daily fare of academic life, as well as descriptions of seasonal coloration: falling leaves, blossoming tulips, love and . . .

Dear Story With Advice II, if "after death" is an actual place, what are the dead wearing these days? Do they wear what they were wearing when they died? Or are the dead naked and unashamed and somehow managing to be beautiful in everyone's eyes, for once? Signed, Woman Who Wants to Prepare Her Closet for Death.

Dear Woman, the first thing I want to stress is that the whole story about how in the moments before you embark on the afterlife you wait in a dimly lit but ethereal holding cell while your dead friends clamor for you, this is Hollywood confection.

This is the Fluffernutter sandwich of afterlife narratives. Not that I want to be the one to burst the bubble. For all I know, you're desperately attached to this idea and are hoping, in the life to come, to meet expired relatives or some boy you loved who, before his car accident, stood under your window and sang. Well, Woman, if your afterlife experience is like mine you don't have a snowball's chance in hell, (and I use this legendary place name with a fearsome purpose), of meeting up with these folks.

Let me remind you, in case you've forgotten, of the particulars of my own story. I was lying on the carpet of my suburban living room gushing from bullet holes, choking to death on my own fountaining insides. This blood, let me point out, had spattered the walnut sofa, the brand new slipcover of which I just paid good money for. What a mess! I was resting one soon-to-be-deceased hand on the sturdy back of the walnut sofa, and I was looking into the eyes of the guy who'd just perforated me. But instead of fretting, Woman, I was thinking mainly about the daily chores that needed to be accomplished. There was some kind of foreign tax certification form I was meant to fill out. I had office hours. I needed to wash the car. The car was sitting out in the turnaround, flecked with grime, while I was bleeding to death. Suddenly, there was in me a chickadee twitter of anxiety, along the following lines, *You're dying! You're dying! You are shot and you are displaying symptoms of the medical condition known as shock, which is good because at this point you don't yet have pain management issues. However, you have only seconds remaining in your not-always-satisfying life, and there are ten thousand things that you have neglected to complete! Among these unaccomplished tasks is going to be explaining to your wife and your sullen teenage son that they made your term here pleasanter!* And so forth. While I was thinking thus, Woman, I was edging closer to a fascinating gray area where I was medically dead but hadn't quite expended the last few electrical impulses that caromed around in the ridges and valleys of my gray matter. In this interval, I wasted yet a further moment or two in the consideration of epic poetry. Was the passage in question from Dante? It must have been from Dante. It's a beautiful passage, too: some Guelph is stabbed to death, but in the moment he passes over he mumbles: *Sorry!* Or the equivalent in medieval Italian. He apologizes for his transgressions, and then he gives up the proverbial ghost.

Guess what? This guy is forgiven by God! All the fucked up stuff he did in his life? Let's say he cheated on his wife a few dozen times, lied on his taxes a fair amount, torpedoed a few colleagues in his department, gossiped like gossip was the air he breathed, lusted after other people's wives, drank to excess several nights a week, stole pot from his son and smoked it, you name it, all the crimes this fellow committed, all the selfishness, the lying, the thoughtlessness, this is all *forgiven,* because this guy remembered to say *Sorry!* before his lips turned blue and his extremities stiffened. So, Woman Who Wants, I am here to say that even though I don't believe in religious mumbo jumbo, even though I have darkened the doorway of churches only for funerals, I too managed, in that moment of my dwindling electrical impulses, to mumble *Sorry!* And apparently this was a shrewd move on my part. Because there's no lake of fire anywhere around here! Not that I can see. The climate in my present locale is temperate around the clock, almost like there's a very reliable thermostat here somewhere!

Now, in order to continue with my remarks, I need to say something briefly about my brother. Back when I was still alive, Woman, I often used my celebrated newspaper advice column to talk about my dead brother. I noted that over the years I'd had complicated feelings about him, competitive feelings, feelings of worthlessness, feelings of exasperation, you name it. These feelings were frustrated or exacerbated by my brother's untimely passing (after a "long battle with" multiple myeloma). As a result, I never managed to put the memory of this particular individual to rest. This individual troubled my sleep. The fact is, I really did find myself, when alive, wishing for some kind of way station or corridor or bus station ticketed-passengers-only waiting room of dead friends and relatives—if only to set things right with my brother at last. I admit it! I hated any movie in which actresses got to consort with their digitally-enhanced dead lovers, etc. I suffered with these feelings both acutely and chronically, the more so as the years passed.

Therefore, as I weltered in gunshot wounds, a victim of violent crime, I did think, in passing, *Goddamit, if I don't get to see my brother I am going to have to complain. Somebody's going to hear about this.* If this constitutes a kind of half-hearted mysticism, Woman, so be it. Because my brother was a really good guy, was the better of the two of us, and I think I can say that if you have had your pick between him and me, you'd have picked him. In the afterlife, under more ideal circumstances, he would have shown me the best spot in the heavenly cafeteria, the section of where Gandhi, Tolstoy, and Hemingway all hung out, shooting the breeze.

Alas, as I've implied, my brother totally failed to show up. Neither were there any other dead pals clamoring for me. This is how I concluded, Woman, that, wherever this place is, I am completely isolated in it. It's just me here, dead author of *Story With Advice,* a column in a small forgettable Connecticut newspaper, a newspaper given over to real estate listings, personals, and advertisements for escort agencies. I guess the afterlife, if I may extrapolate, is as lonely as the ordeal preceding it.

On the other hand, maybe your question is simply about *place,* and about whether there is a place to the time after death.

Woman, suffice to say, the notion of place has too much *location* to be applicable to where I am currently housed. My hypothesis, for today, is that the afterlife is folded onto the reverse of reality like a Disney stage set. The dead and their personal effects, in small mini-storage units, are folded and refolded back onto *what is* until they could fit beneath a hangnail.

As for what I wear, well, this is an interesting question. Since there is no one here excepting myself, there would be no one to wear anything *for*. Without a body, I have no bodily parts to outfit. To put it another way, I don't think I am naked. If I were naked I would have to circumambulate for all eternity with a penis that is decidedly average in terms of its size. I know you are not prepared to reassure me about the size of my penis, and, in fact, none of the women in my life was able to do so while I was living. I'm happy to say that I no longer require them to do so. That I've made my peace with my average-sized cock, however, doesn't mean that I would be prepared to walk around with it for all eternity.

I would like to wear some clothes, however, because I was actually a spiffy dresser while alive. I'm wondering, Woman, if you would consent to bring me some clothes. Maybe we could try a bit of an experiment. If you find yourself dying in the near future, do you think you could bring me up a corduroy blazer, and some black jeans, and, I don't know, a cashmere sweater of some kind? In case of a chill. Any kind of t-shirt or underwear is fine. But, please, no y-front briefs.

Dear Story With Advice II, I need directions to the room with the complete collection of all the objects that I lost while I was alive. Do I need to come with their call numbers written down or will everything will be out on shelves? Also, will I need ID to check them out, or will it be clear that they were my things? Signed, Olive Hedgehog.

Dear Olive, nice to make your acquaintance and thanks for writing to *Story With Advice II: Back From the Dead!* Am I correct in thinking that this is your first time writing to me? Because if it's your first time writing I suppose I can forgive your carelessness about the nature of my pet peeves. However, it's important that you learn the ground rules in case you should like to write again. There are certain kinds of letters, Olive, that we at Story With Advice II call *maledictories*. In these cases, very predictable responses will be forthcoming. You're fortunate that I am now dead, because as a result I am less preoccupied with hot-button issues than I was while breathing.

The particular problem, Olive, concerns *collecting*. Look, I'm willing to bet that you've read your Freud. If so, I'm betting you know which excretory function is, according to that master of psychoanalysis, sublimated in this urge to amass, sort, and name big mounds of possessions. Myself, I have never in my life, and especially not in my afterlife, Olive, given a shit about collecting things. Things are for people who can't hack the demands of their emotional lives. Things are for schizophrenics and two-year-olds, for people who cannot relinquish their death-grip on transitional objects. Admittedly, I did have a brief period with the LP, when I was a teenager, a bit of a collecting period. Later, I had my problems with book ownership. But, Olive, you don't find me prattling on about the fact that I don't have here a first edition of *The Sun Also Rises*, do you?

Things are a seduction down where you are. If there is no longer a *location* to where I am, it then follows, naturally, that there is no shelf space. If there is no shelf space, then there is nowhere to arrange my collection, whatever it might be. Having said this, what I still seem to possess after a fashion, Olive, is the collection of my memories. Would you like to hear a memory of mine?

Because I have a few I'd like to share. The following memory, for example, concerns little league baseball, which I played in the town of Winchester, Massachusetts. I was on a team known as the Dollar Cleaners. I don't know if Dollar Cleaners were better than any of the other cleaners in the neighborhood, but apparently they were cheap. We had a drunken lout for a coach who never let me play. One Saturday, after I had practiced the position of catcher with a guy up the street (how hard could it be?), I was given a chance, by the drunken lout, to fill in for our regular catcher, who left early that day for his boy scout jamboree. Olive, not only did I fail to catch fully one half of the balls pitched in my direction, but I had also a dim awareness, at the time, of the concept of stolen bases. I had no idea that it was my responsibility to prevent stolen bases by throwing out the runners at second base. The upshot was: the Dollar Cleaners were routed in this game, despite the fact that I was removed from the position of catcher after serving out only the fourth and fifth innings. Getting routed was not something the Dollar Cleaners did. In the car pool back home, with a couple of my teammates, it was pointed out to me that I had found an entirely new way to fail at the pastime of baseball. I normally warmed the bench, except when I was a late inning defensive replacement in order to flatter my parents. In my one chance to do otherwise, I had disgraced myself further.

Olive, you do not, in the afterlife, get to keep your books, your records, your dollhouse, your family heirlooms, your silver chest, your art collection, your Kiss action figures, your exotic musical instruments, your plastic handbags, your ceramic bears, your toy pianos, your erotic etchings, your antique furniture, your comical hats. But you do get to keep at hand your memories of childhood disgrace. Why should I have to continue thinking about the Dollar Cleaners? Why should I have to recall the face

of my drunken Little League coach, likewise the self-regard of
the kid who batted .410 and who almost always hit the ball over
the fence? Why?

*Dear Knower of Everything in the Afterlife, I am a very lucky
person, intelligent, talented, educated, healthy enough, good looking
enough for a middle-aged guy. I've got everything one could hope
for—a decent job that allows me to travel, a beautiful house, a nice
car, a wife, a kid, lovers on the side, but I am just not happy to be . . .
a guy. I can't help but think I'd be happier to start life all over again as
a woman. Will my wish be granted in the Afterlife? Signed, Curious
to Cross-Over.*

Dear Curious, I'm thinking maybe you are Olive's husband,
and you wrote this on the sly, because you saw what a good thing
Olive had going on. If this is true, it may gratify you to learn
that during my life I published, in my column, upwards of fifteen
or twenty letters about gender issues. I was a regular fanatic on
the subject. Why, you ask? I'll tell you! Because I loved areas of
inquiry that made people uncomfortable! Had I known that all
you had to do was mumble *Sorry!* at the moment of death in order
to miss out on the whole lake-of-fire business, then I would have
likewise published innumerable letters about self-mutiliating
compulsions, masochism, body dysmorphia, frottage, furries,
erotic asphyxiation, and more. Life is short!

However, my genuine remembrances about sex in the first
world—that disorderly obsession that is the alpha and omega
of youth only to vanish incrementally from your consciousness
later—are beginning to take on the sepia hue of rotogravure
images. Perhaps memory does turn out to be less reliable in
the hereafter than I have indicated in prior missives. I can sort
of remember the various women with whom I performed the

gallant dance of desire, lovers both furtive and public, lovers both brief and attenuated, lovers desperate, lovers gentle and relaxed; I can remember rug burns on my knees and elbows, I remember, in certain circumstances, feeling I was going to suffocate from having someone astride my face in a particular way. I remember driving a hundred miles on the basis of a provocative word or two in some telephone call. I remember sleeplessness, the thunder of my pulse, feelings of shame, fear of discovery. I remember, on occasion, joy. I remember the taste of spermicides and latex. I remember falling asleep, afterward, as though etherized. Was any of this dependent on my gender? Masculinity, retrospectively, does look like some kind of arrested state of psychical development. And yet is femininity preferable? I don't really know.

The question of where I am to go *next*, whether I even have a *next*, is central to these posthumous columns. It's possible that I am due to be reincarnated, according to Hindu philosophy, and this period of letter-answering is simply a purgatorial antechamber on the way to a lackluster episode of rebirth. Perhaps, in some new reincarnated life, if I do not come back as a lizard, I may be lucky enough to be a woman. It's possible because many things are. It's possible, I mean, that dark matter is composed entirely of dead people, that what physicists are looking for—the primordial slurry that perturbs all orbits, that keeps the universe from spasming in upon itself—is just the impossible-to-describe afterlife essence of dead people. However, I doubt it. My advice to you, Curious, is not to expend your days such that you leave behind longing unfulfilled. Those few adventures that you can identify as a lack, search after these experiences, fling off the cares of the day, in pursuit. Because when the Big Forgetting comes, when the Big Forgetting brings with it the wiping clean of all your sentimental experiences—until there's nothing left but eating and shitting—you don't want to have a list of adventures uncompleted. You don't want to remember only the inadvisable journey, the trash-compacted dream.

Yes, transsexuality has something heroic about it. Which is why, I imagine, you're asking about it. Get thee to the slutty lingerie store, buy some provocative outfits, tell your nearest and dearest that, though you have the physique of a linebacker, you feel best when wearing a frock. You will have done something good with your life. Anticipate the Big Forgetting. It will mass on your western flank and sweep mercilessly across you.

Dear Story With Advice II, Do you actually ever roll over in your grave? And if so, can you tell me what would cause you to do a full roll over? Say your granddaughter, a Brooklyn wage slave badly in debt by reason of an overpriced education, sold your treasured armchairs on Craigslist only to use that money to pay for an abortion. Would that be enough to roll over? Signed, A Concerned Granddaughter.

Dear Granddaughter, today's disquisition is on the nature of the influence that the dead exert over the living. It's commonly imagined that the dead exert no particular influence over the living, since they are dead. They're not available for argument in which by cajoling or manipulation they seek to work things out to their decomposing advantage. In most cases, they are incapable of movement. At the same time, Granddaughter, it is assumed by many who are really not worth our prolonged attention that there is HDTV up here in the afterlife, a flat-screen console mounted on the wall in a gigantic common room, and that we are able to watch on this screen round-the-clock programming in which you, you bloody sponge, go about your daily rounds. Granddaughter, remember when you argued with that exterminator about whether his sweet chemicals were going to poison your cat? Do you imagine that the harridan mother of the exterminator, who died eight years ago of congestive heart failure, will be sitting next to your grandfather in the common room just described, watching you argue with this exterminator about the health and welfare of Knuckles, the six-fingered tabby? Do you imagine that because she is concerned about Raoul, the drunken exterminator, while your grandfather is concerned about you, that there will be heavenly fisticuffs, in which cherubim will need to intervene? As I've been trying to make clear, this idea about the dead just doesn't have any *oomph* at all. We have no intention of spending our eternities watching you parallel park.

The influence that the dead exert over the living, Granddaughter, is an internal influence. It's in you, subdermally. The concern in your letter about your grandfather rolling over in the grave, that's a concern that *you* have about the quality of your own luck, though it's fair to say that at this moment, Granddaughter, I probably share your concern. Frankly, while I ardently support a woman's right to choose, and don't believe the state has an obligation to protect a little tadpole, especially when the state murders other animals, right and left, I feel a little worried about your conduct, about whether the pregnancy you describe is owing to a guy you met in a bar. Is my worry justified? Was it true love for seven hours? I am certain that if I were your grandfather, and right now I am as much your grandfather as I am not, I would feel unquiet in the afterlife, and not about armchairs. Distance, you see, is a key ingredient in the molecular construction of the condition known as love. As my distance can be measured in light years, my affection is not insubstantial. Please take note, and adjust your conduct accordingly.

Meanwhile, something is happening here. I feel a need to address this something, while I have the opportunity. It has occurred to me recently that there has been some kind of clerical error or other universal networking glitch that has enabled me to continue posthumously filing these columns in the little newspaper in Connecticut. What do I mean? I mean, Granddaughter, that while I was living I don't recall encountering any letters from dead people in the newspaper. There were occasionally people on talk shows and so forth who claimed to be able to contact individuals in my condition, but I think it is reasonable to assume that those talk-show wannabes were frauds. However, for reasons that I do not understand, Granddaughter, it seems that I truly am a dead journalist able to continue talking with the folks back on earth.

The singularity of my predicament therefore unnerves me. How the fuck is it that I'm doing what I'm doing? It is in the nature of dead things to stay dead! My inability to locate a pneumatic tube, let's say, or Telex or fax machine, any telecommunications device at all, is unsettling. Is there some kind of voice-activated software hidden nearby? Is there, and I admit I am loath to entertain this possibility, some kind of celestial watch-repairman who transmits my ruminations to the audience back home? By now there are probably eight or ten billion people on your planet, most of them speakers of Mandarin or Urdu. I don't have any greater right to be doling out advice than some blogger from Mumbai, some gossip maven from Lahore, and therefore what explains the persistence of my literary voice, as opposed to others?

The thing about singular occurrences, Granddaughter, is that under the pressure of science they collapse. I had no anxiety about dying while I was alive. I was too busy to give it a thought. I had business to look after, columns to write. Then, all at once, I was murdered. I hadn't considered that anyone would murder a second-rate English professor who, upon receiving tenure, had given up doing any substantial academic work. Maybe some of my colleagues wanted to murder me, but they were pacifists. They would have been *more* miserable had they not had the opportunity to belittle me at departmental gatherings.

What I mean is I'm kind of worrying about dying now. After the fact. Imagine, if you will, that consciousness is a radio signal. Not one of those digital satellite signals that always offers good reception. An old-fashioned radio signal. Crackling with interference in a humid night. In just this way, my signal, I believe, is not as clear as it once was. My transmitter is balky. Maybe an adult contemporary station is obliterating me. I can feel this happening. What if my message to you is delayed? What if the answer to your question languishes in theological limbo? Since time, hereabouts, is without periodicity, maybe time will pass and I will miss the local deadline at the paper. What if a decade in your young life races by while my message is gummed up in the interstellar works? Will it then be too late? While I can, I would like to reassure you that I *do* understand. Perhaps in this way, as a caring agency, I can put off from receding from worldly view?

I wish there *were* someone I could appeal to, but to the best of my knowledge there is no congressman, no representative of the innumerable dead to whom I can make formal protest. Granddaughter, I can feel some of the names of persons, places, and things—supreme court justices, obscure rockabilly stars, brands of snack food items—dwindling, as if I could have no possible use for these names. For the time being, faces remain. I can remember that girl who loaned me her windbreaker in the fourth grade, and that guy who had the sister with Down's Syndrome. But how long can I rely upon these last recollections?

Dear Story With Advice II, Several years ago I was walking with a friend through a park in downtown Boston. We came across this group of homely-looking people doing some sort of Renaissance-fair style performance and I began laughing hysterically, particularly at the men in stockings. My friend, who seemed to sympathize with them, said, "Whatever, I bet they have more orgasms than you do." This was at a low point in my life when I'd gone without for nine months. His accusation was correct. Since then, I've wondered if real worth in life is determined not by one's actions or achievements but by numbers of orgasms. I feel you can answer this because you have time to compare notes with other dead people. Signed, Young and Dissolute.

Dissolute, I'm going to try to get this out quickly. There are a number of important things you need to do while you are able and willing. Please find a pen and copy down the following. Whenever possible, buy new socks. Never underestimate the value of listening. The first genuinely warm day in April you should spend outdoors. Peaches can be disappointing, but that's why they are worth the effort. Pet any dog that requests to be petted. If the rain is warm, stand in the rain. Apology, when deployed honestly, will get you far. Every time you are impatient, covet your misery. People who don't read are to be avoided at all cost. Give to whoever asks. Change bedding frequently. Make note of any male cardinal who in April alights in forsythia. Leave no trace.

Michelle Richmond is the author of the New York Times bestseller *The Year of Fog*, the award-winning story collection *The Girl in the Fall-Away Dress*, and the novel *Dream of the Blue Room*. Her most recent novel, *No One You Know*, was published by Delacorte in July 2008. Her stories and essays have appeared in *Glimmer Train, Playboy, Oxford American, The Believer, Salon, The Kenyon Review, The Missouri Review*, and elsewhere. She is the recipient of the 2006 *Mississippi Review* Fiction Prize and the 2000 Associated Writing Programs Award, and has received fellowships from the Millay Colony, the Saltonstall Foundation, and the Sewanee Writers' Conference, among others. A native of Mobile, Alabama, Michelle lives with her husband and son in San Francisco. She is the founding editor of the literary journal *Fiction Attic*, and she serves on the advisory board of the Christopher Isherwood Foundation. "Logorrhea" appeared in the anthology of the same name, edited by John Klima.

He had not been born with the scales. Indeed, the origin of his condition was as enigmatic to the mother who bore him as it was to the scientists who studied him, for nowhere in the family album or in the scientists' vast store of case histories was there another human being so gloriously esquamulose.

He was three years old when the scales began to appear—on his upper legs, at first. Tiny, half-moon shaped bits, hard and thin, the rounded edges paper-sharp. One pediatrician diagnosed it as an allergic rash, another as a severe case of keritosis peritonitis, another as an indeterminable childhood abnormality that would surely right itself with age. But when the scales began to thicken and to stretch up his body—to his groin, his stomach, his arms, shoulders, neck, and eventually, his face, the doctors stopped trying to make a diagnosis. It was like nothing they had seen, it was miraculous, it was horrific.

One thing you should understand: the scales did not cover his skin, they *were* his skin. Unlike hair or fingernails, there was nothing extraneous about them. To rid him of the scales would have been to rid him of his very surface.

The doctors took pictures, they referred him to specialists, they did all of the things one does when an exceptional case is dropped, like a gift of manna, into one's hands. But they offered no answers, only a long series of lotions and pills and dermatological treatments of the abrasive and purative variety, all of which yielded nothing—nothing but a sobbing, put-upon boy.

"No one has ever loved me before," he said, by which he meant no one had ever *made* love to him—and in his mind, the two were one and the same.

All of these things he told me on our first night together. Our first! How could he hold it back, this dark history, when my skin bore the savage marks of his scales, when his flesh literally dug into mine?

It may surprise you to learn that the miracle of that night was not the cuts or his loquaciousness, was not even the fact of our having found each other on a deserted beach in Alabama. The miracle of that night was that I was moved to silence. I, who suffer so plainly from logorrhea, was so enthralled by his story that I dared not interrupt.

In earlier times, surely, a man like him would have been destined to be either a circus freak or a favored showpiece of some royal court. In this modern place and time, protected as he was from indigence by the blessing of disability pay, the effect of his condition had instead been to make him supremely lonely. Because he did not have to go out into the world to make a living, and because he could not be intimate with another human being without causing harm, he had chosen to live a life apart. Before we met, he had passed a decade of bachelorhood in a small house in Fairhope just steps from Mobile Bay, with the aid of a trusted assistant who did his shopping, ran his errands, and occasionally shared his meals.

And then he found me. Or, it should be said, I found him. On the Fairhope Pier, on a typically moonlit night. It is a minor miracle of that particular part of Alabama that the filthy bay is often bathed in a fine moonlight which makes it appear clean, inspiring foolhardy teenagers and tourists to go for midnight swims in the bleak mix of sewage and chemical waste. He appeared to me first as a statuesque figure at the end of the pier, dressed in a long-sleeved shirt and linen pants. I was having a difficult time of it, having recently lost, within the span of a few weeks, a decent job and a beloved pet, not to mention a boyfriend, when I saw him standing there, so still and silent that I first assumed a sculpture had been erected in that familiar spot. I stepped off the warm sand onto the pier, and when the boards creaked beneath me he turned, and that is when I understood that this splendid creature was alive.

For several moments I hesitated. Someone standing in such a way, at such a place, on such a night, surely does not want to be interrupted. Then the moonlight hit his face, and a flash of multicolored light shot off the tip of his elegant nose, and I found myself walking toward him, as the old pier wobbled and groaned.

"Stop," he called out.

It was a slightly scratchy voice, halting, as if it was out of practice.

"Why?" I called back.

"Because," was his reply.

"It's a public pier," I said.

To this, he had no answer. He turned back toward the water and took a step forward. For a moment I thought he might jump. But he didn't. When I reached him, he said, with his back to me, "I came out here to be alone."

"Me too," I said. "I won't bother you." Then I moved to stand beside him, and he lifted a gloved hand to shield his face.

"Please," he said.

But by then, I had already seen.

We stood for a minute or two in silence before I said the only thing I could think of to say, which was, "You're beautiful."

"I'm ghastly," he replied.

"Not to me."

He produced a small paper bag, and when he opened it I could smell hot spice and salt and the sea. It was a strong, wonderful odor particular to the Gulf Coast, and immediately I was happy to be home again, after a long time away.

"Crawfish," he said.

"I know."

I reached into the bag, took one of the hard little shells, and twisted until the tail came clean from the head. I sucked the head, something I hadn't done in years, something that I had deemed in my new life up north to be somewhat barbaric. But the juice was delicious, even more so than I remembered, tangy and sweet in a way no other meat could replicate. The shimmering man followed suit, and it occurred to me that the boyfriend who had just kicked me out of his stylish apartment in the stylish city that had never really felt like home would never have done such a thing. Then I squeezed the tail end of the shell until the tender pink meat came out, popped it into my mouth, chewed luxuriously, licked my fingers, and only after I had swallowed did I have the good grace to thank him.

"No, thank *you*," he said, looking at me directly for the first time. "One should never eat crawfish alone. I've been doing it far too long." The combination of the words and the way he looked at me, as if we were complicit in some dream of love, seemed to cast forward into a future when we would do this together frequently, would, in fact, do many things together. It would not be an exaggeration to say that, at that moment, I understood that the thing we were going to have together would be nothing short of a life.

We sat down on the end of the pier, removed our shoes, our feet dangling in the water, and ate. He produced a couple of warm beers, which seemed to materialize from thin air. We drank them in silence. When the crawfish and the beers were gone, he began to talk. Once he started, it was as if he couldn't stop. And I, who had driven away my last boyfriend and lost my last job because I couldn't shut up, sat and listened. For the first time in my life, I found listening to be effortless. Every now and then I'd feel a school of tiny fish moving past like a gentle wind, the mouths nibbling at my ankles.

When he was finished, I said, "I have something to tell you."

"What is it?"

"I have a problem."

He turned to look at me, and his blue eyes looked strangely dull, contrasted as they were against the glittering scales. "A problem?"

But when I opened my mouth to say it, the words would not come out. Why mar this perfect evening by confessing my worst character trait? I would be for him, that night, the ideal companion. I would let him think that I was the kind of woman a man might be lucky to have. *You'd be a real prize*, my ex had said, sliding his hands over my breasts, my hips, my thighs, *if you had your mouth surgically wired shut.*

"It's nothing," I said. "Never mind."

He shook the last bits of crawfish shell into the water, put the empty bottles into the paper bag, and said, "My house is just down the beach. Do you want to come home with me?"

"Yes."

Walking back with him along the quiet beach, I could not have imagined the physical pain that awaited me. In hindsight, I understand that when he removed his glove and took my hand in his, it was meant as a silent warning. He held my hand as gently as he could, and still I could feel the scales cutting into my palm and fingers. I wondered, but did not ask, whether the affliction covered his entire body. Later that night, pressing my face into a pillow to squelch my screams, I understood that it did.

That first time, I was covered with lacerations. Tiny red marks all over the front of my body, like thousands of paper cuts, and also on my back where his arms had embraced me. All through the night I kept waking in pain, the fresh wounds damp with blood, my body sticking to the soft flannel sheets as if held there by thousands of dots of glue. Beside me, he slept soundly, his scales wet-seeming in the moonlight, his face the picture of peace. I couldn't help but feel, somehow, that I had saved him, although it would occur to me later that it was the other way around. In any event, that first morning-after, when I woke to the sound of his scaled feet clicking softly against the tile floor, I knew that I would stay with him. That I would make a home there in that house by the bay. Maybe it was the disfiguring effect of our first attempt at love—after all, I had never been loved so dramatically. More likely, it was the fact of his having accomplished something no other man had ever been able to do: with him, I had fallen easily, happily, willingly into silence.

I can say without reservation that the weeks that followed were the best weeks of my life. Days, I went out looking for a new job while he concealed himself, as was his routine, in the house, making notes for a memoir he planned to write. He was very secretive about the book, would not let me see so much as a single page, kept the steadily growing manuscript locked away in a file cabinet, behind the locked door of his closet. It was a house of secrets to which I was not privy, but I had my secrets too. I did not mention to him the character flaw that had brought all my previous relationships, romantic and otherwise, to an abrupt and tearful end. I did not tell him that I had laid cruel waste to a long cadre of therapists, professionals who, though trained to listen, could not bear to listen to me. Or that my second-to-last boyfriend had been so put off by my incessant talking that, following our break-up, he'd taken up with a girl who was deaf and mute, a hot little Helen Keller who was fond of fishnets and funny hats. Or that my own mother would not take my calls.

He had fallen in love with a certain girl, the one he met that night at the end of the pier, the one who sat silently and listened to his stories. In order to keep him, I would remain that girl. It was easier than I could have imagined: he held my rapt attention, and I, miracle of miracles, held my fevered tongue.

Following that first night, we went an entire month without making love, during which time my body slowly healed. Mornings and evenings, he dressed the wounds with ointment. Of course, he had to wear gloves, but even so, I felt that I had never been touched so gently. Some nights, while he was sleeping, I stood in front of the bathroom mirror, peeled back the bandages, and examined my shorn skin. It was a source of fascination for me, this pain that made me feel, at the same time, horribly wounded and deeply desired.

Then, at the beginning of our second month together, I came home from work—by then I had landed a gig as a docent at the maritime museum—to find him dressed head-to-toe in a suit of clean white felt.

"Feel," he said, holding an arm out for me to touch. "It's impenetrable. I had it custom-made. The felt is the best one can buy, hand-beaten by Tuvan women in the village of Tsengal in Mongolia."

I stroked his moon-white arm. "So soft," I said. "It's beautiful."

But what I was thinking was that I missed his scales, the way they captured and reflected light, the way, when he moved across a room, he looked like a human chandelier.

Have I mentioned that his scales tinkled? Have I mentioned that, after bathing, while he stood in the middle of the tiled kitchen floor, dripping dry to avoid shredding the towels, he was like a fountain of light?

"There is a necessary flaw in the suit's design," he said, leading me to the bedroom.

"What's that?"

When we reached the bed, he turned to face me and unfastened two buttons on his groin. A flap of felt fell away to reveal that most beautiful part of him, of which I had been in awe from the beginning.

The cock is often described as an obvious and uninspired work of functionality, lacking in beauty. But his was different. It was average in size but exceptional in appearance, covered as it was with scales of many hues, ranging from the palest white to the deepest blue. Although it had been inside me only once, I had admired it often, amazed by the way, when in repose, it lay against his body like a cylindrical jewel. What cruelty, to be blessed with such a beautiful cock, but to be unable to share it with the world!

That night, separated from him by a layer of plush white felt, it was like making love to a pillow, or a human-shaped yurt. Except, of course, for the one part. Our way of making love was to be very, very still, to let the closeness of our two bodies be a substitute for motion; even so, I came away from the event cut and bleeding in the one place where I could feel it most Afterward, it wasn't too bad as long as I was sitting or standing still. But walking around the maritime museum, instructing eager third-graders on the mating habits of sting rays and jumbo Gulf shrimp, proved excruciatingly painful. In a way it was terrible, but in another way it made me feel as though I had happened upon an exceptional love. He was like no man I'd ever been with. I could search for years, and never find anyone like him. It was satisfying to think of the women I knew at work—the secretary with her portentous hair, or the events planner with her eternally disappointed air of someone who has just missed out on a very good party—passing through the days with their ordinary loves, while, in the little house by the bay, my own love waited, freakish and beautiful.

As it turned out, the suit was only an early prototype. Over the months and years it would be followed by many others, each one hand-sewn by a celebrated textile artist across the bay in Mobile, each one an improvement upon the last. An improvement in that each new suit was less obvious, more natural-looking than the one before. The white felt gave way to something thinner and somewhat flesh-colored—also smooth, but with the faint hint of human hair. He gave the textile artist photos of himself as a very young child, before the scales began to appear, and gradually, the color of the suit came to resemble, more and more, the color his skin had been prior to the affliction. That's what he called it, in his more depressive moods, when the memoir was going badly—his *affliction*—and I didn't have the words to tell him that it was the affliction that drew me to him, more so than his personality, which, I came to realize, was rather ordinary, or his intelligence, which tended toward the esoteric, or his cooking, which, it turned out, was limited to boiled crawfish and Oysters Rockefeller, the latter of which I'd never had the stomach for.

The suit's hair, too, became more supple and fine, placed discriminately in the appropriate places—thicker on the legs and upper arms, a lighter patch of it on the chest, and only a few stray hairs, for authenticity's sake, in the small of the back and on the wrists. By and by, the suit began to look alarmingly realistic, so one had to examine it closely to see that something was amiss, that he was wearing not his skin, but rather a suit of simulated skin, designed, ingeniously, to bruise upon impact and to emit faint odors reminiscent of the wearer's last meal and even, under the proper conditions, to sweat.

The suit was so realistic, in fact, that he gained a kind of confidence he'd never known before. Over time, as the suit improved to near perfection, he began to go out in public, to socialize with ordinary folk. Eventually he got a job. He kept his hair long and always wore a hat and scarf, even in the merciless humidity, in addition to a thick makeup that had been designed by the textile artist, who was branching out into clay work. With all of these precautions, he was able to keep his face pretty well concealed, and anyone who might catch a glimpse of scales was likely to think that he was sweating, or that he'd just undergone a very serious exfoliation.

But at night, when he came home from his job at the finance company—something he'd dreamed of his whole life, not least of all because it smacked of normalcy and unobtrusive prosperity— he allowed me to unzip the suit and peel it off of his shimmering skin in the pastel light cast through our windows by the sleeping Gulf, and to rinse the makeup from his face, and to do the one thing I desired most, the one thing that, unbeknownst to him, kept my love for him alive: to look at him, in all his scaled and glittering glory. When he was naked, stripped of the deceptions he had so meticulously acquired in order to pass in polite society, he was nothing short of beautiful.

When it came time to make love, I willingly zipped him into the suit again. With my job, it would have been difficult to endure the all-over scarring that would have occurred if we made love without the suit. Not to mention the fact that some genetic code was at play, some aging process peculiar to the esquamulose was afoot, so that, while his suit grew softer and more pliant with each mutation, his scales grew sharper and more pointed.

During all this time, the suit's one supposed flaw remained: one key part of his body had to remain exposed during lovemaking. According to the textile artist, it had something to do with the chemical makeup of the fabric, which could not sustain exposure to certain types of bodily fluids. So it passed that, year after year, my feminine parts bore the brunt of our lovemaking, the result being that I felt, always, that I was somehow his, that I endured a sacrifice for him. This made our union seem, to me, somehow pure, for what is love if not sacrifice?

And then, one Friday afternoon nearly a decade after that night meeting at the pier, my husband—by then, we had walked down the aisle of a non-denominational church by the sea, and feasted on champagne and crawdads while a local Zydeco band inspired the small group of wedding guests to flail about in the sand—came home to me and said, "It's been solved."

I was sitting at the kitchen table, reviewing the literature for a new live specimen the maritime museum had acquired, the *Tonicella lineate*, or lined chiton, a prehistoric-looking mollusk with a single large foot whose tongue, or *radula* to be precise, is covered with iron teeth. I suppose I didn't properly hear him, or didn't note the enthusiasm in his voice, because rather than asking him what exactly it was that had been solved, I was moved to share with him an interesting fact I'd just discovered in my reading. "It says here that the lined chiton can travel up to three feet on the ocean's surface to scrape algae off nearby rocks. Then it returns to its *home scar*, which is a depression in its own rock that is, get this, shaped just like the lined chiton." I shoved a potato chip into my mouth and kept talking. "I mean, the chiton has used his iron-coated teeth—they get that way, the teeth I mean, by a complicated chemical process called biomineralization—to shave away the rock until it fits his body just so. Like a glove! Like a lover!" I exclaimed, taking a swig of my beer, for by this point I had had really made myself at home on the Gulf Coast, swigging beer and sucking crawfish heads with abandon, occasionally even attending a tent revival, forgetting that I'd ever lived in one of the strange cities of the north or that, in a past life, my beloved cat had, according to the veterinarian, actually committed suicide, "most likely to avoid some trauma at home—is there something traumatic going on at home?" she had asked, looking at me accusingly, to which my boyfriend, the one with the stylish apartment, had replied, "Yeah, this one here won't shut the fuck up. Ever."

"Says here that chitons have flexible shells," I said, " composed of eight articulating valves, which are covered with thousands of tiny eyes called aesthetes. The largest chiton in the world is the *Cryptochiton stelleri*, or gumboot, which can reach thirteen inches and has valves shaped like butterflies. Butterflies, mind you! Never say there isn't poetry in the sea."

My husband, at this point, was staring at me in stunned silence. And why shouldn't he? I'd never strung so many words together the entire time I'd known him. Something strange had happened that long-ago night on the pier; I had, without warning or effort, been cured. What I'd believed at the time to be a temporary reprieve from my own affliction had turned out to be permanent. Weeks turned into months, months to years, and I did not feel the need to talk. Quite the opposite, I felt compelled to silence, so that by the time I returned home each day from the museum, where it was my duty to speak at length about the wonders of the sea, I had little desire to say anything. Instead, I listened. One might argue, of course, that this made my life easier, but I could not help feeling that some important part of me was missing, that I was somehow *less* than I had been before.

"Didn't you hear me?" my husband said, taking a seat beside me at the table, and looking with some disgust at the oily stain the potato chips had left on my paper plate. "I said it has been solved." He was wearing Bermuda shorts, a T-shirt, and thongs—Fridays were mandatory casual day at the finance company—and his suit was so excruciatingly skin-like, so perfectly fitted to his body from neck to fingertips, that, had I not known better, I might think that he too had been cured. By this point we were making love infrequently, once every couple of months at most, and the intimacy we'd once shared had begun to melt away. He had taken to wearing his suit round-the-clock, even to bed, so that I rarely experienced the sweet thrill of disrobing him in the evening after work, peeling away his outer layer to reveal the man I loved.

At that moment, I felt that I was sitting across the table from someone no more familiar to me than the paperboy or the clerk at the 7-11. Then, mercifully, he unwound the scarf that covered his chin, and took off his floppy hat, and brushed back his long hair, and I felt enormously grateful for this glimpse at his private self, this glimpse he allowed to no one but me.

"What's been solved?" I asked.

"This."

He stood and dropped his Bermuda shorts. And there before me stood an entirely natural-looking man, adorned in curly pubic hair and dangling flaccidly in the heat, the scrotal sack appropriately wrinkled, the whole package dismally common.

"How did he do it?" I asked, reaching out to find the zipper.

At which point he began to swell at my touch, saying, "Baby, there's no zipper."

"Well then, how do we get this damn thing off?" I said, tugging at it in a completely utilitarian way, which he mistook for an erotic overture.

"There's no taking it off. I've been sealed into the suit. I can bathe in it, exercise in it, even make love in it."

By now I was using my teeth, trying to tear the wretched false skin away.

"It has to be removed once a year so that the skin can go through an ageing process and any necessary alterations can be made," he panted, as if this thing I was doing with my teeth had something to do with sex, as if it were not a desperate attempt to reveal that most beautiful part of him, that most real and multicolored thing, which was a specimen in its own right, deserving of its own field of scientific study, not to mention an entire school of experimental art and a movement in postmodern literature.

But I was no match for the suit, this soft and lifelike armor. I did not find what I was looking for.

That night, we made ordinary love. While he thrashed and thrusted above me, eventually filling me with a great rush of sperm which seemed to have cooled and coagulated on its journey through the suit, I faked an orgasm for the very first time. And when it was over I had nothing to say. My speech on the mighty chiton, that master of disguise who carved for itself a home in the rock and looked, to any possible predators, like nothing special, like a part of the rock itself—my speech had been a one-time thing. My logorrhea really was gone, relegated like the dead cat the and the ex-boyfriends and the therapists and the big city to my distant past.

Before long, the textile artist came up with a way to disguise my husband's one remaining feature, his face. He fit in so well, even he seemed to forget that the skin he presented to the world was not his own. Eventually he got a promotion, and we moved across the bay to a restored antebellum home in downtown Mobile, keeping the little cottage by the bay for the sake, I suppose, of nostalgia. Mornings, I'd drive the Causeway to the maritime museum in Fairhope, watching the new sun blaze over the silver bay. Afternoons, on the return trip, I'd catch a glimpse of the old warship, the U.S.S. Alabama, sitting placidly in the water, a gigantic relic of some bygone glory, its dull gray cannons barely hinting at the violence they'd once wrought upon the world.

Nights, my husband and I would sit together in our well-appointed living room, reading: he read biographies of captains of industry, while I buried myself in colorful textbooks detailing the wondrous creatures who made their home in the sea: sharp-nosed puffer, oscellated frogfish, mushroom scorpionfish, flying gurnard, dragon wrasse, leafy seadragon. There were pictures of sea stars and urchins, mollusks of many varieties, crustaceans of indescribable beauty.

My husband had long since given up his dream of writing a memoir. After making several attempts to break the lock of the file cabinet in which the manuscript was concealed, I finally called in a locksmith. Upon opening the drawer I saw that the book had never really been started. It was little more than a list of potential titles and chapter headings, accompanied by a few photocopied documents from the medical files of his youth. These documents were characteristically clinical in nature, but among the dull listings of medications and false diagnoses, recommended treatments and such, a little light occasionally shone through. *Upon removal of a small sample of the scales*, one doctor had typed, *the subject bled profusely. Close examination of the scales under a microscope revealed a range of exceptional colors not found in nature.* And then, in nearly illegible handwriting in the margin was a note the doctor had apparently scribbled to himself, an afterthought: *Rare opportunity to witness a thing of wonder. Thanked his mother profusely for bringing him to me. No diagnosis possible. Very clearly one of a kind.*

I returned the files carefully to their places and had the locksmith conceal any sign that the lock had ever been compromised. I did, however, steal from the files the one piece of paper on which the doctor had allowed himself a moment of professional awe. I keep it hidden in a place so secret no one will ever find it. Every now and then, when the ease of our ordinary lives becomes overwhelming, when I think I cannot pass another day in the shadow of my husband's brilliant disguise, I take the paper from its hiding place and review the doctor's words, and I think of the treasure I found that night on the pier in the moonlight. It is almost close enough to touch, this treasure. Sometimes I dream of some point in the future, when some ordinary disease or accident will take my husband's life, and I will lay him down in the good light of our little house by the bay, and I will go exploring. With my fingernails, my teeth, my eyes, I will search until I find his secret seam. Then I will open him up like some splendid fruit, like some creature from the depths of the mysterious sea, and behold, once again, his beauty.

AVE MARIA

Micaela Morrissette

Micaela Morrissette is a senior editor of *Conjunctions*. Her story in this volume was awarded a 2009 Pushcart Prize. She is a fiction reviewer for *Jacket* and *Rain Taxi*, and the editor of a portfolio of works on John Ashbery's domestic environments that appears in *Rain Taxi*'s Summer 2008 online edition. Originally from West Virginia, she lives in Brooklyn, New York. "Ave Maria" first appeared in the special "avian" volume of *Conjunctions*.

> *She herself could once have imitated the notes of any bird.*
> —James Burnett, Lord Monboddo,
> *Of the Origin and Progress of Language*

In summer, in that countryside, there was no dawn, but a sudden sun, that lashed out over the ridge, broke itself upon the sharp peaks, and poured down like rain. The fields swam with wheat, and the wheat bristled and stabbed at the onslaught of the day. On the edge of the fields was a tree, and the sun boomeranged off the glossy leaves and went pinwheeling back to the atmosphere.

In the tree was a bird, and the sun sank into its matted hair, and oozed on its scalp. The sun trickled into the bird's eyes, and the bird raised a scabrous claw to wipe it away.

The ridge to the east, then the field, moving westward, then the tree; beyond the tree, a village. The village had not waited for the sun. It had already begun to draw its water, rob its chickens, stir its coals. Its air was greasy with candle smoke and bacon fat.

In the tree, the bird plucked a caterpillar from a nearby branch. With a nail, it split the caterpillar lengthwise; with a grey tongue, it licked the soft open stomach. The bird tucked the body of the caterpillar between its back teeth and its cheek. A breeze blew the smoke from the village into the tree and the bird sampled the smell. Its eyes were hard and beady. It stared at the roofs of the cottages and hunched its shoulders. Its heart beat very fast.

The arrival of this bird had driven away the other birds. They spiraled around the treetop, screaming and hissing. The bird reached out its claws to them. *Tweet, tweet*, said the bird. *Toowit, toowit. Caw, caw.* A parent whose nestlings remained several branches above the head of the bird screeched and veered in to attack. The bird in the tree flapped its wings wildly before its face, but did not ascend.

A boy led his goats along the edge of the field. Approaching the tree, he watched the birds buzzing angrily around the crown and thought of flies on a corpse.

The bells of the village church were swinging. *Bong, bong*, said the bird softly. *Din, dan, don.* The throats of the villagers were throbbing with singing. *Ave Maria*, croaked the bird, *amen*. The goats were ripping at the wheat in a frenzy, and the bird could smell the dust raised by the clogs of the boy as he pelted down the path back to the village. The bird swallowed thickly. The caterpillar had turned sticky and tough in the back of its mouth.

The sun rose in the sky and melted, drenching the field and

tree and village. A steady procession swam through the syrupy sun to the tree. The rays slithered off the bird's mangy plumage and plopped in long sebaceous strings from its branch to the ground. Observing several villagers reaching out their hands and handkerchiefs to catch these driblets, the priest issued his reluctant pronouncement: the goatherd had in his exulting innocence erred; this was no angel. The bird shifted on its haunches and splattered droppings onto the ground. A sharp jerk and shuddering twist took place inside it, like a hand wringing a goose's long neck. It teetered dizzily on the branch, and squeezed its claws tighter into the bark. *Ave, ave,* whispered the bird. *Tsstsstssss.*

A gendarme strode majestically into the scene. The bird watched his row of glittering buttons; the gendarme himself was a dark velvety cloth against which the buttons were displayed. A box was placed at the foot of the tree, the gendarme mounted it, hoisted himself to the first limb, and, clinging cautiously to the trunk, batted with his stick at the leaves above his head. With "astonishing speed" and "superhuman agility," the bird let go its branch, plummeted down in a flurry of snapped twigs, powdery lichen, and dead bark, yanked off a button from the gendarme's coat, scratched the gendarme's face, pulled the hair from his head, and clambered back up the tree. Reeling, the gendarme lost his grip, and fell to earth.

The bird scraped out the caterpillar where it clung like cotton to the cheek and gums, and tucked the button in its place. The hot metal hissed slightly as it met the flesh, and the bird was rewarded with a small spurt of saliva. The bird swallowed this in clucking gulps. "It's cooing!" cried a child below. *Coo,* whispered the bird. It tucked the hair of the gendarme up safe in its nest, at the Y of the trunk and the limb. There was also a hawk feather, a sheet from an illustrated paper, a dead moth, and bits of a withered funeral wreath, once executed cunningly in the shape of a cross.

Word was sent back to the village that the apparition in the tree was not an angel after all, but a freak escaped from the carnival. Half bird, half human, gender as yet indeterminable, screened modestly by foliage. But tantalizing glimpses had been caught of cruel black talons; hair covering the body, stiff and coarse as quills; teeth pointed and curved like a row of little snapping beaks. As the farmers left their fields and the shopkeepers shuttered their windows for the midday break, the crowd swelled. Some villagers made attempts at capture: a broom was employed, a scythe, several stones. A cat summoned to its duty fled spitting, with its eyes starting out of its head. Seed was scattered on the ground, and everyone moved back a few steps, and waited, but the bird only abandoned its nest and climbed higher in the tree. When the breeze stirred the leaves the bird could be glimpsed, its neck craning, its face turned up toward the sky. The bird observed the passage of the clouds, but saw no pictures there.

The head of the bird was roiling with lice and it sucked hopefully at the ends of its hairs. The edge of a leaf scratched back and forth against its ear. The bark pressed red and white patterns in bas-relief into the legs of the bird and the bird prodded them, watching them swell and flush and fade. The bird's palms were covered with thick calluses and seamed with deep red cracks and the bird moved the palms back and forth against its cheeks to feel the scratching. After a time it fell asleep. Whether it dreamed or not proves nothing.

Around the dinner hour, the gendarme reappeared, escorting Mme. J. Many of the watchers had departed by then; mostly children were left. One had speared an apple on a long stick and was poking it among the branches to tempt the bird. The gendarme had a pail in his hand. Shaking her skirts and fanning her face, Mme. J. banished the children and commandeered the pail. She had a jutting shelf of bosom and a wide, gliding stride.

Her voice was calm and even. "I'm sure it's the same one," she said. She placed the pail at the base of the tree. It was full of cool water, and inside it swam an eel, dark and sinuous as smoke. "If it's her," said Mme. J., "she'll still have the shift we put on her. Not that she likes to wear it, but she wouldn't know how to take it off. Oh yes," she said, in response to the gendarme's inquiry, "my husband was going to report it to the mayor in the morning. But we only had her the one night. She was killing the rabbits in their hutches, and we were ready for her, and caught her. We got her locked in the shed, and got some clothes on her, and gave her a chicken to mangle—she only wanted meat, and only raw. But the next morning she was gone. She broke the lock on the door and the whole frame was bent and scratched—chewed maybe, even." Mme. J. and the gendarme settled themselves in the bushes. "But as you know," she murmured, "we live seventeen miles away, and not a stream between here and there, not a puddle even. Poor thing."

In the pail at the foot of the tree, the serpent luxuriated, stretching, stroking its coils against themselves, rolling, and flicking its muddy belly skyward. The bird cocked its head and heard the water sigh as it caressed the eel. It tilted its head the other way, but the faint whistle of Mme J.'s breath was all one sibilance with the slosh of the water soft against the side of the pail. The bird dropped to a lower limb. Its feet curled and uncurled. The bird hopped quickly. It fluttered to the ground. It huddled very still in the roots of the tree. Its face was in the bucket, and its hands. Its mouth met the mouth of the eel. The eel's tongue flickered. The bird bit down. The eel slithered easily through its gullet and curled itself in the bird's stomach. The bird's face was in the pail, its eyes were shiny and unblinking underwater, then the snick of the noose pulled tight around its feet, and the fluster of wings as the hood slipped over its head.

M'sieu le Docteur ran his fingers over the sharp shoulderblades that jutted from the back of the bird. Solemnly, he counted the vertebrae of the spine. The anklebones were pronounced, like vicious little spurs. He placed his wrist against the bird's wrist, and waited for its pulse to slow to his. He scratched lightly at the horny, twisted, black nails that arched from the bird's enormous thumbs. The knees were buried beneath deep, scaly pads. The smell of the body was pungent but surprisingly sweet, like fruit that has fallen and begun to ferment. M'sieu le Docteur probed at the temples of the bird and felt the blood trembling inside its brain. The bird chewed nervously at its foot, but was otherwise docile. Age was difficult to determine; hair was present around the private parts and under the arms, but the entire torso was hirsute. M'sieu le Docteur tapped at the ribcage; the bones tinkled: a brittle, hollow, tinny sound. A flea emerged from the ear of the bird and raced down its chest and stomach, diving into its navel for cover. The bird cupped its hand protectively over it. The lungs were sound. Excretions were normal, considering the raw diet. Ocular and muscular reflexes were satisfactory.

M'sieu le Docteur settled himself at the small table provided for him and observed the bird. As it did nothing but huddle, squatting against the wall, its arms around its knees, its chin pressed into the hollow of its neck, he turned away his eyes, took up his pen, and wrote:

Upon the apprehension of an apparent specimen of *homo ferus* on the outskirts of the village of S—, I was summoned to evaluate the medical condition of the creature, with a view both to its health and to determining the span of the years it had spent in the wild. With the exception of severe dehydration, the physical examination revealed no disease. Regarding reports made in the last three years of a bird/wolf/ape/devil-like manifestation sighted in the woods and at least twice in the village streets, the physical mutations—presumably adaptations to facilitate a life comprised almost entirely of running, climbing, and hunting—are sufficiently advanced to suggest that the sightings may indeed be assigned to the individual I examined. Whether a child now no more than ten, and at the origination of the sightings only seven years old, could have sustained its own life and defended itself from predators for such an extended period, is a question not easily resolved. Yet it is difficult to imagine that this individual spent so much as seven years in civilization, as it has so far betrayed no knowledge of any social convention or means of human communication.

Human qualities:

The physical form of the creature is by and large human and female, though some of its parts are of exaggerated size (thumbs, feet, knees), and though it does not put all of its parts to their accustomed uses (scratches head with feet; runs on tiptoe with fingertips stabbing the ground at each pace; approaches unfamiliar objects and spaces mouth first, biting the bed, chamber pot, and my hand gently but firmly, in a spirit of investigation rather than attack). If it is in fact not of an altogether new species, then its peculiarities may be plausibly attributed not only to its savage lifestyle, but potentially to a state of idiocy, arising from its isolation or perhaps the original cause of its abandonment.

While there is no evidence that the creature has ever experienced any meaningful interaction with a human being, neither does

anything strongly negate that possibility. If it has no idea of
human diet, hygiene, language, tools, or customs, still it does
not shy away from people as an animal of a truly undomesticated
species might do. I have been able to closely examine the insides
of the ears, the bottoms of the feet, the spaces between the toes,
the back of the mouth, the roots of the hair, without opposition.
Indeed the creature is perhaps more cooperative than the average
human patient of its age. Now that it has resigned itself to its
captivity, its stillness when touched is absolute, extending perhaps
even to the quieting of its heartbeat. It bears an unnerving
resemblance to the quail about to be flushed, more silent than
death, but ready at any moment to explode out of invisibility in a
hysterical churning of feathers.

General bestial qualities:

The creature's strength and agility are so remarkable as to
be perhaps entirely beyond human capabilities, whatever the
demands of the human's environment may have been. A gendarme
who made the original attempt to communicate with it found, to
his disadvantage, that it could race up and down the trunk of
the tree in which it was discovered with all the thoughtless ease
of an ant scurrying up a wall. The creature was coaxed from the
tree and apprehended, but broke away from its captors en route
to the jail, racing blindly (hooded) down the street with such
speed that several women reported that the wind raised in its
wake snatched the caps from their heads. When a mastiff was
released to bring down the escapee, the creature bludgeoned the
dog so violently with its fists that the animal fell helpless in the
dirt, and spectators reported that the prisoner appeared to be
attempting to tear open the dog's throat with its teeth, though
the hood prevented it from doing so.

The creature has eaten a great quantity of raw meat, and was observed to be greedily sucking the blood from the neck of a rabbit it was given to kill. Offerings of raw root vegetables such as turnips and potatoes have been accepted in a desultory manner. It repudiates all cooked meat, cooked fruits and vegetables, and grains.

Although words were spoken to the creature in several languages, it made no response. Its hearing does not appear to be impaired, however, as the squawking of a chicken outside the window claimed its immediate attention. The creature was spoken to harshly, soothingly, commandingly, imploringly, and in accents of terror, but its expression, or lack of one, underwent no change.

Particular avian qualities:

Tucks head under arm in repose or perhaps fear.

Frenzied attacks against mirror.

Nesting: Interested citizens come to view the creature have brought a number of items for its edification and amusement. Some, such as candy, India rubber balls, and chalk, have been ignored, but others are forming a pile under the washstand, where the creature likes to spend the night. These include: a rag doll, a handkerchief, a rosary, a sack of marbles, a robin's egg, and a small brass bell.

When awake, in constant motion, hopping from bed to floor to corner to door to stool to corner to washstand to bed to floor to door.

Beats hands lightly and repeatedly on window glass.

M'sieu le Docteur sighed wearily. Dusk had fallen while he worked out his report, and he had had to light a candle. He laid down his pen and passed his finger back and forth through the flame. After a while, the bird came up and did the same. M'sieu le Docteur stroked the bird gently along the jawbone and behind the ear, and scratched between its eyebrows. The bird chattered its teeth and made a whistling sound in its nose. M'sieu le Docteur continued to pet the bird until he saw its eyelids closing, at which point with great reluctance he draped the hood over its head, and called for the guard to hold the hood until he had gone, lest the bird discover the means by which he opened the door to gain the night.

The carriage went hurtling down the long, smooth drive that led to the palace of the Duke, and inside it the bird hooted loudly and preened itself. It ducked its head to snap in its beak the end of the satin ribbon Mme. J. had tied around its neck. The curtains revealed in snatches the leaves on the trees glowing deep gold and brown like brass buttons. Their shining was like the ringing of bells, and the bird jerked against the silken cord that tethered its ankle to the ring set into the floor of the carriage. "Tsk, tsk," said Mme. J., and the bird said *TtTt* and gently knocked its head against the carriage wall. "Now, now," said Mme. J., and the bird blinked at her rapidly.

The Duke himself, the women with their long smiles and translucent hands, all the scuttling little boys, and the strolling gentlemen flocked around the bird and adored it. Mme. J. and the carriage went rattling back along the drive, farther into the distance, until they were a small black dot disappearing into the orange forest that swelled and thrashed like the sun. The bird watched them shrink and vanish before it veered off the veranda and went swooping to the garden the Duke had created for it.

A giant gazebo was erected, arches woven of twisting twigs crossed at the top and anchored in a generous circle in the ground. These were painted with gold leaf, and a swing was hung inside for the pleasure of the bird. A ladder, too, dangled from the top, woven of thick skeins of silk, and tangled with fuschia, monkeyflowers, hibiscus, and trumpet vines. Beside the ladder, secured firmly to the roof, was the small canvas tent where the bird roosted for the night. When the breeze picked up, the garden burned with the clashing rays of a hundred small round mirrors that were suspended from the ends of thin silver chains attached to the framework of the gazebo. The bird went mad at these moments, leaping into the air with open mouth to bite at the daggers of light where they stabbed the air. There was a splashing fountain, stocked with green frogs that eventually bred and escaped and were soon to be found in every room of the palace, between bedclothes, under cushions, and on tables.

Now the bird began each morning with a cool draught of water in which grapes or figs had stood. It was bathed in milk infused with lavender, and its eyelids, nostrils, and lips were dabbed with Armagnac until its eyes were wide and bright. A bowl of hot blood was brought to it, in which, on Sundays, snails were placed. The bird's hair was brushed until it crackled and the strands rose up into the air and clung to the fingers of its attendants. The hair was plaited loosely, pinned at the back of the neck, and brought forward over the ridge of the skull, swooping down in a thick curl to tease the bird's forehead. The bird wore a brass bracelet on its leg, and peach-colored hose, and long tunics with sweeping, wide sleeves in shining colors. The bird was ruby breasted, green backed, golden throated, chestnut barred, and flame crested. The little boys made chains of coins and wrapped them around the arms of the bird. When it flapped its wings it rang like a morning chorus of a thousand songs rising out of the wheat.

In the afternoons the bird took lessons in dancing. It learned to spread its skirts and arch its back and hurl itself in a circle. It turned its throat to the sky and lifted its arms behind it. Its neck grew long and active, writhing under its head, and its fingers could spread in a circle until the outside of the thumb and pinky were nearly touching. It could hurtle forward in strenuous crouching bounds, so that its legs seemed to buckle sickeningly beneath it even as it was already ricocheting back into the air. At the end of a performance it could bow to the audience in mid-leap, its feet kicking out and its knees tucking into its chest. The bird could sink into the ground with the graceful startlement of a gasp. It could tear at its hair and throw back its shoulders until it was two or three times its natural size.

At dinners the bird perched on a tall stool behind the Duke's chair and was fed morsels by the Duke's own hand. When not being fed, it leaned forward to nibble at his ear or curl its toes comfortably against his back. When the musicians came into the hall at the conclusion of the meal, the bird stood on the stool and keened sharply. All the musicians agreed with the Duke that the sound was uncanny, and they always played in the pitch the bird's screaming suggested. As the programs wound on, the bird would quiet, squatting back down on the stool, clucking its tongue against the back of its mouth, and pressing its face into the Duke's hair.

The bird grew pale and weak not long after the sun went down, so once the meal and entertainment had concluded, the bird would climb onto the Duke's back, and the Duke would bear the bird out into the garden, where it would climb the silken ladder to its tent. The little boys would release the rope and the great canopy would fall and slither over the frame of the gazebo, blotting out the moonlight that might play upon the hundred mirrors. The bird nestled into itself; it twitched at the feeble disturbance of its breath struggling against its feathers, and listened to the slug of its heart striking out at the other smothering organs. Its feet were curled so the toenails scratched the arch. When the bird's eyes closed, it felt the brief sting of the rough inner lid scraping against the lens. It watched red throb and cool, tiny black insects skating across the color, until everything was mottled and dull like mud. Cracks traced idly over the mud, portions of it shifted as if something were tunneling beneath, or a foot were pressing from above. Dark blots came, like drops of rain; a green tinge suffused the whole. A smell of slime and plant life. A kind of tilting in the mud, as if the bird had shifted its perspective. A comfortable tilting, a more agreeable angle, the mud oozed over the eyes of the bird and pressed calmly on its brain. The bird suddenly felt slippage, a plummet, groped wildly for its wings. Then there in its lungs was the aftermath of a tremendous sigh, and the canopy came whisking away, and the sun was sharp with the smell of Armagnac, and lavender, and frothy blood.

The bird had clung to the finger of the Duke with its teeth, with all the strength in its jaw, but now its mouth was empty and the present the Duke had left on the desk, a nest woven of gold wire and containing two warm goose eggs for sucking, had vanished beneath the hand of the Mother Superior. "You must learn to be good and obedient," said the Mother Superior, "and raw meat and shiny toys are just the things to make you agitated. Here we live simply. The habit you wear will be rough, to scratch the itches before they start, and the food will be smooth and soft, to calm your temper."

The bird did not eat the stews and porridges, the salted biscuits or the sharp red wine, and after a week they twisted it in blankets and fed it through a funnel. At first the bird screamed so that the attending sisters could not even hear the chapel bells tolling for prayers, and an exorcist was summoned. Then its throat grew so raw that the brittle shards of sound twisted and dug at its gullet, and the bird quieted. Thick slicks of blood formed inside it and lurched their way out, stumbling from the mouth of the bird in clumsy belches and then in thundering gallops. During these red effusions the bird made a noise as if it were trying to speak through a gag. It licked at the blood clotting on its cheeks and chin, but the taste was rotten. Once the Duke was in the room, making a loud noise, the nuns spiraling away from him like dry leaves caught in a wind. He had the bleeding haunch of a rabbit, which he held to the face of the bird. Everything within the bird leapt and shrank at once in a terrible convulsion. Something held the bird and shook it for several minutes. It felt itself go upside down, then inside out. Then the meat was taken away and the Duke put the tip of his finger in the bird's mouth and sat like that for a while before he crept away. Not long after, a man came to draw the majority of the blood from the bird's body, and this afforded some relief. The bile of the bird became watery and pale and the bird enjoyed a faintness like the sensation of flying. Then like the sensation of sinking. Its body was covered with bruises; peering down, it saw itself hidden in a rose bush. The bird was molting. The air of the room was crowded with strands of its hair; sometimes the breeze picked these up and carried them out into the sky. The teeth of the bird dropped gently from between its lips and rolled onto its neck like a pearly collar. The sisters collected the teeth and also the nails and kept them in a leather pouch.

A sister was always with the bird. Sister Marie-Therese watched in the early morning when the bird was gray. Behind its veil of shadows, she saw its features released, dissolving and shifting, sweetly and gently. Then the light would come in fragments through the tree outside, picking out the beak, which would grow in response, and the eyelids, which glowed red. The bird was naked and pale in the dawn, and came into existence with the advent of the light, the ruff of its neck golden, its arms green as the leaves through which the sun struggled to meet it. The bird woke when the bells tolled for matins, and Sister Marie-Therese would bend over to hide its plumage under the brown blanket.

Sister Marguerite-Marie was most often there in the formless, endless afternoons. She brought lumps of sugar for the bird, sliding them to the back of its mouth. The bird stayed very still, waiting, and felt the sugar rearrange itself, biting at first at the bird's tongue, then spreading, investigating the pockets of the jaw, and traveling in a long procession of granules deep and down. The bird could feel the sugar burning all the way to the pit in the middle of it.

Sister Marguerite-Marie told a story about a girl from China who had a beautiful bird that she loved very much but that one day escaped from its cage. In great distress, the girl resolved to visit a wonderous enchantress and beseech her help finding the bird. On the way, she met various animals in distress. A cat was trapped on an island in the middle of a lake. A rain-dragon was lodged in the arid earth. She helped the animals, and they gratefully came with her to the palace of the enchantress. The enchantress herself was like a bird, a giant blue-black crow. Her palace was of blue and white porcelain, and every inch of it was painted with blue birds. But the girl saw her bird pictured on the wall as well, and she understood that the enchantress had trapped all the birds of the air, and frozen them in the walls of her palace. The enchantress was just reaching out her long claw to snare the girl, when the cat leaped up and swallowed the enchantress whole. Then the dragon flew up into the sky, and rained down water on the palace, and the birds awoke, and turned from blue and white into every imaginable and unimaginable color, and rioted in the air, and the palace crumbled, and the girl put her bird safely back in its cage and they traveled home.

Sister Marguerite-Marie told the bird a story about a great flood that covered the entire earth. One man built a boat to weather it, and brought a male and female of every animal that existed onto the boat. Giraffes and dogs and unicorns. But there was only one dove in the world, and it could not come alone, so it snuck into the boat under an elephant's ear and stowed away. When the captain discovered it, he was wroth, and threatened to feed the dove to the lions, but the dove begged to be spared. So the captain banished the dove from the ship and said it might only return if it came bearing evidence of land. The dove flew over the formless, endless sea, in which no fish swam, and on which no sun shone, so that it could not even watch its own reflection, and after a time it began to doubt its reason, and to suspect that there had never been a ship, a captain, or an elephant, and that it was and had always been the only living creature in the world. And the dove nearly dashed itself into the void of the waters. But at that moment a giant finger pointed out of the clouds in the form of a beam of light and it lit on a sandy beach on the far horizon, and the dove struggled on, and plucked a twig from a tree on the beach, and without pausing for rest or refreshment, veered back to the ship, over the exulting waves. And the ship landed there, and all the animals were saved, and in gratitude to the dove the captain opened his chest and fed his own heart to the bird. And so the captain lived immortal in the dove, which, being the only one of its kind, could never die, but which, having the captain within it, was no longer alone.

Sister Marguerite-Marie told the bird a story about a hungry jackdaw that, observing how well fed was a family of quail, rolled himself in the dust until he was brown and presented himself as a quail. The quail took him in, and fed him and cared for him, until one day the jackdaw was so happy and comfortable that he burst forth in his chattering song. Immediately the quail recognized that he was a jackdaw, and pecking at him mercilessly, they drove him away. The bird crept back to join the other jackdaws, but as he was covered with dirt, they took him for a quail, and attacked him, and bit him until he was dead.

Sister Marguerite-Marie and the bird ate sugar together all through the afternoon, and sometimes she would bring leaves of mint or basil and they would eat those too. Sister Marguerite-Marie would chew her leaves, but, as the bird no longer had any teeth, Marguerite-Marie would roll the herbs between her fingers until the leaf broke and the juice sprang out. She would rub her wet fingers on the bird's lips and nose and behind its ears. The juice would burn like sugar, and the world would be wet and sharp and green.

Sister Marie-Immaculate watched over the bird in the night, telling her rosary. The bird's eyes were open and the dark pressed against them as Sister Marie-Immaculate recited the Apostles' Creed. The bird shifted slightly in the bed and curled its toes around the blanket as Sister Marie-Immaculate recited Our Father. Sister Marie-Immaculate said a Hail Mary for faith, for hope, and for love, and the bird clicked its tongue with the fall of the beads. Sister Marie-Immaculate gave glory to the father, and the bird meditated on the Joyful Mysteries, the Sorrowful Mysteries, and the Glorious Mysteries. Sister Marie-Immaculate offered the Fatima Prayer, and the bird whispered, *Oh, my Jesus.* Sister Marie-Immaculate said, "Hail, Holy Queen, Mother of Mercy, our life, our sweetness, and our hope," and the bird whispered, *Salve Regina.* The bird could hear the hiss of the beads sliding on the string, the scratch of the thumb of Sister Marie-Immaculate rubbing the wood. In the hair of Sister Marie-Immaculate was the ghost of incense; it was not like wood-smoke; it was not like the petals of flowers that have fallen. On the breath of Sister Marie-Immaculate was the rough smell of red wine; the cold salve of lard; the thick odor of beans, like a woman's sweat; the powder of the wafer, like ancient dust. Sister Marie-Immaculate could smell the wool of her own underclothes, damp from the steam of the kitchen; the slick of oil on her face had a palpable weight. She could just see, in the bed, the white of the bird's face, a shock against the night, and the black holes of its eyes. She could hear, in its stuttering breath, a wakefulness. She began again. By the time she came to the Agony in the Garden, she could tell from the whistle in its nose that the bird was asleep.

The Queen of Poland came to visit the bird, and they took communion together. The Queen was disappointed that the bird could not hunt with her, for she had heard that it was faster than a falcon, and that it had returned the Duke's prey to his hand; nonetheless, she caressed it extremely. The bird said, *Gracious lady*, and if the Queen could not at first make out the words, when they were repeated to her by the Mother Superior she was greatly pleased, and favored the bird with a handful of gold coins, which the bird offered to the collection plate, excepting one that it kept in its nest. A poet came to see the bird and recited the poem he had composed in its honor and the bird nodded its head.

Mme. H. was engaged in writing a life of the bird. The bird was able to narrow down its origins to Martinique or Canada. The description it gave of its migration over the dark, inchoate seas was not included in the published work. A man with chapped cheeks and flushed, delicate ears founded a new philosophy on the bird. His coat was resplendent with buttons, but he did not offer one to the bird, and it kept its hands close by its side.

A journalist visited twice, each time with a different companion, each selected with a view toward the appetites of the bird. The first companion was a child, with crepe-like skin webbed with blue veins. Even the journalist was tempted to take a bite. The child's eyes were trembling in their sockets with fear, but the bird patted the fragile skull and begged the child not to be afraid. *God has changed me very much,* said the bird, and when Sister Marie-Therese repeated the words intelligibly, the child crowed with delight and crowded onto the lap of the bird to tug curiously at the long, mournful beak. The second companion of the journalist was a soft, sugary woman whose flesh spilled from her like cream from a pitcher, bubbling out of her clothes, overflowing her chair, in a generous profusion of fat. This time the bird shook its arms about itself in agitation, and had to be removed by the sisters. Marie-Therese informed the journalist that the bird had been overcome not by hunger but by nausea, and that it no longer ate meat in any form, preferring seedcake and communion wafers to all other food. Nonetheless, in the journalist's paper there appeared a long article about the vampirism of the bird, with references to pale young novitiates, and the bird was forced to write a letter to the editor.

After the bird was able to understand years and that they were passing, the Mother Superior invited it to join the convent, but the bird with sorrow declined. It was understood to say: *The rosary is circular and its decades therefore infinite. Nonetheless, eternity is not long enough to expunge the sins I committed when I was in the garden, refusing to eat of the tree that would teach me good from evil.* The Mother Superior spoke more plainly, explaining to the bird that since the death of the Duke, the bird's income would not suffice to cover its board as a guest of the convent. The bird took a small flat in the 12ème arrondissement of Paris and placed an advertisement inviting the curious to come and wonder at what the glory of God had wrought in a savage creature.

The bird arranged twenty chairs in its drawing room and invested in a wardrobe of black silks and velvets, profuse with ruffles, and with long draping sleeves. However, many of those old enough to remember the bird's apprehension in S— found the six flights of stairs too difficult to navigate. Children would sometimes arrive in a giggling band, dart forward to capture a black feather from the bonnet of the bird, and scamper away in hysteria, without leaving any coins. Marie-Immaculate, now Christine, who had left the convent, came on Sundays to take the bird to Mass, bringing baskets of biscuits and wine and pickled cornichons.

The bird often rearranged its nest, polishing its buttons and coins, and crumpling its papers tighter into little balls. It sat with its arm on the sill of the window and sang *Je Mets Ma Confiance* and *Frère Jacques*. It kept a canary named Pierrot.

The bird took long naps in the afternoons. It awoke in the slanted light to see the flocks of dust motes swooping and diving in the breeze. It could feel the warmth of the day wriggling against its skin, tucked beneath its feathers. Twisting its neck to look through the window, it could see saints in white robes and angels with interminable wings drifting and sighing against the sky like clouds. Pigeons burbled comfortably in the eaves and the low hoots of the bird as it yawned did not disturb them.

The bird raked away the covers with its toes and drew itself up on its knees. It would not get out of bed that day to pray. Its chin nestled into its breast and it opened and closed its eyes, watching the light tangle in its lashes. It started and hunched at the sounds of steps in the hall, and continued to watch the door long after they had passed, tucking its hands nervously under its arms.

There were fleas in the bed and the bird watched avidly as they flashed into existence on knee or toe or pillow, blinked out, then reappeared on knuckle or elbow or sheet. One had bitten the bird on the shoulder, and it gnawed with satisfaction at the little welt. On the sidewalk below, a cat was crying forlornly. *Miao*, said the bird.

In the air was the smell of smoke, beer, leather, wet cotton on the line, the stinging scent of the soap with which the girl across the alley was washing her hair. Darker, heavier smells: the overripe peaches in the bowl on the bird's kitchen table, the patch of yellow mildew sprinkled across the corner of the ceiling, the odor of the bird's own skin, sweet sharpness stabbing through a musky closeness, like mud slathered on leaves of basil and mint. The bird's stomach growled. The nails of the rats scratched as they bustled around inside the wall. The bird pressed its very hot palms against its very cold face and felt the temperatures exchange. Its fingers were stiff and cold. Its head was alive with fire. The bells of the church rang with a sound like sun shining.

CHAINSAW ON HAND
Deborah Coates

Deborah Coates lives in Ames, Iowa, with two dogs and no cats. Her fiction has been published in *Asimov's*, *F&SF*, *SCIFICTION*, and *Strange Horizons*, and reprinted in *Year's Best Fantasy*, and *Best New Paranormal Romance*. In her non-writing life, she has been a researcher, a statistician, a farm hand, a factory worker, and an IT professional. She is currently working on a contemporary fantasy novel, also set in South Dakota, involving ghosts, magic, and deputy Sheriffs. "Chainsaw on Hand" is taken from the classic SF/fantasy publication *Asimov's SF Magazine*, edited by Sheila Williams.

This is what winter's like in South Dakota on the plains—you wake up and it's full dark still, maybe five o'clock in the morning and you know without ever throwing the covers off, without ever getting up, that it's at least twenty below zero outside. You can tell by the clean-edged sound of the wind as it hits the corner of the house, as if there's never been a drop of moisture in it, like knives would slice themselves to shreds on a wind like that. You can tell, too, by the feel of the air in the room, the way the frail warmth of the over-stressed furnace is more illusory than real.

It's not possible to be warm on that kind of morning on the plains. Even if you ran the furnace up to eighty. Even if the furnace could get the air up to eighty, it wouldn't be warm—the fragility of surviving on electricity and propane, the understanding that the shiny new wood stove in the kitchen can only really heat a hundred square feet or so in an emergency. All that, the darkness and the cold and the thin edge of knowledge of how close it all is to failure, makes the world close in and makes you hunch your shoulders right on down into your chest as low as you can go.

What you want, on a dark morning like that, with the wind and the cold and the knowledge that you'll never be warm again is to pull the blankets way up over your head and never come out until spring. But this is South Dakota on the plains in winter. There are cattle waiting to be fed, counting on you as their single source of, well, everything. And because you have to get up anyway, you do.

You sit down in a kitchen chair and adjust automatically as it tips sideways where one of the dogs chewed on the leg when he was a puppy. Your work boots are sitting on the mat by the door and you pull them on, yanking the laces tight before tying them. You add a fleece vest, a barn coat and a knit hat with flaps to your flannel shirt, tee-shirt, two layers of long underwear and jeans two sizes too big. Before you put your gloves on, you look at the coffee pot and think about starting coffee, but the day is already too cold and too cruel, doing something human will only make you suffer more when you step outside the door.

The wind sucks your breath and half the brain cells out of your head when you step outside. The thin layer of snow on the ground is so cold and so dry that the soles of your boots squeak when you walk. You check the young stock in the barn and move feed to the pastures and break ice from the heated water troughs that aren't supposed to freeze. The cattle huddle together with their backs to the wind, all shaggy and icy. The dogs are grateful to be allowed in the truck on the ride back to the house and you are grateful for the extra warmth in the cab.

There are two messages on the answering machine when you get back to the house, even though it's only seven o'clock. You call your mother first.

"I'm going to Pierre," she says when she answers.

"Today?"

"Yes, today. Do you want to come?"

"I don't know. Let me think about it."

"Oh, just come." You can almost see her roll her eyes. "No one's going to point and laugh. They don't even know who you are."

"Okay, fine. I'll come."

You shed boots and jackets and hats and gloves. You stand in the kitchen under the florescent lights and take off your jeans and your shirts and your medium-weight long underwear. Then you pull the jeans back on and the flannel shirt. You start coffee brewing in the pot; you take the clothes you shed back upstairs to the bedroom; you pull a town pair of jeans—never been worn for chores—and a white turtleneck and a patchwork knit sweater from the closet for later when you go to town. You make the bed and you put all your things away and you go back down to the kitchen and feed the dogs and pour yourself a cup of coffee. You stare at the phone, then the clock, then the phone again. And then you sigh and pick up the phone and call your ex-husband back.

"Chel?" His voice sounds so normal, deep and certain.

"Bobby."

"There's something I want to show you."

"Now?"

"Well, whenever." There is a sharp flatness in his voice that says yes, he was expecting you to come now.

"I'm going to town," you tell him. "I should be back around three."

"Okay, fine." And he hangs up. There was once a time when Bobby could talk birds out of the trees and mad dogs out of biting and you into marrying him, but that was long-ago Bobby from another life. Present-day Bobby never says more than two words at a time.

By the time you've showered, dressed and fed the dogs, it's time to leave. Even with the sun well up, the cold still hits you like a wall when you leave the house. Your father used to call this religious weather because, he said, you couldn't walk out the door without taking the Lord's name in vain. In Boston where you lived for four years out of college, the snow was wet, but in South Dakota, it's always dry. You can walk all day in the snow in South Dakota and only get wet when you go inside.

When you drive by Bobby's house on your way to your mother's, you notice that he has a new sign on his lawn. Right next to 'Rabbits for Sale' and 'Fresh Eggs' there is now one that simply reads, 'Chainsaw on Hand.'

You don't have much time to think about it before arriving at your mother's. She is, as always, waiting, and comes outside as you pull into the driveway. When you drive back by Bobby's with her in the car, she draws your attention to the sign. "Chainsaw on Hand? What does that mean?"

"Dunno."

"Well, I mean, I suppose it means he has a chainsaw," your mother continues. "But why does he feel the need to announce it to everyone?"

In South Dakota in the winter, your ex-husband is your responsibility until approximately the end of time. His parents don't talk to him anymore. They shop the next town over. His brother sits in the bar on Saturday afternoons underneath old license plates from New Jersey and Arkansas and tells anyone who'll listen that Bobby was always the crazy one. 'He married Chelley Sanderson for hell's sake!" he says in a loud voice that runs scared underneath. "What was he thinking when he did that?"

"I like him, Chelley," your mother has told you over and over and over, as if liking him makes everything all right.

"He talks to people who aren't there," you tell her every time she says it.

"Not people, Chelley," your mother responds as if this is the single fact that saves him.

No, not people; Bobby talks to dreams. Although that's not what he calls them.

The first time he told you they were angels.

"I wish you'd been here, Chel," he said when you returned from three days in Rapid City at a cattle show. "They were golden, absolutely golden."

"Angels, Bobby?" you ask him.

"They stopped everything. They stopped time." He isn't looking at you; his gaze is fixed on something you can never see. "We walked through town, just them and me. It was something."

You try logic. You try reason. You try yelling. Bobby is a sensible man—or at least he was. He knows growing seasons and pole barns and drainage patterns. Bobby is not a man who sees golden angels in time-frozen towns.

And then it happens again.

The next time, you were gone to Iowa State University with Quincy Meadows to take her gelding to the vet school. You are always gone when the angels come—except after the second time Bobby doesn't think they're angels anymore.

"Fairies maybe," he says. "Only big, you know. Or maybe really handsome trolls."

After the fourth time, you ask Bobby to move out. People come up to you in grocery stores and put their hands on your shoulder and stand too close and ask you how Bobby is in that voice that says they might care a little, but mostly they want to be the person who knows the news.

This morning, your mother wants to go to the Pierre Mall and a couple of fabric outlets.

"I'm making Bobby a quilt," she says.

"Why?"

"It's his turn."

"He's not your son-in-law anymore."

"You should be kinder to him," she says while scoping out a parking place at the mall for you. "He's going through a rough patch."

You refrain from pointing out that any rough patch Bobby is going through is his own doing. No one told him to sign over his half of the farm to you, no one told him to quit his job at the mill, no one told him to raise rabbits and sell eggs and scrape an existence out of nothing. Unless the fairies did. Or maybe trolls.

"Maybe it's the devil he talks to, Mom. Did you ever think of that?" You swing into a parking space and sit for a moment with the car running. The day is rounding up on ten-thirty in the morning and it's no warmer than at five. The wind has picked up, too. Welcome to winter in South Dakota.

After the fifth—or maybe sixth—time, the local paper runs an article about the angels, or maybe trolls, with a picture of Bobby out behind the house. Four letters to the editor appear in the next week's edition, double the usual number. Carroll Biedlebaum says it's about TIME—he's been telling everyone for years that there are THINGS in this world both dangerous and hidden. We'd better listen to him and to Bobby or we'll all be sorry. Sallie and Katie Widderman write nearly identical letters pointing out that Jesus and science will determine the truth and offering to set up cameras and recorders and a candle-lit prayer offering the next time the angels come. The fourth letter is from your mother. "Bobby doesn't make things up," her letter says. "He's not creative that way. We ought to listen to him."

You and Bobby have known each other since high school. You dated once or twice back then—the junior prom and the homecoming dance Bobby's senior year. He was a year ahead of you, graduated third in his class, and went off to the University of Minnesota to major in engineering, so normal it could make your teeth hurt. Everyone knew he'd be back after graduation.

"Bobby can build damn near anything," his father would proudly tell anyone who'd listen. "We expect he'll be doing big things one of these days."

You got a full four-year scholarship to the University of Chicago, something that stunned everyone, not least of all yourself (though you never admitted that to anyone, just took the acceptance letter to your room and read it to yourself over and over again).

You told your parents the week before you left that you were going to major in psychology because you wanted to know why anyone would voluntarily live in South Dakota in the winter. "It's like one of those prisoner syndromes," you told them. "Or that boiling frog thing." Your mother smiled as if you'd said something unaccountably brilliant while your father looked at you over the top of his glasses and you knew that they mostly wished you'd stop saying things like that. In Chicago, you discovered academia, research, and thinking that wasn't always interrupted by seeing to the cattle and repairing wire fences and you knew that what you wanted as much as anything was to be a research psychiatrist—medical school and graduate school—MD and PhD—learning and learning and learning until it finally filled you up completely. But then, you got to senior year and you looked $100,000 and $200,000 and maybe even bigger loans in the face and you blinked.

And now, here you are, in South Dakota in the winter.

Since you've been back, you've taken up painting. "It's just like psychology," you tell your mother, "only not." Your mother no longer looks at you as if you're unaccountably brilliant when you say things like that; she just rolls her eyes. You figure that the reason she still likes Bobby in spite of everything is because she half suspects you're the one who drove him around the bend.

Three days after the article in the paper, as the summer sky is just fading to dusk, Bobby's brother comes to see you. You pour ice tea and go out on the back porch and the two of you watch the sky turn red. One of the dogs, which has been lying dead asleep by your chair, leaps up and sprints off the porch after a rabbit.

"What if he really sees something?" Bobby's brother finally asks you, the words bursting out of him like a dam break. "What if there really are angels?"

"Or maybe trolls," you say, mostly hoping to distract him.

"Maybe," he says. There is desperation in his voice and a thin edge of something else, like he knows something that he can't tell you because if he says it out loud then he has to actually admit that it's true. You don't want him to say it out loud, anyway. You don't want to admit to anything.

You sit there together in silence a little longer, then Bobby's brother rises in a spring-loaded motion that echoes the dog. "Here, I—," he presses something into your hand and leaves and never looks back. You haven't seen him since.

Later, you sit at the kitchen table and look at what he left you. It's a gold coin or maybe bronze—it changes in the light—bigger than the new dollar and heavy; it might be real gold. It has symbols on one side that almost look Chinese, but aren't and a landscape on the other that looks a little like the Black Hills and a little like any rugged landscape anywhere. You wonder if Bobby had it made somewhere—it would be a lot of trouble—or maybe he picked it up once at a carnival or someplace. You stick it on the counter above the sink and forget about it, except once in a while when the light hits it in the late afternoon and it glows.

You're home from the mall by 2:30 PM. The wind has sharpened and it's straight out of the north. You let the dogs out and change into long underwear and old jeans and a heavy sweatshirt that used to be Bobby's. The dogs are standing in the yard with as many of their feet off the ground as they can manage, looking as if they're freezing to death, though they run to the house quick enough at your whistle. You're tempted to take them with you to Bobby's so they can stand like a wall between you. But they'd just fight with the pit-bull cross Bobby picked up from somewhere you don't even want to know about so you give them food and water, huddle up in a double-thick fleece vest and freshly laundered barn coat and dive into the bitter cold one more time.

The new sign on Bobby's lawn stands out stark against the bleak winter landscape. 'Chainsaw on Hand.' What does that mean? Then you hate yourself for even wondering because you know you'll be sorry once you know the answer.

You knock on Bobby's side door and walk in. It's never locked. The pit bull knows you and it comes into the kitchen as you enter, waiting to have its head scratched. The kitchen is warm and even humid as if there are pots of spaghetti cooking somewhere just out of sight. Bobby is in the dining room with all the lights on.

"Hey, Chel," he says when you walk in. He's bent over the big dining room table and doesn't look up from what he's doing. You shed your coat, stuffing your gloves in the pockets, but leave the vest on as if that means you won't be staying long.

After a minute, Bobby straightens up and says, "Take a look."

He waves his hand at the dining room table. "It's almost done," he says.

For six and a half months, Bobby has been painstakingly building an exact replica of town and the surrounding countryside. The houses are made of balsa wood and matchsticks. He sculpts the people out of clay. He's recreating the town like it was the first time the angels came. You have avoided asking him why he's doing it, but because it's Bobby, you're pretty sure that he believes if he just lays it all out straight and simple, none of us can help but see what he sees.

Instead of going to the table, you lean against the wall with your arms across your chest. "Is that why you wanted to see me?"

Bobby is tall and lean, lanky like an oversized colt that never grew into its body. He's wearing blue jeans and work boots and nothing more than a faded red t-shirt in spite of the sub-zero air that weaves in around the windows. He has a worn baseball cap, as always, perched on the back of his head which he lifts by the brim, scratching his forehead absently as he looks down on his town. "This?" he says. "No, I—"

The sound of another car pulling into Bobby's driveway cuts across the dry wind outside. "Hold on," Bobby says, like you've been doing anything else for the last year or so. He grabs a jacket off a chair and heads to the back door. You hear him talking to someone in a low voice.

The dining room is cold; you can feel a breeze from the windows and you wish you'd left your jacket on. You wish you'd never come. You could be holed up inside your house, barricaded against the cold—it's not so much where you wish you were, as the only place you have left to be.

You look at the town model Bobby has spread across his dining table. He's painstakingly lettered the signs on old storefronts—Beth's Rings & Things, Shiner Diner, Waterman's Insurance.

He's even—you have to squint to look at it—put the 'Independent Insurance Agent' logo on the bottom half of Waterman's door. There's a car in the middle of the street, one half-pulled out of a parking space, several women walking out of the diner, and Bobby himself at the intersection of Main and North. At least you think it's Bobby, like you would recognize him anywhere, even as a stick figure in a make-believe town. He is completely surrounded by six gold coins.

You reach out and pick up one of the coins. It's heavy, like the one Bobby's brother gave you, and warm against your palm. You close your fingers over it and the warmth of the coin seems to spread all the way up your arm.

You close your eyes.

The back door closes with a loose rattle and, startled, you drop the coin back on the table. It lands with a ringing sound, like metal against crystal, and rolls across the table until it settles with a tiny shudder almost exactly where it was when you picked it up.

"Eggs," Bobby says as he reenters the room and sheds his coat, laying it without looking in the exact spot it was before.

You put your hands in your pockets and look away from the table and the gold coins and miniature Bobby.

"Don't the chickens get cold, Bobby?" you ask despite yourself. He can't make a living from a sign posted in his yard.

"I've got a good place fixed up for them," Bobby says, "You'd be surprised."

You decide that if you're going to be surprised today it's not going to be over chickens. "That new sign, Bobby? 'Chainsaw on Hand?' What's that supposed to mean?"

He cocks his head to one side and looks at you with the ghost of a slow, sweet smile. "What does it mean to you?"

"Nothing," you tell him, irritated with yourself all over again for asking. "It means nothing to me, Bobby. It's just stupid."

Bobby shakes his head sadly. "Then I guess it means nothing," he says.

Exasperation wars with weariness because the truth is you're just plain tired of Bobby and fairies—or maybe trolls—and of being in South Dakota in the bleak depths of endless winter. "No one puts a sign in their yard that says 'Chainsaw on Hand.'"

"I do," Bobby says. "I like to be prepared."

"Bobby, did you want to see me for a reason?"

Bobby looks at you as if he's waiting for something you can't give him. He ducks his head and rubs the back of his neck. "I have something to show you," he says.

"What?" You have a thousand better things to do—stoke the wood stove, feed the dogs, stuff rags around the rattling kitchen window.

"It's outside."

Your shoulders hunch as if you're outside already. "It's goddamned cold outside, Bobby."

"It'll be okay." Like he controls the weather.

You sigh and bite your lip on all the things you want to say, but never do. It's not Bobby you're mad at anyway. You could be living in Boston or Chicago or St. Paul. No one is making you live out in the open. No one is making you do anything.

It takes five minutes to put on your coat and hat and gloves and zip and button everything up to your nose. You can feel the burn of the wind across your cheekbones and you haven't even stepped out the door. The sun is low when you walk outside, flat against the horizon. There are no shadows, just fading half-light slanting blue across the snow.

Your boots and Bobby's squeak on the snow as you walk past the two barns and the tool shed toward the lean-to that houses Bobby's old tractor. Just past that is open pasture, an old cemetery in a grove of dying trees and the creek that divides Bobby's land from his neighbors. The last time you came out this way it was late spring and muddy. Bobby insisted on showing you what he called 'definitive proof of fairy/troll presence.'

Bobby's proof turned out to be three boxes made from some material that looked and felt exotic, but tore exactly like cardboard. All three of them were empty inside except for three cards in the bottom of the largest one that had been printed on both sides with unrecognizable and indecipherable symbols.

"How did they get here?" Bobby asked you.

"I don't know, Bobby, there's a hundred ways they could have gotten here."

"Name one."

"You could have put them here."

"But I didn't."

And then he offered you one of the cards, which you, of course, refused.

You know it's going to be like that again, some lame thing Bobby's made up to convince you of something that only Bobby believes is true. You can feel the cold right through your coat and your fleece vest and your two pair of long underwear. You can feel it in your bones.

In South Dakota in winter the temperature can linger below zero for weeks. Clear skies and weak sun and bone dry wind that grinds your face like sandpaper go on day after day until you don't remember that it's ever been warm, that grass has ever been green. If it were suddenly summer in South Dakota after a week of minus two, you would hate it—it would be too hot and too humid and frightening, like the world was ending in fire instead of ice. In South Dakota in winter, you don't think about seventy degrees or eighty degrees. As far as you're concerned the tropics don't exist; palm trees, blue waters—they're just a television fantasy. Twenty degrees would be enough. If the temperature got up to twenty degrees, you'd unbutton your jacket and shed an entire layer of long underwear. At twenty degrees you'd walk outside without your head covered, with your face turned toward the sun, like you were living in Bermuda. Twenty degrees in South Dakota in winter would give you enough hope to go on.

Right now you can't imagine that it will ever be twenty degrees again.

You stumble on a patch of ice and jerk away from Bobby's offered hand. You realize that you're crying and you don't know when it started. The tears don't freeze on your cheeks, not in cold like this—moisture can't survive. You duck your head so Bobby won't see, but he knows anyway. He puts his hand under your arm and guides you over by the lean-to.

You're out of the wind up against the lean-to wall and just that, just stepping out of the wind, makes it feel half as cold as it was.

"Don't," Bobby says, leaning toward you as if he can block the cold. "I'm sorry."

"I wasn't crying," you say. You rub your hand across your cheek, rubbing away tears that aren't there anyway. "It's not like I care."

Bobby looks away, toward the cemetery and the creek and things you can't see.

"I thought—," he says.

He turns and looks straight at you—you'd forgotten that his eyes are a blue that looks like midnight mixed with summer.

"Bobby—" you begin, because somehow you know that whatever he's going to say, you want to stop him.

He ducks his head as if he wants to say and not-say something at the same time and when he does speak the words come out all in a rush, his voice pitched a half-octave higher than normal. "Maybe I won't see them anymore," he says.

"The fairies?" you ask, your voice half-choked; whatever you expected this isn't it.

"Or whatever."

You forget the cold completely. You look at him as if the world, and not just you, has stopped breathing. You want to ask him—would it be like it was before, would he come back to the farm, would he charm the birds off trees, would he smile—like summer when it's 95 and you can't remember that it's ever been cold, like we'd never been here at all, on this shabby run-down farm with the chickens and the signs and the chainsaw on hand.

Bobby has stepped away from you; he's slouched against the metal wall of the lean-to, his arms across his chest. He isn't looking at you. There is something tight and tense about him, even slouched like that, not the way he's been, as if he doesn't give a damn, almost as if he cares what you will say.

You've thought all along that this was easy for Bobby. He's left you and the farm and his family and his life. He has fairies or angels or trolls who freeze time for him, who make it all right to scrape a living from chickens and rabbits. It can't be cold when the fairies come—that's what you've always figured—there is no need for chainsaws. Bobby gets off easy; everyone else pays the price.

"Why?" you finally ask.

Bobby shrugs. "I'm just saying," he tells you, though he doesn't look your way when he says it.

A blast of pure winter fire flashes through your veins. You were always right and Bobby was always wrong.

After the University of Chicago, you took a job in Boston at a consulting firm running statistics on focus groups and research surveys. In Boston, it gets wet instead of cold. In Boston, no one ever puts a sign in their front yard that says 'Chainsaw on Hand.' In Boston, life never notices you, until one day Bobby shows up out of nowhere and asks you to go whale watching with him.

"Why?" you ask.

"How long have you been here?" he says.

"Four years," you tell him.

"Have you ever seen whales?"

"Well, no."

You should have asked him right then about fairies and angels and trolls. You should have realized what you were getting into. Instead you go whale watching and hiking in New Hampshire and out to dinner at the most expensive restaurant in Boston, which neither of you can afford.

Right now in the shelter of a thin metal wall, with the temperature dropping and every breath burning dry in your throat, you suddenly remember something you forgot, or maybe never even knew—the reason you came back to South Dakota was not because you had nowhere else to go.

"Bobby."

You wipe a hand across your cheek. "Bobby," you say again just so he knows you're really talking to him. And even then, you don't know the words you're going to say until they're already out of your mouth.

"That's not what I want at all."

Five things have surprised you in your life: the first time you saw a calf born in the middle of a green pasture in spring, winning a full scholarship to the University of Chicago just because you were smart enough, when Bobby came to Boston to take you whale watching, finally figuring out how to mix paint the exact color blue of the South Dakota sky on the longest day of summer.

And now this.

"What do you want, Chelley?" Bobby asks. His voice is tired, hopeful, desperate and resigned all in one.

You know, finally, that you have the power to pierce his soul. You know that he has the power to do the same to you.

"I want to see fairies," you tell him, "Or maybe trolls."

Bobby laughs, a sound you haven't heard in longer than you can say. He reaches out his hand and you reach out and take it. You realize, though you should have always known, that warmth doesn't always come from winds out of the south or woodstoves stoked with birch logs or cattle standing huddled in the barn.

You don't know what will happen next. You don't know how to make things work or what it will be like the next time Bobby says the fairies have frozen time. You don't know if Bobby will charm birds again or come back to the farm or smile just because you need him to.

What you know is that even in South Dakota in winter, even with a chain saw, you can never really be prepared for everything.

THE LAST AND ONLY, or, MR. MOSCOWITZ BECOMES FRENCH
Peter S. Beagle

Peter S. Beagle was born in New York in April 1939. He studied at the University of Pittsburgh and graduated with a degree in creative writing in 1959. Beagle's first novel *A Fine and Private Place* (1960) has long been a cult classic. It was followed by the non-fiction travelogue *I See by My Outfit* in 1961, and by his best-known work, the modern fantasy classic *The Last Unicorn* in 1968. Beagle's other books include novels *The Folk of the Air*, *The Innkeeper's Song*, and *Tamsin*; collections *The Fantasy Worlds of Peter S. Beagle*, *The Rhinoceros Who Quoted Nietzsche*, *Giant Bones*, *The Line Between*, several non-fiction books, and a number of screenplays and teleplays. His most recent book is the short novel *I'm Afraid You've Got Dragons*. "The Last and Only..." first appeared in *Eclipse 1*, edited by Jonathan Strahan.

Once upon a time, there lived in California a Frenchman named George Moscowitz. His name is of no importance—there are old families in France named Wilson and Holmes, and the first president of the Third Republic was named MacMahon—but what was interesting about Mr. Moscowitz was that he had not always been French. Nor was he entirely French at the time we meet him, but he was becoming perceptibly more so every day. His wife, whose name was Miriam, drew his silhouette on a child's blackboard and filled him in from the feet up with tricolor chalk, adding a little more color daily. She was at mid-thigh when we begin our story.

Most of the doctors who examined Mr. Moscowitz agreed that his affliction was due to some sort of bug that he must have picked up in France when he and Mrs. Moscowitz were honeymooning there, fifteen years before. In its dormant stage, the bug had manifested itself only as a kind of pleasant Francophilia: on their return from France Mr. Moscowitz had begun to buy Linguaphone CDs, and to get up at six in the morning to watch a cable television show on beginner's French. He took to collecting French books and magazines, French music and painting and sculpture, French recipes, French folklore, French attitudes, and, inevitably, French people. As a librarian in a large university, he came in contact with a good many French exchange students and visiting professors, and he went far out of his way to make friends with them—Mr. Moscowitz, shy as a badger. The students had a saying among themselves that if you wanted to be French in that town, you had to clear it with Monsieur Moscowitz, who issued licenses and *cartes de sejour*. The joke was not especially unkind, because Mr. Moscowitz often had them to dinner at his home, and in his quiet delight in the very sound of their voices they found themselves curiously less bored with themselves, and with one another. Their companions at dinner were quite likely to be the ignorant Marseillais tailor who got all of Mr. Moscowitz's custom, or the Canuck coach of the soccer team, but there was something so touching in Mr. Moscowitz's assumption that all French-speaking people must be naturally at home together that professors and proletariat generally managed to find each other charming and valuable. And Mr. Moscowitz himself, speaking rarely, but sometimes smiling uncontrollably, like an exhalation of joy—he was a snob in that he preferred the culture and manners of another country to his own, and certainly a fool in that he could find wisdom in every foolishness uttered in French—he was marvelously happy then, and it was impossible for those around him to escape his happiness. Now and then he would address a compliment or a witticism to his wife, who would smile and answer softly, "*Merci*," or "*La-la*," for she knew that at such moments he believed without thinking about it that she too spoke French.

Mrs. Moscowitz herself was, as must be obvious, a patient woman of a tolerant humor, who greatly enjoyed her husband's enjoyment of all things French, and who believed, firmly and serenely, that this curious obsession would fade with time, to be replaced by bridge or chess, or—though she prayed not—golf. "At least he's dressing much better these days," she told her sister Dina, who lived in Scottsdale, Arizona. "Thank God you don't have to wear plaid pants to be French."

Then, after fifteen years, whatever it was that he had contracted in France, if that was what he had done, came fully out of hiding; and here stood Mr. Moscowitz in one doctor's office after another, French from his soles to his ankles, to his shins, to his knees, and still heading north for a second spring. (Mrs. Moscowitz's little drawing is, of course, only a convenient metaphor—if anything, her husband was becoming French from his bones out.) He was treated with drugs as common as candy and as rare as turtle tears by doctors ranging from Johns Hopkins specialists to a New Guinea shaman; he was examined by herbalists and honey-doctors, and by committees of medical men so reputable as to make illness in their presence seem almost criminal; and he was dragged to a crossroads one howling midnight to meet with a half-naked, foamy-chinned old man who claimed to be the son of Merlin's affair with Nimue, and a colonel in the Marine Reserves besides. This fellow's diagnosis was supernatural possession; his prescribed remedy would cost Mr. Moscowitz a black pig (and the pig its liver), and was impractical, but the idea left Mr. Moscowitz thoughtful for a long time.

In bed that night, he said to his wife, "Perhaps it is possession. It's frightening, yes, but it's exciting too, if you want the truth. I feel something growing inside me, taking shape as it crowds me out, and the closer I get to disappearing, the clearer it becomes. And yet, it is me too, if you understand—I wish I could explain to you how it feels—it is like, 'ow you say...."

"Don't say that," Mrs. Moscowitz interrupted with tears in her voice. She had begun to whimper quietly when he spoke of disappearing. "Only TV Frenchmen talk like that."

"*Excuse-moi, ma vieille.* The more it crowds me, the more it makes me feel like *me.* I feel a whole country growing inside me, thousands of years, millions of people, stupid, crazy, shrewd people, and all of them me. I never felt like that before, I never felt that there was anything inside me, even myself. Now I'm pregnant with a whole country, and I'm growing fat with it, and one day —" He began to cry himself then, and the two of them huddled small in their bed, holding hands all night long. He dreamed in French that night, as he had been doing for weeks, but he woke up still speaking it, and he did not regain his English until he had had his first cup of coffee. It took him longer each morning thereafter.

A psychiatrist whom they visited when Mr. Moscowitz's silhouette was French to the waist commented that his theory of possession by himself was a way of sidling up to the truth that Mr. Moscowitz was actually willing his transformation. "The unconscious is ingenious at devising methods of withdrawal," he explained, pulling at his fingertips as though milking a cow, "and national character is certainly no barrier to a mind so determined to get out from under the weight of being an American. It's not as uncommon as you might think, these days."

"*Qu'est-ce qui'il dit?*" whispered Mr. Moscowitz to his wife.

"I have a patient," mused the psychiatrist, "who believes that he is gradually being metamorphosed into a roc, such a giant bird as carried off Sindbad the Sailor to lands unimaginable and riches beyond comprehension. He has asked me to come with him to the very same lands when his change is complete."

"*Qu'est-ce qu'il dit? Qu'est-ce que c'est, roc?*" Mrs. Moscowitz shushed her husband nervously and said, "Yes, yes, but what about George? Do you think you can cure him?"

"I won't be around," said the psychiatrist. There came a stoop of great wings outside the window, and the Moscowitzes fled.

"Well, there it is," Mrs. Moscowitz said when they were home, "and I must confess I thought as much. You could stop this stupid change yourself if you really wanted to, but you don't want to stop it. You're withdrawing, just the way he said, you're escaping from the responsibility of being plain old George Moscowitz in the plain old United States. You're quitting, and I'm ashamed of you—you're copping out." She hadn't used the phrase since her own college days, at Vassar, and it made her feel old and even less in control of this disturbing situation.

"Cop-out, cop-out," said Mr. Moscowitz thoughtfully. "What charm! I love it very much, the American slang. Cop-out, copping out. I cop out, *tu* cop out, they all cop out...."

Then Mrs. Moscowitz burst into tears, and picking up her colored chalks, she scribbled up and down and across the neat silhouette of her husband until the chalk screamed and broke, and the whole blackboard was plastered red, white, and blue; and as she did this, she cried "I don't care, I don't care if you're escaping or not, or what you change into. I wouldn't care if you turned into a cockroach, if I could be a cockroach too." Her eyes were so blurred with tears that Mr. Moscowitz seemed to be sliding away from her like a cloud. He took her in his arms then, but all the comfort he offered her was in French, and she cried even harder.

It was the only time she ever allowed herself to break down. The next day she set about learning French. It was difficult for her, for she had no natural ear for language, but she enrolled in three schools at once—one for group study, one for private lessons, and the other online—and she worked very hard. She even dug out her husband's abandoned language CDs and listened to them constantly. And during her days and evenings, if she found herself near a mirror, she would peer at the plump, tired face she saw there and say carefully to it, *"Je suis la professeur. Vous etes l'etudiante. Je suis francaise. Vous n'etes pas francaise."* These were the first four sentences that the recordings spoke to her every day. It had occurred to her—though she never voiced the idea— that she might be able to will the same change that had befallen her husband on herself. She told herself often, especially after triumphing over her reflection, that she felt more French daily; and when she finally gave up the pretense of being transformed, she said to herself, "It's my fault. I want to change for him, not for myself. It's not enough." She kept up with her French lessons, all the same.

Mr. Moscowitz, on his part, was finding it necessary to take English lessons. His work in the library was growing more harassing every day: he could no longer read the requests filed by the students—let alone the forms and instructions on his own computer screen—and he had to resort to desperate guessing games and mnemonic systems to find anything in the stacks or on the shelves. His condition was obvious to his friends on the library staff, and they covered up for him as best they could, doing most of his work while a graduate student from the French department sat with him in a carrel, teaching him English as elementary as though he had never spoken it. But he did not learn it quickly, and he never learned it well, and his friends could not keep him hidden all the time. Inevitably, the Chancellor of the university interested himself in the matter, and after a series of interviews with Mr. Moscowitz—conducted in French, for the Chancellor was a traveled man who had studied at the Sorbonne—announced regretfully that he saw no way but to let Mr. Moscowitz go. "You understand my position, Georges, my old one," he said, shrugging slightly and twitching his mouth. "It is a damage, of course, well understood, but there will be much severance pay and a pension of the fullest." The presence of a Frenchman always made the Chancellor a little giddy.

"You speak French like a Spanish cow," observed Mr. Moscowitz, who had been expecting this decision and was quite calm. He then pointed out to the Chancellor that he had tenure and to spare, and that he was not about to be gotten rid of so easily. Even in this imbecile country, a teacher had his rights, and it was on the Chancellor's shoulders to find a reason for discharging him. He requested the Chancellor to show him a single university code, past or present, that listed change of nationality as sufficient grounds for terminating a contract; and he added that he was older than the Chancellor and had given him no encouragement to call him <u>tu</u>.

"But you're not the same man we hired!" cried the Chancellor in English.

"No?" asked Mr. Moscowitz when the remark had been explained to him. "Then who am I, please?"

The university would have been glad to settle the case out of court, and Mrs. Moscowitz pleaded with her husband to accept their offered terms, which were liberal enough; but he refused, for no reason that she could see but delight at the confusion and embarrassment he was about to cause, and a positive hunger for the tumult of a court battle. The man she had married, she remembered, had always found it hard to show anger even to his worst enemy, for fear of hurting his feelings; but she stopped thinking about it at that point, not wanting to make the Chancellor's case for him. "You are quite right, George," she told him, and then, carefully, "*Tu as raison, mon chou.*" He told her—as nearly as she could understand—that if she ever learned to speak French properly she would sound like a Basque, so she might as well not try. He was very rude to the Marseillais tailor these days.

The ACLU appointed a lawyer for Mr. Moscowitz, and, for all purposes but the practical, he won his case as decisively as Darrow defending Darwin. The lawyer laid great and tearful stress on the calamity (hisses from the gallery, where a sizeable French contingent grew larger every day) that had befallen a simple, ordinary man, leaving him dumb and defenseless in the midst of academic piranhas who would strip him of position, tenure, reputation, even statehood, in one pitiless bite. (This last was in reference to a foolish statement by the university counsel that Mr. Moscowitz would have some difficulty passing a citizenship test now, let alone a librarian's examination.) But his main defense was the same as Mr. Moscowitz's before the Chancellor: there was no precedent for such a situation as his client's, nor was this case likely to set one. If the universities wanted to write it into their common code that any man proved to be changing his nationality should summarily be discharged, then the universities could do that, and very silly they would look, too. ("What would constitute proof?" he wondered aloud, and what degree of change would it be necessary to prove? "Fifty per cent? Thirty-three and one-third? Or just, as the French say, a *soupçon*?") But as matters stood, the university had no more right to fire Mr. Moscowitz for becoming a Frenchman than they would have if he became fat, or gray-haired, or two inches taller. The lawyer ended his plea by bowing deeply to his client and crying, "*Vive* Moscowitz!" And the whole courthouse rang and thundered then as Americans and French, judge and jury, counsels and bailiffs and the whole audience rose and roared, "*Vive* Moscowitz! *Vive* Moscowitz!" The Chancellor thought of the Sorbonne, and wept.

There were newspapermen in the courtroom, and by that last day there were television cameras. Mr. Moscowitz sat at home that night and leaned forward to stare at his face whenever it came on the screen. His wife, thinking he was criticizing his appearance, remarked, "You look nice. A little like Jean Gabin." Mr. Moscowitz grunted. "*Le camera t'aime*," she said carefully. She answered the phone when it rang, which was often. Many of the callers had television shows of their own. The others wanted Mr. Moscowitz to write books.

Within a week of the trial, Mr. Moscowitz was a national celebrity, which meant that as many people knew his name as knew the name of the actor who played the dashing Gilles de Rais in a new television serial, and not quite as many as recognized the eleven-year-old Racine girl with a forty-inch bust, who sang Christian techno-rap. Mrs. Moscowitz saw him more often on television than she did at home—at seven on a Sunday morning he was invited to discuss post-existential film or France's relations with her former African colonies; at two o'clock he might be awarding a ticket to Paris to the winner of the daily *My Ex Will Hate This* contest; and at eleven PM, on one of the late-night shows, she could watch him speaking the lyrics to the internationally popular French song, *Je M'en Fous De Tout Ca*, while a covey of teenage dancers yipped and jiggled around him. Mrs. Moscowitz would sigh, switch off the set, and sit down at the computer to study her assigned installment of the adventures of the family Vincent, who spoke basic French to one another and were always having breakfast, visiting aunts, or making lists. "Regard Helene," said Mrs. Moscowitz bitterly. "She is in train of falling into the quicksand again. Yes, she falls. Naughty, naughty Helene. She talks too much."

There was a good deal of scientific and political interest taken in Mr. Moscowitz as well. He spent several weekends in Washington, being examined and interviewed, and he met the President, briefly. The President shook his hand, and gave him a souvenir fountain pen and a flag lapel, and said that he regarded Mr. Moscowitz's transformation as the ultimate expression of the American dream, for it surely proved to the world that any American could become whatever he wanted enough to be, even if what he wanted to be was a snail-eating French wimp.

The scientists, whose lingering fear had been that the metamorphosis of Mr. Moscowitz had been somehow accomplished by the Russians or the Iranians, as a practice run before they turned everybody into Russians or Iranians, found nothing in Mr. Moscowitz either to enlighten or alert them. He was a small, suspicious man who spoke often of his rights, and might, as far as they could tell, have been born French. They sent him home at last, to his business manager, to his television commitments, to his endorsements, to his ghostwritten autobiography, and to his wife; and they told the President, "Go figure. Maybe this is the way the world ends, we wouldn't know. And it might not hurt to avoid crêpes for a while."

Mr. Moscowitz's celebrity lasted for almost two months— quite a long time, considering that it was autumn and there were a lot of other public novas flaring and dying on prime time. His highwater mark was certainly reached on the weekend that the officials of at least one cable network were watching one another's eyes to see how they might react to the idea of a George Moscowitz Show. His fortunes began to ebb on Monday morning—public interest is a matter of momentum, and there just wasn't anything Mr. Moscowitz could do for an encore.

"If he were only a *nice* Frenchman, or a *sexy* Frenchmen!" the producers and the publishers and the ghostwriters and the A&R executives and the sponsors sighed separately and in conference. "Someone like Jean Reno or Charles Boyer, or Chevalier, or Jacques Pepin, or even Louis Jourdan—somebody charming, somebody with style, with manners, with maybe a little ho-*ho*, Mimi, you good-for-nothing little Mimi..." But what they had, as far as they could see, was one of those surly frogs in a cloth cap who rioted in front of the American Embassy and trashed the Paris McDonald's. Once, on a talk show, he said, taking great care with his English grammar, "The United States is like a very large dog which has not been—*qu'est-ce que c'est le mot?*—housebro*ken*. It is well enough in its place, but its place is not on the couch. Or in the Mideast, or in Africa, or in a restaurant kitchen." The television station began to get letters. They suggested that Mr. Moscowitz go back where he carne from.

So Mr. Moscowitz was whisked out of the public consciousness as deftly as an unpleasant report on what else gives mice cancer or makes eating fish as hazardous as bullfighting . His television bookings were cancelled; he was replaced by reruns, motivational speakers, old John Payne musicals, or one of the less distressing rappers. The contracts for his books and columns and articles remained unsigned, or turned out to conceal escape clauses, elusive and elliptical, but enforceable. Within a week of his last public utterance—"American women smell bad, they smell of fear and vomit and *l'ennui*"—George Moscowitz was no longer a celebrity. He wasn't even a Special Guest.

Nor was he a librarian anymore, in spite of the court's decision. He could not be discharged, but he certainly couldn't be kept on in the library. The obvious solution would have been to find him a position in the French department, but he was no teacher, no translator, no scholar; he was unqualified to teach the language in a junior high school. The Chancellor graciously offered him a departmental scholarship to get a degree in French, but he turned it down as an insult. "At least, a couple of education courses —" said the Chancellor. "Take them yourself," said Mr. Moscowitz, and he resigned.

"What will we do now, George?" asked his wife. "*Que ferons-nous?*" She was glad to have her husband back from the land of magic, even though he was as much a stranger to her now as he sometimes seemed to be to himself. ("What does a butterfly think of its chrysalis?" she wondered modestly, "or of milkweed?") His fall from grace seemed to have made him kind again. They spent their days together now, walking, or reading Chateaubriand aloud; often silent, for it was hard for Mrs. Moscowitz to speak truly in French, and her husband could not mutter along in English for long without becoming angry. "Will we go to France?" she asked, knowing his answer.

"Yes," Mr. Moscowitz said. He showed her a letter. "The French government will pay our passage. We are going home." He said it many times, now with joy, now with a certain desperation. "We are going home."

The French of course insisted on making the news of Mr. Moscowitz's departure public in America, and the general American attitude was a curious mix of relief and chagrin. They were glad to have Mr. Moscowitz safely out of the way, but it was "doubtless unpleasant," as a French newspaper suggested, "to see a recognizable human shape insist on emerging from the great melting pot, instead of eagerly dissolving away." Various influences in the United States warned that Mr. Moscowitz was obviously a spy for some international conspiracy, but the President, who had vaguely liked him, said, "Well, good for him, great. Enjoy, baby." The government made up a special loose-leaf passport for Mr. Moscowitz, with room for other changes of nationality, just in case.

Mrs. Moscowitz, who made few demands on her husband, or anyone else, insisted on going to visit her sister Dina in Scottsdale before the move to France. She spent several days being taught to play video games by her nephew and enjoying countless tea parties with her two nieces, and sitting up late with Dina and her sympathetic husband, talking over all the ramifications of her coming exile. "Because that's the way I know I see it," she said, "in my heart. I try to feel excited—I really do try, for George's sake—but inside, inside..." She never wept or broke down at such points, but would pause for a few moments, while her sister fussed with the coffee cups and her brother-in-law looked away. "It's not that I'll miss that many people," she would go on, "or our life—well, George's life—around the university. Or the apartment, or all the things we can't take with us—that doesn't really matter, all that. Maybe if we had children, like you..." and she would fall silent again, but not for long, before she burst out, "But *me*, I'll miss *me!* I don't know who I'll be, living in France, but it'll be someone else, it won't ever be *me* again. And I did...I *did* like me the way I was, and so did George, no matter what he says now." But in time, as they knew she would, she would recover her familiar reliable calmness and decide, "Oh, it will be all right, I'm sure. I'm just being an old stick-in-the-mud. It *will* be an adventure, after all."

The French government sent a specially-chartered jet to summon the Moscowitzes; it was very grand treatment, Mrs. Moscowitz thought, but she had hoped they would sail. "On a boat, we would be nowhere for a few days," she said to herself, "and I do need to be nowhere first, just a little while." She took her books and CDs about the Vincent family along with her, and she drew a long breath and held onto Mr. Moscowitz's sleeve when the plane doors opened onto the black and glowing airfield, and they were invited to step down among the roaring people who had been waiting for two days to welcome them. "Here we go," she said softly. *"Allons-y.* We are home."

France greeted them with great pride and great delight, in which there was mixed not the smallest drop of humor. To the overwhelming majority of the French press, to the poets and politicians, and certainly to the mass of the people—who read the papers and the poems, and waited at the airport—it seemed both utterly logical and magnificently just that a man's soul should discover itself to be French. Was it not possible that all the souls in the world might be French, born in exile but beginning to find their way home from the cold countries, one by one? Think of all the tourists, the wonderful middle-aged tourists—where will we put them all? Anywhere, anywhere, it won't matter, for all the world will be France, as it should have been long ago, when our souls began to speak different languages. *Vive* Moscowitz then, *vive* Moscowitz! And see if you can get him to do a spread in Paris-Match, or on your television program, or book him for a few weeks at the Olympia. Got to make your money before Judgment Day.

But the government had not invited Mr. Moscowitz to France to abandon him to free enterprise—he was much too important for that. His television appearances were made on government time; his public speeches were staged and sponsored by the government; and he would never have been allowed, even had he wished, to endorse a soft drink that claimed that it made the imbiber twenty-two per cent more French. He was not for rent.

He traveled—or, rather, he was traveled—through the country, from Provence to Brittany, gently guarded, fenced round in a civilized manner; and throngs of people came out to see him. Then he was returned to Paris.

The government officials in charge of Mr. Moscowitz found a beautiful apartment in safe, quiet Passy for him and his wife, and let them understand that the rent would be paid for the rest of their lives. There was a maid and a cook, both paid for, and there was a garden that seemed as big as the Bois de Boulogne to the Moscowitzes, and there was a government chauffeur to take them wherever they wanted to go, whenever. And finally—for the government understood that many men will die without work—there was a job ready for Mr. Moscowitz when he chose to take it up, as the librarian of the Benjamin Franklin library, behind the Odeon. He had hoped for the Bibliothèque Nationale, but he was satisfied with the lesser post. "We are home," he said to his wife. "Having one job or another—one thing or another—only makes a difference to those who are not truly at home. *Tu m'comprends?*

"*Oui,*" said Mrs. Moscowitz. They were forever asking each other that *do you understand me?* and they both always said *yes.* He spoke often of home and of belonging, she noticed; perhaps he meant to reassure her. For herself, she had come to realize that all the lists and journeys of the family Vincent would never make her a moment more French than she was, which was not at all, regardless. Indeed, the more she studied the language— the government had provided a series of tutors for her—the less she seemed to understand it, and she lived in anxiety that she and Mr. Moscowitz would lose this hold of one another, like children separated in a parade. Yet she was not as unhappy as she had feared, for her old capacity for making the best of things surfaced once again, and actually did make her new life as kind and rewarding as it could possibly have been, not only for her, but for those with whom she came in any sort of contact. She would have been very surprised to learn this last.

But Mr. Moscowitz himself was not happy for long in France. It was certainly no one's fault but his own. The government took the wisest care of him it knew—though it exhibited him, still it always remembered that he was a human being, which is hard for a government—and the people of France sent him silly, lovely gifts and letters of welcome from all across the country. In their neighborhood, the Moscowitzes were the reigning couple without really knowing it. Students gathered under their windows on the spring nights to sing to them, and the students' fathers, the butchers and grocers and druggists and booksellers of Passy, would never let Mrs. Moscowitz pay for anything when she went shopping. They made friends, good, intelligent, government-approved friends—and yet Mr. Moscowitz brooded more and more visibly, until his wife finally asked him, "What is it, George? What's the matter?"

"They are not French," he said. "All these people. They don't know what it is to be French."

"Because they live like Americans?" she asked gently. "George—"she had learned to pronounce it *Jhorj,*in the soft French manner—"everyone does that, or everyone will. To be anything but American is very hard these days. I think they do very well."

"They are not French," Mr. Moscowitz repeated. "I am French, but they are not French. I wonder if they ever were." She looked at him in some alarm. It was her first intimation that the process was not complete.

His dissatisfaction with the people who thought they were French grew more apparent every day. Friends, neighbors, fellow employees, and a wide spectrum of official persons passed in turn before his eyes; and he studied each one and plainly discarded him.

Once he had been the kind of man who said nothing, rather than lie; but now he said everything he thought, which is not necessarily more honest. He stalked through the streets of Paris, muttering, "You are not French, none of you are—you are imposters! What have you done with my own people, where have they gone?" It was impossible for such a search to go unnoticed for long. Children as well as grown men began to run up to him on the street, begging, "*Monsieur Moscowitz, regardez-moi, je suis vraiment francais!*" He would look at them once, speak or say nothing, and stride on. The rejected quite often wept as they looked after him.

There were some Frenchman, of both high and low estate, who became furious with Mr. Moscowitz—who was *he*, a first generation American, French only by extremely dubious mutation, to claim that they, whose ancestors had either laid the foundations of European culture, or died, ignorant, in its defense, were not French? But in the main, a deep sadness shadowed the country. An inquisitor had come among them, an apostle, and they had been found wanting. France mourned herself, and began wondering if she had ever existed at all; for Mr. Moscowitz hunted hungrily through all recorded French history, searching for his lost kindred, and cried at last that from the days of the first paintings in the Dordogne caves, there was no evidence that a single true Frenchman had ever fought a battle, or written a poem, or built a city, or comprehended a law of the universe. "Dear France," he said with a kind of cold sorrow, "for all the Frenchmen who have ever turned your soil, you might have remained virgin and empty all these centuries. As far back in time as I can see, there has never been one, until now."

The President of France, a great man, his own monument in his own time, a man who had never wavered in the certainty that he himself was France, wrote Mr. Moscowitz a letter in which he stated, "We have always been French. We have been Gauls and

Goths, Celts and Franks, but we have always been French. We, and no one else, have made France live. What else should we be but French?"

Mr. Moscowitz wrote him a letter in answer, saying, "You have inhabited France, you have occupied it, you have held it in trust if you like, and you have served it varyingly well—but that has not made you French, nor will it, any more than generations of monkeys breeding in a lion's empty cage will become lions. As for what else you may truly be, that you will have to find out for yourselves, as I had to find out."

The President, who was a religious man, thought of Belshazzar's Feast. He called on Mr. Moscowitz at his home in Passy, to the awe of Mrs. Moscowitz, who knew that ambassadors had lived out their terms in Paris without ever meeting the President face to face. The President said, "M. Moscowitz, you are denying us the right to believe in ourselves as a continuity, as part of the process of history. No nation can exist without that belief."

"Monsieur le President, je suis desolée," answered Mr. Moscowitz, He had grown blue-gray and thin, bones hinting more and more under the once-genial flesh.

"We have done you honor," mused the President, "though I admit before you say it that we believed we were honoring ourselves. But you turn us into ghosts, *Monsieur* Moscowitz, homeless figments, and our grip on the earth is too precarious at the best of times for me to allow you to do this. You must be silent, or I will make you so. I do not want to, but I will."

Mr. Moscowitz smiled, almost wistfully, and the President grew afraid. He had a sudden vision of Mr. Moscowitz banishing him and every other soul in France with a single word, a single gesture; and in that moment's vision it seemed to him that they all went away like clouds, leaving Mr. Moscowitz to dance by himself in cobwebbed Paris on Bastille Day. The President shivered and cried out, "What is it that you want of us? What should we be? What is it, to be French, what does the stupid word mean?"

Mr. Moscowitz answered him. "I do not know, any more than you do. But I do not need to ask." His eyes were full of tears and his nose was running, "The French are inside me," he said, "singing and stamping to be let out, all of them, the wonderful children that I will never see. I am like Moses, who led his people to the Promised Land, but never set his own foot down there. All fathers are a little like Moses."

The next day, Mr. Moscowitz put on his good clothes and asked his wife to pack him a lunch. "With an apple, please," he said, "and the good Camembert, and a whole onion. Two apples." His new hat, cocked at a youthful angle, scraped coldly beside her eye when he kissed her. She did not hold him a moment longer than she ever had when he kissed her goodbye. Then Mr. Moscowitz walked away from her, and into legend.

No one ever saw him again. There were stories about him, as there still are; rumors out of Concarneau, and Sète, and Lille, from misty cities and yellow villages. Most of the tales concerned strange, magic infants, as marvelous in the families that bore them as merchildren in herring nets. The President sent out his messengers, but quite often there were no such children at all, and when there were they were the usual cases of crosseyes and extra fingers, webbed feet and cauls. The President was relieved, and said so frankly to Mrs. Moscowitz. "With all respectful sympathy, Madame," he told her, "the happiest place for your husband now is a fairy story. It is warm inside a myth, and safe, quite safe, and the company is of the best. I envy him, for I will never know such companions. I will get politicians and generals."

"And I will get his pension and his belongings," Mrs. Moscowitz said to herself. "And I will know solitude."

The President went on, "He was mad, of course, your husband, but what a mission he set himself! It was worthy of one of Charlemagne's paladins, or of your—" he fumbled through his limited stock of nonpartisan American heroes—"your Johnny Appleseed. Yes."

The President died in the country, an old man, and Mrs. Moscowitz in time died alone in Passy. She never returned to America, even to visit, partly out of loyalty to Mr. Moscowitz's dream, and partly because if there is one thing besides cheese that the French do better than any other people, it is the careful and assiduous tending of a great man's widow. She wanted for nothing to the end of her days, except her husband—and, in a very real sense, France was all she had left of him.

That was a long time ago, but the legends go on quietly, not only of the seafoam children who will create France, but of Mr. Moscowitz as well. In Paris and the provinces, anyone who listens long enough can hear stories of the American who became French. He wanders through the warm nights and the cold, under stars and streetlamps, walking with the bright purpose of a child who has slipped out of his parents' sight and is now free to do as he pleases. In the country, they say that he is on his way to see how his children are growing up, and perhaps there are mothers who lull their own children with that story, or warn them with it when they behave badly. But Parisians like to dress things up, and as they tell it, Mr. Moscowitz is never alone. Cyrano is with him, and St. Joan, Roland, D'Artagnan, and Villon—and there are others. The light of them brightens the road for Mr. Moscowitz to see his way.

But even in Paris there are people, especially women, who say that Mr. Moscowitz's only companion on his journey is Mrs. Moscowitz herself, holding his arm or running to catch up. And she deserves to be there, they will tell you, for she would have been glad of any child at all; and if he was the one who dreamed and loved France so much, still and all, she suffered.

MINUS, HIS HEART
Jedediah Berry

Jedediah Berry is the author of a novel, *The Manual of Detection*, forthcoming from The Penguin Press in spring 2009. His short fiction has appeared in numerous journals and anthologies, including *3rd Bed, Fairy Tale Review, Salon Fantastique*, and *Best New American Voices*. By day, he is an assistant editor at Small Beer Press. "Minus, His Heart" is taken from the literary magazine *The Cincinnati Review*.

1.

The boy was in the house with two doors, alone with his proxy father, the Interminable Richard. The boy leaned in toward the glow of the electric voicebox while the Interminable Richard, trying to soothe his old wound, sat on top of it and flipped frequencies. A whistling, popping sound clotted the air above them. It was the boy's job to watch his proxy father's wound for signs of harmonic sympathy—the creams had done nothing. The old man twisted the knob between his thumb and forefinger. Two hours and the boy could perceive no dimpling, no vibration.

The doorbell rang. The boy took his duffel and went willingly;

212 | JEDEDIAH BERRY

the door, too, did its thing. Nothing beyond but the broad fresh-scrubbed boulevard. He left it and tried the other one. There some lamed tulips failed to look up from their beds.

The boy had left the first door open while he went to the second, and Minus, the Neighborhood Wassailer, yesterday's confetti still in his hair, used this opportunity to slip inside. In the front hall, the proxy father had long maintained statues of the townsfolk, and Minus stood among them, still as a statue of Minus, the Neighborhood Wassailer, for whom there was no statue at this time. His ruse was true and bold. When the boy passed close, Minus grabbed him by the small of the neck and squeezed.

"Fate has brought us together," Minus said. "That, or the old honor between burglar and burgled. You got the jump on me, Billy, but now our platters are switched. How was it encompassed, Jack? Tell me the tale of it."

"Ow," said the boy.

Minus eased his grip. "Speak sooth or I go home with part of you and leave the rest under the tulips."

The boy clutched his duffel and had out with it. "It was at Newbury's All-in-One. You fell asleep on the escalator. Every time you got to the top, some kind shopper would kick you aside and you'd head down the downside, then back up again. Your snoring was ugly and public. I caught you on the rise and felt mean. I opened your coat, meaning to pinch your duffel. Someone had already gotten to it, so I took what I could find. It was blasphemy but I blame my upbringing."

Minus opened his coat and felt around. Something was missing. There in his chestdeck one knob spun while the other didn't. The play button was depressed, but the deck produced only static. "You ejected my tape, Ralph. How will I master toast and ceremony now, tell me that?"

"You have my spine, but I don't have your tape. I hawked it."

Minus clamped down and the boy sputtered, "Or I gave it away, more likely."

"To your sweet number?"

"I'd lie but you'd hurt me for it. The girl has it, yes."

Minus shook his head and a tear loosened from his cheek, went floorward. He'd been crying the whole time. "You lead, Sam, and I steer."

The boy went toward the door. He shouted so his proxy father would hear over the electric voicebox, "I'm being abducted, Dad. This may be your last chance to warm your tone with me."

But the Interminable Richard just caressed his old wound and zeroed in on another frequency.

2.

They went north through the sad part of town. To pedestrians they appeared as man and boy, uncle and nephew, oddly arrayed but not at odds. So the Wassailer's grim intent remained undetected. "Look how he loves his son/nephew/young friend," the pedestrians observed. "Walking hand to nape as was done in days of old." None of them saw how hard he clutched the boy's scruff.

"Is my end before me?" the boy queried.

"As always," Minus said, mistaking fear for philosophy. "The long dark waits crouched in the bushes. The sun sinks at our backs, lonely vermilion. All we can do is gather what shavings of love and splendor our duffels will hold. I see you brought yours with you."

They had come to the playground. It was rusted but serviceable, known throughout the city for having produced several generations of steadfast children. When the merry-go-whirl spun quickly enough, some two or three howling infants per day

214 | JEDEDIAH BERRY

could be jettisoned forth. The sliding whimsy, too, was a fertile mechanism. A mother-to-be might climb the ladder with a small stone in her pouch and hit bottom with a toddler of most any sex. The boy himself had begun here, and returned sometimes to play checkers with his sweet number. If this was Minus's point of origin, the wassailer did not know it.

An unfinished child called from the whirl: "Give us a push. By noon I'll have eyes enough to see you with."

"No tricks now," Minus whispered to the boy, but let him lead over.

The boy kicked the whirl a few times and got its motor running hot. Something blurry clinging to the rails cackled and spat.

"I'm looking for Winsome Jenny," the boy said at the blur. "Has she been this way? We've something to transact."

The almost-child coriolised: "I could give it to you in riddles, as is the right of my kind, but I'll spare you that. She's at the leatherball court with her new team."

The boy knew it was true and he didn't like it. A new team could only mean she was gearing up for the season without him. Hadn't they always coached leatherball together?

The court was wild with freshly tattooed pedestrians. They knocked the ball around with their heads while the goalie tried to kick out their knees. They would make a good team—some might even live through the season. Winsome Jenny stood at the foul line, spitting melon seeds at their errors. In her shorts and sportsweater she was something to behold. When she saw the boy come up with his Wassailer, she shot the rest of her seeds onto the ground at his feet.

"This is not a test," she said, and the boy believed her.

"I just want my tape back." Feeling the pinch at his spine, he added, "Because it isn't mine."

Jenny blew her whistle and the team huddled close. At her

215 HIS HEART | 215

signal they would pounce. The boy had been used as a leatherball once before; he did not care for a rerun of that sad jest.

Jenny said, "This one's a low liar. His mix tape's as phony as a Sunday come-hither. I'd imagined him collecting each soundspot with me in mind, but he stole it wholesale from someone else's chestdeck. Should I let Minus hang him from the monkey bars? Or let you fellows chew off his knees?"

"I vote knees," the goalie said.

The boy pleaded, "What about those quiet walks along the pier, Winsome Jenny? We traded kerchiefs, and I told you the Interminable Richard's unkindnesses? You were such a good listener."

"What?" Jenny said. "I can't hear a thing you're saying."

Minus whispered, "Careful, Jim, she means business."

"I mean business," Jenny said. "I think I'm going to drop the stick."

The boy limped; Minus had to let go of his neck and prop him up with both arms. A few proxy fathers, waiting on a nearby bench for their kids to be finished, whistled at the spectacle. Jenny already had a stick in her hand. She'd had it picked out ahead.

"Please," the boy whimpered. "Don't drop the stick."

Minus shook him. "Don't beg, Jimmy. You'll regret it later."

"Please," the boy said anyway.

Jenny held the stick high above her head. "Yes, I'm really going to drop the stick now," she said.

The merry-go-whirl creaked on its axis. At the base of the sliding whimsy a fresh toddler asked what its name was. The proxy fathers leaned in, dripping spittle.

Jenny dropped the stick.

The team sighed and went back to their leatherball match. Minus let the boy go to the ground, and Winsome Jenny knelt over him and stroked his hair. She said, "I was your bona fide sweet number, so you still get a lastly. What will it be? Mercy kiss? A half-tumble?"

The boy wheezed and stared at the stick. "I just want to know where the tape is," he said.

Jenny found one last melon seed between her teeth and spit it at him. It struck the boy's face and stayed there. "Figures," she said, but told him anyway: "I gave it to Zooman Jubal. He's my sweet number now, the stick having hit ground." She stood up, her knees clicking—she'd forgotten to put on her bracers that morning. "If it makes you feel any better," she said, "I've got your kerchief in my duffel." Then she went looking for fresh melon.

The boy scooped some dirt and tried to eat it, but Minus stopped him. "We're in this together, Roger, my boy. You can't go witless on me now. You used your lastly on my behalf, don't think I didn't notice. Granted, I would have strung you up by your short pants if you'd done otherwise, but what of it? Now hole up your wounds and take that pit off your face."

The boy returned the dirt to the dirt and stood up. "Yes," he said, "we're for the zoo now. But the seed stays where Jenny's sweet spit stuck it." He gave his neck back to Minus and they left the playground which, the Wassailer now remembered, was his native soil. They'd made him out of sand from the pile of it.

3.

On the way to the zoo, Minus told the boy a parable to keep him calm.

"Consider the flybug. How it spins through its brief buzzing life. Consider one flybug, any one. He's been worrying about food and with whom to springoff before he packs in his duffel and forgets how to buzz. He swings low to a bright outdoor bulb, as is his wont. And just then his wings stop working—his legs, too. What's this? An eightlegger traipsed webbing here, because many a flybug swings low in that bright zone. It's a meal-a-minute, that webbing. The flybug sticks, struggles some, and sticks some more.

"Now here's the fetching part. This flybug, just because he's a flybug and is now suffering the fate of generations of flybugs before him, does *not* think to himself, 'Ah, so this is how I'm to go, as many have gone before me. This is one of the ways a flybug forgets his buzz: hungry and unsprungoff, in the web of an eightlegger.' Not at all. You and I know that, but the flybug is not privileged with our point of view, we who light outdoor bulbs. To imagine the flybug cogitating in that fashion would be us-in-them thinking, which is bunkum.

"Is that too tight?" Minus asked, meaning his grip on the boy's scruff.

"No, thank you," said the boy, "the pressure is enough to keep me from running off, but not so strong that it pains me unduly."

"Now where had I got to? Ah yes, the true thoughts of the flybug, there in the doily of the eightlegger. 'What strange stuff is this,' thinks he, 'that sticks me more the more I struggle? I'm not sure I like it, but I'm not sure I fear it, either. Everything is unfamiliar now, everything changed. It is different from being born, that much I know. Or do I?'

"Then comes the machinery of envenoming, enveloping, and engorgement."

"Will you moral it for me, Minus?"

"I will," said he. "It is freshness of feeling that kills, whether by degrees or all at once. Also, woe to the flybug, who twice metamorphoses, both times in a silky bag."

"What is on your cassette tape, Minus? More parables?"

"No, Edward, only love-ditties of the popular sort, performed by my great-uncle on an accordion of his own design. But look, we come now to the zoo. Tickets on me."

4.

The zoophones rang in their cages. A pack of snort clowns trapezed between derricks and tossed snap-crackers. Farther in, a girl was selling inflatable rhino bags. But Minus and his captor had no time for circusing of any kind. Others had been caught in the zoo after closing time—some of them the boy had counted as neighborhood chums, or the brothers of chums. These tardy-tots could be glimpsed now in the ravines between the paths, trundling buckets of sludge-feed to pay their debts, faces big and blue from a stingy breath allowance. The young ones looked old and the old ones looked older.

The boy checked his fold-out guide, which he'd kept in his duffel from a previous visit. Zooman Jubal's Safari Machine was just ahead.

"Parley only at my signal," Minus said. He released the boy's neck so they could pass through the turnstile without injury. There was no line, though a few pedestrians on their way out of the Machine grinned under the walrus-skin canopy as though to say: *I'd trade shoes with you for a nickel!*

The sloop had five rows of seats with four seats to a row. They claimed the middle-most two, and were alone except for Jubal, who crouched at the prow with one hand on the lever and the other on his spyglass.

Zooman Jubal, a collector of minor misrepresentations, held a doctorate in villainy and spoke ill of his dead mother. His left eye had been burned shut in a hot poker duel. He forwent patches, opting instead for a perpetual wink.

He aimed that at his passengers and ruffled his beard. "Clear sailing all the way to Doom-on-Scurvy, gents. Think buoyant thoughts, now."

He leaned on the lever and the sloop groaned on its rails. Wheels churned down below the flotsam and brine. The Zooman ducked as their vessel cut through a screen of blossoming vines. Snakes hissed from above, but they were made of plush and their fangs had been filed down.

Jubal said, "Normally I tell a joke at this stage of the voyage. But since there are only two of you, I'll just give you the punch line: *He was home after all!* Ha. That one always gets them. Now, I need to know whether you want the child's outing or the full safari experience."

Minus said, "Spare us no shrift, Zooman."

"I would have shot you otherwise," Jubal said. He opened three bottles of root fizz but didn't offer to share. Then he put his spyglass to his bum eye and pointed it downstream. "Ahead you'll see what's become of my first sweet number. I thought to set her free but she knew all my secrets. There are pellet-shooters under your seats, in case you want to try your luck."

The sloop creaked around a bend. They saw a lichen-spotted cage hanging by thick chains from a tree limb. Inside, a woman tossed pebbles at a bucket of gin one limb up. Each time a pebble went in, a pebble's worth of gin dripped over the edge and into her open mouth. Her slippers were worn down to the canvas.

Minus handed the boy his pellet-shooter and whispered, "We'd best play trumps, Timothy. Aim low and hope you miss her vitals."

The woman waxed baleful at them and showed her teeth. Minus's shot sang off one of the bars. The boy squinted down the barrel and steadied his breath. He was aiming for the lock on the cage, but he wasn't ready for the recoil. He rolled back over the Wassailer's lap and landed in the aisle. "Wow!" he said to the gun.

The woman laughed with her hands and threw a pebble at the boy. It hit him on the face, nearly dislodging the melon seed.

"Amateurs," Jubal croaked. He unstrapped his own shooter, a large-bore model, and fired from the hip. The pellet hit the pail of gin and sent it whirling into deep woods.

"What'll I do til morning?" the woman wailed.

Jubal quaffed a root fizz and wiped his mouth on his lapel. "Watch the reruns and dream up a stupor, for all I care. I never loved you. I don't think of you sometimes. My duffel is devoid of you-related mementos."

Jubal threw the crank and the sloop went fast into the next Safari zone. The river shallowed out at the edge of a low prairie. Beyond the zoo's border, tenement spires gleamed orange. The boy thought maybe he saw the house with two doors out there. What was his proxy father doing without him? He might have been like the light in the icebox: nothing when the door's closed.

Jubal had the spyglass to his good eye and a new bottle of fizz in his hand. "He's here somewhere," he said.

Minus assisted the boy back into his seat. "I forgot to tell you what my signal is," he said.

"I was worried I'd already missed it," the boy admitted.

"What I'll do is this. I'll tug my right ear, then tug yours."

Minus enacted the signal as he had described it.

The boy tugged back conspiratorially.

"I was not demonstrating," Minus said. He aimed his pellet-shooter at the Zooman. "I was actually giving the signal. Begin the parley now, while he's distracted."

Jubal was still inspecting the open plains.

"Ahem," the boy said.

Jubal took a sip of root fizz and muttered a punch line to himself.

"Ahem," the boy said again. "The Wassailer and I have come to the Safari Machine with something particular in mind."

"Somewhere near this spot is a man who thinks he's a lion," said the Zooman. "Or is it a lion dressed in a man suit? Many times have I shot the beast. Still his secret eludes me."

"We've come about the tape," the boy said. "I stole it from Minus and gave it to Jenny. She betrayed me and gave it to you. We need it back now."

"Madness?" Jubal said. "Or the suit? Which is it? Which?"

Minus said, "I'll shoot if you don't parley."

The Zooman lowered his spyglass and turned his wink on them. "You'd miss," he said. "And anyway, I knew what you were up to from the start. That's why I had the lap buckles removed before you boarded."

"We're steady enough," the boy said.

"This is not a test," said Jubal.

"Careful, Scott, he means business."

"I mean business," said Jubal. "Plus, we're coming up on the waterfall. At bottom are jagged boulder constructs and saw-tooth shark-eaters. The only way is down. And I'm the sole passenger with a lap buckle." He strapped himself in and threw back the rest of his fizz.

The parley was over. Up ahead, something roared.

"That's the waterfall," said Jubal. "If you swim for it now, you have an incomputable chance of survival. The shark-eaters eat things other than sharks, by the way."

"Give us that tape," the boy said.

"Try it on the whirlpools, kid."

Minus pulled the trigger and the pellet ricocheted off the prow and struck the underside of Jubal's knee. He dropped his bottle and grabbed his leg, spitting more punch lines. Then he had his wide bore in his hand. "I'll shoot you and drown you," he said.

He didn't have time to do either. A big-maned man leapt out of the tall grasses and onto the sloop. It was he that had been roaring. He pinched Jubal's left shoulder in his teeth and dragged him leeward. Because the Zooman was belted to his seat, only the top half of him went into the water with his assailant.

The madman or suited lion devoured Jubal in soggy chunks. "Now he know my secret," the beast said. "Now he knows which."

They drifted on along the rails. The waters were calm here. Minus dropped his shooter to the floor of the boat and leaned back in his seat.

"I feel a new life killing me," the boy said. "No longer will I tend to my proxy father's wound. I've had enough of salves and frequencies. Enough of the long haunts at Newbury's all-in-one. And watch this."

The boy took the melon seed off his cheek and flicked it into the water.

Minus patted the boy's neck where before he had clutched. "I'm proud of you, Chip."

"So you do know my name."

The Wassailer's laughter shook the boat, and bits of yesterday's confetti dandruffed out of his hair. "You make me wish I'd read a different rulebook, my boy. Then we'd sit down and bake something good to eat. We'd camp under a drowsy moon and sing old songs to nobody but ourselves. That'd be a plus in our gradebooks, eh?"

But the boy wasn't laughing, and the Wassailer was soon quiet again. They both knew it would never work. The boy already had proxy enough.

"How do we stop this thing?" he asked.

They couldn't find the instructions, and anyway, it was too late. They were going over the waterfall together, all two and a half of them.

5.

The boy woke to accordion music. Winsome Jenny was leaning over him, her tresses tickling his nose. His waterlogged duffel was on the floor beside him, and so was the Interminable Richard. They were back in the front hall of the house with two doors, where the statues of the townsfolk were kept.

"Breathe, breathe!" said Winsome Jenny. "We already pumped enough liquid to water all the tulips."

The boy inhaled her breath. His lungs felt rusty. They creaked as he filled them. He sat up and Jenny patted his back. A little more safari dribbled out of his nostrils.

"I already had my lastly," he said.

"No, you didn't," Jenny said. "I gave the tape to Jubal, but it was you I wanted all along. That was a test."

The boy was on his feet now, dizzy and loud. "You dropped the stick. You said it wasn't a test."

"If I'd said it was a test, then it wouldn't have been a proper test."

The Interminable Richard had one ear to the ground. Minus's heart was playing in the voicebox, and the love-ditties had calmed the old man, calmed him nearly to death. When he saw the boy, though, he got to his feet and stretched his arms out toward him.

The boy couldn't tell if his proxy father wanted to hug him or strangle him. Did he even know the difference? Those arms were shaking, and looked too short for either.

"Where is he?" said the boy. "Where wassails Minus?"

"Son!" the Interminable Richard said. The shakes had spread to the rest of his body, and not because of the old wound. He had a new one—he just didn't know where it was yet.

"Minus took the long plunge," Jenny said. "The big tumble. I could only save one of you."

In the next room a new song started warming the air. The boy felt it would choke him. He wanted to eject the tape but something had paused him in place. *He was home after all!*

"Son!" the Interminable Richard cried.

The boy stood still as a statue of himself.

ABROAD

Judy Budnitz

Judy Budnitz is the author of two story collections, *Nice Big American Baby* and *Flying Leap*, and a novel, *If I Told You Once*. Her stories have appeared in *Harper's*, *The New Yorker*, *McSweeney's*, *Fence*, *Tin House*, *One Story*, and other publications. "Abroad" first appeared in the stylish special volume *Tin House: Fantastic Women*, guest edited by Rick Moody.

The trip was not going as planned. The train was supposed to take us to the white-sand beaches and white hotels high on cliffs and the burnished tans that we could step into and zip up like a second skin. Instead it deposited us in this place where all the buildings looked covered with smudgy fingerprints and the only water in sight was running in the gutters. The sky was overcast, lumpy, a poorly plastered ceiling.

The guidebook says there's a railroad museum here, I said. And a bone church.

We weren't supposed to stop here, he said. He went up to the man caged behind a wire grill selling tickets and spoke with him and came back and said: The next train's in three days.

Three days?

If you don't believe me then you go ask him.

Oh, but I don't want to bother him, I said.

So we went to see the bone church. If you can believe it, that's exactly what it was— a church made entirely of the bleached skulls and preserved leg-bones of some very old people. A row of skulls arched over the door. They all looked alike; I would not have thought that people's bones were so uniform you could stack them up like bricks.

He saw my face and said: Don't be sad, I think they were already dead.

That was his idea of a joke.

We were the only people there except for the boy at the entrance who held out his hand for our admission money. His shorts were too short, his sweater too big for him. A cigarette drooped from his mouth. He spoke sharply at us, I could not understand a word. His face was unreadable, hard and perfectly immobile as if the bones were on the outside.

Don't give him money, I said.

Why not?

How do you know he works here? I mean, he's not wearing a... a *badge* or anything. He could be anyone.

So what?

How do we know we know our money's going to the, the bone church people? He's probably going to keep it for himself.

So what if he does? He's probably related to these bones one way or another. *Look* at him.

I looked and it was true: the boy's head belonged up there with the others. A face hard enough to break your hand.

We spoke in whispers when we went inside. Because of the boy. We whispered because we did not want him to feel left out.

I was surprised by how white they were, I expected old bones to have the stained yellowness of a smoker's teeth. To go inside was like stepping inside the ribcages of a thousand people, hearing their phantom heartbeats fluttering around like moths, or like strolling through the whale skeleton at the natural history museum.

There's a blister on my heel. But these shoes never gave me trouble before.

What are you complaining about now?

Nothing.

Behind the bone church lay a cemetery, which seemed superfluous, why put them in the ground when you could add another wing? I wanted to take a picture but thought it would be rude, like photographing sleeping people. I had bought a camera for the trip, an expensive snouty thing I did not know how to use.

The buses were white and red and did not seem to have any scheduled stops. You had to stand directly in their path to get their attention.

These people, I don't know what to make of them. Their faces are so old, but not in the usual way. They seem to age from the outside in rather than the inside out; rather than a sagging and puckering, it's a buildup of deposits. It's as if anything that life's ever thrown at them has hit them in the face and stuck there.

Your pants are too short, I said.

What's wrong with my pants?

They're wrong. Nobody else's pants look like yours.

I think the problem was in the way he wore them, the set of his hips. They demanded attention, those pants. They were swaggering pants. The men we saw on the streets all had a slow low-stepping shuffle as if they'd wet themselves.

We saw no restaurants. What, do these people never eat? That is why they seem so pure and walk so slowly. We asked some local people, who looked at our clothes and directed us to the McDonald's.

Perhaps they misunderstood us. We did not want to be the kind of abrasive tourists who think that if they speak their own language loudly enough the locals will eventually understand. So instead we spoke apologetically, fumblingly, as if our own language was foreign to us.

A place... to eat? Food.... restaurant? Sit down, inside?

He mimed hands to mouth, a waiter with a tray, pulling out a chair, made the universal check-please gesture.

They were not fooled.

The night came down sudden like a lid being clapped on. We found our hotel, we had not been looking for it but there it was, our landmark was the woman in dark glasses with her flower stand across the street.

Why are flower sellers always blind? he said.

They're born that way, I said.

She waved at us and smiled.

We climbed the stairs to our room; they were so steep we had to use our hands. I looked closely at each stair and each one had a different kind of debris: buckles, beads, beetles. I wanted to lie down and sleep right there. I was exhausted. What do these people want from me? To make me climb all these stairs!

Our room was tall, like two rooms stacked on top of each other, and dark. There was a bulb set in the ceiling but it was so far away its light gave up and died before it reached us where we lay on the bed. There was a long slice of window that ran from floor to ceiling and showed us the spires and towers and crested weathervanes of a city we had never seen before.

It's just a travel poster, he said and tried to scrape off a corner.

We had thought that making love in a strange place, between foreign sheets, would bring us together. But the bed seemed determined to keep us apart, it didn't sag in the middle, it had a sort of hump that kept us sliding away from each other.

I felt more familiar with his body than his face; his body was finite, known, a region explored and mapped and marked with little dots indicating theaters and hot nightspots and restaurants with easy menus.

What's this? he said.

You know... my appendix scar.

What's *this*?

I don't want to talk about that. Don't touch it.

Did you hear about that woman? he said. Now he was touching the lump of fat on my hip. The rest of my body isn't so fat, just that one place. Why does he have to touch me there?

What woman? I said.

The train... I think she was a tourist.

Was she pretty? Was she thinner than me?

I don't know. It was in the paper. She was waiting for the underground. With her husband. They were on their honeymoon, people thought. She had a yellow dress. They were waiting for the train, and she was a tourist, you know, she didn't understand how fast the trains come, and how close, and this one didn't have its lights on for some reason. And she was holding her husband's hand. She was leaning out.

I bet he pushed her!

Why do you say things like that? She fell, and the train came and sliced her clean in half. And this is the strange part. The conductor realizes what's happened and brakes the train. The husband is standing on the platform, and half of the woman's body is on one side of the tracks, half on the other, and the train in between. All the husband can see are her legs. He knows he doesn't have time to dash around either end of the train to be with her head so he leaps off the platform and runs to her legs and holds them, caresses them. Like this.

Oh don't. That's sick.

And the strangest part, the reason I'm telling you this, is that the people on the opposite platform, the ones that could see her head, they *swore* she could feel him, she knew he was touching her. She said his name. Even though the rest of her body was ten feet away. Isn't that amazing?

Did she die?

Well of course she died. But that's not the point.

I think those people were pulling your leg. They were lying because you're a tourist. Did they try to sell you a watch next?

You don't find that story amazing? The power of love?

I think you got it wrong. I think she jumped. I think she had a sudden glimpse of how miserable her life would be married to that man and she decided the only way out was to end it right then.

Why do you ruin everything? A beautiful story and you ruin it.

We slept, with the humped mattress between us and the window casting a long strip of grayish light across our bodies.

I opened my eyes and the clicking went on. Clicks and flashes of light.

What are you doing?

Did you know you smile in your sleep, he said. His hands were holding the black snout to his face. He changed the focus.

Click. Flash. Blackness.

What are you doing?

Preserving the moment.

What moment? What moment?

It's gone. You just missed it.

Then I must have slept, because the next thing I knew was yellow morning light, sounds of people shouting in the street, smells of bread and garbage. I heard shrill little-girl voices singing a pop song with the words all garbled. He was sitting on the edge of the bed rubbing his eyes in a way that would leave them red all day.

Clanking, splashes, heavy breathing. Someone was mopping the hallway, right outside the door, ready to burst in on us at any moment. These people, they won't leave you alone, not even for a minute. They're always trying to get in.

Remember when we first met? I said. We used to talk for hours.

Endlessly, he said. Interminably. It still feels like that sometimes.

Guess who, I said in his ear. His eyelashes were tickling my palms. He twisted away and stood up. I got up too.

How long have we been here? I said.

I forget.

A day? Two days? I said.

Are you going to the train museum?

The guidebook says we have to. It's the only thing to see besides the bone church.

I'll see you tonight, he said and was gone. I sometimes wondered why he didn't just grow a mouth on the back of his head since he seemed to do all his talking turned away from me.

I was going to shower but I didn't, the people here don't seem to bathe at all and they are not too offensive; they smell of cedar, of pine straw and smoke. The young women don't wear underpants, the old women don't wash their hair, they just cover it with greasy scarves and go about their business.

The people here all understand English, they just pretend they don't. You can tell.

The blister's even bigger than yesterday, an amniotic sac of salt water on my heel. But I *want* to wear these shoes.

The train museum was housed in an old station no longer in use; a single room; there were some photographs, maps, model trains, beer served in the back. A big box for donations. All the signs printed in their illegible backwards mirror-writing. No one there. I don't care about trains but I made a point to look at everything.

On the wide front steps there were boys dressed in towels and sandals, playing soccer. I walked through the middle of their game, I did not mean to but honestly there was no other way. They were dribbling the ball up and down the steps, shouting to each other, there were complicated rules involved, some had their hair shaved close, others had hair that had never been touched but you would never mistake them for girls. They have not yet discovered Band-Aids here. Each child was a mass of scabs.

One of them came right at me and I thought I should dodge, I was in the way, but he kept coming. Hey lady, he said, hey lady.

What? I said. Yes? The whites of his eyes were yellowish, jaundiced, and so was his skin, and his hair was dark blond too, he was a mustard-colored boy from head to foot. The others stopped running and listened.

Can I see your camera? he said. I thought he wanted his picture taken; I lifted it to my face and stepped back. I bumped into more boys. They had stepped up behind me. Shouldn't they be in school?

No, give it to me, he said. I thought, what kind of town is this where they've never seen a camera before? And I leaned down so I could hand him the camera without taking off the strap. This brought our faces close.

I'll buy it from you, he said. I looked at his mouth; the teeth were brown and yellow at the edges, there were gaps that were not from lost baby teeth.

He gave the camera one sharp yank and the strap broke at some weak link, and then he was off running and the rest of them with him, their cheap sandals slapping the pavement, all of them raising their hands to their throats with monkey-grimaces of horror as they ran. I looked down and saw my hands doing the same, felt my face constricting. They vanished down alleyways and I felt grateful to them for at least not laughing while I could hear them.

I was not too sorry it happened, I felt relieved of a burden, until I remembered the film in the camera, the pictures I had taken from the window of the train as we arrived, the pictures he had taken in the middle of the night. So much for preserving the moment.

The sky darkened and I did not recognize anything. I did not want to take out my map, because you are not lost until you admit that you are; until then you are exploring, you are admiring scenery.

Why would I ask for directions anyway, since I can't understand a word they say and if I could I know they would only lie to me. I'd ask them for my hotel and they'd direct me instead back to the bone church, and I'd wander in circles there until I died, unable to find my way out, and with each circuit that boy would charge me more money, an admission fee for each lap around the bone church until I was bled dry and footsore and dead. Then they'd take my bones and add them to the steeple, or the pews, or they'd build a little washroom for the priest behind the altar. It's not a church of their ancestors' bones, it's the church of unwanted tourists, it is where the uninvited and uncomprehending go to die. And they'd sell my clothes as relics, as souvenirs, my shoes made into bookends, my buttons into bracelets, my blister sewn into a little change purse with a picture of the bone church embroidered on it.

I saw a group of people on a corner. Beautiful white clothes, raised voices. A pause, the slow telling of a joke, bursts of laughter. Women shifting their weight from hip to hip, men with their sleeves rolled to the elbows. They were drinking from green bottles, the mineral water which according to the guidebook came from a local spring and was supposed to have medicinal properties.

Then I saw the head I knew so well, the curly hair.

He was telling the joke, he was drinking the water.

Even from this distance, I could pick him out of the crowd immediately, the way you always can with a loved one, that sudden rush, that relief. I called his name but I was too far away.

The people around him were too loud, they drowned me out. I walked faster and called again.

Hey, I called and started to run.

I was shouting his name now and waving my arms, I didn't care what they thought of me, what did I care? But as I got close a cab whipped around a corner and paused at the curb, and the whole mob of them swept inside, and the door slammed in my face and the car sped away. It all happened in the space of a breath.

There was a moment when my fist was against the window and his face behind it, just inches away. Our breaths clouded either side of the glass at the same point. Then he turned away and all I saw were taillights.

But it could not have been him.

It was someone who looked a bit like him.

Your mind will do that sometimes, when you want very badly to see someone; your mind will conjure him up before you, will draw your eye to an approximate head of hair, a close-enough pair of shoulders.

The cab was gone but it was all right because suddenly I knew these street lamps, this tobacco shop, that house-dress hung out the window to dry. Here was our hotel. The flower seller waved to me again and showed her teeth. God, she looks even older than yesterday, how does she keep going? And the woman at the front desk glared at me as if to say: what are you doing here now, this place is for sleeping and making love and you're no good at either.

The seasons here are strange and vague. It feels too grotty for spring, too humid for autumn, it's a perpetual waiting, the charged stillness before a thunderstorm. What month is it? But it doesn't matter, we crossed some significant line when we came here, didn't we, so the seasons are the reverse of what they are at home. Or did we lose a day? Gain a day?

I packed my things into my half of the suitcase. We had drawn a line down the middle of it. I wanted to be ready.

I did not hear footsteps on the stairs until evening.

Where have you been? I said.

What? he said. He said: This is Vera.

Vera had the eyes like they all do, and the hennaed hair, and thick white legs. I had never seen anything like them, perfectly smooth, hairless, solid, opaque like marble.

She said something I could not make out.

The room was too crowded, I wanted to rise up and hover in the empty space near the light fixture until I could get my bearings. His face was something I swear I had never seen before. At least the back of his head was familiar.

Come have dinner with us, he said.

Did he say it to her, or me? Which side of *us* was I on?

We drank bottles and bottles of wine, and I was fascinated by the way she ate, pulling things apart with her fingers and sucking out their insides. My throat closed up at the soup which I swear was full of things still alive and swimming. But the candles were nice, and I felt happy and stroked and squeezed his knee under the table and he gave me understanding looks all evening.

What are you talking about? I said.

Yes, I know, it's noisy in here isn't it? he said.

No, I can't... I'm not following the conversation.

He smiled at me. You're drunk, aren't you?

He turned back to Vera but that was all right, he and I did not need to talk, we understood each other. He kept talking to her so that she would not start to feel uncomfortable, shut out. He was considerate that way.

It was not until we were leaving that I saw that what I had thought was his knee was the knobby corner of his chair.

When we went back to our hotel room Vera came with us.

She's very tired, he said. And she lives so far away.

That seemed legitimate. It seemed only right to show her some hospitality, since we were guests in her country.

I tried to express this to her but she blinked her black-rimmed eyes at me impatiently and waited for him to explain. These people, they have no sense of graciousness. Maybe they have no vocabulary for *please* and *thank you*. She slept heavily, deeply, she filled the room with her breath.

The towers outside the window had grown during the day. They blocked more sky than before. I had never been able to find them when I was out walking on the streets, I could see them only from this window.

I suppose this is because the maps they give tourists are not entirely accurate. They want to steer you to certain areas so they can sell you cheap trinkets and marionettes and overpriced film and toothpaste. They want to force you through the gauntlet of jugglers and dancing bears and street artists.

He seemed very far away on the other side of the bed, I could not even feel his cold feet, or the toenails that usually scratched me during his running dreams. The hump in the mattress seemed to have grown, I could hardly see him. There was a tuft of hair, or it could have been the blanket.

Vera came out of the bathroom and asked me something unintelligible, nostrils dancing.

What?

You should try harder to understand, he scolded me. She's speaking perfectly clearly.

I'm trying, I said. When are we leaving?

I have to check the train schedule. Make some room in the suitcase for Vera.

Why?

She's bringing a few things.

But...why?

You can't expect her to use your things all the time, can you?
She's *coming?* What about us?
What about *us?*
His *us* seemed subtly different from mine; his seemed to involve the closed bathroom door. I was not sure though and did not ask again.
I did not see him again until evening when he came back to the room with Vera and Marat. Marat's an *architecture* student, he told me confidingly. She *builds* things.
But *I* used to be an architecture student, I said desperately.
He said: You quit.
Then he said something to the two women that made them laugh. Marat had a black bob and thick bangs that covered her eyebrows and most of her eyes. She was tall and angular, not like most of the women here, but I knew she was one of them.
I watched them talking, the language has such an ugly sound, rough and rattling, they must have crenellated throats.
Marat asked to borrow some of my underwear since she had none of her own. First she asked me, and then when I didn't understand she pantomimed her request with ugly flapping gestures. She and Vera rolled their eyes and snickered.
Why are you being so rude? he said to me.
Why are *you* being so rude? I said.
Now you're just being obnoxious, he said.
Marat snored, and Vera snored. And *he* snored too. I had never noticed that before.
The next night he came bringing Vera, and Marat, and Anna and her twelve-year-old, Lars. The room was too crowded to move, the noise was unbearable. What were they all laughing about?
He came close to me and breathed harsh gutturals in my ear.
What?
He said: Make some more room in the suitcase.

I said: There isn't any more room.

He said: You could take your things out.

But I don't want to.

Then *make* room.

But what are you doing? What about me?

What *about* you?

Don't you care?

What is it? Are you sick? Do you need a Tylenol?

No! What's going on here? I don't understand!

You don't, do you? he said. And you refuse to try.

I don't even understand anything these people are saying.

If you'd try, you'd learn. You're so self-centered.

But I *am* trying, I said. I looked at him and wondered when he had started oiling his hair and wearing his shirt unbuttoned like that, and where had he got that gold medallion? And when had he started speaking with an accent like that? Surely he was putting it on, as a pretension, as a joke, and we'd laugh about it later.

I am trying, I said. Are we breaking up? I whispered.

Break? Break something? he said, and I saw his eyes waver the way the eyes will when a person doesn't quite understand what you're saying but doesn't want to admit it. I know that look, I had it myself in my high school French class: oui, oui, monsieur, les legumes sont tres cheres, il fait beau, non, non, il pleut, cette fille est belle, non? Oui, oui, madam.

Just keep nodding, smiling.

Marat and Anna were lounging on the bed, Vera and Lars were leaning out the window smoking cigarettes. He left to buy wine and came back and passed it around and Marat pointed to the tulip-headed towers in the distance and I suppose she was explaining where they were and who built them and why, she was naming all the gargoyles, and I would have liked so much to know but I had no idea what she was saying.

And the next night they were back, and they brought the blind flower-seller and a bartender named Yves and some girls who were too young to be of consequence, and someone's uncle who needed to leave the country right away, and they all crammed their things into the suitcase so that it became an incredible snarl of hair-dryer cords, make-up cases, diapers (because there was a baby somewhere— you could smell it), rayon scarves, walkman radios, bathing suits, rolling papers, uncooked pasta, pearl necklaces, sunglasses.

And I suppose I should take out my things to make more room for the others but I don't want to, not yet; I suppose we are leaving any day now, any day. The train schedule, where did he put it? He's always losing things, it's one of his endearing quirks. This is something he and I will laugh about later, I am sure, but for now the noise is getting unbearable, the baby crying all night, and these people with their constant talking. What can they possibly have to say to each other?

The room is so crowded that I spend my time walking the streets. But these people everywhere, I don't know them, I don't *want* to know them, it's impossible. It's only natural to want to be with the person who understands you. True communication is the most intimate thing there is; you don't want to share it with everyone.

Earlier today, in a small grocery store, I stood in front of a thick-faced cashier for an hour with a package of crackers in one hand and two bills in the other. She would neither take the money nor acknowledge my presence. A stand-off. I know my mouth was open, I know sounds were coming out. But I had lost the guidebook, with the native phrases spelled out phonetically. I think some boys stole it to roll homemade cigarettes with its pages.

The cashier's eyes followed a fly beating itself against the window. She was in no hurry. The shadows lengthened. Time passed. *Common courtesy*, a voice in my head said over and over.

Common courtesy. I admired her head. A big solid head. It would look good on the bone church.

My own skull, I realize now, would never fit in. It is too oddly shaped. Too pointy.

I suppose if it all gets to be too much I can leave, put my things in a plastic bag, get on the train with the spacious vinyl seats and the empty beer bottle rolling up and down the aisle, go on ahead to the next stop listed in the guidebook, if I can remember it, and he will catch up with me as soon as he can.

But I would hate to leave him here all alone.

The hotel room now is just a mass of bodies, cookstoves, tents, shanties, music, dancing arms and bobbing breasts, boys pitching pennies, stray dogs, the burned smell of someone curling their hair, a bazaar of stalls selling rugs and copper kettles, laundry hanging on lines overhead, the endlessly overflowing toilet. The walls are grease-stained, the bare bulb a small sun. He is still there among them, shaking hands, kissing men on both cheeks, kissing women on the lips as is the custom here. His face is tanned dark mahogany brown though as far as I can tell he never goes outside.

Every time I catch sight of him in the crowd I ask when we are leaving, and he looks past me as a stream of incoherence pours from his mouth. I am sure he just does it so as not to offend the others.

It would make them feel left out.

Matt Bell lives with his wife Jessica in Ann Arbor, Michigan, where he is currently working on his first novel. His stories have appeared in *Hobart*, *Juked*, *Caketrain*, and *McSweeney's Internet Tendency*. He can be found online at www.mdbell.com. Bell's "Mario's Three Lives" appeared in the literary magazine *Barrelhouse* and the podcast *Bound Off*.

The plumber has three lives left or else he is already dead. Maybe he leaps across the gorge with ease, flying high through the air to land safely on the other side. The jump is simple because he's able to check the edge several times, waiting until he is sure of his footing, or else it's impossible because on this world there's an invisible hand pushing him forward, speeding him along, forcing him to leap before he's ready. If that happens then the plumber is going to die. Otherwise he continues his quest, sprinting and jumping to hit blocks with his head and turtles with his ass. The blocks contain either money or food, gold coins or else mushrooms and flowers he can devour to grow bigger or stronger. Sometimes they make him fly and shoot fireballs from his fingertips. Of course, he does not actually eat anything. The closest they ever come to an orifice is when he jumps up and lands on them with his ass, just like he does to the turtles. He eats with his ass. He kills with his ass. His ass is a multi-purpose tool. Why do I have a mouth, he thinks, if I never speak or eat with it? He wonders if it's this way for everyone but there's nobody to ask. The only people he knows are the Princess, who's been abducted, and his brother, who is always missing but who the plumber knows would carry on his quest if he should fail.

The plumber always dies with the same surprised look on his face, his mouth hanging open as he flies upward through the air before being born again at the beginning of the world. He's tiny and frightened without his mushrooms and his fireballs, desperately banging his head against blocks, looking for more. Sometimes, between reincarnations, the plumber thinks he senses God trying to decide whether to give him another chance or to just bag the whole thing. He's scared then, but who wouldn't be? He prays for continuation and then God says Continue and the music plays that means the plumber will live again. Back in the world, he realizes that the God he senses between deaths is there when he's alive too, guiding his motions. His triumphs are God's triumphs but so are his failures. It bothers him that God can fail but he doesn't show it. He is a stoic little plumber, looking for mushrooms and jumping on turtles. He is not a philosopher, or at least not until after the Princess is safe and he has the time to think things through. Still, sometimes when he's alive and running or, heaven forbid, swimming, he realizes that the God Who Continues is possibly not the only god there is. Surely, that god isn't the one who put all the collapsing platforms and strange, angry wildlife everywhere. At first he thinks it's the Turtle King, the one who captured the Princess and started him on this whole adventure, but then he thinks, Who made the Turtle King? Not

God, or at least not his God. Does this prove the existence of the Devil? He doesn't know.

The plumber stomps the tiny mushroom headed foes who wobble towards him, trying to kill him but succeeding only if he's completely careless. He bounces from one head to another, crushing a whole troop of them without touching the ground once. He is an efficient weapon, and these lowliest of enemies are no more than an inconvenience. Crawling through a maze of green pipes, the plumber realizes that he doesn't believe the Devil made the turtles or their king, because that would mean the Devil also made the world and that he will not accept. He hopes he is on the side of good and decides that he must be. He is on a quest to save the Princess, and surely that is a good thing.

Now there is snow covering the land, so he slips and slides precariously down hills toward open crevasses. He springs into the air and bounces off a winged turtle to reach a higher cliff, slipping across the icy landscape. There is money everywhere and although he picks up as much as he can it never gets too heavy. This is because it is constantly disappearing from his pockets, going who knows where. All the plumber knows is that when he's found a lot of gold it makes it easier to come back after he falls down a pit or gets hit by some spiky creature thrown from the sky. The more money he finds, the less he ends up in the Place Where One Waits Between Continues. He hates that place, with its tense anticipation, and so he looks everywhere for gold coins or else green mushrooms, which both make the same music and have the same life-giving effect.

Finally, he sees the castle in the distance. He's passed several fake ones on his way here, convincing replicas built on other worlds, but he knows that this is the real deal. The Princess is there and so is the Turtle King. He enters.

The plumber leaps across lava and disintegrating paths. He

ducks under spikes falling from ceilings and kills every enemy in his path. His mouth, his stupid useless mouth, it is smiling. Soon he will save the Princess. He eats a red mushroom and turns into a giant. He eats a flower and breathes fire. The Turtle King must not defeat him. The music plays and the final fight begins, but the plumber cannot win. He dies until he runs out of lives and then he waits for God to say Continue. He waits for a long time and so he knows that God is frustrated with him. He wants to say, you're the one controlling me. It's your fault too. Give me one more chance, he prays, and I will do exactly as you say. I will jump when you say jump. I will run when you say run. I will hit anyone with my ass that you want me to hit. Please, just say the word and I shall be yours. God ponders and then says Continue, or else he doesn't. The plumber saves the Princess, or else the Turtle King conquers everything. There is no way of knowing what God will do until the moment he does it. He prays and prays. It's all any plumber can do.

THE NAMING OF THE ISLANDS
David Hollander

David Hollander is the author of the novel *L.I.E.*, and his short fiction has appeared or is forthcoming in *McSweeney's, Post Road, Unsaid, Swink, The Black Warrior Review, Sleeping Fish,* and elsewhere. Hollander lives in Brooklyn with his wife, the writer Margaret Hundley Parker, and their daughter, Percy. "The Naming of the Islands" first appeared in *McSweeney's.*

Now in our fourth year of exile, a crew of rogues and reprobates aboard the battered carrack *Scapegrace*, we run our weary figure 8's, slicing through black water and sea foam, searching for a country of our own. Attenuated through hardships uncountable, a thousand miles from our native waters and unable to conceive of a return journey (back into the custody of our condemners, who would not likely take mercy a second time), we trip across the swollen boards, *The Scapegrace* slowly folding in upon her own brittle skeleton. We have yawed beneath towering black waves, survived the screaming violence of moonless storms and sawtooth lightning, our unskilled crew cowering beneath the yards. Lacking the initiative to strike out anew upon the deep, it is among these islands that we must find shelter, or perish. And so we circle and drop anchor, we man our shallops, plugging the holes with salvaged wads of hemp and sealing the seams with wax, and investigate these many beaches. We have never come upon the same island twice, or if we have the islands themselves have metamorphosed. Land masses jut from the sea all around us, most of them scarred and lifeless bedrock, gray-black and canted. And while most of our excursions to these various shores—*The Scapegrace* a bony silhouette at red dawn, our oars digging us to harbor—have revealed nothing but uninhabitable stone peaks and parapets, there have been exceptions both queer and redoubtable. It is these that we have determined to chronicle herein. We name these islands according to Common Law, in the assumption that we are the first examples of civilized men to have infiltrated them, however inadvertently. Our stores run low, and the crew survives on stubs of salt meat and brackish water, the occasional belt of whiskey. Exhausted and bellicose, we lay claim among these islands designed by a deranged and unhappy Creator.

FIRE

For five full days we'd sailed the shallow straits between desolate black crags, growing increasingly certain that no living thing endured this archipelago. Resentment brewed aboard *The Scapegrace* and we quarreled often, a few among us even advocating an improvident return to the open sea. It seemed that our fortunes had improved upon spotting this lonely islet in the middle distance, its shores stippled with flowering vegetation. Cheers went up and joviality briefly prevailed, the promise of food and fresh water quashing any dissent. We lowered down in parties of four, crooning a familiar chantey as we dug for shore. But soon a deathly quiet fell, punctuated only by the lonely splash of our oars.

For we had spotted the inhabitants, their skin blackened and charred, a patchwork of raw meat shining from beneath those jackets of crisp flesh. Their eyes glowed by contrast, two milk-white fishes swimming in the damaged dark. We watched them from our shallops, rowing so close to shore that when a red pyre streamed suddenly from the side of a cliff we were blistered by the heat; recoiling, we saw a wall of blue flame roar fiercely on the beach, then subside a moment later, the white sand scorched into glassy dark scoria. Combustion forced up from the island's buried heart, a place too deep—or so we ultimately decided—to be exposed by our shovels and pick-axes (for we are desperate and arrogant men, and briefly considered the prospect of dousing the flames through such an excavation, pouring casks of seawater over the swollen red interior).

Some of our crew suggest that the island floats atop a tremendous volcano, that trapped lava pushes up through the ground as if through pores in the flesh. Others— contrite men who have found their God on this voyage—insist that we have stumbled upon the gateway to the underworld, that hell itself is twenty fathoms down. They look upon the scorched and lumpen natives as one would the misshapen heretics populating the inferno. But having navigated the island's full perimeter from *The Scapegrace*, having pointed our dinghies toward all beaches, those of us in the scouting parties know better. We have seen them huddle together on a patch of recently destroyed earth, pockets of flame still sizzling in the high branches of blackened trees (which resembled nothing so much as our own sun-seared and emaciated bodies). They did not warn us away, these savages, nor react poorly to our approach. There was no tortured wailing, no gnashing of teeth. Beneath smoking boughs, dancing atop the glowing embers of scorched earth, their bare feet inured to this lesser heat, *they did not hesitate to wave us in.* They called to us in voices hoarse and broken, in a dry, reptilian language we did not recognize as human. The message, however, was clear. *It is safe to land*, their haunted eyes conveyed. *Come to us.*

We did not set foot upon their floating furnace, but watching these aborigines fry was a sport we could not deny ourselves. Our smaller boats retrieved aboard *The Scapegrace*, a half mile off shore, we enjoyed the blazes by evening, red and orange and blue, the island undergoing its terrible ablutions beneath the silver glow of a crescent moon. Dark figures ran screaming into the shallows, the scent of their cooked flesh drifting out to our salivating men. We watched a dozen of them burn that night, making hollow wagers—for what would we actually proffer up?—our mirth bubbling on the hot night air. By morning, we were gone.

BLOCK

A half-day's treacherous sail through coarse channels and around rocky promontories delivered to us this uninhabited flatland. We dropped anchor and reconnoitered the island through a halcyon night, eager now to avoid any of the earth's dark business. Satisfied, we stepped upon the sand at dawn, extending our hands into a veil of thick green fog and stumbling blindly until the sun vaporized the noxious haze. Then we lowered our makeshift weapons and pivoted like synchronized gears in the loose yellow sand.

All around us, geometric forms rose from the earth, great blocks and spheres and pyramids of seamless design, without brick or mortar, constructed of the same pale sand from which they scaled. Sometimes three hundred feet in height, these shapes arranged themselves into the distance and obscured the horizon. We trekked on, leaving behind the silhouette of *The Scapegrace* and descending deeper into the island's interior, hoping to discover something *other*, for surely some race of fantastic mathematicians and engineers had preceded us here. Dazed and without compass, we wandered through an enormous geometry of shadows, stopping only to sip our rationed water and to chew a bit of dried fish beneath squares and rhomboids of impossible dimension. The silence was as dense as cream. No bird chirped; no breeze stirred; the sun roasted our bare backs whenever we abandoned the shade. We found nothing, of course, and by the time we thought to retreat to *The Scapegrace* dusk had arrived, and with it the same smothering fog. A few of our men (the vain and superstitious) panicked, invoking old myths of angry Gods and their maledictions, insisting that we make for our ship immediately. But without recourse to our own path, nor to sun nor constellations, we could do nothing but make camp. Fitful sleep overcame us beneath the rough walls of a tremendous rectangle, its outlines lost in the darkening haze, which grew heavier and took on the smell of smoke and rum.

In the night, whilst we dreamt of devils and beheadings, the island rearranged itself.

We had nodded off within yards of each other, but woke to find ourselves dispersed. The great rectangle no longer towered above us, though other blocks and semicircles had emerged nearby, as if the island had been renovated by a race of nocturnal giants. Scattered hundreds of yards apart, we began shouting into the warm air, slowly reconvening to find ourselves short one man, Ernest Penton, who had committed a patricide so grisly that even his peers aboard *The Scapegrace* shuddered to hear the details. The fog was beginning to burn off, and after gathering our meager possessions— a few swords, a single gunpowder matchlock loaded with pebbles, our remaining provisions—we set out after him, moving as a human wall through the remaining haze.

We found him impaled atop a great pyramid which had risen in the night, his bright blood streaming down its sides, his face turned back toward the distant ground, his innards strung from the hole in his torso like holiday streamers. He seemed about to ask us a question.

When we tried scaling the sides, hoping to retrieve him, we found them slick as ice and just as solid. We might have waited another day, allowed for the possibility of his body's return via the same silent mechanism that rendered him airborne. Instead we abandoned his corpse with feelings of spite and envy, huffing recklessly eastward until we sighted *The Scapegrace* floating like a gargantuan oak casket, happy to welcome the moribund back upon her familiar creaking decks.

HART

A day to the south, through smaller, rocky outcroppings that none among us recognized (despite our charts, which suggest our having crossed these latitudes previously), our hopes were again stirred by a lush green island, a forest of tall trees at its center and a smooth crescent bay inviting our approach. By now the pattern was familiar, each incipient uprising aboard the *Scapegrace* ended precipitously by some new promising islet bobbing in the black. Redolent honeysuckle clung to the warm breeze as we pulled toward shore, famished but certain that here there would be meat and fresh water, that our bodies (if not our pruned souls) would be renewed. Sure enough, not fifteen feet from shore we spied a tremendous sea turtle basking in the shallows. Watson leapt into the lapping surf and grappled with the lazy monster. Two more men followed, and soon we'd slit the leathery throat and shared the warm blood from the stump of its neck, stowing the carcass in the bottom of our boat to be later roasted, carapace and all.

So satisfied were we with the blood in our bellies and thoughts of turtle meat that we did not immediately notice the drumming. But now, sated and staring into dense green brush pocked with erotic color, we bristled with awareness of a steady pounding that could mean only one thing: if we wanted this island, and already we did, we would have to take it by violence. With pointed spears and chipped shortswords, we crept from white sand into soft foliage and crooked scrub pines, their sweet-smelling sap running red from knots and twisted roots.

Huge black flies swarmed around us; the soil was dark and rich; purple berries clung to shrubs and we chewed them greedily, surprised by the thickness of the juice that ran down our chins and necks. The unceasing drumming called us forward through brush that now grew thick and thorny, and when finally a stubborn branch caught Thompson across the bridge of his nose he swung his sword angrily into the thicket.

At once the severed branches began spouting bright red blood. Glowing, it cascaded across Thompson's bare chest and onto the black soil of the canopy floor. We will die, I am sure, with this image in our minds: vegetation spraying gore, its salty odor cutting through the fecundity of an accursed forest.

And yet what could we do but push importunately forward? Aboard *The Scapegrace* a dozen of our comrades awaited our return, starving and jaundiced, mouths ripe with rotten teeth. We lowered our blades and slid gingerly through this dense woodland. The drumming was ominously regular, *ONE-two-three, ONE-two-three...* it's rhythm etched into our movements. Insects buzzed and bit; we slapped at our flesh and left their pasted carcasses there, a pox of winged viscera upon skinny sunburnt bodies. The needles shivered in the pines and the brush squeezed tighter against us, until after a time (one hour? five?) we penetrated a clearing of strange, nacreous sand, at the center of which was a small pond perhaps twenty feet in diameter.

Submerged beneath a clear syrupy liquid—not water, but something more akin to honey in consistency—there pounded a tremendous heart, the size of three men. From beneath this fist-shaped apparatus shoots and scions ran out and into the soil, their gnarled bark throbbing. Black seams in thick bark spread with each contraction to reveal a lurid red skin. And then one of us—Aiden Hart, who in our homeland had brutally raped and murdered a seamstress—took his spear and pushed it through that clarified honey, gently piercing this enormous, pulsing organ which, puckering, released a stream of bubbles into its liquid amnion.

The percussive tempo increased immediately, that same *ONE-two-three* but in double time now, and higher in pitch. We stood perfectly still. A moment passed. And another. A fly landed silently on Watson's forehead. And then the entire island began to hemorrhage.

We spun and ran. All around us, leaves and pods began to explode, making small hissing noises and spraying thick heliotrope liquid into the air. Pine needles emitted a fiery drizzle as we sprinted through thornbushes, swinging our swords indiscriminately now, rampaging through fountains of blood, a high sun baking it to our burnt skins, the pungency of slaughtered hogs hanging ripe in the hot, wet air. There were men among us screaming, if I recall correctly, and the island trembled as if built upon an uncertain foundation.

Our shallop awaited us, the turtle's carcass a quainter form of butchery, its severed head's dead eyes chronicling our departure into water stained violet, the dye running out in an immense cloud, the island dying in our wake. Rowing away, we watched it happen: trees reduced to crisp yellow husks, vegetation crumbling to black ash, black soil bleached pale as the living island bled out. After a moment, we remembered the turtle, and our thoughts turned to whether or not we were responsible for sharing this meager sustenance with those left behind on *The Scapegrace*, which we approached as if from the most wicked of battles, painted in the colors of warfare and massacre.

ABOARD

By now the decks of our carrack simmer with violence. Hungry pugilists swing tumid fists and we all take sides, eager for blood. None among us can countenance a return to the sea, but those who had once advocated such a course now openly vow murder upon those responsible for our vagaries among these dire straits. The astrolabe was found destroyed yesterday at dawn, the celestial bodies chiseled from its face and the device entire nailed to the foremast. A futile act of protest, or else crude misanthropic humor. This log is now kept fast and secreted from harm; it is our last precious connection to the realm whose liberties we squandered. Nights pass beneath a waning sulfur moon and our desiccated bodies give out one by withered one. And yet the Almighty toys with us. Just as weapons are drawn aboard our creaking decks, just as men declare their blood pacts with parched and swollen tongues, we sight some previously undiscoverable bit of earth. It is as if these islets were humps on the spine of an enormous serpent that rolled lazily near the surface, renewing our dimwitted hopes before descending again into the drink. But must every island mete out some new variety of punishment? Can there not be that one upon whose shores even such men as these might find redemption? We lower down again and again, in search of that single palatable fate.

RAT

More rock than island, this craggy mound of feldspar glinted and shimmered from a distance of two miles, persuading us to turn the bow of our sluggish and beloved carrack and make cautiously for the reflected light. Riding a deep sluice of black water, the smell of sulfur rising, we drifted to within two hundred yards. We lowered a boat and rowed to within a stone's throw, only to confirm the supposed illusion: this rocky wafer—barely larger than our own *Scapegrace*—was covered in them. Rats. They swarmed over every inch of ground, their skins like hot tar, ten thousand oily rodents with pink tails swinging serpentine. On this stony hummock they fornicated with and devoured one another (as if these acts were synonymous), twin-chisel teeth tearing madly into the pink flesh of a lover, a child, a parent. A frenzied mass of sex and carnage, blood and semen, writhing on mounds of their own ripe excrement, the testicles of the larger males dangling like dark plums.

We did not land, but we approached the pernicious shoreline, reaching out to snatch two dozen of the little demons, risking fingers and suffering filthy puncture wounds, whipping them by unctuous tails against the shallop's pine boards. And then we rowed back with our eldritch cargo, Thompson vomiting over the side, though with our shrunken stomachs even the bile has dried up, so that he wretched a sort of yellow ash.

But this meal of rat meat cut our hunger and delivered another tentative peace. We gutted them on the decks of *The Scapegrace*, roasted them whole. We devoured them down to the bones, which we chewed on for days, sucking at the greasy pink marrow that tasted like sweat and treacle, surprisingly sweet. We have tried in vain to return to Rat Island, to feast again on this bounty. Alas—it, too, has disappeared.

The Twins

Not three full days ago, we sailed through a shallow breech between identical islands, their silver shores tapered down from low green hills, mirror images of fecundity. And yet we know well enough to distrust these first giddy impressions. Our bodies wasted down to kindling (just that day our numbers dwindled to ten, as two more succumbed to starvation accelerated by enteric disease, their corpses still warm and flushed with fever hours after their passing, when we dumped them over the side), we flipped a coin stamped with our beloved monarch's image to choose between islands, and the five strongest among our fast-expiring crew lowered down and dug in. We beached the shallop in soft sand, hopping barefoot upon the island, our bodies pocked with pink sores and blue bruises.

Once on land, we immediately took to halfhearted quarreling. Should we seek out the island's fresh water, our fundamental commodity, of which we had but a few days supply remaining? Or should we concentrate our efforts on food, the gathering of roots and berries, or the possible (though unlikely) discovery of jungle boar rippling with muscle?

As we bickered, swollen bees zipped by like striped bits of pastry, an emerald forest one hundred yards inland exuding humidity like a sweet liqueur. Watson was the first to identify the rustling in the branches. We noticed him staring into the greenery, and one by one we shut our mouths and joined him in scrutiny. A moment later a call went up, too loud and too shrill to be the voice of any shore bird. The arrows followed, a hundred or more, soaring from the forest in a slow, high arc, and then emerging just behind them a phalanx of painted aborigines, their spears piercing the warm air, their war cries cleaving the hazy sunlight, a verdict of sorts. We had found our cannibals.

In a harried dance we dodged the lazy arrows, all of us but Watson. His thigh skewered, he dropped to the beach, a thin fountain of blood erupting from the wound as the rest of us boarded the shallop and pushed off. Ah, Watson! He tried to rise, his wasted body all wire and parchment. We watched them overtake him as we pulled wildly at our oars, unprepared after all for true warfare, made fainthearted by our more private battles with dysentery, intestinal flu, scurvy, and sea fever. The savages enveloped him like ants dismantling a piece of gristle.

We did not set out immediately for *The Scapegrace*, however. The four of us made instead for the second island, drifting beneath the shadow of our carrack's bow (where no man stood watch). Already the ordeal seemed unreal to us, resembling as it did the architecture of our many fevered dreams.

Still, when we found his body—on the *second* island—his face half-eaten, his limbs severed and strewn about, his trunk eviscerated, our cowardice was as palpable as a furry moth. He stared at us through enormous eyes, his serpent tattoo the clearest indicator that it was in fact our shipmate, Watson. From where we stood, the first island was a yellow hump in the middle distance. Fearful of the savages' return, we loaded the carcass piece by bloody piece into the shallop, figuring burial at sea was the least we could offer one of our own. Before pushing off, Hart could not help but perform the simplest of experiments. He raised his hackbut toward the sky and pulled the matchlock, firing its single shot. Sure enough, a second powder blast could be clearly heard, an instant later, from the other island, where a tiny puff of smoke drifted upward. Another set of ourselves stood there, performing this same experiment, feeling as we did that theirs was the power of autonomy, and that these men across the channel were mere reflections, shadows, phantom twins risen from mysterious ether.

Adrift

Rowing back for *The Scapegrace* we descried our doubles returning from *their* island, and some strange conflux seemed all but assured. But the nearer we approached, the less substantial their forms became, dissipating into the same ether from which they had congealed. Not even the ripple of their oars survived our arrival alongside our carrack, which we boarded with eerie suspicions regarding our own solidity. Watson's blood stained our flesh and we felt certain that we were being watched, aware not only of our vanished twins but also of their own invisible *Scapegrace* which endured some uncanny permutation of our fruitless odyssey.

We have since spotted, in the near distance, a long flat island whose barrier beach displays a sunken forest of scrub pines. Toward this next inevitability we creep, with tattered sails clutching at a slight easterly breeze and our carrack moaning, seemingly chagrined. Above deck the last of our fevered crew debate the surest channel through treacherous shallows, their rusting weapons at the ready, would-be malcontents and mutineers but shipmates above all else, bound together by fate and by character. Does suffering in one precinct of the cosmos alleviate the burden elsewhere? Is there a single Almighty, or rather a multitude thereof, each working in mad isolation on His own dubious project? This chronicle exists under lock in the ship's binnacle, and also in the minds of a thousand doppelgangers, whose more fortunate destinies exist, unwritten, in the recesses of my own internal seascape. Momentarily, we pull again for shore.

THE DROWNED LIFE
Jeffrey Ford

Jeffrey Ford's first published story, "The Casket," appeared in John Gardner's magazine *MSS* in 1981, and since then his work has appeared in numerous magazines and anthologies and has won the Nebula, Fountain, Edgar Allan Poe, and World Fantasy Awards. He is the author of seven novels and three short story collections, including, most recently, *The Shadow Year* and *The Drowned Life*. He is a professor of writing and literature at Brookdale Community College in New Jersey, and he has been an instructor at the Clarion Workshop. "The Drowned Life" is from the Jonathan Strahan-edited *Eclipse 1* anthology.

1

It came trickling in over the transom at first, but Hatch's bailing technique had grown rusty. The skies were dark with daily news of a pointless war and genocide in Africa, poverty, aids, desperate millions in migration. The hot air of the commander in chief met the stone cold bullshit of congress and spawned water spouts, towering gyres of deadly ineptitude. A steady rain of increasing gas prices, grocery prices, medical costs, drove down hard like a fall of needles. At times the mist was so thick it baffled the mind. Somewhere in a back room, Liberty, Goddess of the Sea, was tied up and blind folded—wires leading out from under her toga and hooked to a car battery. You could smell her burning, an acid stink that rode the fierce winds, turning the surface of the water brown.

Closer by, three sharks circled in the swells, their fins visible above chocolate waves. Each one of those slippery machines of Eden stood for a catastrophe in the secret symbolic nature of this story. One was *Financial Ruin*, I can tell you that – a stainless steel beauty whose sharp maw made Hatch's knees literally tremble like in a cartoon. In between the bouts of bailing, he walked a tightrope. At one end of his balancing pole was the weight of the bills, a mortgage like a Hydra, whose head grew back each month, for a house too tall and too shallow, taxes out the ass, failing appliances, car payments. At the other end was his job at an HMO, denying payment to people with legitimate claims. Each conversation with each claimant was harrowing for him, but he was in no position to quit. What else would he do? Each poor sop denied howled with indignation and unallied pain at the injustice of it all. Hatch's practiced façade, his dry, "Sorry," hid indigestion, headaches, sweats, and his constant, subconscious reiteration of Darwin's law of survival as if it were some golden rule.

Beyond that, the dog had a chronic ear infection, his younger son, Ned, had recently been picked up by the police for smoking pot and the older one, Will, who had a severe case of athlete's foot, rear ended a car on route 70. "Just a tap. Not a scratch," he'd claimed, and then the woman called with her dizzying estimate. Hatch's wife, Rose, who worked 12 hours a day, treating the people at a hospital whose claims he would eventually turn down, demanded a vacation with tears in her eyes. "Just a week, somewhere warm," she said. He shook his head and laughed as if she was kidding. It was rough seas between his ears and rougher still in his heart. Each time he laughed, it was in lieu of puking.

Storm Warning was a phrase that made surprise visits to his consciousness while he sat in front of a blank computer screen at work, or hid in the garage at home late at night smoking one of the Captain Blacks he'd supposedly quit, or stared listlessly at Celebrity Fit Club on the television. It became increasingly difficult for him to remember births, first steps, intimate hours with Rose, family jokes, vacations in packed cars, holidays with extended family. One day Hatch did less bailing. "Fuck that bailing," he thought. The next day he did even less.

As if he'd just awakened to it, he was suddenly standing in water up to his shins and the rain was beating down on a strong southwester. The boat was bobbing like the bottom lip of a crone on Thorozine as he struggled to keep his footing. In his hands was a small plastic garbage can, the same one he'd used to bail his clam boat when at eighteen he worked the Great South Bay. The problem was Hatch wasn't eighteen anymore, and though now he was spurred to bail again with everything he had, he didn't have much. His heart hadn't worked so hard since his 25th anniversary when Rose made him climb a mountain in Montana. Even though the view at the top was gorgeous – a basin lake and a breeze out of heaven—his t-shirt jumped with each beat. The boat was going down. He chucked the garbage can out into the sea and *Financial Ruin* and its partners tore into it. Reaching for his shirt pocket, he took out his smokes and lit one.

The cold brown water was just creeping up around Hatch's balls as he took his first puff. He noticed the dark silhouette of Captree Bridge in the distance. "Back on the bay," he said, amazed to be sinking into the waters of his youth, and then, like a struck wooden match, the entire story of his life flared and died behind his eyes.

Going under was easy. No struggle, but a change in temperature. Just beneath the dark surface, the water got wonderfully clear. All the stale air came out of him at once – a satisfying burp followed by a large translucent globe that stretched his jaw with its birth. He reached for its spinning brightness but sank too fast to grab it. His feet were still lightly touching the deck as the boat fell slowly beneath him. He looked up and saw the sharks still chewing plastic. "This is it," thought Hatch, "not with a bang but a bubble." He herded all of his regrets into the basement of his brain, an indoor oak forest with intermittent dim light bulbs and dirt floor. The trees were columns that held the ceiling and amid and among them skittered pale, disfigured doppelgangers of his friends and family. As he stood at the top of the steps and shut the door on them, he felt a subtle tearing in his solar plexus. The boat touched down on the sandy bottom and his sneakers came to rest on the deck. Without thinking, he gave a little jump and sailed in a lazy arc ten feet away, landing, with a puff of sand, next to a toppled marble column.

His every step was a graceful bound, and he floated. Once on the slow descent of his arc, he put his arms out at his sides and lifted his feet behind him so as to fly. Hatch found that if he flapped his arms, he could glide along a couple of feet above the bottom, and he did, passing over coral pipes and red seaweed rippling like human hair in a breeze. There were creatures scuttling over rocks and through the sand – long antennae and armored plating, tiny eyes on sharp stalks and claws continuously practicing on nothing. As his shoes touched the sand again, a school of striped fish swept past his right shoulder, their blue glowing like neon, and he followed their flight.

He came upon the rest of the sunken temple, its columns pitted and cracked, broken like the tusks of dead elephants. Green sea vines netted the destruction – two wide marble steps there, here a piece of roof, a tilted mosaic floor depicting the Goddess of the Sea suffering a rash of missing tiles, a headless marble statue of a man holding his penis.

2

Hatch floated down the long empty avenues of Drowned Town, a shabby, but quiet city in a lime green sea. Every so often, he'd pass one of the citizens, bloated and blue, in various stages of decomposition, and say, "Hi." Two gentlemen in suits swept by but didn't return his greeting. A drowned mother and child, bugling eyes dissolving in trails of tiny bubbles, dressed in little more than rags, didn't acknowledge him. One old woman stopped, though, and said, "Hello."

"I'm new here," he told her.

"The less you think about it the better," she said and drifted on her way.

Hatch tried to remember where he was going. He was sure there was a reason that he was in town, but it eluded him. "I'll call, Rose," he thought. "She always knows what I'm supposed to be doing." He started looking up and down the streets for a payphone. After three blocks without luck, he saw a man heading toward him. The fellow wore a business suit and an overcoat torn to shreds, a black hat with a bullet hole in it, a closed umbrella hooked on a skeletal wrist. Hatch waited for the man to draw near, but as the fellow stepped into the street to cross to the next block, a swift gleaming vision flew from behind a building and with a sudden clang of steel teeth meeting took him in its jaws. *Financial Ruin* was hungry and loose in Drowned Town. Hatch cowered backward, breast stroking to a nearby dumpster to hide, but the shark was already gone with its catch.

On the next block up, he found a bar that was open. He didn't see a name on it, but there were people inside, the door was ajar, and there was the muffled sound of music. The place was cramped and narrowed the further back you went, ending in a corner. Wood paneling, mirror behind the bottles, spinning seats, low lighting and three dead beats – two on one side of the bar and one on the other.

"Got a pay phone?" asked Hatch.

All three men looked at him. The two customers smiled at each other. The bartender with a red bow tie, wiped his rotted nose on a handkerchief, and then slowly lifted an arm to point. "Go down to the grocery store. They got a pay phone at the Deli counter."

Hatch had missed it when the old lady spoke to him, but he realized now that he heard the bartender's voice in his head, not with his ears. The old man moved his mouth, but all that came out were vague farts of words flattened by water pressure. He sat down on one of the bar stools.

"Give me something dry," he said to the bartender. He knew he had to compose himself, get his thoughts together.

The bartender shook his head, scratched a spot of coral growth on his scalp, and opened his mouth to let a minnow out. "I could make you a Jenny Diver…pink or blue?"

"No, Sal, make him one of those things with the dirt bomb in it… they're the driest," said the closer customer. The short man turned his flat face and stretched a grin like a soggy old doll with swirling hair. Behind the clear lenses of his eyes, shadows moved, something swimming through his head.

"You mean a Dry Reach. That's one dusty drink," said the other customer, a very pale, skeletal old man in a brimmed hat and dark glasses. "Remember the day I got stupid on those? Your asshole'll make hell seem like a backyard barbecue if you drink too many of them, my friend."

"I'll try one," said Hatch.

"Your wish is my command," said the bartender, but he moved none too swiftly. Still, Hatch was content to sit and think for a minute. He thought that maybe the drink would help him remember. For all of its smallness, the place had a nice relaxing current flowing through it. He folded his arms on the bar and rested his head down for a moment. It finally came to him that the music he'd heard since entering was Frank Sinatra. "The Way You Look Tonight," he whispered, naming the current song. He pictured Rose, naked, in bed back in their first apartment, and with that realization, the music went off.

Hatch looked up and saw that the bartender had turned on the television. The two customers, heads tilted back, stared into the glow. On the screen there was a news show without sound but the caption announced *News From The War*. A small seahorse swam behind the glass of the screen but in front of the black and white imagery. The story was about a ward in a makeshift field hospital where army doctors treated the wounded children of the area. Cute little faces stared up from pillows, tiny arms with casts listlessly waved, but as the report obviously went on, the wounds got more serious. There were children with missing limbs, and then open wounds, great gashes in the head, the chest, and missing eyes, and then a gaping hole with intestines spilling out, the little legs trembling and the chest heaving wildly.

"There's only one term for this war," said the old man with the sunglasses. "Clusterfuck. Cluster as in cluster and fuck as in fuck. No more need be said."

The short man turned to Hatch, and still grinning, said, "There was a woman in here yesterday, saying that we're all responsible."

"We are," said the bartender. "Drink up." He set Hatch's drink on the bar. "One Dry Reach," he said. It came in a big martini glass – clear liquid with a brown lump at the bottom.

Hatch reached for his wallet, but the bartender waved for him not to bother. "You must be new," he said.

Hatch nodded.

"Nobody messes with money down here. This is Drowned Town…think about it. Drink up, and I'll make you three more."

"Could you put Sinatra back on," Hatch asked sheepishly. "This news is bumming me out."

"As you wish," said the bartender. He pressed a red button on the wall behind him. Instantly, the television went off, and the two men turned back to their drinks. Sinatra sang "Let's take it nice and easy," and Hatch thought, "Free booze." He sipped his drink and could definitely distinguish its tang from the briny sea water. Whether he liked the taste or not, he'd decide later, but for now he drank it as quickly as he could.

The customer further from Hatch stepped around his friend and approached. "You're in for a real treat, man" he said. "You see that little island in the stream there." He pointed at the brown lump in the glass.

Hatch nodded.

"A bit of terra firma, a little taste of the world you left behind upstairs. Remember throwing dirt bombs when you were a kid? Like the powdery lumps in homemade brownies? Well you've got a dollop of high grade dirt there. You bite into it, and you'll taste your life left behind – bright sun and blue skies."

"Calm down," said the short man to his fellow customer. "Give him some room."

Hatch finished the drink and let the lump roll out of the bottom of the glass into his mouth. He bit it with his molars but found it had nothing to do with dirt. It was mushy and tasted terrible, more like a sodden meatball of decay then a memory of the sun. He spit the mess out and it darkened the water in front of his face. He waved his hand to disperse the brown cloud. A violet fish with a lazy tail swam down from the ceiling to snatch what was left of the disintegrating nugget.

The two customers and the bartender laughed, and Hatch heard it like a party in his brain. "You got the tootsie roll," said the short fellow and tried to slap the bar, but his arm moved too slowly through the water.

"Don't take it personally," said the old man. "It's a Drowned Town tradition." His right ear came off just then and floated away, his glasses slipping down on that side.

Hatch felt a sudden burst of anger. He'd never liked playing the fool.

"Sorry, fella," said the bartender, "but it's a ritual. On your first Dry Reach, you get the tootsie roll."

"What's the tootsie roll?" asked Hatch, still trying to get the taste out of his mouth.

The man with the outlandish grin said, "Well, for starters, it ain't a tootsie roll."

3

Hatch marveled at the myriad shapes and colors of sea weed in the grocery's produce section. The lovely wavering of their leaves, strands, tentacles, in the flow soothed him. Although he stood on the sandy bottom, hanging from the ceiling were rows of fluorescent lights, every third or fourth one working. The place was a vast concrete bunker, set up in long aisles of shelves like at the Super Shopper he'd trudged through innumerable times back in his dry life.

"No money needed," he thought. "And free booze, but then why the coverage of the war? For that matter why the tootsie roll?

Financial Ruin has free reign in Drowned Town. Nobody seems particularly happy. It doesn't add up." Hatch left the produce section, passed a display of anemone, some as big as his head, and drifted off, in search of the Deli counter.

The place was enormous, row upon row of shelved dead fish, their snouts sticking into the aisle, silver and pink and brown. Here and there a gill still quivered, a fin twitched. "A lot of fish," thought Hatch. Along the way, he saw a special glass case that held frozen food that had sunk from the world above. The hot dog tempted him, even though a good quarter had gone green. There was a piece of a cupcake with melted sprinkles, three French fries, a black Twizzler, and a red and white Chinese take out bag with two gnarled rib ends sticking out. He hadn't had any lunch, and his stomach growled in the presence of the delicacies, but he was thinking of Rose and wanted to talk to her.

Hatch found a familiar face at the lobster tank. He could hardly believe it, Bob Gordon from up the block. Bob looked none the worse for wear for being sunk, save for his yellow complexion. He smoked a damp cigarette and stared into the tank as if staring through it.

"Bob," said Hatch.

Bob turned and adjusted his glasses. "Hatch, what's up?"

"I didn't know you went under."

"Sure, like a fuckin stone."

"When?" asked Hatch.

"Three, four months ago. Peggy'd been porking some guy from over in Larchdale. You know, I got depressed, laid off the bailing, lost the house, and then eventually I just threw in the pail."

"How do you like it here?"

"Really good," said Bob and his words rang loud in Hatch's brain, but then he quickly leaned close and these words came in a whisper, "It sucks."

"What do you mean?" asked Hatch, keeping his voice low.

Bob's smile deflated. "Everything's fine," he said, casting a glance to the lobster tank. He nodded to Hatch. "Gotta go, bud."

He watched Bob bound away against a mild current. By the time Hatch reached the deli counter, it was closed. In fact, with the exception of Bob, he'd seen no one in the entire store. An old black phone with a rotary dial sat atop the counter with a sign next to it that read: Free Pay Phone. NOT TO BE USED IN PRIVACY!

Hatch looked over his shoulder. There was no one around. Stepping forward he reached for the receiver, and just as his hand closed on it, the thing rang. He felt the vibration before he heard the sound. He let it go and stepped back. It continued to ring, and he was torn between answering it and fleeing. Finally, he picked it up and said, "Hello."

At first he thought the line was dead, but then a familiar voice sounded. "Hatch," it said, and he knew it was Ned, his younger son. Both of his boys had called him Hatch since they were toddlers. "You gotta come pick me up."

"Where are you?" asked Hatch.

"I'm at a house party behind the 7-11. It's starting to get crazy."

"What do you mean it's starting to get crazy?"

"You coming?"

"I'll be there," said Hatch, and then the line went dead.

He stood at the door to the basement of his brain and turned the knob, but before he could open it, he saw way over on the other side of the store, one of the silver sharks, cruising above the aisles up near the ceiling. Dropping the phone, he scurried behind the Deli counter, and then through an opening that led down a hall to a door.

4

Hatch was out of breath from walking, searching for someone who might be able to help him. For ten city blocks he thought about Ned needing a ride. He pictured the boy, hair tied back, baggy shorts and shoes like slippers, running from the police. "Good grief," said Hatch and pushed forward. He'd made a promise to Ned years earlier that he would always come and get him if he needed a ride, no matter what. How could he tell him now, "Sorry kid, I'm sunk." Hatch thought of all the things that could happen in the time it would take him to return to land and pick Ned up at the party. Scores of tragic scenarios exploded behind his eyes. "I might as well be bailing," he said to the empty street.

He heard the crowd before he saw it, faint squeaks and blips in his ears and eventually they became distant voices and music. Rounding a corner, he came in sight of a huge vacant lot between two six story brown stones. As he approached, he could make out there was some kind of attraction at the back of the lot, and twenty or so Drowned Towners floated in a crowd around it. Organ music blared from a speaker on a tall wooden pole. Hatch crossed the street and joined the audience.

Up against the back wall of the lot, there was an enormous golden octopus. Its flesh glistened and its tentacles curled, unfurled, created fleeting symbols dispersed by schools of tiny angel fish constantly circling it like a halo. The creature's sucker disks were flat black as was its beak, its eyes red, and there was a heavy, rusted metal collar squeezing the base of its lumpen head as if it had shoulders and a neck. Standing next to it was a young woman, obviously part fish. She had gills and her eyes were pure black like a shark's. Her teeth were sharp. There were scales surrounding her face and her hair was some kind of fine green seaweed. She wore a clam shell brassiere and a black thong. At the backs of her heels were fan-like fins. "My name is Clementine," she said, and this beside me is Madame Mutandis. She is a remarkable specimen of the Midas Octopus, so named for the beautiful golden aura of her skin. You see the collar on the Madame and you miss the chain. Notice, it is attached to my left ankle. Contrary to what you all might believe, it is I who belong to her and not she to me."

Hatch looked up and down the crowd he was part of – an equal mixture of men and women, some more bleached than blue, some less intact. The man next to him held his mouth open, and an eel's head peered out as if having come from the bowels to check the young fish woman's performance.

"With cephalopod brilliance, non-vertebrate intuition, Madame Mutandis will answer one question for each of you. No question is out of bounds. She thinks like the very sea itself. Who'll be first?"

The man next to Hatch stepped immediately forward before anyone else. "And what is your question asked the fish woman?" The man put his hands into his coat pockets and then raised his head. His message was horribly muddled, but by his third repetition Hatch as well as the octopus got it – "How does one remove an eel?" Madame Mutandis shook her head sac as if in disdain while two of her tentacles unfurled in the man's direction. One swiftly wrapped around his throat, lurching him forward, and the other dove into his mouth. A second later, the Madame released his throat and drew from between his lips a three foot eel, wriggling wildly in her suctioned grasp. The long arm swept the eel to her beak, and she pierced it at a spot just behind the head, rendering it lifeless. With a free tentacle, she waved forward the next questioner, while, with another, brushing gently away the man now sighing with relief.

Hatch came to and was about to step forward, but a woman from behind him wearing a kerchief and carrying a beige pocketbook passed by, already asking, "Where are the good sales?" He wasn't able to see her face, but the woman with the question, from her posture and clothing, seemed middle aged, somewhat younger than himself.

Clementine repeated the woman's question for the octopus. "Where are the good sales?" she said.

"Shoes," said the woman with the kerchief. "I'm looking for shoes."

Madame Mutandis wrapped a tentacle around the woman's left arm and turned her to face the crowd. Hatch reared back at the sudden sight of a face rotted almost perfectly down the middle, skull showing through on one side. Another of the octopus's tentacles slid up the woman's skirt between her legs. With the dexterity of a hand, it drew down the questioner's underwear, leaving them gathered around her ankles. Then, wriggling like the eel it removed from the first man's mouth, that tentacle slithered along her right thigh only to disappear again beneath the skirt.

Hatch was repulsed and fascinated as the woman trembled and the tentacle wiggled out of sight. She turned her skeletal profile to the crowd, and that bone grin widened with pleasure, grimaced in pain, gaped with passion. Little spasms of sound escaped her open mouth. The crowd methodically applauded until finally the object of the Madame's attentions screamed and fell to the sand, the long tentacle retracting. The fish woman moved to the end of her chain and helped the questioner up. "Is that what you were looking for?" she asked. The woman with the beige pocketbook nodded and adjusted her kerchief before floating to the back of the crowd.

"Ladies and gentleman?" said the fish-woman.

Hatch noticed that no one was too ready to step forth after the creature's last answer, including himself. His mind was racing, trying to connect a search for a shoe sale with the resultant.. what? Rape? Or was what he witnessed consensual? He was still befuddled by the spectacle. The gruesome state of the woman's face wrapped in ecstasy hung like a chandelier of ice on the main floor of his brain. At that moment, he realized he had to escape from Drowned Town. Shifting his glance right and left, he noticed his fellow drownees were still as stone.

The fish-woman's chain must have stretched, because she floated over and put her hand on his back. Gently, she led him forward. "She can tell you anything," came Clementine's voice, a whisper that made him think of Rose and Ned and Will, even the stupid dog with bad ears. He hadn't felt his feet move, but he was there, standing before the shining perpetual motion of the Madame's eight arms. Her black parrot beak opened, and he thought he heard her laughing.

"You're question?" asked Clementine, still close by his side.

"My kid's stuck at a party that's getting crazy," blurted Hatch. "How do I get back to dry land?"

He heard murmuring from the crowd behind him. One voice said, "No." Another two said, "Asshole." At first he thought they were predicting the next answer from Madame Mutandis, but then he realized they were referring to him. It dawned that wanting to leave Drowned Town was unpopular.

"Watch the ink," said Clementine.

Hatch looked down and saw a dark plume exuding from beneath the octopus. It rose in a mushroom cloud, and then turned into a long black string at the top. The end of that string whipped leisurely through the air, drawing more of itself from the cloud until the cloud had vanished and what remained was the phrase *322 Bleeter Street* in perfect, looping script. The address floated there for a moment, Hatch repeating it, before the angel fish veered out of orbit around the fleshy golden sac and dashed through it, dispersing the ink.

The fish-woman led Hatch away and called, "Next." He headed for the street, repeating the address under his breath. At the back of the crowd, which had grown, a woman turned to him as he passed and said, "Leaving town?"

"My kid…" Hatch began, but she snickered at him. From somewhere down the back row, he heard, "Jerk," and "Pussy." When he reached the street, he realized that the words of the drowned had crowded the street number out of his thoughts. He remembered Bleeter street and said it six times, but the number… Leaping forward, he assumed the flying position, and flapping his arms, cruised down the street, checking the street signs at the corners and keeping an eye out for sharks. He remembered the number had a 3, and then for blocks he thought of nothing but that last woman's contempt.

5

Eventually, he grew too tired to fly and resumed walking, sometimes catching the current and drifting in the flow. He'd seen so many street signs—President's Names, different kinds of fish, famous actors and sunken ships, types of clouds, waves, flowers, slugs. None of them was Bleeter. So many store fronts and apartment steps passed by and not a soul in sight. At one point, tiny star fish fell like rain all over town, littering the streets and filling the awnings.

Hatch had just stepped out of a weakening current and was moving under his own volition when he noticed a phone booth wedged into an alley between two stores. Pushing off, he swam to it and squeezed himself into the glass enclosure. As the door closed, a light went on above him. He lifted the receiver, placing it next to his ear. There was a dial tone. He dialed and it rang. Something shifted in his chest and his pulse quickened. Suffering the length of each long ring, he waited for someone to pick up.

"Hello?" he heard; a voice at a great distance.

"Rose, it's me," he screamed against the water.

"Hatch," she said. "I can hardly hear you. Where are you?"

"I'm stuck in Drowned Town," he yelled.

"What do you mean? Where is it?"

Hatch had a hard time saying it. "I went under, Rose. I'm sunk."

There was nothing on the line. He feared he'd lost the connection, but he stayed with it.

"Jesus, Hatch… What the hell are you doing?"

"I gave up on the bailing," he said.

She groaned. "You shit. How am I supposed to do this alone?"

"I'm sorry, Rose," he said. "I don't know what happened. I love you."

He could hear her exhale. "OK," she said. "Give me an address. I have to have something to put into Mapquest."

"Do you know where I am?" he asked.

"No, I don't fucking know where you are. That's why I need the address."

It came to him all at once. "322 Bleeter Street, Drowned Town" he said. "I'll meet you there."

"It's going to take a while," she said.

"Rose?"

"What?"

"I love you," he said. He listened to the silence on the receiver until he noticed in the reflection of his face in the phone booth glass a blue spot on his nose and one on his forehead. "Shit," he said and hung up. "I can take care of that with some ointment when I get back," he thought. He scratched at the spot on his forehead and blue skin sloughed off. He put his face closer to the glass, and then there came a pounding on the door behind him.

Turning, he almost screamed at the sight of the half gone face of that woman who'd been goosed by the octopus. He opened the door and slid passed her. Her Jolly Roger profile was none too jolly. As he spoke the words, he surprised himself with doing so – "Do you know where Bleeter Street is?" She jostled him aside in her rush to get to the phone. Before closing the door, she called over her shoulder, "You're on it."

"Things are looking up," thought Hatch as he retreated. Standing in the middle of the street, he looked up one side and down the other. Only one building, a darkened store front with a plate glass window behind which was displayed a single pair of sunglasses on a pedestal, had a street number—621. It came to him that he would have to travel in one direction, try to find another address and see which way the numbers ran. Then, if he found they were increasing, he'd have to turn around and head in the other direction, but at least he would know. Thrilled at the sense of purpose, he swept a clump of drifting seaweed out of his way, and moved forward. He could be certain Rose would come for him. After 30 years of marriage they'd grown close in subterranean ways.

Darkness was beginning to fall on Drowned Town. Angle jawed fish with needle teeth, a perpetual scowl and sad eyes, came from the alleyways and through the open windows of the apartments, and each had a small phosphorescent jewel dangling from a downward curving stalk that issued from the head. They drifted the shadowy street like fireflies, and although Hatch had still to see another address, he stopped in his tracks to mark their beautiful effect. It was precisely then that he saw *Financial Ruin* appear from over the rooftops down the street. Before he could even think to flee, he saw the shark swoop down in his direction. Hatch turned, kicked his feet up and started flapping. As he approached the first corner, and was about to turn, he almost collided with someone just stepping out onto Bleeter Street. To his utter confusion, it was a deep sea diver, a man inside a heavy rubber suit with a glass bubble of a helmet and a giant nautilus shell strapped to his back, feeding air through two arching tubes into his suit. The sudden appearance of the diver wasn't what made him stop, though. It was the huge gun in his hands with a barbed spear head as wide as a fence post jutting from the barrel. The diver waved Hatch behind him as the shark came into view. Then it was a dagger toothed lung, a widening cavern with the speed of a speeding car. The diver pulled the trigger. There was a zip of tiny bubbles, and *Financial Ruin* curled up, thrashing madly with the spear piercing its upper pallet and poking out the back of its head. Billows of blood began to spread. The man in the suit dropped the gun and approached Hatch.

"Hurry," he said, "before the other sharks smell the blood."

6

Hatch and his savior sat in a carpeted parlor on cushioned chairs facing each other across a low coffee table with a tea service on it. The remarkable fact was that they were both dry, breathing air instead of brine, and speaking at a normal tone. When they'd both entered the foyer of the stranger's building, he hit a button on the wall. A sheet of steel slid down to cover the door, and within seconds the sea water began to exit the compartment through a drain in the floor. Hatch had had to drown into the air and that was much more uncomfortable than simply going under, but after some extended wheezing, choking, and spitting up, he drew in a huge breath with ease. The diver had unscrewed the glass globe that covered his head and held it beneath one arm.

278 | JEFFREY FORD

"Isaac Munro," he'd said and nodded.

Dressed in a maroon smoking jacket and green pajamas, moccasins on his feet, the silver haired man with drooping mustache sipped his tea and now held forth on his situation. Hatch, in dry clothes the older man had given him, was willing to listen, almost certain Munro knew the way back to dry land.

"I'm in Drowned Town, but not of it. Do you understand," he said.

Hatch nodded, and noticed what a relief it was to have the pressure of the sea off him.

Isaac Munro lowered his gaze and said as if making a confession, "My wife Rotzy went under some years ago. There was nothing I could do to prevent it. She came down here, and on the day she left me, I determined I would find the means to follow her and rescue her from Drowned Town. My imagination, fired by the desire to simply hold her again gave birth to all these many inventions that allow me to keep from getting my feet wet, so to speak." He chuckled and then made a face as if he were admonishing himself.

Hatch smiled. "How long have you been looking for her?"

"Years," said Munro, placing his tea cup on the table.

"I'm trying to get back. My wife Rose is coming for me in the car."

"Yes, your old neighbor Bob Gordon told me you might be looking for an out," said the older man. "I was on the prowl for you when we encountered that cut purse leviathan."

"You know Bob?"

"He does some leg work for me from time to time."

"I saw him at the grocery today."

"He has a bizarre fascination with that lobster tank. In any event, your wife won't make it through, I'm sorry to say. Not with a car."

"How can I get out?" asked Hatch. "I can't offer you a lot of money, but something else perhaps."

"Perish the thought," said Munro. "I have an escape hatch back to the surface in case of emergencies. You're welcome to use it if you'll just observe some cautionary measures."

"Absolutely," said Hatch and moved to the edge of his chair.

"I take it you'd like to leave immediately?"

Both men stood and Hatch followed through a hallway lined with framed photographs that opened into a large space, like an old ball room with peeling flowered wallpaper. Across the warped wooden floor scratched and littered with, of all things, old leaves and pages of a newspaper, they came to a door. When Munro turned around, Hatch noticed that the older man had taken one of the photos off the wall in the hallway.

"Here she is," said Isaac. "This is Rotzy."

Hatch leaned down for a better look at the portrait. He gave only the slightest grunt of surprise and hoped his host hadn't noticed, but Rotzy was the woman at the phone booth, the half faced horror mishandled by Madame Mutandis.

"You haven't seen her, have you?" asked Munro.

Hatch knew he should have tried to help the old man, but he thought only of escape and didn't want to complicate things. He felt the door in front of him was to be the portal back. "No," he said.

Munro nodded and then reached into the side pocket of his jacket and retrieved an old fashioned key. He held it in the air, but did not place it in Hatch's outstretched palm. "Listen carefully," he said. "You will pass through a series of rooms. Upon entering each room, you must lock the door behind you with this key before opening the next door to exit into the following room. Once you've started you can't turn back. The key only works to open doors forward and lock doors backward. A door can not be opened without a door being locked. Do you understand?"

"Yes."

Munro placed the key in Hatch's hand. "Then be on your way and godspeed. Kiss the sky for me when you arrive."

"I will."

Isaac opened the door and Hatch stepped through. The door closed and he locked it behind him. He crossed the room in a hurry, unlocked the next door and then passing through, locked it behind him. This process went on for twenty minutes before Hatch noticed that it took less and less steps to traverse each room to the next door. One of the rooms had a window, and he paused to look out on some watery side street falling into night. The loneliness of the scene spurred him forward. In the following room he had to duck down so as not to skin his head against the ceiling. He locked its door and moved forward into a room where he had to duck even lower.

Eventually, he was forced to crawl from room to room, and there wasn't much space for turning around to lock the door behind him. As each door swept open before him, he thought he might see the sky or feel a breeze in his face. There was always another door but there was also hope. That is until he entered a compartment so small, he couldn't turn around to use the key but had to do it with his hands behind his back, his chin against his chest. "This has got to be the last one," he thought, unsure if he could squeeze his shoulders through the next opening. Before he could insert the key into the lock on the tiny door before him, a steel plate fell and blocked access to it. He heard a swoosh and a bang behind him and knew another metal plate had covered the door going back.

"How are you doing, Mr. Hatch?" he heard Munro's voice say.

By dipping one shoulder Hatch was able to turn his head and

see a speaker built into the wall. "How do I get through these last rooms?" he yelled. "They're too small and metal guards have fallen in front of the doors."

"That's the point," called Munro, "you don't. You, my friend are trapped, and will remain trapped forever in that tight uncomfortable place."

"What are you talking about? Why?" Hatch was frantic. He tried to lunge his body against the walls but there was nowhere for it to go.

"My wife, Rotzy. You know how she went under? What sunk her? She was ill, Mr. Hatch. She was seriously ill but her health insurance denied her coverage. You, Mr. Hatch, personally said No."

This time what flared before Hatch's inner eye was not his life, but all the many pleading, frustrating, angry voices that had traveled in one of his ears and out the other in his service to the HMO. "I'm not responsible," was all he could think to say in his defense.

"My wife used to tell me, 'Isaac, we're all responsible.' Now you can wait, as she waited for relief, for what was rightly due her. You'll wait forever, Hatch."

There was a period where he struggled. He couldn't tell how long it lasted, but nothing came of it, so he closed his eyes, made his breathing more steady and shallow, and went into his brain, across the first floor to the basement door. He opened it and could smell the scent of the dark wood wafting up the steps. Locking the door behind him, he descended into the dark.

7

The woods were frightening, but he'd take anything over the claustrophobia of Munro's trap. Each dim light bulb he came to was a godsend, and he put his hands up to it for the little warmth it offered against the wind. He noticed that the creatures prowled around the bulbs like waterholes. They darted behind the trees, spying on him, pale specters whose faces were masks made of bone. One he was sure was his cousin Martin, a malevolent boy who'd cut the head off a kitten. He'd not seen him in over thirty years. He also spotted his mother-in-law, who was his mother-in-law with no hair and short tusks. She grunted orders to him from the shadows. He kept moving and tried to ignore them.

When Hatch couldn't walk any further, he came to a clearing in the forest. There, in the middle of nowhere, in the basement of his brain, sat twenty yards of street with a brownstone situated behind a wide sidewalk. There were steps leading up to twin doors and an electric light glowed next to the entrance. As he drew near, he could make out the address in brass numerals on the base of the banister that led up the right side of the front steps – 322.

He stumbled over to the bottom step and dropped down onto it. Hatch leaned forward, his elbows on his knees and his hands covering his face. "That's not me," he said, "it's not me," and he tried to weep till his eyes closed out of exhaustion. What seemed a second later, he heard a car horn and looked up.

"There's no crying in baseball, asshole," said Rose. She was leaning her head out the driver's side window of their SUV. There was a light on in the car and he could see both their sons were in the back seat, pointing at him.

"How'd you find me?" he asked.

"The internet," said Rose. "Will showed me Mapquest has this new feature where you don't need the address anymore, just a person's name, and it gives you directions to wherever they are in the continental United States."

"Oh, my god," he said and walked toward Rose to give her a hug.

"Not now Barnacle Bill, there's some pale creeps coming this way. We just passed them and one lunged for the car. Get in."

Hatch got in and saw his sons. He wanted to hug them but they motioned for him to hurry and shut the door. As soon as he did, Rose pulled away from the curb.

"So, Hatch, you went under?" asked his older son, Will.

Hatch wished he could explain but couldn't find the words.

"What a pile," said Ned.

"Yeah," said Will.

"Don't do it again, Hatch," said Rose. "Next time we're not coming for you."

"I'm sorry," he said. "I love you all."

Rose wasn't one to admonish more than once. She turned on the radio and changed the subject. "We had the directions, but they were a bitch to follow. At one point I had to cut across two lanes of traffic in the middle of the Holland Tunnel and take a left down a side tunnel that for more than a mile was the pitchest pitch black."

"Listen to this, Hatch" said Ned and leaned into the front seat to turn up the radio.

"Oh, they've been playing this all day," said Rose. "This young woman soldier was captured by insurgents and they made a video of them cutting her head off."

"On the radio, you only get the screams, though," said Will. "Check it out."

The sound, at first, was like from a musical instrument, and then it became human – steady, piercing shrieks in desperate bursts that ended in the gurgle of someone going under.

Rose changed the channel and the screams came from the new station. She hit the button again and the same screaming. Hatch turned to look at his family. Their eyes were slightly droopy and they were very pale. Their shoulders were somehow out of whack and their grins were vacant. Rose had a big bump on her forehead and a rash across her neck.

"Watch for the sign for The Holland Tunnel," she said amid the dying soldier's screams as they drove on into the dark. Hatch kept careful watch, knowing they'd never find it.

LIGHT
Kelly Link

Kelly Link is the author of two collections, *Stranger Things Happen* and *Magic for Beginners*. Her short stories have appeared in *The Magazine of Fantasy and Science Fiction*, *Conjunctions*, *A Public Space*, and *Best American Short Stories 2005*. With her partner, Gavin J. Grant, she runs Small Beer Press as well as producing the zine *Lady Churchill's Rosebud Wristlet*. She and Gavin co-edit the fantasy half of *Year's Best Fantasy and Horror* (St. Martin's). She lives in Northampton, Massachusetts. "Light" first appeared in *Tin House: Fantastic Women*.

two men, one raised by wolves

The man at the bar on the stool beside her: bent like a hook over some item. A book, not a drink. A children's book; dog-eared. When he noticed her stare, he grinned and said, "Got a light?" It was a Friday night, and the Splinter was full of men saying things. Some guy off in a booth was saying, for example, "Well, sure, you can be raised by wolves and lead a normal life but—"

Lindsey said, "I don't smoke."

The man straightened up. He said, "Not that kind of light. I mean a *light*. Do you have a *light*?"

"I don't understand," she said. And then because he was not bad-looking, she said, "Sorry."

"Stupid bitch," he said. "Never mind." The watercolor illustration in his book showed a boy and a girl standing in front of a dragon the size of a Volkswagen bus. The man had a pen. He'd drawn word bubbles coming out of the children's mouths, and now he was writing in words. The children were saying—

The man snapped the book shut; it was a library book.

"Excuse me," she said, "but I'm a children's librarian. Can I ask why you're defacing that book?"

"I don't know, *can* you? *Maybe* you can and *maybe* you can't, but why ask me?" the man said. Turning his back to her, he hunched over the book again.

Which was really too much. She opened her shoulder bag and took out her travel sewing kit. She palmed the needle and then jabbed the man in his left buttock. Very fast. Her hand was back in her lap and she was signaling the bartender for another drink when the man howled and sat up. Now everyone was looking at him. He slid off his stool and hurried away, glancing back at her once in outrage.

There was a drop of blood on the needle. She wiped it on a bar napkin.

At a table behind her three women were talking about a new pocket universe. A new diet. A coworker's new baby: a girl, born with no shadow. This was bad, although, thank God, not as bad as it could have been, a woman—someone called her Caroline—was saying.

A long, lubricated conversation followed about over-the-counter shadows—prosthetics, available in most drugstores, not expensive and reasonably durable. Everyone was in agreement that it was almost impossible to distinguish a prosthetic shadow from a real one.

Caroline and her friends began to talk of babies born with two shadows. Children with two shadows did not grow up happy. They didn't get on well with other children. You could cut a pair of shadows apart with a pair of crooked scissors, but it wasn't a permanent solution. By the end of the day the second shadow always grew back, twice as long. If you didn't bother to cut back the second shadow, then eventually you had twins, one of whom was only slightly realer than the other.

Lindsey had grown up in a stucco house in a scab-raw development in Dade County. Opposite the house had been a bruised and trampled nothing. A wilderness that grew, was razed, then grew back again. Banyan trees dripping with spiky epiphytes; tunnels of coral reef barely covered by blackish, sandy dirt that Lindsey—and her twin, Alan, not quite real enough, yet, to play with other children—lowered herself into, to emerge skinned, bloody, triumphant. Developers' bulldozers made football field–size depressions that filled with water when it rained and produced thousands and thousands of fingernail-size tan toads. Lindsey kept them in jars. She caught blue crabs, Cuban lizards, yellow-pink tobacco grasshoppers the size of toy trucks. They spat when you caged them in your hand. Geckos with their papery clockwork insides, ticktock barks; anoles whose throats pulsed out like bloody fans; king snakes coral snakes *red and yellow kill a fellow, red and black friendly Jack corn* snakes. When Lindsey was ten, a lightning strike ignited a fire under the coral reef. For a week smoke ghosted up. They kept the sprinklers on but the grass cooked brown. Alan caught five snakes, lost three of them in the house while he was watching Saturday-morning cartoons.

Lindsey had had a happy childhood. The women in the bar

didn't know what they were talking about.

It was almost a shame when the man who had theories about being raised by wolves came over and threw his drink in the face of the woman named Caroline. There was a commotion. Lindsey and the man who had theories about being raised by wolves went for a walk on the beach. He was charming, but she felt his theories were only that: charming. When she said this, he became less charming. Nevertheless, she invited him home.

"Nice place," he said. "I like all the whatsits."

"Most of it belongs to my brother," Lindsey said.

"Your *brother*. Does he live with you?"

"God, no," Lindsey said. "He's . . . wherever he is."

"I had a sister. Died when I was two," the man said. "Wolves make really shitty parents."

"Ha," she said, experimentally.

"Ha," he said. And then, "Look at that," as he was undressing her. Their four shadows fell across the bed, sticky and wilted as if from lovemaking that hadn't even begun. At the sight of their languorously intertwined shadows, the wolf man became charming again. "Look at these sweet little tits," he said over and over again as though she might not ever have noticed how sweet and little her tits were. He exclaimed at the sight of every part of her; afterward, she slept poorly, apprehensive that he might steal away, taking along one of the body parts or pieces that he seemed to admire so much.

In the morning, she woke and found herself stuck beneath the body of the wolf man as if she had been trapped beneath a collapsed and derelict building. When she began to wriggle her way out from under him, he woke and complained of a fucking terrible hangover. He called her "Joanie" several times, asked to borrow a pair of scissors, and spent a long time in her bathroom with the door locked while she read the paper. "Smuggling ring

apprehended by___ . Government overthrown in___ . Family of twelve last seen in vicinity of___ . Start of hurricane season___ ."
The wolf man came out of the bathroom, dressed hurriedly, and left.

She found a spongy black heap, the amputated shadow of his dead twin and three soaked, pungent towels, on the bathroom floor; there were stubby black bits of beard in the sink. The blades of her nail scissors were tarry and blunted.

She threw away the reeking towels. She mopped up the shadow, folding it into a large ziploc bag, carried the bag into the kitchen, and put the shadow down the disposal. She ran the water for a long time.

Then she went outside and sat on her patio and watched the iguanas eat the flowers off her hibiscus. It was 6:00 A.M. and already quite warm.

no vodka, one egg

Sponges hold water. Water holds light. Lindsey was hollow all the way through when she wasn't full of alcohol. The water in the canal was glazed with light, which wouldn't hold still. It was vile. She had the beginnings of one of her headaches. Light beat down on her head and her second shadow began to move, rippling in waves like the light-shot water in the canal. She went inside. The egg in the refrigerator door had a spot of blood when she cracked it into the pan. She liked vodka in her orange juice, but there was no orange juice and no vodka in the freezer, only a smallish iguana.

The Keys were overrun with iguanas. They ate her hibiscus; every once in a while she caught one of the smaller ones with the pool net and stuck it in her freezer for a few days. This was supposedly a humane way of dealing with iguanas. You could even eat them, although she did not. She was a vegetarian.

She put out food for the bigger iguanas. They liked ripe fruit. She liked to watch them eat. She knew that she was not being consistent or fair in her dealings, but there it was.

men unlucky at cards

Lindsey's job was not a particularly complicated one. There was an office, and behind the office was a warehouse full of sleeping people. There was an agency in DC that paid her company to take responsibility for the sleepers. Every year, hikers and cavers and construction workers found a few dozen more. No one knew how to wake them up. No one knew what they meant, what they did, where they came from.

There were always at least two security guards on duty at the warehouse. They were mostly, in Lindsey's opinion, lecherous assholes. She spent the day going through invoices, and then went home again. The wolf man wasn't at the Splinter and the bartender threw everyone out at 2:00 A.M.; she went back to the warehouse on a hunch, four hours into the night shift.

Bickle and Lowes had hauled out five sleepers, three women and two men. They'd put Miami Hydra baseball caps on the male sleepers and stripped the women, propped them up in chairs around a foldout table. Someone had arranged the hands of one of the male sleepers down between the legs of one of the women. Cards had been dealt out. Maybe it was just a game of strip poker and the two women had been unlucky. It was hard to play your cards well when you were asleep.

Larry Bickle stood behind one of the women, his cheek against her hair. He seemed to be giving her advice about how to play her cards. He wasn't holding his drink carefully enough, and the woman's neat lap brimmed with beer.

Lindsey watched for a few minutes. Bickle and Lowes had gotten to the sloppy, expansive stage of drunkenness that, sober, she resented most. False happiness.

When Lowes saw Lindsey he stood up so fast his chair tipped over. "Hey now," he said. "It's different from how it looks."

Both guards had little, conical, paper party hats on their heads.

A third man, no one Lindsey recognized, came wandering down the middle aisle like he'd been shopping at Wal-Mart. He wore boxer shorts and a party hat. "Who's this?" he said, leering at Lindsey.

Larry Bickle's hand was on his gun. What was he going to do? Shoot her? She said, "I've already called the police."

"Oh, fuck me," Bickle said. He said some other things.

"You called the police?" Edgar Lowes said.

"They'll be here in about ten minutes," Lindsey said. "If I were you, I'd leave right now. Just go. It isn't as if I can stop you."

"What is that bitch saying?" Bickle said unhappily. He was really quite drunk. His hand was still on his gun.

She took out her own gun, a Beretta. She pointed it in the direction of Bickle and Lowes. "Put your gun belts on the ground and take off your uniforms, too. Leave your keys and your ID cards. You, too, whoever you are. Hand over your ID and I won't press charges."

"You've got little cats on your gun," Edgar Lowes said.

"Hello Kitty stickers," she said. "I count coup." Although she'd only ever shot one person.

The men took off their clothes but not the party hats. Edgar Lowes had a purple scar down his chest. He saw Lindsey looking and said, "Triple bypass. I need this job for the health insurance."

"Too bad," Lindsey said. She followed them out into the parking lot. The third man didn't seem to care that he was naked. He didn't even have his hands cupped around his balls, the way Bickle and Lowes did. He said to Lindsey, "They've done this a couple of times. Heard about it from a friend. Tonight was my birthday party."

"Happy birthday," she said. She watched the three men get into their cars and drive away. Then she went back into the warehouse and folded up the uniforms, emptied the guns, cleaned up the sleepers, used the dolly to get the sleepers back to their boxes. There was a bottle of cognac and plenty of beer. She drank steadily. A song came to her, and she sang it. *Tall and tan and young and drunken and—* She knew she was getting the words wrong. *A midnight pyre. Like a bird on fire. I have tried in my way to be you.*

It was almost 5:00 A.M. The floor came up at her in waves, and she would have liked to lie down on it.

—

The sleeper in Box 113 was Harrisburg Pennsylvania, a young boy. The sleepers were named after their place of origin. Other countries did it differently. Harrisburg Pennsylvania had long eyelashes and a bruise on his cheek that had never faded. The skin of a sleeper was always just a little cooler than you expected. You could get used to anything. She set the alarm in her cell phone to wake her up before the shift change.

In the morning, Harrisburg Pennsylvania was still asleep and Lindsey was still drunk. She'd drooled a little on his arm.

All she said to her supervisor, the general office manager, was that she'd fired Bickle and Lowes. Mr. Charles gave her a long-suffering look, said, "You look a bit rough."

"I'll go home early," she said.

She would have liked to replace Bickle and Lowes with women, but in the end she hired an older man with excellent job references and a graduate student, Jason, who said he planned to spend his evenings working on his dissertation. (He was a philosophy student, and she asked what philosopher his dissertation was on. If he'd said "Nietzsche" she might have terminated the interview. But he said, "John Locke.")

She'd already requested additional grant money to pay for security cameras, but when it was turned down she went ahead and bought the cameras anyway. She had a bad feeling about the two men who worked the Sunday-to-Wednesday day shift.

as children, they were inseparable

On Tuesday, there was a phone call from Alan. He was yelling something in LinLan before she could even say hello.

"*Berma lisgo airport. Tus fah me?*"

"Alan?"

He said, "I'm at the airport, Lin-Lin, just wondering if I can come and stay with you for a bit. Not too long. Just need to keep my head down for a while. You won't even know I'm there."

"Back up," she said. "Where are you?"

"The airport," he said, clearly annoyed. "Where the planes are."

"I thought you were in Tibet," she said.

"Well," Alan said. "That didn't quite work out. I've decided to move on."

"What did you do?" she said. "Alan?"

"Lin-Lin, please," he said. "I'll explain everything tonight. I'll make dinner. House key still under the broken planter?"

"*Fisfis meh,*" she said. "Fine."

The last time she'd seen Alan in the flesh was two years ago, just after Elliot had left for good. Her husband.

They'd both been more than a little drunk and Alan was always nicer when he was drunk. He gave her a hug and said, "Come on, Lindsey. You can tell me. It's a bit of a relief, isn't it?"

The sky was low and swollen. Lindsey loved this, the sudden green afternoon darkness as rain came down in heavy drumming torrents so loud she could hardly hear the radio station in her car, the calm, jokey pronouncements of the local weather witch. The vice president was under investigation; evidence suggested a series of secret dealings with malign spirits. A woman had given birth to a dozen rabbits. A local gas station had been robbed by invisible men. Some religious cult had thrown all the infidels out of a popular pocket universe. Nothing new, in other words. The sky was always falling. U.S. 1 was bumper-to-bumper all the way to Plantation Key.

Alan sat out on the patio behind her house, a bottle of wine under his chair, the wineglass in his hand half full of rain, half full of wine. "Lindsey!" he said.

"Want a drink?" He didn't get up.

She said, "Alan? It's raining."

"It's warm," he said and blinked fat balls of rain out of his eyelashes. "It was cold where I was."

"I thought you were going to make dinner," she said.

Alan stood up and made a show of wringing out his shirt and his peasant-style cotton pants. The rain collapsed steadily on their heads.

"There's nothing in your kitchen. I would have made margaritas, but all you had was the salt."

"Let's go inside," Lindsey said. "Do you have any dry clothes? In your luggage? Where's your luggage, Alan?"

He gave her a sly look. "You know. In there."

She knew. "You put your stuff in Elliot's room." It had been her room too, but she hadn't slept there in almost a year. She only slept there when she was alone.

Alan said, "All the things he left are still there. Like he might still be in there too, somewhere down in the sheets, all folded up like a secret note. Very creepy, Lin-Lin."

Alan was only thirty-eight. The same age as Lindsey, of course, unless you were counting from the point where he was finally real enough to eat his own birthday cake. She thought he looked every year of their age. Older.

"Go get changed," she said. "I'll order takeout."

"What's in the grocery bags?" he said.

She slapped his hand away. "Nothing for you," she said.

close encounters of the absurd kind

She'd met Elliot at an open mike in a pocket universe near Coral Gables. A benefit at a gay bar for some charity. Men everywhere, but most of them not interested in her. Elliot was over seven feet tall; his hair was canary yellow and his skin was greenish. Lindsey had noticed the way that Alan looked at him when they first came in. Alan had been in this universe before.

Elliot sang the song about the monster from Ipanema. He couldn't carry a tune, but he made Lindsey laugh so hard that whiskey came out of her nose. He came over and sat at the bar. He said, "You're Alan's twin."

He only had four fingers on each hand. His skin looked smooth and rough at the same time.

She said, "I'm the original. He's the copy. Wherever he is. Passed out in the bathroom, probably."

Elliot said, "Should I go get him or should we leave him here?"

"Where are we going?" she said.

"To bed," he said. His hair was feathers, not hair. His pupils were oddly shaped.

"What would we do there?" she said, and he just looked at her. Sometimes these things worked and sometimes they didn't. That was the fun of it.

She thought about it. "Okay. On the condition that you promise me that you've never fooled around with Alan. Ever."

"Your universe or mine?" he said.

Elliot wasn't the first thing Lindsey had brought back from a pocket universe. She'd gone on vacation once and brought back the pit of a green fruit that fizzed like sherbet when you bit into it and gave you dreams about staircases, ladders, rockets, things that went up and up, although nothing had come up when she planted it, although almost everything grew in Florida.

Her mother had gone on vacation in a pocket universe when she was first pregnant with Lindsey. Now people knew better. Doctors cautioned pregnant women against such trips.

For the last few years Alan had had a job with a tour group that ran trips out of Singapore. He spoke German, Spanish, Japanese, Mandarin Chinese, passable Tibetan, various pocket-universe trade languages. The tours took charter flights into Tibet and then trekked up into some of the more tourist-friendly pocket universes. Tibet was riddled with pocket universes.

"You lost them?" Lindsey said.

"Not all of them," Alan said. His hair was still wet with rain. He needed a haircut. "Just one van. I thought I told the driver Sakya but I may have said Gyantse. They showed up eventually, just two days behind schedule. It's not as if they were children. Everyone in Gyantse speaks English. When they caught up with us I was charming and full of remorse and we were all pals again."

She waited for the rest of the story. Somehow it made her feel better, knowing that Alan had the same effect on everyone.

"But then there was a mix-up at customs back at Changi. They found a reliquary in this old bastard's luggage. Some ridiculous little god in a dried-up seedpod. Some other things. The old bastard swore up and down that none of it was his. That I'd snuck up to his room and put them into his luggage. That I'd seduced him. The agency got involved and the story about Gyantse came out. So that was that."

"Alan," she said.

"I was hoping I could stay here for a few weeks."

"You'll stay out of my hair," she said.

"Of course," he said. "Can I borrow a toothbrush?"

more like Disney World than Disney World

Their parents were retired, living in an older, established pocket universe that was apparently much more like Florida than Florida had ever been. No mosquitoes, no indigenous species larger than a lapdog, except for birdlike creatures whose songs made you want to cry and whose flesh tasted like veal. Fruit trees that no one had to cultivate. Grass so downy and tender and fragrant that no one slept indoors. Lakes so big and so shallow that you could spend all day walking across them. It wasn't a large universe, and nowadays there was a long waiting list of men and women waiting to retire to it. Lindsey and Alan's parents had invested all of their savings into a one-room cabana with a view of one of the smaller lakes. "Lotus-eating," they called it. It sounded boring to Lindsey, but her mother no longer e-mailed to ask if Lindsey was seeing anyone. If she were ever going to remarry and produce children. Grandchildren were no longer required. Grandchildren would have obliged Lindsey and Alan's parents to leave their paradise in order to visit once in a while. Come back all that long way to Florida. "That nasty place where we used to live," Lindsey's mother said. Alan had a theory that their parents were not telling them everything. "They've become nudists," he insisted. "Or swingers. Or both. Mom always had exhibitionist tendencies. Always leaving the bathroom door open. No wonder I'm gay. No wonder you're not."

—

Lindsey lay awake in her bed and listened to Alan make tea in the kitchen. Alan hanging up his clothes in Elliot's closet. Alan turning the television on and off. At two in the morning, he came and stood outside her bedroom door. He said, softly, "Lindsey? Are you awake?"

She didn't answer and he went away again.

In the morning he was asleep on the sofa. A DVD was playing; the sound was off. Somehow he'd found Elliot's stash of imported pocket-universe porn, the secret stash she'd spent weeks looking for and never found. Trust Alan to turn it up. But she was childishly pleased to see he hadn't found the gin she'd hidden in the sofa.

When she came home from work he was out on the patio again, trying, uselessly, to catch her favorite iguana. "Be careful of the tail," she said.

"Monster came up and bit my toe," he said.

"That's Elliot. I've been feeding him," she said. "Probably thinks you're invading his territory."

"Elliot?" he said and laughed. "That's sick."

"He's big and green," she said. "You don't see the resemblance?" Her iguana disappeared into the network of banyan trees that dipped over the canal. The banyans were full of iguanas, leaves rustling greenly with their green and secret meetings. "The only difference is he comes back."

The next morning Alan drove her to work and went off with the car. In the afternoon Mr. Charles came into her office. "Bad news," he said. "Jack Harris in Pittsburgh went ahead and sent us two dozen sleepers. The new kid, Jason, signed for them down at the warehouse. Didn't think to call us first."

"You're kidding," she said.

"'Fraid not," he said. "I'm going to call Jack Harris. Ask what the hell he thought he was doing. I made it clear the other day that we weren't approved with regards to capacity. He'll just have to take them back again."

"Has the driver already gone?" she said.

"Yep. Maybe you could run over to the warehouse and take a look at the paperwork. Figure out what to do with this group in the meantime."

There were twenty-two new sleepers, eighteen males and four females. Jason already had them on dollies.

"Where were they before Pittsburgh?" she asked.

Jason handed over the dockets. "All over the place. Four of them turned up on property belonging to some guy in South Dakota. Says the government ought to compensate him for the loss of his crop."

"What happened to his crop?" she said.

"He set fire to it. They were underneath a big old dead tree out in his fields. Fortunately for everybody his son was there too. While the father was pouring gasoline on everything, the son dragged the sleepers into the bed of the truck, got them out of there. Called the hotline."

"Lucky," she said. "What the hell was the father thinking?"

"People your age—," Jason said and stopped. Started again. "Older people seem to get these weird ideas sometimes. They want everything to be the way it was. Before."

"I'm not that old," she said.

"I didn't mean that," he said. Got pink. "I just mean, you know . . . "

She touched her hair. "Maybe you didn't notice, but I have two shadows. So I'm part of the weirdness. People like me are the people that people get ideas about. Why are you on the day shift?"

"Jermaine's wife is out of town so he has to take care of the kids. What do we do with the sleepers now?"

"Leave them on the dollies," she said. "It's not like it matters to them."

She tried calling Alan's cell phone at five thirty, but got no answer. She checked e-mail and played solitaire. She hated solitaire. Enjoyed shuffling through the cards she should have played. Playing cards when she shouldn't have. Why should she pretend to want to win when there wasn't anything to win?

At seven thirty she looked out and saw her car in the parking lot. When she went down to the warehouse he was flirting with Jason while the other guard, Hurley, ate his dinner.

"Hey, Lin-Lin," Alan said. "Come see this. Come here."

"What the hell are you doing?" Lindsey said. "Where have you been?"

"Grocery shopping," he said. "Come here, Lindsey. Come see."

Jason made a don't-blame-me face. She'd have to take him aside at some point. Warn him about Alan. Philosophy didn't prepare you for people like Alan.

"Look at her," Alan said.

She looked down at a sleeper. A woman dressed in a way that

suggested she had probably been someone important once, maybe hundreds of years ago, somewhere, probably, that wasn't anything like here. Versailles Kentucky.

"I've seen sleepers before."

"No. You don't see," Alan said. "Of course you don't. Hey, Lin-Lin, this kind of haircut would look good on you."

He fluffed Versailles Kentucky's hair.

"Alan," she said. A warning.

"Look," he said. "Just look. Look at her. She looks just like you. She's you."

"You're crazy," she said.

"Am I?" Alan appealed to Jason. "You thought so, too."

Jason hung his head. He mumbled something. Said, "I said that maybe there was a similarity."

Alan reached down into the container and grabbed the sleeper's bare foot, lifted the leg straight up.

"Alan!" Lindsey said. She pried his hand loose. The prints of his fingers came up on Versailles Kentucky's leg in red and white. "What are you doing?"

"It's fine," Alan said. "I just wanted to see if she has a birthmark like yours. Lindsey has a birthmark behind her knee," he said to Jason. "Looks like a battleship."

Even Hurley was staring now.

The sleeper didn't look a thing like Lindsey. No birthmark. Funny, though. The more she thought about it the more Lindsey thought maybe she looked like Alan.

not herself today

She turned her head a little to the side. Put on all the lights in the bathroom and stuck her face up close to the mirror again. Stepped back. The longer she looked the less she looked like anyone she knew.

Alan was right. She needed a haircut.

The kitchen stank of rum; Alan had the blender out. "Let me guess," he said. "You met someone nice in there." He held out a glass. "I thought we could have a nice, quiet night in. Watch the Weather Channel. Do charades. You can knit. I'll wind your yarn for you."

"I don't knit."

"No," he said. His voice was kind. Loving. "You tangle. You knot. You muddle."

"You needle," she said. "What is it that you want? Why are you here? To pick a fight?"

"*Per bol tuh*, Lin-Lin?" Alan said. "What do *you* want?" She sipped ferociously. She knew what she wanted. "Why are *you* here?"

"This is my home," she said. "I have everything I want. A job at a company with real growth potential. A boss who likes me. A bar just around the corner, full of men who want to buy me drinks. A yard full of iguanas. And a spare shadow in case one should accidentally fall off."

"This isn't your house," Alan said. "Elliot bought it. Elliot filled it up with his junk. And all the nice stuff is mine. You haven't changed a thing since he took off."

"I have more iguanas now," she said. She took her rumrunner into the living room. Alan already had the Weather Channel on. Behind the perky blond weather witch, in violent primary colors, a tropical depression hovered off the coast of Cuba.

Alan came and stood behind the couch. He put his drink down and began to rub her neck.

"Pretty, isn't it?" she said. "That storm."

"Remember when we were kids? That hurricane?"

"Yeah," she said. "I probably ought to go haul the storm shutters out of the storage unit."

"That kid at your warehouse," he said. His eyes were closed.
"Jason?"

"He seems like a nice kid."

"*Kid* being the key word. He's a philosophy student, Lan-Lan.
Come on. You can do better."

"Do better? I'm thinking out loud about a guy with a fine ass,
Lindsey. Not buying a house. Or contemplating a career change.
Oops, I guess I am officially doing that. Perhaps I'll become a
do-gooder. A do-better."

"Just don't make my life harder, okay? Alan?"

"He has green eyes. Jason. Really, really green. Green as that
color there. Right at the eye. That swirl," Alan said, draining his
third rumrunner.

"I hadn't noticed his eyes," Lindsey said.

"That's because he isn't your type. You don't like nice guys." He
was over at the stereo now. "Can I put this on?"

"If you want to. There's a song on there, I think it's the third
song. Yeah. This one. Elliot loved this song. He'd put it on and
start slithering all over the furniture."

"Oh yeah. He was a god on the dance floor. But look at me. I'm
not too bad either."

"He was more flexible around the hips. I think he had a bendi-
er spine. He could turn his head almost all the way around."

"Come on, Lindsey, you're not dancing. Come on and dance."

"I don't want to."

"Don't be such a pain in the ass."

"I have a pain inside," she said. And then wondered what she
meant.

"It's such a pain in the ass."

"Come on. Just dance. Okay?"

"Okay," she said. "I'm okay. See? I'm dancing."

Jason came over for dinner. Alan wore one of Elliot's shirts. Lindsey made a perfect cheese soufflé, and she said nothing when Jason assumed that Alan had made it.

She listened to Alan's stories about various pocket universes as if she had never heard them before. Most were owned by the Chinese government and, as well as the more famous tourist universes, there were ones where the Chinese sent dissidents. Very few pocket universes were larger than, say, Maryland. Some had been abandoned a long time ago. Some were inhabited. Some weren't friendly. Some pocket universes contained their own pocket universes. You could go a long ways in and never come out again. You could start your own country out there and do whatever you liked, and yet most of the people Lindsey knew, herself included, had never done anything more venturesome than go for a week to someplace where the food and the air and the landscape seemed like something out of a book you'd read as a child; a brochure; a dream.

There were sex-themed pocket universes, of course. Tax shelters and places to dispose of all kinds of things: trash, junked cars, murder victims. People went to casinos inside pocket universes more like Vegas than Vegas. More like Hawaii than Hawaii. You must be this tall to enter. This rich. Just this foolish. Because who knew what might happen? Pocket universes might wink out again, suddenly, all at once. There were best-selling books explaining how that might happen.

Alan began to reminisce about his adolescence in a way that suggested it had not really been all that long ago.

"Venetian Pools," he said to Jason. "I haven't been there in a couple of years. Since I was a kid, really. All those grottoes that you could wander off into with someone. Go make out and get such an enormous hard-on you had to jump in the water so nobody noticed and the water was so fucking cold! Can you still get baked ziti at the restaurant? Do you remember that, Lindsey? Sitting out by the pool in your bikini and eating baked ziti? I heard you can't swim now. Because of the mermaids."

The mermaids were an invasive species, like the iguanas. People had brought them back from one of the Disney pocket universes, as pets, and now they were everywhere, small but numerous in a way that appealed to children and bird-watchers. They liked to show off and although they didn't seem much smarter than, say, a talking dog, and maybe not even as smart, since they didn't speak, only sang and whistled and made rude gestures, they were too popular with the tourists at Venetian Pools to be gotten rid of.

Jason said he'd been with his sister's kids. "I heard they used to drain the pools every night in summer. But they can't do that now, because of the mermaids. So the water isn't as clear as it used to be. They can't even set up filters, because the mermaids just tear them out again. Like beavers, I guess. They've constructed this elaborate system of dams and retaining walls and structures out of the coral, these elaborate pens to hold fish. Venetian Pools sells fish so you can toss them in for the mermaids to round up. The kids were into that."

"They sing, right?" Lindsey asked. "We get them in the canal sometimes, the saltwater ones. They're a lot bigger. They sing."

"Yeah," Jason said. "Lots of singing. Really eerie stuff. Makes you feel like shit. They pipe elevator music over the loudspeakers to drown it out, but even the kids felt bad after a while. I had to buy all this stuff in the gift shop to cheer them up."

Lindsey pondered the problem of Jason, the favorite uncle who could be talked into buying things. He was too young for Alan. When you thought about it, who wasn't too young for Alan?

Alan said, "Didn't you have plans, Lindsey?"

"Did I?" Lindsey said. Then relented. "Actually, I was thinking about heading down to the Splinter. Maybe I'll see you guys down there later?"

"That old hole," Alan said. He wasn't looking at her. He was sending out those old invisible death rays in Jason's direction; Lindsey could practically feel the air getting thicker. It was like humidity, only skankier. "I used to go there to hook up with cute straight guys in the bathroom while Lindsey was passing out her phone number over by the pool tables. You know what they say about girls with two shadows, don't you, Jason?"

Jason said, "Maybe I should head home." But Lindsey could tell by the way that he was looking at Alan that he had no idea what he was saying. He wasn't even really listening to what Alan said. He was just responding to the vibe that Alan put out. That *come hither come hither come a little more hither* siren song.

"Don't go," Alan said. "Stay a little longer. Lindsey has plans, and I'm lonely. Stay a little longer and I'll play you some of the highlights from Lindsey's ex-husband's collection of pocket-universe gay porn."

"Alan," Lindsey said. Second warning. She knew he was keeping count.

"Sorry," Alan said. He put his hand on Jason's leg. "*Husband's* collection of gay porn. She and Elliot, wherever he is, are still married. I had the biggest hard-on for Elliot. He always said Lindsey was all he wanted. But it's never about what you want, is it? It's about what you need. Right?"

"Right," Jason said.

How did Alan do it? Why did everyone except for Lindsey fall for it? Except, she realized, pedaling her bike down to the Splinter, she did fall for it. She still fell for it. It was her house, and who had been thrown out of it? Who had been insulted, dismissed, and told to leave? Her. That's who.

Cars went by, riding their horns. Damn Alan anyway.

She didn't bother to chain up the bike; she probably wouldn't be riding it home. She went into the Splinter and sat down beside a man with an aggressively sharp cologne.

"You look nice," she said. "Buy me a drink and I'll be nice, too."

—

there are easier ways of trying to kill yourself

The man tried to kiss her. She couldn't find her keys, but that didn't matter. The door was unlocked. Jason's car still in the driveway. No surprise there.

"I have two shadows," she said. It was all shadows. They were shadows too.

"I don't care," the man said. He really was very nice.

"No," she said. "I mean my brother's home. We have to be quiet. Okay if we don't turn on the lights? Where are you from?"

"Georgia," the man said. "I work construction. Came down here for the hurricane."

"The hurricane?" she said. "I thought it was headed for the Gulf of Mexico. This way. Watch out for the counter."

"Now it's coming back this way. Won't hit for another couple of days. You into kinky stuff? You can tie me up," the man said.

"Better knot," she said. "Get it? I'm not into knots. Can never get them untied, even sober. This guy had to have his foot amputated. No circulation. True story. Friend told me."

"Guess I've been lucky so far," the man said. He didn't sound too disappointed, either way. "This house has been through some hurricanes, I bet."

"One or two," she said. "Water comes right in over the tile

floor. Messy. Then it goes out again."

She tried to remember his name. Couldn't. It didn't matter. She felt terrific. That had been the thing about being married. The monogamy. Even drunk, she'd always known who was in bed with her. Elliot had been different, all right, but he had always been the same kind of different. Never a different kind of different. Didn't like kissing. Didn't like sleeping in the same bed. Didn't like being serious. Didn't like it when Lindsey was sad. Didn't like living in a house. Didn't like the way the water in the canal felt. Didn't like this, didn't like that. Didn't like the Keys. Didn't like the way people looked at him. Didn't stay. Elliot, Elliot, Elliot.

"My name's Alberto," the man said.

"Sorry," she said. She and Elliot had always had fun in bed.

"He had a funny-looking penis," she said.

"Excuse me?" Alberto said.

"Do you want something to drink?" she said.

"Actually, do you have a bathroom?"

"Down the hall," she said. "First door."

But he came back in a minute. He turned on the lights and stood there.

"Like what you see?" she said.

His arms were shiny and wet. There was blood on his arms. "I need a tourniquet," he said. "Some kind of tourniquet."

"What did you do?" she said. Almost sober. Putting her robe on. "Is it Alan?"

But it was Jason. Blood all over the bathtub and the pretty half-tiled wall. He'd slashed both his wrists open with a potato peeler. The potato peeler was still there in his hand.

"Is he okay?" she said. "Alan! Where the fuck are you? Fuck!"

Alberto wrapped one of her good hand towels around one of Jason's wrists. "Hold this." He stuck another towel around the other wrist and then wrapped duct tape around that. "I called 911," he said. "He's breathing. Who is this guy? Your brother?"

"My employee," she said. "I don't believe this. What's with the duct tape?"

"Go get me a blanket," he said. "Need to keep him warm. My ex-wife did this once."

She skidded down the hall. Slammed open the door to Elliot's room. Turned on the lights and grabbed the comforter off the bed.

"*Vas poh!* Your new boyfriend's in the bathroom," she said. "Cut his wrists with my potato peeler. Wake up, Lan-Lan! This is *your* mess."

"*Fisfis wah*, Lin-Lin," Alan said, so she pushed him off the bed.

"What did you do, Alan?" she said. "Did you mess with him?"

He was wearing a pair of Elliot's pajama bottoms. "You're not being funny," he said.

"I'm not kidding," she said. "I'm drunk. There's a man named Alberto in the bathroom. Jason tried to kill himself. Or something."

"Oh fuck," he said. Tried to sit up. "I was nice to him, Lindsey! Okay? It was real nice. We fucked and then we smoked some stuff and then we were kissing and I fell asleep."

She held out her hand, pulled him up off the floor. "What kind of stuff? Come on."

"Something I picked up somewhere," he said. She wasn't really listening. "Good stuff. Organic. Blessed by monks. They give it to the gods. I took some off a shrine. Everybody does it. You just leave a bowl of milk or something instead. There's no fucking way it made him crazy."

The bathroom was crowded with everyone inside it. No way to

avoid standing in Jason's blood. "Oh fuck," Alan said.

"My brother, Alan," Lindsey said. "Here's a comforter for Jason. Alan, this is Alberto. Jason, can you hear me?" His eyes were open now.

Alberto said to Alan, "It's better than it looks. He didn't really slice up his wrists. More like he peeled them. Dug into one vein pretty good, but I think I've slowed down the bleeding."

Alan shoved Lindsey out of the way and threw up in the sink.

"Alan," Jason said. There were sirens.

"No," Lindsey said. "It's me. Lindsey. Your boss. My bathtub, Jason. Your blood all over my bathtub. My potato peeler! Mine! What were you thinking?"

"There was an iguana in your freezer," Jason said.

Alberto said, "Why the potato peeler?"

"I was just so happy," Jason said. He was covered in blood. "I've never been so happy in all my life. I didn't want to stop feeling that way. You know?"

"No," Lindsey said.

"Are you going to fire me?" Jason said.

"What do you think?" Lindsey said.

"I'll sue for sexual harassment if you do," Jason said. "I'll say you fired me because I'm gay. Because I slept with your brother."

Alan threw up in the sink again.

"How do you feel now?" Alberto said. "You feel okay?"

"I just feel so happy," Jason said. He began to cry.

not much of a bedside manner

Alan went with Jason in the ambulance. The wind was stronger, pushing the trees around like a bully. Lindsey would have to put the storm shutters up.

For some reason Alberto was still there. He said, "I'd really like a beer. What've you got?"

Lindsey could have gone for something a little stronger. Everything smelled of blood. "Nothing," she said. "I'm a recovering alcoholic."

"Not all that recovered," he said.

"I'm sorry," Lindsey said. "You're a really nice guy. But I wish you would go away. I'd like to be alone."

He held out his bloody arms. "Could I take a shower first?"

"Could you just go?" Lindsey said.

"I understand," he said. "It's been a rough night. A terrible thing has happened. Let me help. I'll stay and help you clean up."

Lindsey said nothing.

"I see," he said. There was blood on his mouth too. Like he'd been drinking blood. He had good shoulders. Nice eyes. She kept looking at his mouth. The duct tape was back in a pocket of his cargo pants. He seemed to have a lot of stuff in his pockets. "You don't like me after all?"

"I don't like nice guys," Lindsey said.

There were support groups for people whose shadow grew into a twin. There were support groups for women whose husbands left them. There were support groups for alcoholics. Probably there were support groups for people who hated support groups, but Lindsey didn't believe in support groups.

By the time Alan got back from the hospital it was Saturday night; she'd finished the gin and started in on the tequila. She was almost wishing that Alberto had stayed. She thought about asking how Jason was, but it seemed pointless. Either he was okay or he wasn't. She wasn't okay. Alan got her down the hall and onto her bed and then climbed into bed too. Pulled the blanket over both of them.

"Go away," she said.

"I'm freezing," he said. "That fucking hospital. That air-conditioning. Just let me lie here."

"Go away," she said again. "*Fisfis wah.*"

When she woke up, she was still saying it. "Go away, go away, go away." He wasn't in her bed. Instead there was a dead iguana, the little one from the freezer, on the pillow beside her face.

Alan was gone. The bathtub stank of blood and the rain slammed down on the roof like nails on glass. Little pellets of ice on the grass outside. Now the radio said the hurricane was on course to make land somewhere between Fort Lauderdale and Saint Augustine sometime Wednesday afternoon. There were no plans to evacuate the Keys. Plenty of wind and rain and nastiness due for the Miami area, but no real damage. She couldn't think why she'd asked Alberto to leave. The storm shutters still needed to go up. He had seemed like a guy who would do that.

If Alan had been there, he could have opened a can and made her soup. Brought her ginger ale in a glass. Finally, she turned the television on in the living room, loud enough that she could hear it from her bedroom. That way she wouldn't be listening for Alan. She could pretend that he was home, sitting out in the living room, watching some old monster movie and painting his fingernails black, the way he had done in high school. Kids with conjoined shadows were supposed to be into all that Goth makeup, all that music, so Alan was into it. When Alan had found out that twins were supposed to have secret twin languages, he'd done that too, invented a language, LinLan, and made her memorize it. Made her talk it at the dinner table. *Ifzon meh nadora plezbig* meant *Guess what I did? Bandy Tim Wong legkwa fisfis, meh* meant Went all the way with Tim

Wong. (Tim Wong fucked me, in the vernacular.)

People with two shadows were *supposed* to be trouble. They were supposed to lead friends and lovers astray, bring confusion to their enemies, bring down disaster wherever they went. (She never went anywhere.) Alan had always been a conformist at heart. Whereas she had a house and a job and once she'd even been married. If anyone was keeping track, Lindsey thought it should be clear who was ahead.

Monday morning Mr. Charles still hadn't managed to get rid of the sleepers from Pittsburgh. Jack Harris could shuffle paper like nobody's business.

"I'll call him," Lindsey offered. "You know I love a good fight."

"Good luck," Mr. Charles said. "He says he won't take them back until after the hurricane goes through. But rules say they have to be out of here twenty-four hours before the hurricane hits. We're caught between a rock—"

"And an asshole," she said. "Let me take care of it."

She was in the warehouse, on hold with someone who worked for Harris, when Jason showed up.

"What's up with that?" Valentina was saying. "Your arms."

"Fell through a plate-glass door," Jason said.

"That's not good," Valentina said.

"Lost almost three pints of blood. Just think about that. Three pints. Hey, Lindsey."

"Valentina," Lindsey said. "Take the phone for a moment. Don't worry. It's on hold. Just yell if anyone picks up. Jason, can I talk to you over there for a moment?"

"Sure thing," Jason said.

He winced when she grabbed him above the elbow. She didn't loosen her grip until they were a couple of aisles away. "Give me one good reason why I shouldn't fire you. Besides the sexual harassment thing. Because I would enjoy that. Hearing you try to make that case in court."

Jason said, "Alan's moved in with me. Said you threw him out."

Was any of this a surprise? Yes and no. She said, "So if I fire you, he'll have to get a job."

"That depends," Jason said. "Are you firing me or not?"

"*Fisfis buh*. Go ask Alan what that means."

"Hey, Lindsey. Lindsey, hey. Someone named Jack Harris is on the phone," Valentina said, getting too close for this conversation to go any further.

"I don't know why you want this job," Lindsey said.

"The benefits," Jason said. "You should see the bill from the emergency room."

"Or why you want my brother."

"Ms. Driver? He says it's urgent."

"Tell him one second," Lindsey said. To Jason: "All right. You can keep your job on one condition."

"Which is?" He didn't sound nearly as suspicious as he ought to have sounded. Still early days with Alan.

"You get the man on the phone to take back those six sleepers. Today."

"How the fuck do I do that?" Jason said.

"I don't care. But they had better not be here when I show up tomorrow morning. If they're here, you had better not be. Okay?" She poked him in the arm above the bandage. "Next time borrow something sharper than a potato peeler. I've got a whole block full of good German knives."

"Lindsey," Valentina said, "this Harris guy says he can call you back tomorrow if now isn't a good time."

"Jason is going to take the call," Lindsey said.

everything must go

Her favorite liquor store put everything on sale whenever a hurricane was due. Just their way of making a bad day a little more bearable. She stocked up on everything but only had a glass of wine with dinner. Made a salad and ate it out on the patio. The air had that electric, green shimmy to it she associated with hurricanes. The water was as still as milk, but deflating her dock was a bitch nevertheless. She stowed it in the garage. When she came out, a pod of saltwater mermaids was going out to sea. Who could have ever confused a manatee with a mermaid? They turned and looked at her. Dove down, although she could still see them ribboning there, down along the frondy bottom.

The last time a hurricane had come through, her dock had sailed out of the garage and ended up two canals over.

She threw the leftover salad on the grass for the iguanas. The sun went down without a fuss.

Alan didn't come back, so she packed up his clothes for him. Washed the dirty clothes first. Listened to the rain start. She put his backpack out on the dining room table with a note. *Good luck with the philosopher king.*

In the morning before work she went out in the rain, which was light but steady, and put up the storm shutters. Her neighbors were doing the same. Cut herself on the back of the hand while she was working on the next to last one. Bled everywhere. Jason's car pulled up while she was still cursing, and Alan got out. He went into the house and got her a Band-Aid. They put up the last two shutters without talking.

Finally Alan said, "It was my fault. He doesn't usually do drugs at all."

"He's not a bad kid," she said. "So not your type."

"I'm sorry," he said. "Not about that. You know. I guess I mean about everything."

They went back into the house and he saw his suitcase. "Well," he said.

"*Filhatz warfoon meh*," she said. "*Bilbil tuh.*"

"*Nent bruk*," he said. No kidding.

He didn't stay for breakfast. She didn't feel any less or more real after he left.

The twenty-two sleepers were out of the warehouse and Jason had a completed stack of paperwork for her. Lots of signatures. Lots of duplicates and triplicates and fucklipates, as Valentina liked to say.

"Not bad," Lindsey said. "Did Jack Harris offer you a job?"

"He offered to come hand me my ass," Jason said. "I said he'd have to get in line. Nasty weather. Are you staying out there?"

"Where would I go?" she said. "There's a big party at the Splinter tonight. It's not like I have to come in to work tomorrow."

"I thought they were evacuating the Keys," he said.

"It's voluntary," she said. "They don't care if we stay or go. I've been through hurricanes. When Alan and I were kids, we spent one camped in a bathtub under a mattress. We read comics with a flashlight all night long. The noise is the worst thing. Good luck with Alan, by the way."

"I've never lived with anybody before." So maybe he knew just enough to know he had no idea what he had gotten himself into. "I've never fallen for anybody like this."

"There isn't anybody like Alan," she said. "He has the power to cloud and confuse the minds of men."

"What's your superpower?" Jason said.

"He clouds and confuses," she said. "I confuse and then cloud. The order makes a big difference."

She told Mr. Charles the good news about Jack Harris; they had a cup of coffee together to celebrate, then locked the warehouse down. Mr. Charles had to pick up his kids at school. Hurricanes were holidays. You didn't get snow days in Florida.

On the way home all the traffic was going the other way. The wind made the stoplights swing and flip like paper lanterns. She had that feeling she'd had at Christmas, as a child. As if someone was bringing her a present. Something shiny and loud and sharp and messy. She'd always loved bad weather. She'd loved weather witches in their smart, black suits. Their divination kits, their dramatic seizures, their prophecies that were never entirely accurate but always rhymed smartly. When she was little she'd wanted more than anything to grow up and be a weather witch, although why that once had been true she now had no idea.

She rode her bike down to the Splinter. Had a couple of whiskey sours and then decided that she was too excited about the hurricane to get properly drunk. She didn't want to be drunk. And there wasn't a man in the bar she wanted to bring home. The best part of hurricane sex was the hurricane, not the sex, so why bother?

The sky was green as a bruise and the rain was practically horizontal. There were no cars at all on the way home. She went down the middle of the road and ran over an iguana almost four feet long, nose to tail. Stiff as a board, but its sides went out and in like little bellows. The rain got them like that sometimes. They got stupid and slow in the cold. The rest of the time they were stupid and fast.

She wrapped her jacket around the iguana, making sure that the tail was immobilized. You could break a man's arm if you had a tail like that. She carried it under her arm, walking her bike, all the way back to her house and decided it would be a good idea to put it in her bathtub. She went out into her yard with a flashlight.

Checked the storm shutters to make sure they were properly fastened and discovered three more iguanas. Two smaller ones and one real monster. She brought them all inside.

By 6:00 P.M. it was pitch-dark. The hurricane was still two miles out at sea. Picking up water to drop on the heads of people who didn't want any more water. She dozed off at midnight and woke up when the power went off.

The air in the room was so full of water she had to gasp for breath. The iguanas were shadows stretched along the floor of the living room. The black shapes of the liquor boxes were every Christmas present she'd ever wanted.

Everything outside was clanking or buzzing or yanking or shrieking. She felt her way into the kitchen and got out the box with her candles and flashlight and emergency radio. The shutters banged away like battle.

"Swung down," the announcer was saying. "How about that—and this is just the edge, folks. Stay indoors and hunker down if you haven't already left town. This is only a Category 2, but you betcha it'll feel a lot bigger down here on the Keys. It's 3:00 A.M. and we're going to have at least three more hours of this before the eye passes over us. This is one big baby girl, and she's taking her time. The good ones always do."

Lindsey could hardly get the candles lit; the matches were that soggy, her hands greasy with sweat. When she went to the bathroom, the iguana looked as battered and beat, in the light from her candle, as some old suitcase.

Her bedroom had too many windows for her to stay there. She got her pillow and her quilt and a fresh T-shirt. A fresh pair of underwear.

When she went to check Elliot's room there was a body on the bed. She dropped the candle. Tipped wax onto her bare foot.

"Elliot?" she said. But when she got the candle lit again it wasn't Elliot, of course, and it wasn't Alan either. It was the sleeper. Versailles Kentucky. The one who looked like Alan or maybe Lindsey, depending on who was doing the looking.

She dropped the candle again. It was exactly the sort of joke Alan liked. Not a joke at all, that is. She had a pretty good idea where the other sleepers were—in Jason's apartment, not back in Pittsburgh. And if anyone found out, it would be her job too. No government pension for Lindsey. No comfy early retirement.

Her hand still wasn't steady and she was running low on matches. When she held up the candle, wax dripped onto Versailles Kentucky's neck. But if it were that easy to wake a sleeper, Lindsey would already know about it.

In the meantime, the bed was against an exterior wall and there were all the windows. Lindsey dragged Versailles Kentucky off the bed.

She couldn't get a good grip. Versailles Kentucky was heavy. She flopped. Her head snapped back, hair snagging on the floor. Lindsey squatted, took hold of the sleeper by her upper arms, pulled her down the dark hall, trying to keep her head off the ground. This must be what it must be like to have murdered someone. She would kill Alan. Think of this as practice, she thought. Body disposal. Dry run. *Wet* run.

She dragged Versailles Kentucky through the door of the bathroom and leaned the limp body over the tub's lip. Grabbed the iguana. Put it on the bathroom floor. Arranged Versailles Kentucky in the tub, first one leg and then the other, folding her down on top of herself.

Next she got the air mattress out of the garage; the noise was worse out there. She filled the mattress halfway and squeezed it through the bathroom door. Put more air in. Tented it over the tub. Went and found the flashlight, got a bottle of gin out of the freezer. It was still cold, thank God. She swaddled the iguana in a towel that was stiff with Jason's blood. Put it into the tub again. Sleeper and iguana. Madonna and her very ugly baby.

Everything was clatter and wail. Lindsey heard a shutter, somewhere, go sailing off to somewhere else. The floor of the living room was wet in the circle of her flashlight when she went to collect the other iguanas. Either the rain beginning to force its way in under the front door and the sliding glass doors, or else it was the canal. The three iguanas went into the tub too. "Women and iguanas first," she said, and swigged her gin. But nobody heard her over the noise of the wind.

She sat hunched on the lid of her toilet and drank until the wind was almost something she could pretend to ignore. Like a band in a bar that doesn't know how loud it's playing. Eventually she fell asleep, still sitting on the toilet, and only woke up when the bottle broke when she dropped it. The iguanas rustled around in the tub. The wind was gone. It was the eye of the storm or else she'd missed the eye entirely, and the rest of the hurricane as well.

Light came faintly through the shuttered window. The batteries of her emergency radio were dead, but her cell phone still showed a signal. Three messages from Alan and six messages from a number that she guessed was Jason's. Maybe Alan wanted to apologize for something.

She went outside to see what had become of the world. Except that what had become of the world was that she was no longer in it.

The street in front of her house was no longer the street in front of her house. It had become someplace else entirely. There were no other houses. As if the storm had carried them all away. She stood in a meadow full of wildflowers. There were mountains in the far distance, cloudy and blue. The air was very crisp.

Her cell phone showed no signal. When she looked back at her house, she was looking back into her own world. The hurricane was still there, smeared out onto the horizon like poison. The canal was full of the ocean. The Splinter was probably splinters. Her front door still stood open.

She went back inside and filled an old backpack with bottles of gin. Threw in candles, her matchbox, some cans of soup. Her gun. Padded it all out with underwear and a sweater or two. The white stuff on those mountains was probably snow.

If she put her ear against the sliding glass doors that went out to the canal, she was listening to the eye, that long moment of emptiness where the worst is still to come. Versailles Kentucky was still asleep in the bathtub with the iguanas, who were not. There were red marks on Versailles Kentucky's arms and legs where the iguanas had scratched her. Nothing fatal. Lindsey got a brown eyeliner pencil out of the drawer under the sink and lifted up the sleeper's leg. Drew a birthmark in the shape of a battleship. The water in the air would make it smear, but so what. If Alan could have his joke, she would have hers, too.

She lowered the cool leg. On an impulse, she picked up the smallest iguana, still wrapped in its towel.

When she went out her front door again with her backpack and her bike and the iguana, the meadow with its red and yellow flowers was still there and the sun was coming up behind the mountains, although this was not the direction that the sun usually came up in and Lindsey was glad. She bore the sun a grudge because it did not stand still; it gave her no advantage except in that moment when it passed directly overhead and she had no shadow. Not even one. Everything that had once belonged to her alone was back inside Lindsey where it should have been.

There was something, maybe a mile or two away, that might have been an outcropping of rock. The iguana fit inside the basket on her handlebars and the backpack was not uncomfortably heavy. No sign of any people, anywhere, although if she were determined enough, and if her bicycle didn't get a puncture, surely she'd come across whatever the local equivalent of a bar was, eventually. If there wasn't a bar now, then she could always hang around a little while longer, see who came up with that bright idea first.

Rachel Swirsky is a graduate of Clarion West 2005 and holds an MFA in fiction from the University of Iowa. Her fiction has appeared in a number of magazines and anthologies, including *Subterranean Magazine*, *Weird Tales*, *Interzone*, and Rich Horton's *Year's Best Fantasy*, 2007. She is the editor of PodCastle, the world's first audio fantasy magazine, which releases audio versions of previously published fantasy stories every week at http://podcastle.org. She wrote this story after dreaming the battles of the insect men, and is disgruntled that her subconscious has not recently been so generous with plot-oriented dream imagery.

Part One – The Apocalypse of Trees

During the first million years of its existence, mankind survived five apocalypses without succumbing to extinction. It endured the Apocalypse of Steel, the Apocalypse of Hydrogen, the Apocalypse of Serotonin, and both Apocalypses of Water, the second of which occurred despite certain contracts to the contrary.

Mankind also survived the Apocalypse of Grease, which wasn't a true apocalypse, although it wiped out nearly half of humanity by clogging the gears that ran the densely-packed underwater cities of Lor, but that's a tale for another time.

Humans laid the foundation for the sixth apocalypse in much the same way they'd triggered the previous ones. Having recovered their ambition after the Apocalypse of Serotonin and rebuilt their populations after the Apocalypse of Grease, they once again embarked on their species' long term goal to wreak as much havoc as possible on the environment through carelessness and boredom. This time, the trees protested. They devoured buildings, whipped wind into hurricanes between their branches, tangled men into their roots and devoured them as mulch. In retaliation, men chopped down trees, fire-bombed jungles, and released genetically engineered insects to devour tender shoots.

The pitched battle decimated civilians on both sides, but eventually—though infested and rootless—the trees overwhelmed their opposition. Mankind was forced to send its battered representatives to a sacred grove in the middle of the world's oldest forest and beg for a treaty.

Negotiations went slowly since the trees insisted on communicating through the pitches of the wind in their leaves, which astute linguists played back at 1,000 times normal speed in order to render them comprehensible to human ears. It took a day for a sentence, a week for a paragraph, a month for an entire stipulation.

After ten years, a truce was completed. To demonstrate its significance, it was inked in blood drawn from human victims and printed on the pulped and flattened corpses of trees. The trees agreed to cease their increasing assaults and return forevermore to their previous quiescent vegetable state, in exchange for a single concession: mankind would henceforth sacrifice its genetic heritage and merge with animals to create a new, benevolent sentience with which to populate the globe.

After the final signatures and root-imprints were applied to the treaty, the last thing the trees were heard to say before their leaves returned to being mere producers of chlorophyll was this: *At least it should keep them busy for a millennium or two, fighting among themselves.*

Part Two – The Animals Who Lived as Men

Mankind, as history had known it, was no more. The new hybrids wore bodies constructed like those of mythological beasts, a blend of human and animal features. They scattered into the world's forests, deserts, jungles, and oceans, where they competed with unmixed animals for food and territory.

If some ancient legends were to be believed, men were only returning to their ancient roots as dolphin and lizard, raven and grizzly bear. Other traditions would have been appalled that man had cast himself down from his place at the apex of the chain of being and been consigned to the lesser links below.

Intellectuals became the whale men, who kept their faces, but lost their bodies for the streamlined shape of cetaceans. Their sentience blended with the intelligence already inhabiting those massive, blubbery forms. They indulged in abstract philosophy as they swam through the ocean depths in a silence created by the first absence of shipping lines in five hundred thousand years.

Pilots and acrobats became glider men, acquiring huge eyes, wing flaps, and nocturnal habits which served them well as they arrowed from tree to tree in forests that echoed with their eerie, sonar calls. Eight-armed crab men spent their days skittering up and down beaches dancing for the gulls; spotted jaguar men skulked through forests; cold-blooded turtle men inched through years; flattened stingray men lurked on river bottoms, awaiting unwary travelers.

For the first twenty thousand years, mankind peacefully coexisted in all its forms. After that, the buried genetic contribution of the human mind bubbled to the surface.

"The treaty is an outgrown shell to be discarded," young crab men gestured defiantly with their third and sixth arms. Crab matrons clacked their claws in outrage, but who could control the youth?

The most extreme of the crab men formed a rebel sect called the Weeders. They wove strands of kelp around their eyestalks and ritually cut their seventh arms, searing the wounds with a mixture of brine and gull guano. At first, they expended their rage on symbolic targets: dumb unblended seabirds, or rocks shaped like dolphin men. And then a juvenile Weeder called Long Stalks found an injured seal man bleeding on the beach and dragged him home in time for the evening convocation. The Weeders tore him to pieces, rubbing themselves with his blubber and parading in his fur. The meat they left to rot.

When they discovered the decaying corpse, the crab matrons went to the seal men with offerings and apologies, but the seal men refused to hear diplomacy. They clipped off the delegation's claws and sent the mutilated ambassadors home with a terse condemnation: "You didn't even have the courtesy to eat him."

Seal and crab men hunted each other to extinction in less than a decade. The last crab man sidled four hundred miles inland to a camp of parrot men before expiring with a curse on his lips.

Soon it was hyena man versus eagle man and frog man versus capybara man, then tiger and spider and cockatiel men against snake and giraffe and ostrich men. Amidst the hectic formation and betrayals of alliances that seethed on the battlefield, only one order created a stable federation. These were the insect men, greatest of all the species of men in their variety and achievements.

Their infantry were the mosquito men, fearsome female warriors with the muscular bodies of amazons topped by tiny, blood-sucking heads. They marched wherever battle raged, drinking the blood of fallen soldiers. They were sliced and swatted, crushed and grasped in giant crocodilian jaws, but still the indomitable parasites survived to carry samples of their victim's blood back to their superiors, the butterfly men.

Oh, the tragedy of the butterfly men, wisest of the insect men, whose useless jewel-colored wings draped from their slender shoulders like robes. These were the descendents of the geneticists who engineered the destruction of mankind, innocent victims of their ancestor's self-flagellation. Forced to subsist on honey and chained to a lifespan of less than a week, these shrewd but ephemeral leaders did not even enjoy the consolation of flight. Instead they lingered in forest glades looking pale and melancholy. Liable to terrible moods, they made love in the underbrush one moment and shredded each other's wings the next.

Yet the geneticist's legacy was not entirely bad, for they had left their descendents the gift of instinct: inscribed into the rapid pathways of their ephemeral brains lay an intricate understanding of DNA and genetic manipulation. Using this knowledge, the butterflies divined their enemy's secret anatomical weaknesses from the blood samples which the mosquito men brought to them. Generations of butterfly men scrutinized each vial in order to create fatal viruses which would massacre their enemy's ranks.

Only when the last disease had been designed did the butterfly men let loose the fruits of their labor. Simultaneously, a hundred deadly plagues seized their victims, sweeping across the earth in a single night. By morning, only the insect men remained.

High on an isolated cliff in a desert that had once been the Amazon, a cluster of hardy Joshua trees broke their ancient silence to speak once more. Wind rushed through the prickly tufts of their leaves, rustling out a single sentence: *That didn't take long, did it?*

Part Three – The Reign of Insects

Though the butterfly men's cunning won the war, their flighty emotions and brief life spans made them unsuitable for leading a world, and so it was that the cockroach men became the rulers of the earth. Tough enough to survive dismemberment because their brain processes were spread throughout their becarapaced bodies, and possessed of the keen and supernatural senses of scavengers who had once lived among creatures many hundreds of times their own size, the cockroaches had the desire and capacity to enact a reign of fascism on the other insect men the like of which had never been seen before.

Ant men and bee men filled the roles of farmers and drudges. Atlas and rhinoceros beetle men provided brute force. Flea and mite men accomplished those tasks requiring agility.

Mosquito men served as the secret police. The cockroach men sent them to swarm on enemies of the state and drain them dry – and there was never a lack of traitors to keep them fed.

Alas, the plight of the butterfly men was only to become worse, for the cockroach men were loathe to risk the same end which had befallen their enemies. To ensure their safety from the butterfly's dangerous knowledge, they imprisoned the butterfly men in a dark chain of underground caves where they lived their brief, miserable lives out of the sun's reach. Within a season and twelve generations, all conscious knowledge of how to create viruses from blood was gone, but the butterfly men's unhappy descendents remain incarcerated in their underground cells today.

Above ground, bees and ants marched to the cockroach's well-timed rhythm, carrying crops from outlying farms into the hills of the city. Caravans of traveling gypsy moth men departed each hour on the hour, and the cockroach men began great civil works projects to erect bridges and statues and roads and memorials and temples. Larvae were taken away from their hatcheries and forced to work at back-breaking labor past adulthood; dragonfly men journalists reported only that news which drifted on the prevailing winds of fascism; hives were routinely broken up to redistribute the working population. While the other insect men lived poor and wintry lives subsisting on meager grain, the cockroach men gorged on honey, orange peels and moldy bread. Those who dissented disappeared, only to be found as blood-drained corpses swinging from study branches.

Yet all this might have endured, were it not for the deadliest sin of the cockroach men. Ancestrally predisposed to look favorably upon debris, the cockroach men allowed their wastes to build up in giant landfills. Junkyards choked out the fields; garbage seeped into the ground water; rotting trash provided breeding grounds for the nastiest, most virulent epidemics and hemorrhagic fevers. When the first wave of ant men died of a plague that turned their exoskeletons scarlet, at first the cockroach men suspected their old accomplices the butterfly men, but when they went to interrogate them, no one could remember where that unhappy species had been stashed.

The trees cried out against what was happening to them. New bacteria chewed through leaves and blocked out photosynthesis;

roots withered in poisoned soil. Things would only get worse, they knew – oh, how they would suffer. Across the globe it would be the same for all things natural: seas would rumble, ecosystems shatter; even the iron-breathing archeans in the deepest volcanic vents would perish if the cockroach men were allowed to continue on their path. *This will hurt you too, earth*, the trees wailed, not in the language of wind-in-leaves which they had used to communicate with the humans, but in the language of roots-in-ground and life-in-soil.

And the earth heard their plight. It shivered, cracking the super-continent down the middle like a slice of lightning splitting the sky. *I have seen enough of mankind's ability to make trouble*, it rumbled to itself in the language of magma-under-crust, and it initiated the seventh apocalypse, the Apocalypse of Darkness.

The Apocalypse of Darkness was the most terrible yet suffered by mankind. Untold agony wiped out almost the entire population of the globe.

Three cricket men survived. They woke quaking into the dawn, antennae shivering down their backs. They were two females and a male, and they might have carried their line into future generations, but the three of them regarded each other with dark, compound eyes that reflected the same understanding.

"We must never bear children," said the oldest and wisest, "Or someday we might tell them what we have experienced, and we must never damn another soul to see what we have seen, even by picturing it in their minds."

The others agreed, and the three of them leapt off the tallest cliff they could find, dying in silence. Though the details of the Apocalypse of Darkness are known, it would be disrespectful to the cricket men's sacrifice to record them.

Interlude – Whisperings from Branch to Branch

So, little rootlings, little seedlings, little starting-to-grows, that is why the earth is quiet now. Feel the snails trail across your bark. Listen to the birds trilling in your branches and the insects nibbling your leaves. Hear the snap of monkeys brachiating from branch to branch. With mankind gone, we are free to enjoy these things. Are they not good?

Ah, but by now you've guessed, the time of man is not entirely behind us. Why else would we whisper this tale on a fine spring morning, with winter's frosts sweetly melted?

Before the Apocalypse of Darkness, we did not tell each other stories. Through necessity, we have learned the skill. Next year, you will help us tell the starting-to-grows about The Great Cathedral Mother who stood in the center of the world until her children sprouted up in a ring around her and sucked up all the sunlight. Her trunk remains where she once grew, swollen with dead leaves and congealing sap and blind grubs. Someday, lightning will strike all the way through the earth, piercing her in two, and each half will grow into a tall, straight pine with a tip like a spear: one going up, one going down. And when this happens, everything we think we know about the world will change.

The year after that, we will tell the great love story of The Garlanded Tree and the hive of bees who fertilized her.

But this is our most important tale. Like winter, man will return in his season. By the time he does, little rootling, you may have a great solid trunk like your mother. Or perhaps you will have grown and perished, and it will be your children standing. Or your children's children. Whoever grows when mankind returns must remember how to drop their leaves and huddle naked in the snow.

And also, when man comes back, we wish to return to him his history so that he may hold and regard it like a spring bloom budding on a new-leafed branch, new and yet also old, a gift not unlike the one given last spring. Who knows? Maybe this will be the time mankind can learn from stories.

Part Four –

Hands Yearning Upward Through the Surface of the Earth

Stretch your roots into the ground, little seedlings. Listen. Can you hear life rustling under the soil?

Who else but the butterfly men? The Apocalypse of Darkness did not faze them. Having become accustomed to their miserable state, they could no longer be depressed by the black. They crept anxiously through their underground dwellings, their bright wings beautiful and unseen, and whispered to each other, "Do you feel that? What's happening?"

When the Apocalypse was over, without knowing the reason for it, the butterfly men wept together for twenty-four full hours in cosmic mourning for the human race of which they were now the sole representatives. But since their quixotic moods were often given to fits of communal sorrow, they failed to understand the uniqueness of the occasion.

After that, it was as though a pall had lifted from the butterfly men. They no longer had surface cousins to envy, so they went about making their lives in the dark. Their society flourished. Their stymied flight sense muddled their sense of direction, so they built joyously everywhere, not knowing up from down. They laughed and fought and made love in the mud and created an entire caste system based on the texture of the useless flight powder that dusted their wings.

Sometimes an unusual prophet among them dreamed of the surface and spoke of things called light and sun, and usually she was buried alive - but occasionally she wasn't, and then a new religion started and some of the butterflies marched off through the dark to pursue their cult in a different set of caves.

In the past millennia, these cults have gained power. Everyone has lost a sister or a cousin or a parent to their undeniable allure. Whispers among the fine-powdered aristocracy indicate that the cults have even gained sympathy among the inbred monarchy in their velvet-draped cocoons. Soon perhaps, every butterfly will believe.

The cults employ a diverse array of dogmas, rituals, taboos, gods and mythologies, but they all share two common traits. All tell of an eighth apocalypse when the earth will open up into a chasm so terrifying that it will unlock a new sensation – a sixth sense – to accompany hearing, smell, touch, taste and desire. And all require their devotees to spend one day of their week-long lives meditating to discern which direction is up, and then to raise their arms toward it, and start digging.

RECOMMENDED STORIES FROM 2007

"Bar Joke, Arizona" by Sam Allingham
One Story 97

"Monsters of Heaven" by Nathan Ballingrud
Inferno edited by Ellen Datlow (TOR Books)

"The Forest" by Laird Barron
Inferno edited by Ellen Datlow (TOR Books)

"North Of" by Marie Bertino
Mississippi Review, vol. 35, no. 1&2

"Twilights in the Softening City" by Sarah Blackman
Diagram 7.4

"Bears" by Leah Bobet
Strange Horizons, November 5

"The King of the Big Night Hours" by Richard Bowes
Subterrannean 7

"The End of the Age is Upon Us" by Austin Bunn
American Short Fiction, Spring

"The Egg Market" by Sheila Heti
Ninth Letter, Fall/Winter

"Piranha-Otter" by Trevor J. Houser
Zyzzyva, Spring

"Hell" by Stanya Kahn
Userlands edited by Dennis Cooper (Akashic Books)

"North of North" by John Lindgren
Chelsea 82/83

"The Monster in Winter" by Norman Lock
New England Review 28.3

"The Tower" by Steven Millhauser
McSweeney's 25

"The Miracles of St. Boggio of Piedmont" by Tom Miller
Notre Dame Review, Summer/Fall

"If Giants are Thunder" by Steven Mills
Tesseracts 11

"Acid and Stoned Reindeer" by Rebecca Ore
Clarkesworld, November

"No Good Deed" by Patricia Russo
Not One of Us 37

"The Invisibles" by Hugh Sheehy
Kenyon Review, Fall

"Daredevils" by Benjamin Warner
Meridian, January 2007

PUBLICATIONS RECEIVED

In addition to online sources and printed materials sought out by the guest editors and series editor, the following websites, journals, and anthologies were sent to *Best American Fantasy* for consideration.

A PUBLIC SPACE
323 Dean Street
Brooklyn, NY 11217
apublicspace.org

ALASKA QUARTERLY REVIEW
University of Alaska, Anchorage
3211 Providence Drive
Anchorage, AK 99508
aqr.uaa.alaska.edu

ASIMOV'S SCIENCE FICTION
475 Park Avenue South, 11th floor
New York, NY 10016.
asimovs.com

AT EASE WITH THE DEAD
Ash-Tree Press
P.O. Box 1360
Ashcroft, BC
Canada V0K 1A0

BACKWARDS CITY REVIEW
PO Box 41317
Greensboro, NC 27404
backwardscity.net

BLACK GATE
New Epoch Press
815 Oak Street
St. Charles, IL 60174
blackgate.com

BLACK WARRIOR REVIEW
University of Alabama
Box 862936
Tuscaloosa, AL 35486
webdelsol.com/bwr

BRIAR CLIFF REVIEW
Briar Cliff University
3303 Rebecca Street
P.O. Box 2100
Sioux City, IA 51104
briarcliff.edu/campus_info/bcu_review/home_bcu_review.asp

CALYX
P.O. Box B
Corvalles, OR 97339-0539
calyxpress.com

CHELSEA
P.O. Box 773
Cooper Station
New York, NY 01276-0773

CONJUNCTIONS
21 East 10th St.
New York, NY 10003
conjunctions.com

THE COYOTE ROAD
Viking
Penguin Group
345 Hudson Street
New York, NY 10014

ECOTONE
Creative Writing Department
University of North Carolina Wilmington
601 South College Road
Wilmington, NC 28403-3297
ecotonejournal.com

ELECTRIC VELOCIPEDE
P.O. Box 5014
Summerset, NJ 08873
electricvelocipede.com

FAIRY TALE REVIEW
Department of English
University of Alabama
Tuskaloosa, AL 35487
fairytalereview.com

FANTASY & SCIENCE FICTION
P.O. Box 3447
Hoboken, NJ 07030
fsfmag.com

FANTASY MAGAZINE
9710 Traville Gateway Drive, #234
Rockville, MD 20850
fantasymag.com

FICTION
Department of English
City College of New York
Convent Avenue at 138th Street
New York, NY 10031
fictioninc.com

THE GEORGIA REVIEW
The University of Georgia
Athens, GA 30602-9009
uga.edu/garev

GLIMMER TRAIN
1211 NW Glisan, Suite 207
Portland, OR 97209-3054
glimmertrain.org

HAWAII REVIEW
Kuykendall 402
1733 Donaghho Road
Honolulu, HI 96822
english.hawaii.edu/journals/journals.html

HOBART
P.O. Box 1658
Ann Arbor, MI 48103
hobartpulp.com

INFERNO
TOR Books
175 Fifth Avenue
New York, NY 10010
tor.com

INTERFICTIONS
Interstitial Arts Foundation
P.O. Box 35862
Boston, MA 02135
interstitialarts.org

THE KENYON REVIEW
Kenyon College
104 College Drive
Gambier, OH 43022-9623
kenyonreview.org

LADY CHURCHILL'S ROSEBUD WRISTLET
176 Prospect Avenue
Northampton, MA 01060
lcrw.net

MCSWEENEY'S
826NYC
372 Fifth Ave.
Brooklyn, NY 11215
mcsweeneys.net

MERIDIAN
University of Virginia
P.O. Box 400145
Charlottesville, VA 22904-4145
readmeridian.org

MISSISSIPPI REVIEW
University of Southern Mississippi
118 College Drive, #5144
Hattiesburg, MS 39406-0001
mississippireview.com

NEW ENGLAND REVIEW
Middlebury College
Middlebury, VT 05753
go.middlebury.edu/nereview

NEW GENRE
P.O. Box 270092
West Hartford, CT 06127
new-genre.com

THE NEW YORKER
4 Times Square
New York, NY 10036-6592
newyorker.com

NINTH LETTER
University of Illinois at Urbana-Champaign
234 English Building
608 South Wright Street
Urbana, IL 61801
ninthletter.com

/NOR
New Ohio Review, English Department
360 Ellis Hall
Ohio University
Athens, OH 45701
ohiou.edu/nor/

NORTH CAROLINA LITERARY REVIEW
East Carolina University, Department of English
2201 Bate Building
Greenville, NC 27858-4353
ecu.edu/nclr

NOT ONE OF US
12 Curtis Road
Natick, MA 01760
not-one-of-us.com

ON SPEC
P.O. Box 4727
Edmonton, AB
Canada T6E 5G6
onspec.ca

ONE STORY
P.O. Box 150618
Brooklyn, NY 11215
one-story.com

PARADOX
P.O. Box 22897
Brooklyn, NY 11202-2897
paradoxmag.com

PHANTOM
9710 Traville Gateway Drive, #234
Rockville, MD 20850

PLEIADES
Pleiades Press/Department of English and Philosophy
University of Central Missouri
Warrensburg, MO 64093
ucmo.edu/englphil/pleiades/

PORCUPINE
P.O. Box 259
Cedarburg, WI 53012
porcupineliteraryarts.com

REDIVIDER
Emerson College
120 Broylston Street
Boston, MA 02116

ROSEBUD
N3310 Asje Road
Cambridge, WI 53523
rsbd.net

SHIMMER
P.O. Box 58591
Salt Lake City, UT 84158-0591
shimmerzine.com

SOU'WESTER
Department of English
Box 1438
Southern Illinois University, Edwardsville
Edwardsville, IL 62026-1438
siue.edu/ENGLISH/SW/

THE SOUTHERN REVIEW
Old President's House
Louisiana State University
Baton Rouge, LA 70803
lsu.edu/thesouthernreview

SUBTERRANEAN
P.O. Box 190106
Burton, MI 48519
subterraneanpress.com

SUBTROPICS
Department of English, University of Florida
P.O. Box 112075
Gainesville, FL 32611-2075

TESSERACT BOOKS
P.O. Box 1714
Calgary, Alberta
Canada T2P 2L7

TEXT:UR – THE NEW BOOK OF MASKS
Raw Dog Screaming Press
rawdogscreaming.com/

TIN HOUSE
P.O. Box 10500
Portland, OR 97296-0500
tinhouse.com

WEIRD TALES
9710 Traville Gateway Drive, #234
Rockville, MD 20850
weirdtales.net

ZAHIR
315 South Coast Highway 101
Suite U8
Encinitas, CA 92024
zahirtales.com

PUBLICATION HISTORY

ABOUT THE EDITORS

Matthew Cheney has published fiction and nonfiction with *One Story*, *Strange Horizons*, *Locus*, *Rain Taxi*, *Failbetter*, and others. He has served on the jury for the Speculative Literature Foundation's Fountain Award, and his weblog, mumpsimus. blogspot.com, was a finalist for the 2005 World Fantasy Award. He lives in New Hampshire.

Ann VanderMeer is the fiction editor for *Weird Tales*, an award-winning publisher, a columnist for io9.com, and co-editor with her husband, Jeff, on *Fast Ships*, *Black Sails* (pirates), *Steampunk*, *New Weird*, and many more. Together, they have taught writing workshops and given lectures all over the world. This literary "power couple" (Boing Boing) has been profiled on Wired.com, NYT blog, and on national NPR. Ann is a frequent guest of honor at events around the world, including Utopiales (France) and the Brisbane Writers Festival (Australia).

Jeff VanderMeer is a multiple-award winning author with books published in over 20 countries. His work has made the year's best lists of *Publishers Weekly*, *LA Weekly*, *Amazon*, *The San Francisco Chronicle*, and many more. Jeff reviews books for, among others, *The Washington Post Book World*, *The Huffington Post*, and *The Barnes & Noble Review*, as well as being a regular columnist for the Amazon book blog. Current projects include *Booklife: Strategies and Survival Tips for Twenty-First Century Writers* and the novel *Finch*. He currently serves as assistant director for Wofford College's Shared Worlds writing camp for teens. For more information, visit jeffvandermeer.com.

LaVergne, TN USA
08 January 2010
169335LV00001B/106/P